KU-502-381

The Love Child

AMANDA BROOKFIELD

PENGUIN BOOKS

FIFE COUNCIL
LIBRARIES

HJ318813	
Askews & Holts	01-Feb-2013
AF	£7.99
GEN	AN

PENGUIN BOOKS

Published by the Penguin Group

Penguin ... Ltd, 80 Strand, London WC2R 0RL, England
Penguin Gr... Group (USA) Inc., 375 Hudson Street, New York, New York 10014, USA
... a division of Pearson Penguin Canada Inc.) ...anada M4P 2Y3

Penguin ... 25 St Stephen's Green, Dublin 2, Ireland (a division of Penguin Books Ltd)
Pen... ...Australia) ... ...stralia

Penguin Boo... ... 110 017, India
Pen... Group (NZ), 67 Apollo Drive, ... Auckland 0632, New ...aland
(a division of Pears... ...nd Ltd)

... Books (South Africa) (Pty) ... Block D, Rosebank Office ...rk,
...ernas Avenue, Parktown ..., Gauteng 2193, South Afr...

Penguin Books Ltd, Registered Offices: 80 Strand, London WC2R 0RL, England

www.penguin.com

First published 2013
001

Copyright © Amanda Brookfield, 2013
All rights reserved

The moral right of the author has been asserted

Set in 12.5/14.75 pt Garamond MT Std
Typeset by Jouve (UK), Milton Keynes
Printed in England by Clays Ltd, St Ives plc

Except in the United States of America, this book is sold subject
to the condition that it shall not, by way of trade or otherwise, be lent,
re-sold, hired out, or otherwise circulated without the publisher's
prior consent in any form of binding or cover other than that in
which it is published and without a similar condition including this
condition being imposed on the subsequent purchaser

ISBN: 978–0–718–19234–1

www.greenpenguin.co.uk

MIX
Paper from
responsible sources
FSC® C018179

Penguin Books is committed to a sustainable
future for our business, our readers and our planet.
This book is made from Forest Stewardship
Council™ certified paper.

ALWAYS LEARNING   **PEARSON**

For Jean Bray

So we beat on, boats against the current, borne
back ceaselessly into the past.

F. Scott Fitzgerald

PART ONE

Chapter One

'I thought she might be with you.'

'And why would you think that?'

'Because I just . . .' Janine faltered, biting her lip, already regretting the call. The phone felt hot against her ear. She was sitting on her top stair in her pyjamas, one eye on the front door below her, the other on the porthole of a window by her elbow, where a branch of snowy blossom bobbed against the murky night sky, shedding petals like confetti. Along the landing behind her she could hear the hum of the TV through the open door of the bedroom where Mike was watching a late-night news round-up, waiting for her to join him. He had been his usual lovely self, doing as good a job as he could of providing reassurance. It was only twenty minutes past the curfew. Stevie was a wilful fifteen-year-old, headstrong, but also a north London girl, streetwise. If she wasn't picking up it was probably because she was haring home, full of guilt.

'Stevie isn't staying with me until the weekend after next,' Dougie reminded Janine with some venom, 'because you and Mike have decided to take her out on a *treat* this Saturday . . .'

'Yes. Sorry. I know the timing's not ideal for you.'

There was a pause. The sound of Dougie regrouping, allowing himself to engage. 'How late is she anyway?'

'Twenty minutes . . .' Janine checked her watch. 'Twenty-four minutes. We agreed on eleven and it's almost half past.'

'It's probably fine. She's nearly sixteen, after all.'

'Yes, I know. But it's impossible not to worry, isn't it?'

There was another, heavier, silence, while they both considered, but did not mention, the deeper reasons why this might be so. Two years of separation, divorce, had the seen the end of many things, but not the business of knowing one another.

The left leg of Janine's pyjamas had rucked up to her knee, exposing the silvery thread of an old scar: the result of a childhood bike accident, a broken bottle lurking in a patch of grass. She traced the familiar ridge of knotted skin under her fingers, trying to draw comfort from the memory of her own cavalier youth, the irritation at her parents' protectiveness, how she had rebelled against it, doing more singing than studying at uni, working her way through boyfriends with abandon, the trouble she had got into as a result. And yet here she was, two decades later, caught in the very same predicament of motherhood that she had so signally failed to understand as a teenager. Life was a series of circles, Janine reflected wistfully, wishing she knew whether this was a matter for comfort or despair.

Dougie started to speak again, but the front door swung open in the same instant, revealing their daughter, every striking nuance of her formidable legs – the slim, strong curves of the thigh and calf muscles, the neat bulges and indents of her knees – clearly outlined in skinny-fit jeans. Her small feet were in the usual scruffy plimsolls, her heavy chestnut hair bunched out over the collar of her fitted red denim jacket. 'Oh, she's here,

4

Doug,' Janine whispered. 'She's here, thank God. Sorry.' She closed her phone softly, craning her neck to get a proper look before Stevie became aware of the scrutiny. Late and guilty her daughter might have been, but there was no suggestion of haste or unease in her manner. On the contrary, she closed the front door with great precision, using her key and both hands, before slinging her jacket onto one of the wall-hooks and shaking out threads of hair that had snagged inside her shirt collar. She then paused, hands on hips, saying in the tone of one resigned to castigation, and without so much as a glance up the stairs, 'Hey, Mum.'

Janine stood up, the tremble of relief still upon her. 'You're later than we agreed. Thirty minutes later. That is not good. What is even *less* good is not answering your phone.'

'Dead battery, okay?' Stevie waved her mobile, like a piece of court evidence, and launched herself up the stairs, releasing a huff of irritation when Janine blocked her path.

'No, Stevie. Not okay. If you can't make sure you go out with a charged phone, then you can't go out at all.'

'Mum, for Christ's sake —'

'And you've been smoking.'

'Yeah, like *one* cigarette. It's no big deal.' She ducked under Janine's arm and skipped onto the landing.

Janine turned and followed her, feeling powerless, but knowing she mustn't show it. Further reprimand was called for, but it was hard, when all she really wanted was to pull Stevie to her chest and tell her how glad she was to have her safely home. 'Stevie. I'm talking to you.'

'And I'm listening.' She flopped against the wall next to her bedroom door folding her arms.

'No, you're not. You're too busy being pissed off. You're still too young to smoke, not just according to me, but *legally*. In fact . . .' Janine blustered, hating the moment, the antipathy, the look of disdain on Stevie's beautiful open face '. . . in fact, I've a good mind to tell Mike to give those Jason Stobart tickets back to the box office.'

The moment the words were out Janine regretted them. Aside from being a weak threat, it wasn't hers to make. The Saturday night excursion to see the new young sell-out comedian of the year – the cause of such irritation to Dougie – had been a surprise hatched solely by Mike, the latest in a string of endearing efforts to win the affections of his girlfriend's prickly daughter.

'Fine. Go ahead.' Stevie met Janine's gaze, her dark blue eyes defiant. She unfolded her arms and picked at something on her shirt. 'I didn't ask Mike to take us out, did I?'

Janine wished even harder that she had thought more carefully before speaking. She glanced along the landing behind her, fearful Mike could hear this messed-up attempt at discipline. In the few months since he had moved in he had already gently pointed out how hopelessly lenient she was. 'Look, Stevie.' She sucked in some extra breath. 'I didn't mean that . . . about Saturday. I shouldn't have said it. Just have the grace to understand why I was worried tonight, could you? No answer on your phone . . . If you're running late, I need to know. Do you understand that, darling? I *need* to know.'

Stevie nodded, looking meek suddenly, the fight gone

out of her. 'Yeah. Right. Sorry.' She turned for her bedroom, trailing one finger behind her along the wall.

'And smoking,' Janine called after her. 'It's so bad for you and *such* waste of money. Why should I give you pocket money if that's what you're going to spend it on?'

'It wasn't mine. I never buy them.'

'Good. Don't.' Janine hesitated, wondering if she was lying. Stevie had paused, her back against the door. She looked so hunched, so sullen. It was impossible not to want to do something about it. 'Did you enjoy the film?' she ventured, watching her daughter's face carefully as it turned, seeing the reluctance with which her expression softened and recognizing within it the little girl who had once loved her mother so unreservedly that she would insist on twenty kisses every night – solemnly counted out loud – before the exaction of a sworn undertaking that the same duty would be performed in the morning.

'Yeah, it was dumb, really, but funny . . .' Stevie shook her head, giggling. 'There was this cute dog in it that could do, like, the most amazing things.' She laughed again, more loosely, her face lighting up, as if a switch had been pressed somewhere deep inside. 'You'd like it, Mum.'

Janine smiled. 'Good. One to remember for a DVD, then.'

'But I *so* need a new phone.' Stevie groaned, her attention flicking to the mobile still clutched in her hand. 'I *did* charge it, honestly, but it, like, *dies* in seconds. Dad has said he'll get me a new one for my birthday – the very latest – but with Dad . . .' She glanced at Janine, uncertain as ever of her right to ask for reassurance on the subject. 'Night, then,' she murmured instead, quickly propelling herself backwards through the door and releasing a sigh that seemed to contain all Janine's own lost hopes where Dougie was concerned.

A drink: that was what he needed. Dougie sat on the edge of his bed in his boxers as he confronted the notion, telling himself it was a factual, rational possibility instead of the first step towards a certain head-on collision with disaster. The intrusion of Janine's phone call deserved solace, he reasoned. Selfishly, she had worried him before it was necessary, waking him up, when she knew he always had trouble going back to sleep. A drink would help him over that hurdle, too. A slug of whisky, say. Yes, that would do the job nicely, dull the quick-fire tedium that went on in his brain, the gallops of panic about money, about work (or lack of it), about Stevie – seeing her, not seeing her – about how the hell a divorced, penurious, failed restaurateur went about the business of being a good father.

Dougie was aware of his pulse quickening. The idea of the drink was taking hold: he could feel its tight little roots lashing themselves to the knots inside his stomach. One drink. Why not? He ran the tip of his tongue round the inside of his teeth. His mouth had gone dry in the sticky way it did at such times. His mind, meanwhile – ever the treacherous, co-operative rebel – had started, excitedly, to assess the options. He kept no alcohol in the house, these days, but the late-night corner shop would be open. The boy with the glossy dark hair on his upper lip would be manning the till, his face pasty under the neon strip-lights. Kentish Town Road was only a five-minute walk away.

From there it was two minutes to the corner shop. Another two minutes to make the purchase. Nine minutes. Then the return walk. That made sixteen minutes in total. Sixteen minutes and he would be opening a bottle. A half-bottle. Scotch. No need to go mad.

Dougie reached for his jeans and shook the change out of his pockets. There wasn't enough. There was never enough. He knew already that his wallet was empty. Apart from credit cards. Which he mustn't use. Not until he got his new business plan off the ground anyway. Private catering services and cooking lessons: a feeble, flimsy plan, maybe, but it was all he had. He slumped back down onto the bed, his shoulders dropping as he allowed his gaze to drift slowly, greedily, to the money jar on the window sill. His 'Stevie' jar. The fund for her birthday phone. Four hundred it was going to cost, even off the cheapest site. The jar didn't contain nearly that much yet – a couple of tenners, some fives, a fistful of pound coins – but it was a start. Enough for whisky.

Dougie flung the jeans across the floor and fell backwards onto the bed, squeezing his fists and his eyes shut. Ten months of sobriety and still they came, these moments, each its own monster, each needing to be wrestled to the ground. He lay rigid, digging his nails into his palms, seeing fireworks under his eyelids, his head thrumming. Even taking a breath was an effort. He had to force every inhalation, every release, as if his own body was turning against him.

He watched his chest rise and fall, trying to focus on the good things. Things like Stevie, who was safe and would visit soon in spite of the recent sabotage; and his new work venture, which, thanks to an advertising contact, now had a modest soon-to-go-live website. He might owe two months' rent and six grand of rising, un-payable debt on his credit cards, but – for the time being at least – he still had a kitchen. And what did a cook need other than a kitchen? He was putting it to its first 'professional' use the following night: his oldest friends, Simon and Gary, plus a friend of Gary's called Richard, were coming round for a class. It had been Simon's idea – a dummy-run, he had called it, though they were paying thirty quid a head and Dougie knew that that was just Simon being Simon, trying to help out. Using an old journo-stalwart mate of his called Danny to line up a feature in *North London Life* had been another. Some local advertising would promote the new cooking venture, Simon had insisted, give it that first vital kick-start. A keen, baby-voiced girl called Laura Munro had phoned Dougie that morning to arrange an interview. In his stronger moments he was almost looking forward to it.

And there was always the *finca*, Dougie reminded himself, his thoughts flying with their customary desperation to the holiday house he still owned in Spain, the one potential 'golden goose' in his otherwise dire finances, cleverly ring-fenced for him during the divorce and bankruptcy settlements by a wily accountant. For a while the source of vital income, the place had stood empty for months. No one wanted to rent it. No one wanted to buy it. More like a millstone than a bloody goose. But at least it was *there*, Dougie consoled himself; something solid in the quicksand.

He had stopped the deep breathing, Dougie realized.

And he wasn't so thirsty. He was just a man lying on a bed who couldn't sleep. A lonely thirty-eight-year-old man, who knew little about anything except the preparation of food. From nowhere a tune broke inside his head, a track from the old Exeter days. An image joined it: of Janine standing at a mike in a denim mini skirt and Dr Martens, her voice smoky, the chestnut tones in her long hair glinting under the lights; Simon, Gary, Victoria seated round him, as they always had been back then; the student bar heaving; Janine's eyes on his through the mist of cigarette smoke. It was before they had met. Before love and success and life taking shape. Before everything had gone wrong.

Chapter Two

Hopper once said, 'Maybe I'm not very human. What I wanted to do was paint sunlight on the side of a house.' Yet in all Hopper's work light does so much more than illuminate a scene: it is an emotion, a metaphor. In these later paintings the abstract fall of light takes on geometric forms, rectangular shafts that penetrate interiors, bathing their subjects in a celestial glow . . .

Victoria lifted her head from her screen and flexed her fingers. Bands of sunlight were falling through the balcony windows of the flat, lined up across the sitting-room carpet, as solid as a balustrade. She felt a sudden and ridiculous urge to leave her position at the dining-room table and plant herself in the middle of it; maybe even take off her clothes like Hopper's *A Woman in the Sun*, one of the many highlights of the series she was trying to describe. *Celestial glow* . . . yes, she could do with some of that, all right. Victoria bulged her cheeks, then blew out the air slowly.

With a click she enlarged Hopper's picture of the nude to full screen. The woman's eyes were wide open and she was staring directly into the sun as it poured through the window. She looked extraordinarily powerful, almost goddess-like, with the light shaping the bold swells of her thighs, her buttocks, her breasts . . . powerful, ripe, *fecund* – yes, that was the word.

Victoria kicked off her shoes and curled her toes into the carpet as she resumed typing. She had got up early to tackle the Hopper text because she was having lunch with her father, which meant the best of the afternoon would be lost.

In fact, she had all that week to work on the Hopper copy, not to mention the one after. She was ahead of the game as usual, staying on top of deadlines before they got on top of her, pushing herself a little too hard, as was her wont. Otherwise, she had found, life slipped past, like sand through an egg-timer; action, keeping busy, was what gave it shape. Even so, time seemed to be progressing at breakneck speed. Her thirties, so dreaded, had briefly felt safe. But now, suddenly, they were almost done. She was thirty-eight. *Thirty-eight*. It was as if the decade had been one of those hateful rollercoaster rides, lumbering upwards to a midway peak, then tearing down the other side, covering the same distance in a fraction of the time.

Victoria rubbed her eyes, which ached a little, then the nape of her neck, which was stiffening as it always did. Working at the dining-room table wasn't ideal, but in spite of its spacious luxury, the north London flat (a wedding gift to her and Simon from her parents) had only one room that obviously offered service as a study and that had been consigned to Simon. That he rarely *used* the place was neither here nor there. It was Simon's 'space', recognized by both of them as an important piece in the chess game of co-habitation. For that reason it was allowed – unlike any other inch of the flat – to be messy.

Victoria re-read her sentence about fecundity, her mind blank suddenly as to how to proceed. The ache in her neck seemed rooted in her shoulders that day, invisible branches of pain, probably because she had slept fitfully, at odd angles, waiting for Simon to get back from his men-only cooking class at Dougie's, then being unable to go back to sleep once he had. She picked at a fleck on the table next to her laptop, half tempted to abandon the catalogue copy and devote some time to looking nice instead. Her father liked femininity – dresses, makeup; he was old-fashioned like that.

The balustrade of sunlight was still blazing across the carpet. Behind it she could make out the shimmering upper torso of the Post Office Tower – a lone sentinel against the backdrop of blue sky. Like a lighthouse . . . A lighthouse, of course. Victoria scrolled back to her opening. Hopper's lighthouses – that was how she should start the catalogue commentary. Early on he had painted loads of the damn things. They embodied the seeds of his fascination for light and shadow, for human solitariness. Her fingers flew over the keys.

'I thought you were meeting your dad.'

'I am.' Victoria glanced up. She didn't know how long she had been working. Simon was in his dressing-gown, his hair scuffed, his feet bare.

He shook his head at her in fond wonderment. 'Only you could lose track of time with quite such thoroughness, did you know that?'

'Like what? Why?' Victoria looked about her wildly. She had left her watch in the bathroom after her morning shower. 'What time is it?'

'Midday.'

'Christ – why didn't you say?'

'I did,' Simon cried. 'I just have.'

'No, *before* – why didn't you say *before*?' Victoria scrabbled with her papers and buttons, saving her documents and shutting down tabs.

'No need to panic. The old man won't mind. It's his club, isn't it? He'll have all his old pals to talk to while he waits.' Simon stopped, holding himself very still while the knot of his hangover momentarily tightened, then released again.

'So, last night was fun, I take it?' Victoria gave him a beady look. 'This is a late morning, even for you.'

'I know.' Simon hung his head ruefully. 'I'm a disgrace. Lucky you're so keen on me, isn't it?'

Victoria slid her laptop into its case and briskly zipped it shut. She did indeed love her husband's laid-back attitude to life, an attitude given free rein by his somewhat haphazard career as a mostly freelance journalist. With her own rather over-driven nature, she had always recognized the importance of the balance Simon's much more easy-going personality provided. She tried to think about this as she ducked under the table, swiping for her shoes. 'What did you cook?'

For one terrible moment Simon couldn't remember. There was an underlying accusatory tone to this wifely inquisition, something he knew he wasn't getting and which he was pretty certain had nothing to do with his late night in Dougie's kitchen. 'Oh, basically it was fish to start.' He paused, as the evening came back into focus. 'Trout, then duck, then a rhubarb thing, with a sort of honey and ginger mousse. Dougie was like a major general. Tetchy, barking orders – we rushed round like idiots.

Then, of course, we had to eat it all – though I have to say, it was bloody good.' He grinned sheepishly.

Victoria slipped her feet into the leather pumps with ballet tassels, which she had retrieved from under the table. 'Wow, very advanced stuff.' She studied her feet for a moment, briefly pondering whether to dig out some heels instead. After a decade with Simon, who barely touched five foot six, she rarely bothered. Even without shoes she was still taller than him by a good three inches. 'So when do I get to enjoy the benefits?' she murmured, deciding to leave the shoes. 'Duck, hmm . . . I quite fancy that.'

'Whoa! It's still early days,' Simon protested, more cheerful now, having sensed a lightening in her mood. 'I think I need a few more lessons first.'

'More lessons? I thought it was a one-off.'

'It was going to be. But we've all agreed to another. Dougie needs the money,' he explained, his face crumpling with concern. 'Vic – he really does.'

'I see.' She disappeared into the bedroom and returned in a mulberry-coloured fitted linen jacket that sat snugly over the waistband of her black trousers. 'And will all these "lessons" go on so late, do you think?' She tugged sharply at the jacket sleeves. 'I waited as long as I could, Simon . . . I bloody *waited* . . .'

Simon slapped his forehead, understanding the traces of sourness at last. 'You waited.' He groaned. 'Oh, God – of course you waited . . . Of course you did. I'm so sorry, Vic, I completely forgot.'

'Two o'clock, Simon. It was two o'clock in the morning. Not that you were in any fit state by then anyway.'

'No. Shit. I am an idiot.' Simon shook his head mournfully. 'You told me – you reminded me. I know you did.'

Victoria could feel herself relenting. He looked so hopeless – he *was* hopeless – with his hair sticking up and his eyes owl-wide without his glasses. And his efforts at helping Dougie made her want to forgive him too. As an early investor in the Black Hen, the now defunct Notting Hill restaurant responsible for shooting Dougie, briefly, to celebrity-chef stardom, Simon had lost many thousands of pounds; but she hadn't heard him complain about it once. On top of which, he famously loathed anything to do with food except eating it. To subject himself to some culinary tuition because his oldest friend had fallen on seriously hard times was the greatest, sweetest testimony of affection Victoria could imagine.

'Yes, you're hopeless,' she conceded, reflecting on the degree to which the friendship between the two men had taxed her over the years. Early on, she had often felt like an unwanted third point of a triangle, trying to keep Simon on track with his uni studies while Dougie seemed hell-bent on steering him off, usually to great effect. The young Dougie Easton had been a formidable force, with his towering height and wild good looks – ice-blue eyes set under a mop of sandy hair and a manner that exuded effortless *laissez-faire* charm. With him in attendance, even the most innocent gathering could – and usually did – degenerate into a riotous party. Janine, always more of a free spirit, kicking out against her square, northern family, had been so much better at going with the flow, leaving Victoria to feel like the kill-joy of their little student group, the one stifling yawns with half an eye on the clock, wishing they could all just go home.

But after she and Simon had completed their degrees and set up home in London, everything had got easier. She had embarked on her D.Phil. on Byzantine art and Simon had started getting his articles and stories into print, at the same time landing a job with a niche art magazine called *London Culture*. By the time Dougie arrived, lashed to the accelerating juggernaut of his restaurant successes, they were married and on a wavelength of their own. As the friendship between the two men resumed, Victoria had learned to respect rather than resent it and, barring a few early gatherings that had involved her and Janine, had been more than happy to let Dougie and Simon meet on their own terms. Late nights, heavy drinking, old in-jokes – it was hardly her scene. Simon would get something out of his system, then come home to her afterwards. That was the main thing. Unlike Dougie, who (as evinced by the occasional desolate enquiring call she received from Janine in the small hours) began to find his way back to his own doorstep less and less. The eventual double crash of Dougie's personal and public life had had a dreadful inevitability to it, even given Simon's loyally limited disclosures about what was going on. Victoria had been proud of how Simon had stood by his old friend as the débâcle had unravelled. Her own tentative efforts to offer Janine support had been rebuffed. There was a man called Mike now – Victoria knew that much but had never met him – and Stevie, by all accounts, had survived and adjusted, as children did to such situations. She was now, apparently – incredibly – soon to embark on her final two years of school.

Victoria returned her attention to her husband. He was

hung-over: she could tell not just because he had slept so late but because of the way he was standing, making an effort to hold his eyes wide, to look focused. She peered into her handbag, checking for keys and phone. 'Maybe we could find a moment for a *siesta* later on this afternoon,' she murmured, trying to remember what her getting-pregnant book had said about body temperature and windows of opportunity.

'Or now?' Simon shuffled towards her. 'Your dad can wait, surely.' He slipped his arms round her waist and nestled the side of his face into the crook of her collarbone.

Victoria traced a finger over the crown of his head, following the familiar thick circular growth of brown hair, still, in spite of his thirty-nine years, as springy and resilient as a teenager's. There was no question of agreeing to sex. Her father would be irritated as it was. She nuzzled Simon's neck, liking the smell of him even through the faint aroma of alcohol; liking, too, the way he was so obviously trying to make amends. He didn't often initiate full-blown physical intimacy. He was more of a stroking-and-cuddles kind of man. It was one of the reasons she had resorted to buying the how-to-conceive book. Two or three times a month had been their mutually comfortable average for years. But lately it had dawned on Victoria that if she was serious about the business of making a baby – which she was, very – it was going to take a little more applied commitment to the mechanics of the task. To improve their statistical chances, if nothing else.

'Sorry, sweetie.' She kissed the top of his head and prised herself free, wishing suddenly that Simon had more of an air of motivation about him, a deadline to meet, a story to chase. *London Culture* had finally succumbed to the dot.com boom a few years before, while his freelance commissions had been getting fewer and further between. It maddened her that he didn't seem to mind. 'But I'd better not. You know Dad. I'm going to have to throw myself in front of a taxi as it is.' She picked a piece of fluff off his dressing-gown.

Simon accepted the rejection with a meek smile. 'Say hi to the old man from me. Tell him golf soon.'

The moment he was alone Simon's hangover surged. He listened as the clatter of Victoria's feet receded down the stairs (there was a lift but she insisted that the four flights kept her fit), and then opened the fridge, peering much as Cortez must have peered at the New World. The only faintly appealing item he could see was ham – freshly sliced, folded in cellophane. He picked it up and put it down again. What he wanted was bacon. But Victoria didn't buy bacon, these days, she bought 'pancetta' and then only if her menu plans for the week included a carbonara. There was a carton of pineapple juice but Simon wasn't sure his stomach could take it. He grabbed the ham again, tearing off the wrapping and shovelling several slices straight into his mouth. He chewed ravenously, keeping the fridge door open with his elbow, wondering whether to drag himself to his desk or simply write off the day as a lost cause.

There was standstill traffic stretching from Hyde Park Corner all the way to St James's. Victoria eventually got out of her taxi and walked the last few hundred yards, at such speed that in spite of the brisk April wind, reminding her at every tug that her linen jacket was too thin, she arrived at her father's club in a lather of perspiration.

'Daddy, I'm here but I'm going to the loo. See you in the dining room.' She kissed the top of his head over the back of his usual leather chair in the lounge and made her way along the carpeted corridor to the Ladies. The décor inside was as sumptuous as any boudoir's, the air thick with scent, vases of arching orchids skirting the basins between bottles of luxury hand creams and piles of starched linen napkins. To Victoria's relief, the place was empty – no other guests or any sign of the squat, raven-haired girls in waitress uniforms who liked to hover by their saucer of pound coins, rubbing at imaginary smears on the mirrors.

Victoria planted a hand on either side of the central basin and warily surveyed her reflection, wondering at what unnoticed moment girlish high colour had segued into a complexion that could have benefited from concealer. But thank God for her hair. She had her mother's – long, ram-rod straight, somewhere between auburn and blonde. She would have liked bigger eyes, wider apart, but they were an unusual light green and easily sharpened by mascara and a little shadow. Rummaging in her bag, she found lipstick and a comb and applied a few brusque strokes of both.

Soon she was settling herself into one of the wide uncomfortable chairs in the dining room opposite her father.

'You look tired, petal.'

'Thanks, Dad, you look great.' She leant back to let a waiter flick a napkin across her knees. 'How's Mum?'

'The same. You know.'

'Yes.' Victoria pressed her palms hard against the napkin, feeling the heat of her legs through the linen. Her mother had depression, the kind that pills didn't really sort out.

'Up and down. That hellish winter we had hasn't helped. But the garden is coming to life at last – thank goodness. Camellias and wisteria both out in full force, even though we're only halfway through April. She'd love a visit from you.'

'Of course. We're planning one.' Victoria smiled, trying to banish selfish thoughts about the traffic on the M4 and the blank expression of indifference that would greet her at the other end. If her mother enjoyed being visited by her only daughter she had long since lost the capacity to show it.

'Have the oysters, petal – they'll be excellent.'

'I'm sure they will, Dad, but I don't like oysters, do I?'

'Well, you should. Everybody should. The ocean in one gulp – bloody delicious.'

Victoria scanned the menu, pressing away familiar fond surges of irritation. Her father was the sort of man who, if he liked something, could rarely be deflected from the purpose of persuading others to like it too. Oysters, offal, malt whisky, American politics, golf, Wagner: to dare to contradict the merits of such passions was like standing alone in the face of a high gale. It was admirable in many ways, forming the bedrock of his success as a driven businessman and his capacity, still, to spring around the planet like a twenty-year-old instead of a man only just shy of seventy.

And yet it was exhausting too, Victoria mused, as the waiter was summoned and barked at. One of the things that had drawn her to Simon was his ability to move through life at a slow, steady pace, allowing life to happen to him rather than seizing it by the lapels. So what was she doing fretting about her husband's lack of ambition? she scolded herself, casting the waiter a smile of encouragement as he scurried away with their order, and embracing the happy notion that, when it came to parenthood, a chilled, stay-at-home dad was going to prove very useful indeed.

'You're working too hard,' Charles Lambert accused her, a short while later, wagging an empty oyster shell at her.

Victoria had chosen crayfish, five extravagantly whiskered creatures laid out in a straight line across her plate, next to a small pot of mayonnaise and a finger bowl floating with crescents of fresh lemon.

'And I admire you for it, sweetheart. All those brains you've got, all those wonderful exhibitions you do those catalogues for – I couldn't be more proud, but there also comes a time . . .' He paused to tip the contents of the last shell down his throat, swallowed noisily, then took a swig of the wine – something buttery and delicious, which Victoria had been savouring in tiny sips. '. . . for a woman, I mean, when it's important to slow down, to realize that a career has its place . . .'

Victoria was glad of the crayfish. They took a lot of attention and work – care, too, since their shells were sharp. Her father was telling her to have a baby, which he did from time to time. A few years ago it had made her want to storm off, affronted. Now it was the fear of jinxing her and Simon's chances that kept her quiet. 'Si wants to fix up some golf, by the way. He told me to say.'

'Splendid.' Charles pressed his napkin to his lips. Rarely did he lunch without a purpose, even with his daughter. 'And now I have some news. About your mother.'

Victoria glanced up sharply. Their empty first-course plates had quickly been removed and replaced with their mains. She had stuck with fish – a Dover sole, draped across the entire width of the plate, with a side portion of spinach that seemed suddenly to be sticking to her teeth. 'What about her?'

'She's decided . . . There's a place – a residence . . . She would like to spend some time there.'

'What residence? Where?'

'Scotland. Inverness-shire. A beautiful place – lakes, mountains, clean air, peace. As you know she's found it hard . . . since . . .'

'Since Miles.'

'It's in Scotland,' he repeated.

Victoria sat very still. She had said her brother's name and he had ignored her. She wasn't sure she dared say it again.

'It's only for a few weeks, longer if she wants.'

Afterwards Victoria walked to Baker Street, needing to clear her head before the plunge into the tube. Everywhere she looked there seemed to be pushchairs and prams, sprouting the chubby limbs of infants brandishing rattles and bottles, kicking off blankets and shoes. She didn't want one of those. She wanted her own. Hers and Simon's. It would be earnest and quiet and sweet. It would have Simon's full quirky lips and her thin, straight hair.

And yet, life wasn't such a tidy parcel, was it? Things invariably didn't add up. Like her mother, who, presumably, had once experienced the same yearning for a child. And yet one wouldn't know it now, with her stiff welcome smile and dead eyes. Where was the motherly love in that? Victoria leant against a boarded-up shop as the pavement heaved. She felt too full, a little queasy. It had been a mistake to drink, to choose such rich food.

By the time she stepped through the door of the flat the feeling had merged with other emotions and she was crying. Simon was stretched out on the sofa with his laptop on his knees, his nose in a website on urban gardens that he was researching for an article. 'Oh, no,' he cried, sliding the laptop onto the carpet. 'What did he say?'

'Nothing ... no ... At least, he wouldn't talk about Miles ...'

'He never talks about Miles.'

'And Mum, she's going somewhere for a few weeks – a *residence* in Scotland –'

'Scotland? What sort of residence?'

'I don't know – for depressives. Maybe it'll be good. I just ...' Victoria fell to her knees next to the sofa, flinging her arms round his waist. 'Simon ... wanting a baby ... it's not just me, is it?'

Simon struggled upright so he could get a better hold of her. 'Of course not, Vic.'

'Because if it is, I'm not sure I can manage. There's too much that can go wrong. And even afterwards – remember what happened to Janine –'

'That was years ago and you're not Janine.'

'And Miles . . . I mean, however old you are, whatever you do, you're always someone's *child.*'

'Vic, you're not thinking straight. You're just upset –'

'But if we're going to do this – to become *parents* – I need you *with* me for *ever.* Till death. And don't say I'm being dramatic – I *feel* dramatic.'

'And I'm with you, Vic,' Simon cried, recognizing that it was no moment to delve into any of his dim reservations about parenting; most of them were the obvious, despicable selfish ones, although there were others that related to the knottier problem of not having enjoyed his own childhood sufficiently to feel confident about repeating the exercise. It was Victoria's certainty that had won him round, a tidal wave that had swept all his indecision away. 'A baby with you, Vic,' he said gently, 'how could I not want that? Whenever I think about it my heart stops.'

'Really, Si?' She had sat back on her heels and was staring at him as if her life depended on it, red-eyed, her lips full, her long lashes gluey with tears.

'Really. Now, sit here.' He took hold of her hands and gently pulled her onto the sofa next to him. 'Put your feet up while I make us some tea.' He disappeared into the kitchen, emerging a few minutes later with two steaming mugs. 'By the way, Gary broke the news last night that he and Ruth are expecting – Oh, no.' Simon stopped at the sofa, gripping the mugs to his chest, looking crestfallen. 'That was tactless, wasn't it, mentioning that now? Bugger. Talk about thoughtless –'

'No, it's fine, you're not thoughtless, you're lovely.' Victoria reached for her tea, noting happily that he had used what he knew was one of her favourite mugs, of butterflies and lilies. 'How wonderful for Gary and Ruth.'

'I brought shortbread too. Look.' Simon brandished the packet of biscuits he had wedged under his arm, making sure she took one before he helped himself. He had been eating all day, craving sweetness, and was feeling a lot better as a result. 'She's several months gone, Gary said. They'd been keeping it quiet. He's clearly chuffed to bits. Budge up. I want to hug my wife. Can I hug my wife?'

'You can.' Victoria tucked her legs up to one side and nestled against him. 'Wow. Gary, the last of the original Dougie Easton set, thoroughly domesticized – talk about a bunch of late starters.'

'*Domesticized?*' Simon teased, despatching a second piece of shortbread in two wolfish bites. 'Is that even a word? I've a good mind to look it up. How's it going with your man Hopper, by the way? You were clearly very into it this morning.'

'Oh, yes, I was.' Victoria ducked free of his arm and stretched out on the sofa, tucking a scatter cushion under her head and burrowing her feet under Simon's thigh. He was always good at asking her about her work. Just as she was good at knowing he didn't much like being quizzed about his, not even during his busy patches. It was one of those dovetailing things they had learnt about each other over the years without ever needing to discuss it, intuiting each other's differences and accommodating them, being okay with them. 'There's such bleakness to Hopper,' she went on eagerly, 'but such colour too . . . such energy . . .' She paused, wondering if she could do justice to the naked goddess-like woman and deciding she couldn't.

'I'm glad Gary's happy, but Ruth's not exactly my kind of woman,' she confessed instead, reverting to the earlier subject.

'I like her.'

'So do I, but she thinks I'm posh and privileged.'

Simon peered fondly at her over the tops of his glasses. 'Which you are.'

'Which I am. But sometimes I'm not sure Ruth sees beyond that. And she doesn't like Picasso. How can anyone not like Picasso?'

'Don't tell me you preferred Lulu.'

They caught each other's eye and burst out laughing. Lulu had been an impossible princess of a model who had run rings round Gary for almost a decade. Gary had met Ruth with a move to a new advertising agency three years before and married her within six months. Neither of them yet knew her very well, Gary's love of socializing having diminished in proportion to his new-found contentment in his private life. Victoria's reservations were based on a couple of loose comments Ruth had made early on about middle-class wealth and the inferiority of figurative art.

'You're right. Ruth is fine,' Victoria conceded, tunnelling her toes deeper under Simon's leg, enjoying the companionable sense of their shared past. 'Hey, Si, you haven't told Dougie we're trying for a baby, have you?'

'Of course not.'

'Good.' She put her empty mug on the carpet.

'Another cup? I'm having one.'

'No, thanks.' There was a catch in her voice, not of sadness this time, but he didn't hear it. Victoria watched as he left the room, willing him to turn round. It wasn't more tea she wanted, but to make love. To be fucked senseless, in fact, left gasping, impregnated. The Hopper woman flashed across her mind again, so strong and radiant in the sunlight.

On his return Simon retrieved his laptop from the floor and slumped back onto the sofa, idly tapping the keys with one hand and holding his mug against his lips with the other. She sat up and slid one hand up inside his trouser leg, moulding her palm round the smooth hard ridge of his calf muscle. He might not be the tallest man, her husband, but she had always found his figure appealingly compact, his legs toned and perfectly proportioned. 'Simon . . .'

'Yup?'

'I don't suppose you feel like . . . ?'

'I most certainly do. Give me a mo, okay? I just need to get out of this.' He held out his arm and she wriggled back under it. A few minutes later she was fast asleep.

Chapter Three

The estate agent was quiet for a Friday morning. The one viewing in Janine's diary had been cancelled, the woman having phoned to say she had been up all night with a sick child. She had sounded stressed, as if there was a lot more she would have liked to discuss other than looking round houses. With only a couple of walk-in enquiries, Janine had spent the time tidying up her email inbox and clearing old specs out of her files. By midday the sun was streaming so thickly through the window behind her, that it was hard to see her computer screen properly. Donna, who sat at the desk in front of her, had already pulled out a salad tub and was eating it in the slow, meticulous way of one for whom no meal could ever last too long. The other two desks were empty, since both Dale and Vince, the manager, were out on calls.

Janine looked at the wall clock, which had edged closer to one o'clock. She didn't mind not being busy. Lulls in life, she had learnt to value them. There had been too many dramas over the years, cudgels in the dark, often just when one had dared to hope the world might be safe. And when it got to one o'clock Mike was going to call. He had said he would and he always did what he said. Janine loved the certainty of that. The certainty of Mike.

After talking to him, she would eat her own lunch – a tuna sandwich with rocket and mayonnaise, which she had made the night before, as usual, wrapping it in cling-film and putting it in the fridge to keep fresh. It saved time in the mornings, she found. With the three of them – her, Mike and Stevie – trying to get out of the little house, bumping into each other, it was always a rush. She had offered to make one for Stevie, but she had said no, thanks, using the sharp tone that Janine knew had nothing to do with the sandwich. Tension crackled between them con-stantly now, no matter how hard she tried to circumvent it. Restored peace never lasted. In the two days since the late cinema return there had already been countless fresh causes for confrontation, not just over predictable things, like chores and television, but often the most innocent attempts at conversation. The previous evening a new pair of denim shorts had been the trigger. Tatty, eye-catchingly tight, Stevie had changed into them after school, pulling them on over a pair of extravagantly lad-dered tights and thumping her way downstairs in high heels.

Was she going out? Janine had asked, a studiedly bland enquiry to which Stevie had nevertheless retorted with such a scathing 'No,' that Mike had intervened, telling her not to be rude to her mother before exacerbating matters by saying he guessed she couldn't have been going out anywhere because she only appeared to be half dressed.

Janine got up and pulled the blind down to block out the worst of the sun. There were bound to be rows, she reminded herself. They were a new household still, all three of them trying to find their way. And Stevie, as she kept having to remind herself, was still only fifteen, push-ing at barriers. Clothes with attitude – heavens, she had done her share of that once upon a time, and a lot more besides. Janine twiddled with the blind, letting her thoughts drift, with their usual irksome predictability, to Dougie. She had read somewhere recently that embracing difficult emotions was better than trying to ignore them and had been doing her best to put the advice into practice. It was difficult, though, like opening a door to a stranger one wasn't certain about, then finding they wouldn't leave. Her emotions about Dougie were always like that: good and bad, invariably strong, invariably outstaying their welcome. She had never loved anyone more fiercely or been so hurt by them. That she could still remember both states of being so vividly, so separately, was a contradiction that was as baffling as it was painful.

Behind her Donna was on the horoscope page of her magazine. 'You're a Capricorn, aren't you?'

Janine nodded, smiling, glad of the interruption. 'January the sixteenth. What does it say?'

Donna sucked her plastic fork. 'It's one of those stupid ones, about planets being lined up . . . but it gets better . . . Hang on . . . Issues that have been –'

Janine's mobile *tring*ed inside her handbag. One o'clock exactly, she noticed, her heart swelling with affection. Murmuring apologies to Donna, she hurried outside to take the call, pressing a finger in her free ear to drown the hum of the high-street traffic.

'Hey, babe.'

'Hi, Mike.'

'How's your day going?'

'Okay. Quiet. Yours?'

'Busy. But fine. I shouldn't be late tonight . . . six thirty, sevenish.'

'Great. I thought we'd have that chicken thing – with spaghetti and mascarpone.'

'Sounds good.'

He said something else but a bus lumbered by and she had to ask him to repeat it.

'It was just about what we discussed the other day. I was wondering if . . .'

'I'm still thinking about it, Mike, okay? It's still a possibility. Like I said, I need to run it past Dougie.'

'Of course.'

Janine heard the guardedness creep into his tone. It always did when she used Dougie's name. 'Stevie's got that parents' evening coming up,' she reminded him gently. 'I thought I'd mention it then. That way, I get a bit more time to think things through myself.'

'Good idea. I didn't mean to bully you. We've got a couple of months yet till a decision needs to be made. So, no pressure, okay?'

Janine smiled to herself. No pressure indeed. But it was nice pressure, good pressure for the right reasons. 'Okay.'

'I just want you to be happy, you know that, don't you, my love?'

'Yes, Mike, I know that. It's one of the reasons I'm so mad about you.'

'And I want Stevie to be happy too.'

Through the window Janine could see Donna slowly, reverently, unwrapping the metal foil from a long thin bar of chocolate. 'Sweetheart, I know that too – really I do.'

'I'm so pleased we're all going out on Saturday,' he

33

blurted. 'Finding something she would enjoy, managing to get tickets – being able to sort it. I love that.'

'Oh, and she's *so* excited.' Janine turned her back on Donna, hugging herself and feeling blessed all over again that Mike had come into her life. Walking through the door wanting to look at flats and asking her out in the space of ten minutes – he had been endearingly bold. He had such a good heart, such a desire to please.

'Not that I'm trying to buy your daughter's affections or anything,' he added, with a chuckle. 'It's her mother I'm really interested in.'

When Janine stepped back inside the office Donna was on the final mouthful of her chocolate. She pressed her fingers against her big soft lips when she swallowed, as if, now that she had a witness, it was a pleasure that warranted concealment. 'Was that your man?'

'Yes, it was.'

'He phones a lot, doesn't he?'

'Yes, he does.'

'So I guess it's, like, *serious* between you, then?'

Janine nodded, grinning. 'Oh, yes, it is. Very serious. But also a little bit complicated.' She sighed. 'Somehow it always gets complicated, doesn't it?'

The journalist was even younger than Dougie had expected, and strikingly attractive, with sharp cheekbones, white-blonde hair, swept up in a loose ponytail, deep-set grey eyes, and legs so long in clinging jeans and leather boots that he had to make a conscious effort to keep his eyes off them. Where the flap of her jacket had fallen open he could see that she had a decent chest too, appealingly criss-crossed by the straps of her bag and camera, and centred by a lovely gully of cleavage, the skin creamy smooth. 'Laura Munro? Come on in.' He held the door wider, ushering her past his bike. 'I guess, all things considered, we should conduct our business in the kitchen. Follow me. It's a basement conversion and easily the best thing about the house.' She trotted behind him, her boots clomping on the stairs. 'Tea? Coffee?'

'No thanks. Just a glass of tap water would be great.' She slipped off the camera and rummaged in the bag, plucking out a small digital recorder. 'Okay with this?'

'Sure.' Dougie ran the tap for her water (bad plumbing meant it took a while to get properly cold) and quickly set about preparing coffee for himself. Beans, the grinder, the percolator – since he'd packed in the booze it had become something of a treasured ritual. 'I'll be right with you.'

'No worries.'

From the corner of his eye he could see her exploring the kitchen, picking things up and putting them down, peering through the glass pane of the back door. He was nervous, he realized. Nervous. It was ridiculous. In the old days he had taken the media in his stride like everything else. Even sniping reviews, not to mention snatches of tabloid gossip, had proved healthy for business. The Black Hen and its predecessors had thrived on publicity, good and bad.

But now things were different. There was too much at stake, not just the need for this young woman's help in getting his feeble cooking enterprise off the ground but also the new, despicable fear of making a fool of himself, losing what sometimes felt like the only thing he had left to lose, which was pride.

Laura had returned her attention to the room. 'So this is where it all happens.' She didn't sound enthused and Dougie could hardly blame her. The kitchen was large and clean but undeniably dingy, the grey walls and ugly square units darkened by age. The worktops running between them were unattractive and cheap *faux*-marble, covered with knife cuts from previous careless tenants. There was a sturdy six-ringed gas hob and fan-assisted double oven, both encrusted with scars. The fridge was cadaverous and free-standing, with a decent-sized freezer, but pressed into an awkward position against the wall beside the stairs.

The journalist had returned to the back door and was peering through its mottled glass panel. It looked out onto the sunken well of concrete from which metal steps led up to the garden. 'Any chance we could go outside? It would be better for the photo.'

'If you like – though, be warned, it's not exactly Kew Gardens and we'll have to take a couple of these.' Dougie left his coffee simmering and hooked his arms through two of the kitchen chairs. He used the garden a lot, but only to smoke in. Even above the concrete stairwell it was a sorry sight – grass lost to weeds, borders of brambles, and two lopsided poles presumably intended, once upon a time, as markers for a washing line. The whole house was like that – full of intentions gone to seed. He should probably have settled for a poky flat, somewhere a lot cheaper and further north than Kentish Town. But a poky flat wouldn't have given Stevie a decent-sized bedroom, or a front door that didn't have to be shared, or a garden to wander into (even if it was a little on the rough side);

and Kentish Town was at least within cycling distance of her Camden school, not to mention the small three-bedroomed terraced house in Chalk Farm that Janine had managed to buy with her much larger share of the divorce settlement.

Laura held the door open for him and the chairs. 'Where I come from,' she said, 'any scrap of sunshine and we're out there worshipping it.' Arriving after him at the top of the metal steps, she tipped her face skyward. 'Oh, yes, that's so good.'

Dougie set the chairs on the flattest section of ground. It had been a dry spring and the earth was too hard and compacted even for the weeds to get a decent grip. He fetched his coffee and lit a cigarette, studying her through the film of smoke while she settled herself. 'So where's that, then, this sun-worshipping place you come from? Scotland?'

She tossed her ponytail off her neck and flicked open her notebook. 'No, Sweden.'

Dougie slowly exhaled as various hackneyed associations—natural blondes, nudity, saunas, free love—scrolled through his mind. He had been to Sweden once during the high-flying times, checking sources for seafood, but it had also been a good excuse to get away, from the restaurant, from the bad stuff between him and Janine. He had taken a young Polish waitress with him — Carla? Carma? Carda? — an elfin thing with dyed black hair who had ruined the trip with an upset stomach and an inability to hold her drink. They had stayed in Gamla Stan, Stockholm's old town, lit up like a fairy tale with Christmas markets and street lights. One of Dougie's prime memories of the visit was staring down at the enticing view of it from his hotel room, wishing he had come alone.

Laura pressed a button on her mini-recorder and clicked open her biro. 'Okay, shall we get going?' She tucked a stray lock of hair behind her ear. 'You're starting a cooking company?'

'Not exactly.' Dougie took a deep breath and launched into a description of his plans, doing his best to make them sound both plausible and interesting, and giving several plugs to the website, which had gone live that morning. The designer, who was a friend of Gary's, was still refusing to discuss costs.

'So, are you, like, banking on people remembering your name from when you ran a successful restaurant?'

'Well, yes, I suppose that is part of the idea . . .' It was hard not to flinch at the girl's bluntness. 'It's a well-trodden path, of course,' Dougie blustered on, 'celebrity chefs branching out into other areas. Though I'm also working on a book, as it happens.' He paused to breathe, smiling. The book was hazy – a few notes, some sketchy titles: *Out to Dinner*, *Simple & Delicious*, *Food Made Easy*, *Dougie Easton's Dining Delights*. Once he had nailed the name he was sure the rest would follow. 'The idea is that it will all link up,' he went on, improvising madly, 'the book, the website, some apps in due course . . .'

'So you don't want to open another restaurant?'

Dougie sat back in his chair and folded his arms. 'God, no. Been there. Done that. It's no life, trust me.' He smiled again, more tightly.

'But it was up there, wasn't it?' She sifted some papers at the back of her notepad. 'The Black Hen, in Notting

Hill, "the venue other chefs eat at", and wasn't it where Guy Rawlings proposed to Lily Champ, getting you to put the ring in a Baked Alaska or something, going on one knee in front of everybody?'

'It was a compôte – blueberries.'

'Don't you miss that? The buzz, the publicity, the –'

'No. No, I don't at all.'

She looked disappointed. 'I suppose that's because of . . . er . . . how things panned out.'

'I thought we were here to talk about my new business venture.' It was taking some effort now to hang on to the smile.

'We are. But background is always good. Context. People will be more interested if they know where you're coming from. Like with the Black Hen – where it all went wrong.'

'Something to cheer up readers over their cornflakes, eh?' Dougie quipped, aiming for a tone of joviality that didn't quite come off.

'Look,' she said, the briskness back in her voice, 'just tell me about the turning point – when you realized the place couldn't be saved, when you hit rock bottom.'

Dougie drew so deeply on his cigarette butt he could feel the smoke burning his lips. Rock bottom. There was a phrase. Every time he'd thought he'd reached it there had been further to go, more levels. Near the journalist's chair leg a lone daffodil had pushed its way up through a large crack in the concrete – a blinding yellow, such beauty, such resilience. It sent a sudden wave of sadness through him, of humiliation.

'Or we could go further back?'

39

The afternoon spring sun was suddenly too hot. Dougie could feel sweat breaking out on his upper lip and under the thick front mess of his hair. Through the biggest of the gaps in the fence he glimpsed his neighbour, clad in her usual baggy jogging bottoms and one of her weird woolly hats, pegging out some washing – a pair of black tights, a grey bra. Her fat black cat was by her feet, rolling in a patch of sun. 'Cooking was just something I found easy. My mother . . .' he hesitated, aware he was about to give her exactly the sort of detail she wanted '. . . she died when I was just a kid and Dad wasn't too domesticated, so culinary skills kicked in pretty young. I gave uni a go, but soon dropped out, started skivvying in kitchens and never looked back.'

'And you have an ex-wife.' She checked her notes again. 'Janine? She used to sing in a band called the Rules. When you met she was pregnant by someone else but you got married and became the father of the child?'

'Well, haven't you done your research well?'

'I like to get the facts straight.' Laura threw him a businesslike smile. 'And you've got a younger brother who –'

'James, yes. A soldier, so I don't see much of him.' Dougie swigged the last dreggy mouthful of his coffee and shifted his chair so that both his frumpy neighbour and the daffodil were out of his eye-line. 'But if you're so keen on getting your facts straight, perhaps I could save you a little time.' He was aware of some small barrier inside him giving way, giving up the fight. What was there to be afraid of, after all? Why not speak some of the truth? There were enough other things that the journalist – and the rest of the world – would never know. 'I had everything, you see, Laura – a wife and family, a good business, talent, money. And I lost them all. Because I drank too much. Okay? It was crap for a time but I've put it behind me. Now I'm launching a new business based on catering for private events and teaching folk how to cook. A bit of money, the simple life, good health – that's all I'm after now.'

'Do you see your daughter?'

Dougie recalled the recent late-night phone call from Janine, the flurry of panic. Stevie being a cause for worry was new territory for both of them. Predictable territory, but no easier for that. Stretched out on his sofa a couple of weekends before, he had glimpsed two gold loops puncturing the neat rim of her tummy button. Two. That he had managed not to mention them was a fact of which he was still inordinately proud. 'Yes, thank you, I do.'

'Are you in a new relationship?'

'Are you?'

She laughed. 'Oh, I get it, you're telling me I'm getting too nosy. Well, actually, I'm *between* relationships at the moment. The last one wanted to get serious and I didn't.'

'Right. Well, so am I. For similar reasons.' Clare Beazley, cloying, intense . . . God, he was well out of that – and sufficiently unnerved to have vowed to steer clear of women completely for a while. Dougie sat back in his chair, shaking his head, smiling in spite of himself. Christ, what had he expected from this journalist woman anyway? There was no publicity that wasn't prurient these days and she had been right: reminding readers of his former glory would do the opposite of harm. 'Rock bottom, since you asked about it, was waking up in the small hours, alone on a pavement, in a pool of my own vomit. A cold pool. I'll never forget that, how cold it was. And lumpy. It's always lumpy, isn't it?'

She scribbled madly, even though her tape was still running.

Chapter Four

Janine gripped the handle of Stevie's bedroom door and turned it slowly so as not to make a noise. A couple of hours earlier her daughter had stumbled into the kitchen clutching her stomach and saying she wasn't up to school. It was now mid-morning and her curtains were still drawn. Only the upper half of her face was visible above the top of the duvet. Her skin looked chalky and her eyes were closed. Her long thick hair was in wild arrows across the pillow. The air smelt stuffy and faintly acrid. Janine was about to retreat when the bedclothes moved. 'Hey, darling, I just wondered if you were feeling any better.'

'A bit.'

'It's the usual, I suppose?'

'Yup.'

'Do you want anything? Tea? Water? Juice?'

'Uh-uh.'

Janine hovered in the doorway, pondering all the new tensions between them, aware that they appeared to be solidifying into something permanent. 'Do you want to chat or be left alone?'

There was a grunt, which Janine decided to take as sufficient encouragement to sit on the end of the bed. She squeezed the lump of the foot nearest her under the duvet. 'School's OK, is it? You're not worried about the parents' evening, are you? Or your exam results?'

'Mum, school is *fine*.'

Janine looked out of the window, fighting the urge to open the curtains, let in some light. Somewhere outside a bird was singing, a piercingly repetitive whistle, as if it was desperate to be heard, to be understood. 'Very good on Saturday, wasn't it? Such a funny, talented man. Mike did well to –'

Stevie pulled the foot free and wriggled upright, peering at her mother through haystack hair. 'Actually . . . could I have a juice? Orange?'

'Sure. Of course. I won't be a tick.'

Stevie slumped back against the headboard, glumly contemplating the galvanizing effect of her request and despising herself for engineering it. She should have gone to school. Day one of her period was never great, but seldom unbearable. Janine taking the morning off hadn't been part of the plan. It meant she had to pretend to be as poorly as she claimed, instead of doing what she had really wanted, which was to veg out with food in front of the telly.

Her mother reappeared a few minutes later with a tall glass of juice and a Digestive biscuit, which Stevie did her best to ignore, but then picked bits off, trying not to look as if she was enjoying it. 'The Panadol helped,' she mumbled, when she had finished, fearing that the consumption of the biscuit nonetheless needed explaining. 'Are you taking the whole day off?' she added cautiously.

'No. I just said I'd be in late. I was worried about *you*. A mother's lot, worrying.' She pulled a face. 'And Mike,' she added, rushing the words, so Stevie could tell at once that they had been rehearsed, 'he worries about you, too. He likes you a lot. You know that, don't you?'

Stevie let her eyes glaze while her mother plunged into one of her now familiar Mike speeches – there had been a lot of them lately, which just made her less inclined to listen. It ended back where it had started, with the business of the Jason Stobart tickets, Mike's 'fantastic' treat, which had indeed been fantastic but –

'So I think a letter might be nice.'

Stevie focused properly, unable to conceal her disdain. 'A *letter*?'

Janine fidgeted with her cardigan cuffs, like even she knew it was a naff idea. 'Well, a card, anyway. I've got one you could use … Look, sweetie,' she gabbled, 'I know how grateful you were, but I just think that Mike might enjoy the reassurance of a proper thank-you.'

'I've given him a proper *thank-you* to his face about a *million* times –'

'No, you have not,' Janine retorted, showing her true colours, Stevie decided bitterly, her true loyalties.

'How do you know *what* I've said to Mike or *when*?' she scoffed. 'It's not like you're with us the whole time, is it? If you must know, I've told him literally hundreds of times what a brilliant surprise it was …' Stevie faltered as the glaring logic of the situation dawned on her. 'He's *told* you I'm not grateful enough, hasn't he? He's told you and that's why you're here now, ordering me to write him a stupid letter.'

'Showing proper gratitude is not stupid.'

'Yes, it is, when it's so fake. And it wasn't like I asked to see Jason bloody Stobart anyway, was it? Mike needn't have done it. Just because he's got so much money compared to us, he loves any excuse to flash it around.'

'Now that is simply not fair,' Janine gasped, folding her arms tightly across her chest, as if it was the only way to stop herself exploding.

'And what is the point,' Stevie went on viciously, raising her voice, aware that she was half enjoying the row, as she had recently discovered could happen if she took the brakes off and stopped trying to second-guess or worry about her mother's reactions, 'what is the *point* in doing something nice if you're just going to use it as a reason to bitch about someone behind their back? Mike is just trying to get you on his side against *me*. He's got that swanky house in Surrey, hasn't he? He wanted to buy a flat in London, didn't he? So why did he have to go and ruin everything by moving in here?'

'Enough,' Janine shrieked. She flung out a finger, pointing it at Stevie like a weapon, the whole arm trembling visibly. 'I will not have you talking about Mike like that —'

'Go away, then,' Stevie retorted miserably. 'I feel crap. Go away. Leave me alone.' When Janine did not move, she pulled the duvet over her head and sat under the hot tent of it, breathing hard until she heard the door close.

Soon after, there were footsteps on the stairs and then the slam of the front door. A couple of minutes later her phone buzzed with a text. *Sorry. I just want you and M to be friends. I hope you feel better soon. Reheat the pasta if u up to lch. Xx*. Feeling guilty, resenting the guilt, Stevie snatched a piece of paper out of the computer printer in the spare bedroom and wrote a few fast and furious words to Mike, hoping the scrawl alone would tell him of the arm-twisting that lay behind them: *Thanks again for Saturday – it was brilliant. S.*

Unable to face the hunt for an envelope, she folded the paper in two, wrote his name in capital letters on one side and propped it on the newel post where he always slung his coat. She then texted her mother, saying, *I've done it,* all the while cursing the fact of being able to hate someone so much, yet still feel an obligation to do their bidding.

Her dad was so much easier to handle, so much less demanding, she reflected angrily, taking two more biscuits and settling in front of the telly. He just let her be herself. He never made her feel like he had this private list of things he was trying to get her to be or do. And though he had girlfriends, he had never yet forced any of them on her, let alone asked them to move in with him. On their weekends together they just hung out, playing games, watching films, eating brilliant food. In fact, Stevie sometimes caught herself being glad about all the bad things that had happened – the split from her mum, losing his job – because he had time for her now in a way that he had never had before. Before, even when he was there, it often felt like he might as well not have been.

The light changed to red, but Dougie, seeing the coast was clear, kept on pedalling. The driver of the car he passed put up a middle finger, but amiably, more as if out of duty to the unwritten rules of traffic warfare than because he really cared. There was a slight slope in the road and Dougie cruised down it, letting go of the handlebars and steering expertly with a combination of balance and gentle pressure from his thighs, relishing the notion that even a penurious cyclist could own the road a little. The sun beat pleasantly on his back and his panniers bulged with fresh produce from the market.

It was Wednesday, a week after his *North London Life* interview with Laura Munro, and he had an afternoon class to prepare for, of ten-year-olds. It wasn't much, but it was a start. A 'Birthday Cook', the mother had called it, phoning after getting the number off the website, to make cakes, but only after they had eaten something healthy using fruit and vegetables. Could he make vegetables fun? Did he know how?

She had sounded desperate and Dougie, improvising as he seemed to at every turn now, had assured her he could provide exactly what was required. In truth, he was still working on a few motley ideas – maybe fresh peas (the kids would enjoy the shucking); a salad of raisins, grated carrot, apples (perhaps bobbed for from a bucket to make it more of a game); banana boats; chunky chips cut into funny faces – a potato was a vegetable, after all. But for three hundred quid (thirty quid a head with ten kids for two hours) he was prepared to give anything a go. The cakes would be easy: cupcakes, lots of them, with fla-voured icings – banana, vanilla, lemon – decorated with bits of fresh fruit and a shake of sugar for added crunch. Back in the day, before body-piercing and iPhones, Stevie had always been a sucker for a good cupcake, preferably chocolate, preferably sprinkled with silver balls.

Dougie resumed control of the handlebars and patted his fleece pocket, checking for the precious little clutch of business cards he had been distributing during the course of his morning's shopping – to hairdressers, newsagents, dry cleaners, any outlet, indeed, prepared to display them. The only target now left in his sights was the library.

It had been a hassle doing the cards, fiddling with settings on his computer, getting the paper properly aligned. It had reminded him of the trouble he and Janine had had in printing off their menus in the early, prehistoric days – amateur efforts, sometimes going out with dreadful howlers. *Dick* à l'orange, brandy *slaps* – how they had laughed. Everything had been easier to laugh at then, with life still feeling like there was everything to hope for and nothing to lose. The original Hen had been a mere five tables on the ground floor of their tiny rented Cornwall cottage, expanding to seven via the pavement if the weather was fair (which it wasn't often). It had taken a full evening of covers to make any money. He and Janine rarely snatched more than a few hours' sleep. And yet it had never seemed to matter much, or to detract from the pleasure of sitting at their small, rickety kitchen table at the end of each long day, sipping glasses of wine while they counted their takings, their eyes popping with exhaustion, Stevie asleep on the sturdy old sofa next to them, fenced in with cushions to keep her safe.

Dougie slowed as the library came into sight, marvelling that a period in his life that had felt so like a beginning had – in the unblemished-happiness stakes, at least – been so close to the end. By the following year the group Janine sang in had disbanded and he was on his second premises, an expensive rental, but in a popular fishing village, tucked under the lip of a cliff, beside a cobbled path down to the sea. The first summer was hot and tourists had flocked to be fed. Penny-counting became a more serious business, done via paper and a bank account rather than round a table among the debris of a meal. Under pressure he worked well – creatively – especially, he had found, if he had a drink or two along the way. Established foodies started to mention his name. Stevie began nursery and Janine got a part-time job in a clothes shop as well as managing front-of-house. Backstage, he hired someone to wash up, someone to prep, as well as two waitresses to spin in and out of the dining room.

The following summer, millennium year, a Polish student had come to help out with the skivvying: scarlet hair, black lipstick, short skirts, pink Converse trainers, attitude. She'd had a way of lingering over tasks that required any physical stretching or bending, waggling her backside as if inviting him to check her out. After late-night shifts she would sit against the wall by the bins, smoking a spliff and sipping a Coke, before getting on the rusting moped that took her back to wherever it was she called home. Petra, her name was. Petra Koswolski. Dougie had started drinking more by then, using the kick it gave with more calculation, more need, to wind up, to wind down, whatever was required. One night as he was closing up, dropping a last bag into a bin, a little bleary-eyed after the usual long day, Petra had appeared from nowhere, uncoiling like a snake from the dark and wrapping herself around him. They had stumbled down the path and had sex against a tree in the shadows of a boathouse, the beat of the night waves in their ears.

Furtive, fast, grubby, born of opportunism rather than discontent and therefore unforgivable, it was an act of disloyalty that might nonetheless have been forgiven had it been confessed to. Instead, it had stayed locked up, got-away-with. The effect on Dougie had evolved over time, from guilt to regret, then relief and a sort of elation. It wouldn't happen again, he vowed. But a year later it had. And then again ten months after that. And again after that. It was almost as if that first lapse had opened the door to something rotten inside him, a pebble releasing an avalanche. A pattern was born; a habit of gratification – bad, unstoppable, another way of feeling high when his stress levels were up and the world was spinning. It was testimony to the strength of what they had started with that Janine hung on as long as she did. Dougie knew that, and there had been patches when they'd almost got it back again, when he had kept the drinking down and stopped the playing around. One patch in particular when . . .

Dougie squeezed the bike brakes, jolting to a stop with unnecessary force. He didn't want to think about that. He never wanted to think about that. It made the rock bottom he had mentioned to Laura Munro feel like a bit of fun.

The library looked forlorn. A single loose banner advertising an upcoming event had been inexpertly pinned above the crescent of red bricks over the entrance. On it Dougie could just make out the words 'Reading' and 'Free!' The bike rack was empty, adding to the impression of an institution in decline. Dougie slid his bike into a middle slot and hesitated, fearing for the welfare of his party-shopping, bulging out of his panniers, the lush green carrot heads trailing like plants from a window-box.

If it was all nicked he'd be in trouble. There was a fiver left in his wallet and he was at the edge of his overdraft limit. He squatted down to unstrap the bags, but then left them where they were, overcome by a sort of revulsion at how his world – his mind-set – had shrunk. To be afraid of losing a few root vegetables. It was too pitiful.

He took the steps two at a time and strode into the library. All he wanted was to pin a business card to a board – it was hardly likely to take more than a few minutes. The board in question was in the main foyer and already swarming with notices and flyers: painting, flower arranging, Pilates, yoga, private tuition, gardeners, baby-sitters, cleaners, accountants, house-clearers. Dougie stared at the dense collage for a few moments, fighting the fear that his little advert, even with the jaunty miniature logo of a chef's hat that had been such a fiddle to get right, would be totally lost – a flake in a snowstorm.

'Hi.'

'Hi.' Dougie cast a cursory glance sideways, registering a headscarf, tightly bound, gypsy-style, round a bleached-looking face and two huge hoop earrings. He quickly edged away, heading for the main reception area, which was set further into the foyer. As he walked he plucked one of the cards out of his fleece pocket, checking it for smudges or creases. It might feel pointless but he still had to try. He needed business, he needed *money*. Through some swing doors on his left a child started howling.

The reception area comprised a ring of desks containing several chairs and computer terminals. A vast, jowly blancmange of a man, his body spilling over the sides of his small wheeled chair, appeared to be in sole charge.

As Dougie approached, he slid away to attend to an elderly lady on the other side, using his feet to steer across the carpet. The lady was trying to use an out-of-date library card and reluctant to be persuaded of the fact. Dougie waited, first trying not to look impatient but then switching tack and looking as impatient as possible, foot-tapping, watch-checking, hair-tugging. The large man glided several more times between desks, pulling out different forms from different drawers, wheeling back again. He clearly loved the chair. And what an admirably sturdy piece of furniture it must be, Dougie observed darkly, his impatience thickening to antipathy as the show continued.

'Hi there.'

It was the gypsy woman again. She was in a curious wigwam of a dress. Beneath the hem Dougie glimpsed a flash of a very white foot encased in an unflattering flat open-toed sandal, with wide leather straps and a chunky rubber sole.

'I live next door to you,' she prompted. 'Number fifty-four?'

'You do? Oh, right . . . God – sorry, of course you do. I was miles away.' Dougie forced a smile. 'Small world.' He looked at his watch, experiencing a pang of concern for his panniers. 'I'm going to have to come back another time.'

'Perhaps I could help. I work here.'

'Really? Blimey – that's a stroke of luck.' He brandished the business card. 'I just want to put this up on the board – advertise my services.'

'Oh, fine. It's two quid a week.'

'Is it? Wow.'

'Oh, is that a lot?'

'No, it's fine. Thanks very much.' She had no lashes or eyebrows, Dougie noticed, and a puffiness round her eyes and mouth that made him think, cruelly, of a badly blown-up beach ball. He recalled all the limp bras pegged to the washing line, telling himself he should feel sorry rather than repelled.

'I'm Nina, by the way. Nina Carmichael.'

'Dougie Easton – nice to meet you.' Dougie dug into his jeans pocket for his wallet, glad it ruled out the possibility of any silly formality, like shaking hands.

'I enjoyed the article, by the way.'

'The article, right . . . Hang on, what article?' He handed over a two-pound coin, noting as he did so that, within the puffiness, her eyes were a clear almost translucent blue, and that, unless he was imagining it, also faintly amused. 'You mean in *North London Life?*'

'Yup, that's the one.'

'When?'

'Today.'

'Today?' It was far sooner than Laura had led him to expect.

'There's a copy in the library.'

'Is there?'

'I'll show you if you like.'

'Thanks, yes, I'd like that very much.'

She set off down the corridor, stopping at a sitting area in an alcove near a water machine. A woman in a *burqa* was in one of the chairs reading the *Daily Mail.* 'Here we are.' She shook out a paper from a magazine rack and handed it to Dougie. 'I had no idea I was living next door to a *celebrity*, I must say. And with such an interesting life-history. Good picture too, especially as . . .' she had to stand on tiptoe to point across his arm '. . . Sam's in it. Look.'

'Sam?'

'My cat.' There was a trace of affront in her voice at having to spell out something so obvious.

Dougie studied the photo. Sure enough, the black cat was lying like some giant sea-slug across the top of the fence, slightly out of focus, very much in the background, but most definitely there. It was indeed a good shot of himself, though – an ironed T-shirt for once, hair a little messed up but not weird, his face creased in a half-smile – knowing but not arrogant. Yes, he could live with that, all right.

Come-back Cook Dougie Easton Stirs Up a Storm

Oh, Lord. A glib précis of his life followed, reading like the plot of a shallow novel. The facts were straight enough – he had to give Laura credit for that – even if there were rather more of them than he would have liked, especially about the early shenanigans surrounding Stevie. Janine had been single and just pregnant when they'd got together, an unwitting parting gift from a fling with an Australian surfer. It was unusual, but hardly the oddest scenario on the planet. To Dougie, loving Stevie had been integral to loving her mother, yet any newsprint version of the story (inevitably, there had been a few over the years) somehow managed to sully these good, simple things, as if salacious unknown details had to be lurking in the shadows somewhere. So he was a stepfather. So bloody what?

Dougie liked Laura's closing paragraph best. The website address was in bold, as was his phone number, while her final line comprised a private recommendation so warm that it sounded as if she had had a cooking session herself instead of disdainfully sipping a glass of his lukewarm tap water and firing provocative questions.

Dougie looked round to thank Nina but she had gone. He scanned the piece a second time, enjoying it more. He should drop Laura an email, he decided, express his gratitude properly. Maybe even suggest a return-the-favour meal. An enticing image slid into his mind, of the journalist in her knee-high boots and not much else. Hadn't she said she was between partners, dropping in the unnecessary detail that it was because the last one had wanted to get *serious*? Would an attractive female divulge such an enticing nugget of information without at least a hint of an ulterior motive?

Dougie returned the paper to its pile, throwing the veiled *Daily Mail* reader a sweet smile that belied the far from sweet urges suddenly raging in his lower abdomen. Pledging to stay away from relationships was one thing, but no sex was proving quite another matter. He felt ill from it sometimes, to the point of pain.

His panniers were intact. He pedalled home whistling, stopping en route to scoop up a copy of *North London Life* from a newsagent. He then set about preparing for his children's cooking party in earnest, devising an ingenious game-plan of entertainment that involved not only a wide variety of fruit and vegetables, but a witty treasure hunt of clues and simple culinary instructions.

As a result, and rather to Dougie's amazement, the two

hours with the ten-year-olds flew by. 'They're in the garden,' he told the two mothers who appeared on the doorstep for the pick-up. He led them downstairs where they were soon cooing over the few uneaten cupcakes and Laura's article, which (with a little shame at his own cunning) he had left open on the kitchen table.

'I had them eating out of my hand,' he joked to Simon, over the phone, a couple of hours later.

'That's great, mate, though be careful you don't get stuck with the tag of being a children's entertainer. You're far too good for that, Doug, and you know it.'

Dougie laughed. 'Of course I do.'

'You must take what you can at the moment – I get that, really, and I'm not knocking it. Just . . . just don't let go of what you are – *who* you are – in the process, okay?'

Dougie hesitated. For the first time in a while he had been feeling really up-beat and Simon was in danger of ruining it. And yet who but Simon could issue such warnings? The man was his truest, oldest friend. Their allegiance had started as sixth-formers when Simon had turned up as a late arrival after being kicked out of a much higher-profile school for achieving an insufficient number of top grades. Arrogant, uncompromising, and with his markedly diminutive size, he had been ignored or picked on until Dougie had come to his aid, a rescue spurred by an instinctive recognition of loneliness and the realization that behind Simon's glib comments there lurked a unique and enjoyably dry take on the world. Repayment had come in the form of the steadiest companionship anyone could have hoped for. Through good times and bad Simon had always been there – a safety net, supportive, unquestioning, not to mention generous, to the extent lately that Dougie had been finding it almost too much to bear. 'Okay, point taken,' he replied carefully. 'But I tell you,' he added, as the success of the afternoon came surging back, 'those chattering mums are going to be key to stirring up local business. The Kentish Town grapevine is probably a-buzz even now. This time tomorrow they'll be queuing round the street. And that *North London Life* piece came out today –'

'Oh, good,' said Simon, lightly. 'I'm glad. Did they make a good job of it?'

'Not bad at all. Thanks again for that, Simon.'

'No probs. I must make sure I pick up a copy.'

'Or look at mine when you come round.'

Simon groaned. 'Oh dear, yes, the next *cooking* session looms.'

'Si, there's no obligation on that as you well know,' Dougie assured him hurriedly, some of the awkwardness at being so beholden resurfacing. 'You've helped so much already.'

'Shut up, man. I'll be there. As will Gary and Richard. Set in stone.'

Dougie put down his mobile and peered over the back of the sofa into the street. He was in his sitting room for once, at the front of the house, stretched out on the same piece of furniture that had served as a bed for Stevie fifteen years before. Of soft grey velvet, grand and comfortable, one of Janine's earliest clever bargain-spots, he had not expected to remain its lucky owner, but during the ugly process of dividing up belongings Janine had surprised him with several of the items she surrendered. They were embarking on new lives, she had said bitterly, so how much did it really matter what either of them left behind? Dougie pressed his fingers into the soft, worn seat cushion as the memory hardened. He could still picture her face as she had said the words: the small tight lines round her mouth, the accusing hurt in her deep brown eyes. He had so nearly reached for her, so nearly tried, again, to offer the impossibility of fixing all that had gone wrong. It had felt like a last chance, vanishing the moment it was recognized.

Out in the street there was no sign of anything very much, let alone a queue of would-be cooks. Dougie felt in his back pocket for the wad of money the mums had given him – cash as agreed – and it felt good. A drop in several oceans, but still good. He would keep fifty to see him through the week, pay two hundred towards his rent debt and put the rest towards the never-ending challenge of keeping his credit cards at bay. He had to be patient, that was the thing, patient and careful, with money, with himself.

A car shot past, music thumping out of its windows. Although it was a sunny evening, a wind had picked up, forcing the spindly street trees to spill yet more of their blossom and making the polythene over the half-completed loft conversion across the street flap like a loose sail. A yellow Styrofoam box bounced into view on the pavement, slapping up against the wheel of a parked car. A moment later Nina, his neighbour-librarian, stepped into the frame, wielding a large pair of garden shears, with which she began scissoring viciously at the trailing overgrowth of her front hedge. She was still in the wigwam dress but had an anorak pulled over it and a purple pom-pom hat in place of the gypsy headscarf.

Dougie slid deeper into the sofa and reached for his laptop. It had been a good day but, with the phone call to Simon over and the evening stretching ahead, empty but for the TV and the predictable contents of his own head for company, he was aware of having arrived at the tail-end of his buoyant mood. Circling in its place, like a vulture after carrion, was the familiar shadow of half-bored loneliness, the one that once would have served as one of many pretexts for twisting the top off a fresh bottle of Jack Daniel's. Dougie hurriedly logged into his emails, stabbing at the keys, wishing he could drum out the background rasp of Nina Carmichael's garden shearing, which was intermittent and jarring, as if neither the blades nor their operator were up to the job.

There were two new messages. The first was from Rentinc, the company that managed the business for his landlord: a formal notification that his arrears stood at £1,300 and that, without immediate settlement, legal action would be taken to evict him from the property. Dougie read it quickly, the dryness in his throat worsening. This wasn't the first warning. But it was still only an email, he consoled himself. The letter on the doormat would signal that the endgame had really begun. He replied with as much confidence as he could, offering a painstaking explanation about imminent returns on recent investment in his new business and promising four hundred pounds by the following day. The sum was woefully short of what was required, and would tip him onto the wrong side of his overdraft limit, but might at least buy him a little more time.

The second message was from Janine, reminding him of Stevie's parents' evening the following Tuesday. She wished to talk to him afterwards, she said, a half-hour at most, at her place, if that would be convenient. Dougie read the brief paragraph twice, the knots in his stomach tightening. The meetings with the teachers would be fine – enjoyable, even: he never missed those. He would be co-operative and attentive as usual – play the Good Dad – but also do his best to catch Stevie on the hop, stir her up a little, make her laugh, show her he cared. An audience with Janine was quite another matter. It meant money, Dougie guessed, not for her – after the settlement she had sworn never to ask on her own behalf and had so far kept her word – but for Stevie. There was a language-improvement trip to Valencia coming up in the summer, he remembered. Yes, it had to be that, he decided grimly; a deposit of some kind – small but, given his current circumstances, potentially crippling.

Doggedly, using the usual four fingers, Dougie tapped out a jolly reply: he would see her at the school gates and be available to talk afterwards. No problemo. Gritting his teeth, he then composed a rather less carefree note to Xavier, the Spanish agent supposedly in charge of the *finca*, asking if there had yet been any progress towards either a rental or a sale. Finally, with the winged black shadow hovering ever closer, and the dryness having become a raging thirst, tightening its grip as it always did when he was low and there was cash in his pocket, Dougie scrolled back through his old messages to pick out the email address of the *North London Life* journalist.

Hi Laura,

Just to say thank-you for the piece today – it was a very pleasant surprise that it came out so soon. I thought you did a great job – words and picture. My phone hasn't stopped ringing . . . Well, it hasn't started ringing yet, to be honest, but I'm sure it will! In the meantime, I wondered if you would allow me to thank you in person? We could meet for a drink or, perhaps more appropriately, I could cook you dinner. What about tomorrow?

If you can't/don't want to, no worries.

Cheers,
Dougie

Dougie pressed 'send' and sat back. Deep in the dark of him now there was a murmur of something else – excitement, anticipation, diversion. Holding on to the feeling, fearing what might happen if he let it fade, Dougie then picked up his mobile and dialled the number of his father's terraced house on the outskirts of Tonbridge. When the call-minder message kicked in, he said a silent prayer of gratitude and left a hasty message, dutiful filial platitudes, before returning his attention to his computer screen. To his astonishment, Laura had already fired back a reply:

I'm glad you liked it. Dinner tomorrow would be good. I'll see you at 8.

Laura x

PS I'm a vegetarian

Chapter Five

Victoria was about to get out of the car when a slim young blonde woman in dark blue drainpipe jeans, platform shoes and a bright green T-shirt emerged from the front door. She had a leather satchel slung over one shoulder, and a black jacket over the other. Once the door was open, she turned back to kiss Dougie, standing on tiptoe to reach, her long ponytail swinging like a silvery pendulum between her shoulder blades. Instinctively Victoria glanced away, feeling like an interloper, a spy. But when she looked again the embrace was still going on, a more entwined version now, which seemed to involve Dougie trying to coax the girl back into the house.

Victoria would have driven off if she could. She had come on impulse, after her fingers had hovered over her phone. It was Friday and she was supposed to be going to the supermarket, the big one that always had queues at the checkouts but was worth it for the choice. But Dougie had already seen her, making eye contact as he gave a final wave to his girlfriend. He sauntered over to where she was parked, his fingers casually sheathed in his jeans pockets, his slim hips so full of swagger that she wanted to scream. After what Simon had said, she had expected him to look more down somehow, more in need of pity.

'To what do I owe *this* pleasure?' he asked, putting his grinning face down to her open window, his voice imbued with the lazy tone of one already embarked on a fabulous day.

'Hello, Dougie.' Victoria grinned back, determined not to give him the satisfaction of mentioning the girl – only in her mid-twenties by the look of it, but devilishly pretty, as the ones she had glimpsed over the years always had been. The long-suffering Janine was certainly well out of it, she mused, winding up the window and getting out of the car. 'I was just passing – I wanted a word about something, if you have time.' She found her gaze drifting down the street, where the latest squeeze had just disappeared into the Saturday shoppers streaming up and down the road.

'I always have time for you, Victoria,' Dougie declared gallantly. 'I'm going to Broadway Market but I've got so held up already, what with one thing and another. Thirty more minutes won't make any difference. Come in for a coffee.'

Victoria hesitated, tracing cracks in the pavement with the toe edge of her flip-flop. 'I don't really need coffee . . . It's just, well, I've a favour to ask.' She was shy now the moment had come, put off her stride by Dougie's familiar laid-back charm. It was intriguing to see him sober too; not between-binges sober – she had seen a few of those in the past – but thoroughly dried-out sober. He looked well, his blue eyes bright, his skin faintly luminous, as if it had been scrubbed on the inside as well as out.

'Coffee,' he commanded, turning for the house, leaving her little option but to follow. A few minutes later he had directed her to a chair in his kitchen and promptly begun working his way through a large stack of washing-up. Victoria sprang up to help but was firmly steered back to her place. 'Sit down, for God's sake. It's my mess. I'll do it till the coffee's ready.'

'No gloves, I see,' she remarked, obediently flopping back into her seat but feeling both in the way and feeble. 'Doesn't your skin get sore?'

Dougie turned briefly to waggle his hands at her, dripping fat blobs of foam on the floor. 'Yes, it does.' He pulled a tortured face. 'But I'm very, very brave.'

'Idiot.' Victoria shook her head, smiling, observing that Dougie's hands looked as they always had – large and muscled, backed with fine sandy hairs. From nowhere an image slid into her mind of him using them to caress his petite young Slavic-featured girlfriend; he was such a gentle giant of a man, with a touch that was strong, deft, tender . . . Victoria hastily checked herself, faintly appalled, glad Dougie had his back turned. She had sex on the brain at the moment. She blamed Hopper – all that fecundity, burning up her innards, merging with the hunger for a child. Simon was being sweet – at his most attentive and loving – but so far the sweetness had yet to translate into any obvious signs of heightened physical need. In fact, it was now twenty-seven days since they had made love. Twenty-seven days. Once happy with the quieter patches of their sex life, Victoria had lately found herself counting and analysing them with the rigour of a mathematician. Even after the lunch with her father a couple of weeks before, when her cycle had been so perfectly poised and Simon's apologies so heartfelt, even then, their afternoon closeness on the sofa had somehow evolved into nothing more than an evening of sleepily loafing around, followed by a chaste night in bed.

'So, this favour of yours . . .' Dougie gripped the percolator tightly as he poured, aware that it was going to be one of those days when he had to control the shake in his hands. It happened still when he was tired. And that morning he was worn out, but also wired, as if he had done a night on speed. Laura had been voracious, unquenchable. It had been great for a while, but by the small hours worms of doubt and impatience had begun creeping into his lovemaking, about whether he had satisfied her, about why, in spite of coming once, twice, three times, she wouldn't fall asleep. For the final encounter in the early hours he had had to resort to a few old tricks to keep going – other thoughts, nothing to do with Laura, ways of holding his own while she worked her way towards the state of nirvana she was trying to achieve, nails stapling his skin, jaw grinding, eyes closed, clearly in a mental place that was just as removed as his was from her.

'Ah, yes. My favour.' Victoria took a small sip from the mug he had set in front of her and then a much larger one because it tasted so good. It was a relief to feel she had Dougie's full attention at last. 'It's about your Alicante house. The *finca*. Simon mentioned that it's been empty for a while and it gave me this idea.' She looked him squarely in the face, confident now the moment had come. 'Simon's fortieth – I was wondering if you would allow us to use it for a long-weekend house-party type thing. I picture just a small group, a bit like that time we went before – do you remember? – however many years ago it was, but with the difference that on this occasion we would be using your services *professionally*, for a fee . . . I mean, a really *decent* fee.'

'I see. Simon's birthday. Okay.' Dougie tapped his index finger against his lip in a show of ponderous thought, while inside his brain raced. To rent the *finca* for four days for several people, with big meals and good wine thrown in, would indeed warrant a big fee. Thousands. He would have to do the sums. Given his current situation, it was certainly appealing. And yet ... He studied Victoria's expectant expression, fearing that the plan might be another act of charity hatched by Simon. It struck him in the same instant how worn out his friend's wife was looking. An air of what appeared to be permanent tiredness seemed to have fallen round her clear green eyes. She had been a fine-looking woman, Victoria, towering, fearless, flashing energy. It was a shame to see it start to fade.

'Simon doesn't know,' she said, as if half reading his mind.

'The straight answer is yes, in principle,' Dougie replied carefully. He was bursting for a cigarette, but couldn't face the palaver of asking Victoria to accompany him outside. Never relaxing company at the best of times, she was now watching him like someone in a trance, which made it harder to marshal his thoughts. 'It's a fine idea, Vic. Very fine. And in theory I'd be more than happy to play my part. But the truth is I'm trying to get rid of the place and if I get an offer it'll have to take precedence. I can't afford for it not to,' he added gruffly, looking away. 'Which means it wouldn't be fair on you –'

Victoria was hugging herself, clearly thrilled. 'That's a yes, then?'

'I'm not sure you've been listening.'

'I have, I have.' She nodded vigorously, visibly loosening

the two Victorian mother-of-pearl combs keeping her long hair off her face. 'If we have to pull out, so be it. I'll take that risk – sort something else out. I'm good at sorting.' She talked fast, her eyes glazing slightly as the plans took shape in her head. 'But mid-July isn't far off, is it? Simon's actual birthday falls on the Saturday, which is handy. I was thinking four nights, Thursday to Monday. Probably six-ish people. That's a lot of food and drink. Then there's your flight too – of course I shall pay for that. You'll need time to think through all the costs. Imagine you're a five-star hotel and charge accordingly.' She paused to grin, providing a rare flash of the full extent of her smooth, tightly packed teeth. 'I want the best, you see, Doug,' she warned merrily, deftly tightening the grip of the combs and suddenly seeming somewhat less exhausted.

'Okay. I'll think through some rough costs and get back to you,' Dougie promised, glad she was being so professional. With the desire for a smoke corroding his insides, he retrieved her empty coffee mug and rinsed it out, hoping she would take the hint. But when he turned round she was still in her chair looking pensive, her legs knotted from thigh to ankle, like entwined vines, her diamanté-studded flip-flops dangling.

'Can we keep it between ourselves for now?'

'However you want to play it, Vic.'

'I was thinking of asking Gary and Ruth too. Simon doesn't have many friends really, does he? Apart from you – and Gary, of course. He used to get on well with my brother but . . .'

Dougie knew all about druggy Miles from Simon: the attempts at rescue that had failed, the dirty squats, the needles, the grisly death. Dougie and his friends had all done their share of drugs in their time, Gary especially, but none of them had ever got sucked into the really hard stuff. Victoria had turned away, her eyes glassy. 'I'll keep schtum, I promise,' he said briskly, 'until commanded otherwise.'

She picked up her handbag at last and he herded her to the door. But on the step she paused again, fiddling with the strap of the bag, an expensive box shape of livid mustard leather with a thick gold buckle. 'One more thing, if you don't mind my asking . . .'

'Yes?' Dougie leant against the door, doing his best to look relaxed. He wanted her gone so he could enjoy a smoke, get to the market. He was also wary of any questions that began with a preface about the fear of causing offence, such fears in his experience invariably proving justified.

'When they drink like that,' Victoria blurted, 'like when they were cooking with you the other night – Simon and the others – do you find it hard?'

'You mean, not drinking?' Dougie bluffed, caught further off guard than he had expected. 'Not really. Sometimes. There's the odd moment when . . . but then it passes . . . at least . . .'

'Good. That's good.' She kissed him quickly on the cheek. 'You've done so well. I'm really pleased for you. And if that sounds at all patronizing –'

'No – it's fine. Compliment received. Over and out. We'll talk soon.'

Fifteen minutes later Victoria glided her Audi into a slot in the supermarket car park. She then sat staring through the windscreen with the engine on and the air-con running. The late burst of spring warmth had stretched into early summer. The sun was high and hot. After her coffee with Dougie, the car had been like a sauna. Yet the supermarket would be too cold, she knew, especially round the freezer cabinets and dairy shelves. In her skirt and flip-flops she would soon be shivering. A blur of blue in one of the trees behind the recycling bins caught her eye. She craned her neck to get a better look, recalling an article she had read about exotic parakeets breeding in various pockets of London, escaped captives going it alone.

But it wasn't a parakeet: it was a plastic bag, ripped and tangled between the branches. Victoria blinked and looked away, disappointment washing through her, not for the silly bag, but for all the things that, in a parallel universe, she would really have liked to ask her husband's best friend, things not to do with Simon's fortieth-birthday celebrations so much as with Simon himself. Things like whether he had, in fact, mentioned that they were trying for a child; and if he hadn't, what Dougie thought about such hopes, whether he could even picture his undeniably self-centred oldest mate becoming a parent. And could it be pressure from her that was putting Simon off? Yes, she would have loved to ask that, too.

The courage to initiate such a conversation had to remain a pipe-dream, of course. It would have felt disloyal to Simon – and Dougie, she was certain, wouldn't have offered any straight answers anyway. He and Simon went back too far. They had that wavelength, the one she couldn't access. The one she had learnt to leave alone.

The weekly shop required concentration. And she had

forgotten her list. Victoria wheeled her trolley quickly up and down the aisles, plucking items off the shelves, remembering half of one planned meal, then another. She found her thoughts drifting to Dougie's villa in Spain, picturing its handsome terracotta roof tiles and white-washed walls from the time she and Simon had visited before. Was it five years or six? There were two terraces, she remembered, linked via an attractive set of curling stone steps, and a large kidney-shaped pool inlaid with mosaics of leaping dolphins. Gary had been there with Lulu, and Dougie with Janine. It had been one of those magical times when all the respective couples had seemed to get on, with each other and everyone else. She and Simon had begun each day with a swim, naked, if the hour was early enough and the rest of them still in bed.

Victoria stood before the rows of packet pasta, letting the colours blur as she summoned the creamy feel of the cold water on her bare skin. A shudder of desire passed through her, a wave of ecstasy in anticipation. Simon's birthday aside, they needed a holiday, she realized. Prefer-ably in the sun. The summer before, they had gone to Tuscany and it had rained for seven days out of ten – a miracle that had delighted the locals in charge of the parched countryside but left countless holidaymakers like themselves feeling cheated. Perhaps they should stay in Spain, she mused, go on somewhere after the birthday weekend – turn the venture into a proper two weeks.

She swept out of the supermarket car park with fresh purpose, all the windows of the car open, her long straight hair flying. Seeing a space outside the antiques shop where she had wavered over a birthday gift for Simon the week

71

before – a small exquisite *faux*-bronze clay sculpture of a young girl riding a swan – she pulled up and bought it in the space of five minutes. The sales assistant wrapped it in tissue paper and wedged it into a large box, which she insisted on carrying out to the car, standing by while Victoria dug a space for it among the bags of shopping. Arriving outside the flat twenty minutes later, she took the precaution of phoning the landline – checking Simon wasn't in – before loading the bags into the lift for the ride up to the fourth floor. She carried the box in her arms, enjoying how heavy it was, the sense of having done something good.

Chapter Six

Stevie was standing with a group of other year-elevens when she spotted Dougie swinging his leg off his bike and chaining it to the school railings. She kept her back to him, laughing out loud at something one of her school mates had said, even though it wasn't very funny. It was a failsafe trick she had learnt early on: not looking as if she wanted her father's attention so there was no loss of face if she didn't get it and a lovely bubble of joy if she did.

'Hello, ladies.' Her dad patted the wind out of his hair as he strolled towards them, behaving as if he owned the place, which was cool but also irritating. Stevie gave him a half-glance, wondering why he had to do the thing of looking different – wearing scruffy shorts and his beaten-up loafers, when every other parent she had seen had made an obvious effort to be smart. He tugged at a clump of her hair. 'Aren't you going to say a proper hello?'

'Hey, Dad.'

He kissed the top of her head, grinning at her friends. 'Hey, you lot. Now, who do I know here? Jude, Amelia, Merryl – how's it going? Are you all in for a roasting for not working hard enough? I bet Stevie is.' He rubbed his palms together gleefully.

'*Dad.*'

'Only joking, my little chickadee. Your mock results were pretty solid from what you told me at the weekend . . . or was that an edited version? Come on, the truth . . . now.' He poked her ribs and she squirmed away.

Merryl had a hand to her mouth and was giggling. 'Stevie . . . little? She's, like, the *tallest* in our year.'

'Yes, but she's still small compared to me, isn't she?' Dougie slung an arm across Stevie's shoulders, pulling her back to his side, feeling her relax.

In truth, Dougie had found himself doing a double-take as he crossed the school forecourt. It was a few months since he had last seen such a troupe of Stevie's classmates gathered together and in that time it was clear that, quite apart from any temperamental changes he and Janine might have been noticing, something of a physical group metamorphosis was also taking place. While the puppy fat still hung off some of them, and Merryl's pink railtrack braces bulged endearingly inside her small mouth, the general impression was no longer of schoolgirls so much as preening young women, tossing their hair, lips glossed, skirts short.

If there was any sort of race going on, though, Stevie was clearly winning it, Dougie observed ruefully – leggier, bustier than her cohorts, her pinned-up mane of hair more sophisticated, her expression more knowing. And yet there was still such a touching innocence to her, too, the artlessness of one embarking on a game not yet fully understood. Her school skirt was by no means the shortest, but she kept yanking it down, perhaps in the hope of concealing the smudgy crescent of a birthmark across the back of her left thigh. Her 'lucky' sign, he and Janine had christened it, during the memorable bathtime at least a decade before when Stevie had discovered the blemish and its resistance to soap, which her four-year-old self had found hilarious.

She had done something new to her eyebrows, Dougie noticed suddenly – tweezered them to thin crescents; a brutal grooming that drew attention to the unquestionable beauty of her wide-set blue eyes (the only obvious physical legacy of the Australian beach-bum who had fathered her, but which had always pleased Dougie for being so like his own). The rest of her, fortunately, was pure Janine, the long, pointy nose, the olive skin, the chestnut hair and willowy build. In fact, apart from the colour of their eyes (Janine's were brown), she was growing into the closest thing to a clone he had ever seen.

'Dad, Mum's here – let's go.' Stevie tugged at his shirt and set off at a lope across the tarmac, looking suddenly – reassuringly – like the gangly girlish stick of a thing she still was.

Janine was standing on the steps at the main entrance, her shining brown hair loose on her bare shoulders, her slim legs visible as faint shadows through the thin cotton of a long, floral halter-neck summer dress. She tried to hug Stevie, who ducked away, and waved a hello to Dougie, deploying the now familiar nod designed to indicate that the post-divorce absence of hostility between them did not extend to the intimacy of a kiss.

'Let's crack on, shall we?' She seemed tense. 'There's only five minutes with each teacher.' Her tone was the one Dougie had learnt to be most wary of, all falsely breezy and business-like. 'If we're late for the first we'll be behind all night. It's Mrs Hepple. English. And you're still okay to talk afterwards, Dougie, aren't you? Back at my place?'

'Yes, boss.' Dougie caught Stevie's eye and pulled a face. Inside his spirits plunged. A horrible conversation lay ahead, he knew. A conversation about money. Janine would ask for the deposit for Stevie's language-improvement trip and he would say he couldn't give it to her. His financial position remained parlous. There had been two more large, lucrative cooking classes – one for some of the mums he had boasted to Simon about, and another children's birthday party – as well as catering for a friend of Richard's celebrating a tenth wedding anniversary, but the profits on all three jobs had been instantly vacuumed up by day-to-day bills and another stalling payment on his rent debt. The only serious injection of cash he had to look forward to was Victoria's Spanish surprise for Simon. But July was two long months away; a lifetime, it felt like.

Janine had done her speed-walking thing and reached the end of the corridor. Stevie, trotting to catch up, turned and signalled at Dougie to hurry.

'Remember, the bark is never worse than the bite,' he murmured, arriving at her side and peering through the glass door panels into the hall where the teachers were arranged, with intimidating military precision, in rows behind desks, each sporting a sign to advertise their name and subject. Dougie had to quell a moment of queasiness as some of the unpleasantness of his own schooldays surged back at him – the last-minute never-quite-good-enough results, the ringing silence of disappointment from his father. 'I'd prefer to be facing this lot than your mum, I can tell you,' he whispered, mustering playfulness and earning a hiss and an elbow-dig for his pains.

As it turned out the teachers' reports were mostly

positive, the results of the recent mock GCSEs being the main yardstick for comment. Stevie sat squirming on a seat between her parents through most of it, chiselling at her cuticles with her teeth, showing little emotion, whether being told that she was going to have to pull all the stops out to get a top grade in maths and physics, or that her essay writing was exceptional and would stand her in good stead for her choice of A levels, now confirmed as Spanish, English and history. Dougie let Janine ask most of the questions. He focused on Stevie, endeavouring to look more cheerful than he felt while experiencing a profound pity for the monotony of revision and exams that lay ahead of her, not to mention the weird cross-section of individuals with whom she would have to keep company in the process. There was a new physics master, who was especially repellent – lank-haired with oily skin and a curious whistle to his voice, as if he was blowing air through his teeth as he talked. He had a way of saying Stevie's name, peering at her intently over steepled fingertips, that made Dougie extremely glad his daughter wasn't a scientist.

'Blimey, is he from Planet Creep, or what?' he muttered, as they walked away. Stevie hung on his arm, giggling, while Janine shook her head, tightening her lips to hide the first possibility of a smile he had seen all evening. Dougie tried to catch her eye, wanting to force the smile into being, yearning for just one moment when the ugliness of their past might fall away to reveal a glimpse of the naïve, happy threesome they had started out as sixteen years before. But Janine either didn't notice or pretended not to, and twenty minutes later Dougie was labouring on his bike up the final steep stretch of the road towards her small terraced house in Chalk Farm.

'*My* place', Janine had called it. Recalling the unmistakable note of defiance in her voice as she had deployed the words, Dougie marvelled at the still peculiar business of trying to feel separate even after separation; how one missed irksome things as well as good, how hard one had to fight sometimes against the temptation to play the corrosive, pointless game of what-if. Sometimes he truly wished they had gone through one of those divorces based on spitting injustice and hate. How much simpler it would have been to rant and rage, to vent anger, to feel hard-done-by; or to have no contact at all, just the proverbial clean slate. But there was no chance of that. Not just because of Stevie, but because, when all was said and done, his behaviour – on every conceivable level – had been unforgivable.

On the doorstep there was a bit of a last-minute shuffle, thanks to Mike turning up – unexpectedly, from the expression on Janine's face – just as Dougie was being ushered inside.

'Dougie and I will pop down the road to the wine bar,' she said at once, her voice fluid and conciliatory. 'We won't be long. Okay, sweetie?'

'Sweetie'? Dougie stayed leaning against the door jamb with his arms crossed, watching the proceedings unfold. Mike was stocky but muscular, with one of those closely shaved heads designed to make the best of acute hair loss. He had to be thirty-three or -four. He was wearing a suit with pinstripes that were a little too wide and carried a briefcase as big as a holdall. He travelled a lot, Dougie knew, mostly to Scandinavia, for a company that had something to do with renewable fuels.

'Or I can take myself upstairs – keep out of your way,' Mike suggested eagerly. 'The afternoon meeting was cancelled so I got an earlier flight.' He put his arm round her waist and kissed her on the lips, lingering for a second longer than it looked as if Janine was expecting him to. Deeper in the hall Dougie saw Stevie's face emerge briefly round the kitchen door, then duck away. A moment later she was scampering up the stairs, clutching what looked like several slices of toast. He called out a goodbye, but she didn't break stride.

'You'll see her soon,' Janine murmured.

Dougie nodded, surprised and glad that she had not only noticed the subtle daughterly rebuff but cared enough to offer reassurance. The effortless connection, the exclusion of Mike – those also felt good.

'We won't be long.' She kissed Mike on the cheek, and pulled her jacket off the peg next to the door.

'We could have postponed,' Dougie muttered, as she fell into step beside him. 'And you might as well know that I'm more than usually broke at the moment anyway,' he blurted. 'The buggering *finca* is still empty. The wild boar will be moving in soon. Though Xavier assures me he's on top of things, keeping it nice. It might take till the autumn, he says.' Dougie paused, wondering whether to mention Victoria's July birthday plan, but thinking better of it. He didn't want to raise hopes when the project might yet run aground. He concentrated his energies instead on walking with studied casualness, keeping his hands loosely in his shorts pockets, scuffing the pavement with his heels, painfully aware of how hard it was to feel natural without Stevie between them and nothing ahead but the dull inevitability of disappointment and confrontation.

They were soon at the wine bar. It was a hateful establishment, in Dougie's view, with an overpriced menu of ineptly cooked food and sloppily washed floors to which the soles of one's shoes stuck. Worse, it had formed the backdrop to one of his more pitiful displays of public drunkenness during the course of the separation. There had been alcohol-fuelled sobbing (by him), a broken glass (his), falling on bended knee (him). Janine had sat stony-eyed through it all, letting his energies play themselves out, the disdain on her face telling him, and those watching from behind their menus at other tables, that she had seen it all too many times before to be moved.

'Oh, but this isn't about money,' Janine said airily, getting to the door first and holding it open for him.

'No?' Dougie couldn't hide his relief. 'Oh, good. I only thought . . . because of that Valencia jaunt she's going on –'

'It's not a jaunt,' Janine corrected him testily, leading the way to a table at the back of the room. 'It's to improve her Spanish by spending a week with a family. Anyway, I've paid the deposit – it was peanuts. The flights are cheap and there'll be nothing else apart from a little extra pocket money. We can settle up later.'

'I see. Okay.' Dougie filled his lungs and exhaled slowly. They ordered two apple juices and the waiter brought a bowl of Bombay mix, which he tackled ravenously. He hadn't eaten since a plain omelette mid-afternoon, the few more interesting ingredients in his fridge being destined for stomachs other than his own.

'What I wanted to talk about was Stevie.'

'You don't say.' He licked the salt off his lips and scooped out a second handful of the mix. The earlier twinges of nostalgia had given way to a mounting and unpleasant sense of being jerked around – by Mike, driving them off the doorstep, and now Janine, all glassy-eyed and inscrutable, ready to guilt-trip him into something new. She didn't even look that pretty any more, he decided churlishly. She was just a thirty-seven-year-old in a dress, with a hawk-like expression on her face and hours-old lipstick worn to a dull pink line round the edges of her mouth.

'This isn't going to be easy, Dougie, so please don't make it harder. You should eat something, by the way,' she added stiffly. 'You're clearly starving. You're never good when you're starving.'

'Oh, aren't I? What a sweet, wifely observation – I shall treasure it.'

She closed her eyes. 'Dougie, please . . .'

Dougie ignored her, signalled to a waiter and ordered a steak with chips. The desire for a drink kicked in at the same time, sharper and stronger than it had been for days, making the hunger feel like nothing. He took a vicious swig of his apple juice and folded his arms. 'Okay, spit it out.'

Janine had been looking out of the window, her attention caught by the passing whine of an ambulance siren. She slowly turned her head to meet his gaze. 'Mike's been offered a job in Sweden. Stockholm.'

Dougie blinked, marvelling at the way places either previously unknown, or not thought about for years, could suddenly start cropping up in unexpected contexts. It took a second longer for the wider implications to sink in. He opened his mouth, releasing a growl of protest while his brain scrambled for the best, most inarguable way of saying that no daughter of his, the only good thing to rise from the rubble of their limping marriage, could be transplanted across the Baltic at the whim of a surly near-bald stranger with a poor taste in tailoring; a stranger with no priorities other than his own self-advancement.

'I want to give her the option of living with you.'

A steak was delivered to the table next to them. The meat looked rubbery and threaded with gristle, the chips thick and soggy. Dougie took a preparatory breath, but then didn't know where to start.

Janine sat back in her chair to watch the struggle. Her eyes were hot, but she had vowed not to cry. She would not cry. Some men were good with female weeping, but not Dougie. He would twitch and look away. For years she had thought it was due to deficiency of sympathy, until it had dawned on her that it simply made him feel shut out, helpless.

And there was nothing to cry about anyway. Mike had given her time to think the situation through and that was exactly what she had been doing, unflinchingly, from every possible angle, for several weeks. The conclusion she had arrived at in the end had been simple. She had found someone she wanted to spend the rest of her life with. That someone was going abroad for his work and she wanted to go with him. It would be the first purely selfish major decision she had made in her life. Stevie did not like Mike. And though Janine wished with all her heart that the situation was otherwise, she was starting to accept that it was one she could neither change nor ignore. Forcing Stevie to write thank-you notes for Mike's acts of generosity was both futile and detrimental. The harder Mike tried, the more Stevie resisted. And Janine could understand exactly why, too. Mike, probably because he had no children of his own, had got it wrong from the start, ricocheting between attempts at being a disciplining grown-up one minute and a 'best friend' the next. If Stevie had been three years younger, or five, or ten, it wouldn't have mattered. As it was, her daughter was showing all the signs of pulling away from her anyway, fighting for an independence that Janine could remember only too well wanting herself at a similar age. Two more years and school would be behind her. To announce that those two years were to be spent on an island on the outskirts of Stockholm, away from their patch of north London and friends, some of whom she had known since primary school, simply felt too cruel.

Mike, sweetly, frantically, had done some research into various international schools. Stockholm was full of foreign families, he said, lots of them English, lots American. Children from all walks of life quickly settled in. But Mike, Janine knew, was only saying what he thought she needed to hear. Because he loved her. He might have seen a lot of the sulking surliness of which Stevie was capable, but he still had no notion of how difficult the situation would be. He thought the iciness in Stevie's sharp blue eyes was normal, that all the time she spent in her bedroom was because she was quiet and studious. He didn't know the extent to which he was loathed and Janine couldn't bring herself to enlighten him.

That Mike was only really interested in her was what Janine loved most about him. It was a long time since she had had a man chase her, had been the one in charge, the one with the power. Even during the early days with Dougie the balance of control had been all his. The thrill of loving, rather than being loved, was what had consumed her. And Dougie had been so easy to love: handsome, talented, ambitious, wild, funny, but with an earnestness about his cooking – about her – that had stormed her heart with its power. He had proved his commitment by sitting through an endearing number of her gigs, too, many of them in grimy, half-empty bars, tapping his feet to the beat, waiting patiently to whisk her back to his bedsit where he would produce some glorious concoction on the two-ringed metal box that passed for a stove, fixed so close to the bed that the smells of the cooking permeated the linen as they made love afterwards. And such love-making . . . Her lion, Janine had always thought of him, as savage as he was tender, as demanding as he was generous. Even now the memory of being in Dougie's arms could sometimes blow her off her feet.

But improbably it was Stevie that clinched things. She had been just pregnant when they'd met, the dreadful, hapless Australian gone, the termination booked, and it had been Dougie who had persuaded her to keep the baby, promising on one subsequent, vertiginously unforgettable night that he would care for it as his very own.

Dougie's finest hour, without a doubt. Janine eyed her ex-husband steadily, squeezing her glass of apple juice so hard her fingers slid on the glass. Sixteen years on, the fact of that promise having been kept, the ferocity with which Dougie loved his adopted daughter, still had the power to move her beyond words. He had been a hopeless husband in so many ways and terrible things had happened as a result, some of them still hard to think about even now. But never once, not even during the worst times, had he done anything to endanger Stevie. When sober, he had been the gentlest, most loving and protective father; when soaked with alcohol the same instincts had made him keep out of her way.

'Stevie live with me?' Dougie had formulated a sentence at last and was gawping.

'You are her father. She and I have been at loggerheads for months. Her and Mike, they . . . It's hard for both of them. And you've got your life sorted out now, haven't you.' It was a statement not question.

Janine dropped her gaze to her lap, not wanting the inevitable reflex of doubt to show. There had been other false starts in the past, other broken pledges, including the one in particular that she kept in a locked cabinet at the back of her mind. Only for consideration when she had the strength. But this time he really did seem different – cleaned up and determined in a way that almost reminded her of the man she had fallen in love with. 'And please don't say it's selfish,' she rushed on. 'It *is* selfish, but . . .' She hesitated, fighting all the reservations she had been battling against for weeks. Mike was her second chance. The love was different, less intense – nothing could ever match what she had felt for Dougie – but no less real. She had every right to grasp it, to ask Dougie to step up as a parent and take his turn. 'Mike and I – we get on. And as for living abroad, you remember, surely, how much I always wanted to give that a go. I'm not going to tell Stevie she *can't* come – I'd love her to. I just want to give her the choice. I need this, Dougie,' she faltered, 'but it will only work if Stevie can be happy, too.'

'Yes, but *Sweden*?'

'Mike's company has found us this house on an island called Lidingö – that's how Stockholm is, apparently, several islands joined to the mainland by bridges. It sounds incredible, just nine miles long, full of forests and lakes –' Janine broke off, fearful of sounding too eager, of being diverted from the main point of the conversation. 'You used to say,' she went on quietly, 'that if we split you wanted Stevie. Remember how you always said that? Well, now . . .'

'Now I'm sober enough for the job,' Dougie snapped. 'Is that it?' He dropped his head into his hands, running his palms down over his face. 'And what does Stevie want?' he asked softly. 'Have you even asked her?' His food had arrived and even looked faintly appetizing, the chips fresh, the meat lean, but he couldn't bring himself to touch it.

'Not yet. I wanted to run it by you first. But . . .' Janine was twisting her hands in her lap, biting her lower lip '. . . I'm going to wait till after her GCSEs, before she goes for that week in Valencia. However she responds, I shall suggest that she postpones a final decision until after she's been out to stay with Mike and me later in the summer, see how she likes it. As I said, the important thing is for Stevie to feel she has a choice. It will only be for a couple of years. We'll be home again before she knows it.'

'Fine. All sorted, then.' Dougie picked up his empty juice glass and dropped it back onto the table.

'I thought you might even be pleased,' Janine ventured, her voice small and tight, her face fighting disappointment.

'I am pleased.' He stabbed a chip with his fork, then pushed the plate away. 'Just caught on the hop . . . as usual.'

Janine's eyes were burning again. She wanted to go home. She hadn't wanted her apple juice. She had only ordered it to be supportive. What she really wanted was wine. Warm, cold, any colour. At such moments she realized that there was a finer line between her and Dougie's drinking habits than she sometimes liked to imagine. Self-discipline was all it amounted to in the end, the power to stop. She glanced at the tawdry grey and purple décor of the wine bar, also remembering the hateful evening of the broken glass and spilt bottle, with Dougie kneeling among the mess, embarrassing himself – embarrassing them – with his boozy sobbing. Her heart hadn't softened for a moment. She had agreed to the meeting because Dougie had promised he wanted to talk sensibly about what had happened, about all the things that had brought them to such a brink. Instead, drunk on arrival, the evening had provided a panoply of all the moods he passed through whenever the alcohol brakes were off: loving, conciliatory, argumentative, angry, manic, penitent, incoherent – all the phases she had come to dread, not one of them ever easier to deal with for the fact of being familiar. To be able to walk away that night, to leave him to it, had been one of the most liberating moments of her life.

Chapter Seven

'Four days in Spain mid-July? Hmm . . . that's just seven weeks away. Perfect.' Ruth peered at the still modest bulge of her belly, giving it a little pat. She was lying on the sofa, both feet propped on a cushion, speed-reading the novel she was supposed to have finished for her book club, which was being hosted that evening by its founder Richard's wife, Katie. Gary was also going out, for the second cooking session at Dougie's.

'I'll be almost seven months gone by then,' she continued dreamily. 'At seven months you're not supposed to fly, Katie says, and she should know, with her and Rich having notched up four. And yet she'd still have another, she claims – if they could afford it. Five times doing this . . .' Ruth glowered. '*Five* . . . can you imagine?' She flopped back against the sofa cushion. 'The flying rule is all about insurance apparently – the airlines don't want to pay up if labour starts and things go wrong.'

'It'll be perfect timing, then,' Gary pointed out quickly, hoping to keep his wife on the subject of Simon's birthday treat rather than any blood-and-guts stories to do with babies and aeroplanes. Ruth seemed impervious, but he had no stomach for them. He was too excited – too terrified. It had been like that since the moment Ruth had announced the pregnancy – the feeling that he was embarking on the greatest adventure of his life. 'Dougie's in the process of trying to sell the place,' he went on, 'so it could be everybody's last chance to pay it a visit.'

'And my *only* chance because you went there before, didn't you – with *Lulu*?' Ruth grinned to indicate that recollection of the woman who had preceded her in her husband's affections held no terrors for her.

'And Victoria said it was a secret from Simon, so I mustn't let anything slip during the cooking tonight,' Gary continued quickly, hating to be reminded of his ex-girlfriend, as Ruth well knew. They had been insane years – drugs and partying, a lot of it with Dougie, a lot of it in the manic subterranean underbelly of the advertising world, awash as it had been then with money rather sense. Lulu had been at the heart of it all, a beautiful, crazy, cruel, coke-head model, as manipulative as she was compelling. It was a ten-year period that Gary had never once looked back on with anything other than gladness that it was done with.

'Ah, yes, your cooking class with Dougie.' Ruth peered over the top of her book, her hazel eyes glinting with the faintest suggestion of admonition. She liked it that she had Gary had separate friends, separate hobbies, but since the pregnancy she had lost some of her patience with things like being woken up by inebriated door-slamming homecomings in the small hours. 'Not so late this time, okay? Or so noisy, come to that. Oh, and could you possibly walk Lois before you go?'

Hearing her favourite word, their English bull mastiff plodded to the armchair in which Gary was sitting and placed her chin on his knee, her pink-rimmed eyes pleading. Gary patted the wide, flat head, tutting affectionately.

Acquired eighteen months before – his and Ruth's first big step as a couple – he loved the creature so unconditionally it made him dizzy to think how much he would be capable of loving his own child. 'It's actually a bit late for me to squeeze that in, Ruthie . . .'

'But look at my ankles,' she wailed. 'They're not supposed to do that yet. It's because it's been so bloody hot . . . Since when has May ever been this hot?' She lifted her bare legs, flexing her feet. They weren't long but were attractively shaped, with neat knees and full calves, below which Gary, looking hard, could just make out a slight thickening round the ankle bones. 'And it's all because of that endless bloody client presentation I was made to do,' she went on crossly, 'standing in front of storyboards singing for my supper for the entire afternoon.' She let both legs drop back onto the cushion, creating a tide of air that lifted the hem of her skirt. 'Really, if the account team can't pitch a few ideas on their own then what's the point of them? Talk about spoon-feeding. And you know what Di will do anyway, don't you? She'll give in to every one of the client's inane requests, as she always does. Bigger pack shot? Yes Brian. Longer pack shot? Yes, Brian. Slash the production budget? Yes Brian. That's what Di does. Every bloody time.'

'I could take Lois with me, I suppose,' Gary conceded, realizing that his wife was more uptight than he had first thought, and feeling for her over Di, who was the most lily-livered of all the agency's account directors. 'I'll walk to Dougie's instead of driving. It's only a couple of miles. And presumably you're going to need the car anyway, to get to your book thing.'

'So I will. Oh, Gary, you darling.' Ruth clambered off the sofa and plonked herself on her husband's lap, gently pushing the dog out of the way with her foot. 'And I've still got to finish the blooming book, which I'm hating – murder, child slavery, bonnets and bodices. Katie's choice, needless to say. She always picks rubbish things.'

'Poor Ruthie.' Gary closed his eyes because she was kissing them. She was a woman who blew off steam easily; storms and sunshine, you always knew where you were with her. It was one of the many things he adored about her. Although what had first caught his eye was her electrifying appearance – layered clothes of crimson, yellow, purple, black, gold, with huge bangles and baubles hanging off her wrists and ears, her short dark hair streaked with red and skewered into messy spikes, her eyes and lips a brilliant scarlet. She had literally lit up the room. She had arrived in the advertising world via Central St Martins art college, a fact that sometimes prompted Ruth to worry she had sold out, but which had proved a springboard for a swiftly earned reputation as one of the best art directors in the industry. Every year her press and TV creations were up for awards. Gary, who occupied the duller role of copywriter and who had never won anything, often wished his own art-director work partner showed half as much flair.

'I'd better go, then,' he said, making no effort to move.

'Aw, shucks.' Ruth ran her fingers through his hair, still in the long curls that had been the first thing to catch her eye when he had wandered into her office to seek an opinion three years before.

Gary peered at his watch, wondering if there was time

to make love, and glimpsed Lois, who was studying them with the unnerving intensity of a mind-reader seeking evidence of betrayal. Ruth's mouth had drifted to his forehead, brushing her lips along his skin in a way that told him she was just as interested. Gary twisted so their mouths met. Hers tasted of the chocolate biscuit she had had with her cup of tea. Moreish and delicious. But as he deepened the kiss Lois began head-butting his knees, as if she was trying to alert him to the fact that, with his gallant relinquishment of the car, they had precisely twenty minutes to walk two miles. Reluctantly, Gary pulled out of the kiss. 'Sorry, Ruthie, but I don't think there's time.'

He gently extricated himself from the chair and eased Ruth into his place. He didn't want to be late, not just because it would piss Dougie off but because he was genuinely looking forward to the lesson. Since meeting Ruth, he had really got into cooking. He had already tried the trout from the first session and Ruth had been goggle-eyed with praise. He had also tried, with less success, to replicate some of Dougie's skills at the chopping board: a knife blade whisking sea salt and a garlic clove to paste, herbs chopped, at mesmerizing speed, almost to powder, a fish gutted in three slashes – the sheer dexterity had been astounding and impossible to reproduce. Gary had eaten enough of Dougie's food in the past, but never before seen it prepared at such close quarters. After the first class he had actually found himself feeling bad about that, as if he had overlooked something vital. It had made him admire his friend properly all over again instead of feeling sorry for him, as had been the inevitable tendency in recent years. And the way Dougie was trying to pick himself up, Gary admired that too. The man had slipped publicly to the bottom of a very tall ladder. If his own life had capsized quite so dramatically Gary wasn't sure he would have shown half so much resilience or guts.

He found the dog lead and then, recalling Dougie's generous insistence on the subject, a bottle of wine. Noticing the sky had darkened, he delved into the under-stairs cupboard and pulled out an anorak. With Lois doing a clumsy dance at his heels, making the wheezy noises she reserved for her highest state of excitement, he then put his head back round the sitting-room door. 'See you later – happy book-clubbing.'

'Laters, sweetheart.' Ruth waved, not looking up from her page.

'I've rung the bell,' Richard shouted, in his amiable bari-tone, as Gary and Lois arrived at Dougie's front gate. He was standing on the doorstep, still in his work suit, his tie poking out of his pocket, his tar-brush hair more vertical than usual from a recent cut. 'But I'm not sure he heard.' He peered through the door's glass panel, then leant on the bell again, pushing his bodyweight behind his thumb.

Dougie, halfway up the kitchen stairs in response to the first ring, slowed his pace. Simon had been settled in the kitchen for some time, drinking one of the beers he had brought with him, burping merrily as he flicked through the now dog-eared copy of *North London Life* and casting acerbic Simon comments about the state of the world while Dougie rummaged for chopping boards and knives.

The evening should be fun, Dougie reminded himself, squaring his shoulders as he approached the door. He squinted through the glass, wishing he could blink away the grit of fatigue under his eyelids. He hadn't been sleeping well, that was the trouble, not since Janine's bombshell news about leaving England. Whether Stevie would decide to go with her, how he would cope if she did, how he would cope if she didn't – his head had fizzed for ten straight nights. On top of which, like a tap slowly turning, the initial trickle of work bookings was thickening to real demand. His days were full again, buzzing, stressful. He had been accepting anything and everything, driven not just by the still pressing need to clear his debts, but the new possibility of becoming a full-time dad. Pocket money, extras, another mouth to feed, the fresh chance to prove himself – suddenly the slog of being alive was in danger of making a little sense.

'Aha, my two remaining students – greetings.' He flung wide the door, which took its usual two tugs because it was badly warped. He shook Richard's hand, ushering him in first, then hugged Gary, remarking wryly, as he caught sight of Lois, 'Is she paying her way too?'

'Sorry, Doug, I knew you wouldn't like it.' Gary dragged, then lifted the dog over the threshold. 'But she did need the walk and Ruth had her book club. She'll be no trouble, I promise. Hey, by the way . . .' he lowered his voice, casting a conspiratorial glance down the passageway where Richard had stopped to inspect the large black-and-white photo of Stevie that hung over the kitchen stairwell '. . . Ruth and I are totally up for the house-party in Spain. Great idea. Final fling before the baby.' He shook his big curly head as if he couldn't quite believe his own words.

When Dougie reached the stairwell photo he found

himself pausing, too. It showed Stevie, aged ten, spread-eagled mid-bounce over a trampoline, her arms and legs stuck out like planks, her socks in uneven doughnut rolls around her skinny ankles. Gary had every right to look awestruck, he reflected, with a twist of wistfulness: he and Ruth were at the beginning of something huge, something he had already had and had half screwed up; something he might never know again. He clenched his fists. Stevie had to stay in England. She just had to.

'Hey, what is it, man?' Gary punched his arm playfully. 'You look pissed off. Is it Lois?'

'No, of course not.' Dougie laughed quickly. 'I love your blooming mutt.' He bounded on down the stairs and into the kitchen, issuing commands as he assessed all the things that had to be done and in what order. He had planned langoustine in wine and tomato sauce for the starter; a hot-water-crust pork pie with French beans and almonds for main, with custard gooseberry fool and homemade vanilla biscuits to finish. For a bunch of amateur cooks it was a wildly ambitious evening's work. If he wasn't careful he would end up doing most of it himself. But Gary was good, he remembered. Gary listened and didn't piss around. Dougie set him to work on the pie pastry, which was tricky, and allocated Richard the lighter duty of topping and tailing the gooseberries.

'Er . . . all hands on deck, mate,' he said, turning to Simon last. 'I thought you could take charge of the first course. Those need cutting up to make a start on the sauce,' he pointed to two carrots and an onion he had put on the third chopping board, 'and these fellas need washing.' He set the bag of shellfish next to the sink.

Simon slowly folded the newspaper away and drained his beer bottle. 'I did the fish the last time. Those bloody trout. I washed them.'

'Ah, but with such panache,' Dougie countered, noting the hint of obstinacy in his friend's response and being reminded of the chippy, defensive sixth-former he had befriended twenty years before, as adept at riling teachers as he was classmates. Simon did not like being told what to do, that was the thing, not even over trivial matters. It was almost as if he equated any sort of obedience with being seen as a push-over. Small-man syndrome, Janine had called it once, after they had witnessed a row between Simon and Victoria over some petty request at which he had taken offence – fetching the car, feeding coins into a meter? Dougie couldn't remember. Simon cared too much about being taken seriously, Janine had said. It made him dig in his heels over nothing, or sometimes stand too close when he was making a point, or laugh too loudly when someone cracked a joke. Dougie never minded, she claimed, because he towered too high above Simon to notice how close he was standing and because it was invariably his jokes that were being laughed at.

'Shouldn't we pay our tuition fees before we start labouring?' Simon went on now, still not moving from his perch. 'Thirty quid. There's mine.' He took a wad of notes out of his back pocket and slowly counted three tens. 'Bloody hell,' he went on, eyes widening with surprise as he peered at the scrawl of appointments in Dougie's work diary. 'Look at this lot. It's a wonder you could fit us in.'

'Yes, isn't it?' Dougie replied, sensing, as he had on the phone a couple of weeks before, a dim thread of something

97

odd and negative in Simon's attitude and wondering at its origins. He might even have pressed for an explanation had Lois not chosen that moment to start hurtling between chair legs and cupboards, yelping like a spoilt toddler.

'Okay, okay.' Gary dropped his roll of pastry and dusted his hands. 'I'll get rid of her.' He clicked his fingers and shooed the dog outside, where she promptly started barking much more loudly, barrelling her squat body against the door with such force that the hinges shook.

'She'll stop soon,' Gary muttered, not looking up as he resumed his work with the rolling pin.

'Alternatively . . . anyone got a gun?' hissed Simon from the sink, where he was tussling with the langoustines. He already had a cut finger to show for his pains – a mere scrape but it was stinging.

Dougie, as irritated as the rest of them by Lois but resolved not to show it, strolled over to inspect his progress. 'Actually, you'd be better off starting on the veg first, Si. Cut up the onion and carrot, then fry them together – just till they're softened, keeping the lid on, then add some water –'

'How much water?'

'Oh, I don't know – a cup, a glass, some.'

'*Some?*' Simon snorted. 'When it comes to that cookbook of yours, mate, you might find your editors asking you to be a little more specific. Us plebs, you know, we can't do it by guesswork.'

'This glass, then, okay?' Dougie ran the cold tap with unnecessary force, reminding himself that friendship and business were always a tricky combination. Overestimating how he could mix the two had been a pertinent element to his downfall as a restaurateur: tables for pals, free drinks, mates' rates – by the end the Black Hen had become one mad, continuous party with him footing the bill.

'Use the pan with the blue handle, okay?' he instructed, as Simon dithered. 'And when you're done you can help Gary with the meat – trim the fat off that pork, ready for mincing. Richard, if you ever get to the end of those gooseberries – which might be midnight at the rate you're going – they need to be washed, drained and put in that pan there with a dollop of water and a spoonful of caster sugar. Cook them gently for a few minutes at most, with the lid *on*. Got it? Right. I'm going out for a fag. And I might kill that beast of yours while I'm at it, Gary.' He opened the back door and deftly slipped through the gap before Lois could scoot inside.

The air was fresh and damp – wonderful. Lois fell silent immediately and scrambled after him up the steps onto the main body of the garden. When Dougie picked his way to the end fence she followed, her claws scraping on the ruptured concrete.

'Christ, but you're a grim-looking thing.' Dougie chuckled, cupping a hand round his chin as he lit up. Next door a light in an upstairs room went out, converting Nina Carmichael's house into a hunch of grey in the dark. In comparison, his own place was ablaze with life. This was good, Dougie decided, something to relish, be proud of. He smoked greedily and steadily, watching the plumes disperse, trying to empty his brain. He must work hard, but not slip back into letting things get on top of him, that was the key. He had come a long way. The worst stuff was done with, buried. His life had focus again. It was important not to try to take more than one day at a time.

He tipped his head back to hunt for the moon, finding only a grey thumbprint in a murk of night cloud. It stirred a wave of fondness for Spain where, in his memory at least (it was a good three years since his last visit), the sky was always clear and vividly coloured – black or blue – none of the in-between ugliness of England. It would be good to go there again; good to touch base with the old place one last time before he got shot of it.

And what were the skies like in Sweden, he wondered suddenly, lighting a second cigarette off the first, trying and failing to summon any memories on the subject from his work trip. Sweden. Stockholm . . . the foreign place that was going to swallow Janine. And Stevie too, probably. Both of them gone for a good two years . . . Two years. Dougie hunched forwards, gripping the fence, crushing the cigarette between his fingers. His knuckles were bluish-white in the dark, the bones bulging. His heart was leaping, like something caged and crazed – it seemed faintly incredible that there was no visible sign of it pummelling under his shirt. He had been agonizing over whether Stevie would go, of course. Lost sleep over it. But Janine as well? They were the only two people in his life who had ever really mattered.

Behind him the kitchen door burst open and shut, releasing a brief volley of light and noise. Lois charged towards the steps and stopped as Simon appeared at the top of them, grinning impishly. 'Bit of a situation developing in there . . . Hey, Doug, are you okay?'

'Yup. Fine.' Dougie nodded vigorously to make up for a momentary inability to speak. 'Be right there,' He winced, pushing off from the fence.

Simon picked his way towards him, rubbing his arms against the night chill. 'Doug? Are you sure you're all right? Sorry if I was a bit of an arse before . . . Was I an arse?'

Dougie grimaced. 'You bloody were.'

'It's cooking. You know I hate the whole fucking business.'

'I know. So never again, okay?'

'Never again,' Simon agreed, laughing, slinging an arm across Dougie's back as they drew level.

'And what you lost in the Hen,' Dougie went on thickly, glad of the arm but a combination of pride and shyness also making him keen for it to be gone, 'I just want you to know that I'll pay you back one day. I will,' he insisted fiercely, as Simon started to protest. 'Now.' He set off quickly towards the house. 'What exactly do you mean by a "situation"?'

'A visitor,' Simon explained, adding, with some glee, 'One Laura Munro? She says she *interviewed* you. Would that have been before or after your recent vow of chastity, I wonder?'

'Fuck off,' Dougie countered amiably, hopping down the steps and trying to peer through the steam of the kitchen window.

Simon was a step behind him and still chuckling. 'Look, I don't blame you, mate. I mean, bloody hell, she's hot.'

'We had a one-off thing but, as far as I was concerned, that was the end of it, okay?'

'Well, it looks to me like she might have a different view,' Simon warned drily, giving Dougie's back a final slap of support as they went inside.

Laura was perched on the end of the kitchen table sipping a glass of white wine, her long legs bare and swinging free of a very short skirt. Her top half was sheathed in a tight black T-shirt and her silky hair knotted, ballerina-style, in a neat ball on the crown of her head. The two other men were on either side of her, Richard hovering over his precious pile of topped-and-tailed gooseberries, Gary kneading what Dougie could see at a glance was already a hopelessly overworked dry lump of dough.

'But I want to cook too,' Laura cried, when Dougie explained that she had to leave. 'As a *paying* customer.' She whipped out three ten-pound notes and slotted them into the back pocket of his jeans. 'A customer who will not take no for an answer,' she pleaded, in a husky voice, raising the wide dark pools of her eyes so close to his face that Dougie realized she had probably done a few lines of coke before deciding to arrive unbidden on his doorstep.

'Okay,' he glanced at his companions, aware they were lapping up the scene, 'but you'll have to pull your weight.'

The cooking class resumed but with rather more of a party atmosphere. Lois was banished upstairs to the sitting room and Simon switched on Dougie's iPod, which lived on top of the fridge, settling on some soft jazz. Rather to Dougie's surprise, Laura proved a decided asset, both as a quick learner who did not need orders repeating, and because of the effect she had on her fellows: flirting, co-operative, competitive, the other three men jostled around her, like bees at a flower, showing off with anything that came to hand, whether it was sparkling repartee, a perfect pie mould or swiftly and stiffly beaten egg whites.

It was nearly eleven when they finally sat down to eat. Dougie was racked with tiredness to a point beyond hunger, and wishing he could skip the meal and despatch all four of them back to their homes with doggy-bags.

Around him, however, thanks largely to Laura, the party began to gather fresh momentum. More wine was opened, finger-bowls called for on account of the langoustines, Simon applauded for his tasty tomato sauce and Gary for his only slightly heavy pastry. As if fearing the conversation might turn dull, Laura found some club music on the iPod, turned up the volume and started shimmying round the table, twisting her hips and arms.

'Okay, everybody must *sing*,' she shrieked, kicking off her shoes and climbing onto her chair, 'or there will be forfeits.' She pointed at Simon, who dutifully leapt from his seat and hopped round the table, yodelling nonsense lyrics because he didn't know the song. Richard and Gary, not to be outdone, hammed up their own version of the tune, performing like a comic operatic duo, cheeks close, mouths wide.

Dougie shrank deeper into his chair. He was beginning to feel more and more like a charioteer who had lost control of his horse, a once bold, heroic charioteer no longer in touch with either his courage or his mojo. There had probably been no single moment in his life when he had felt less like singing. He didn't have a good voice anyway. Exercising it in the old days had been guaranteed to send Stevie and Janine running for cover, palms pressed to their ears. He would seek refuge in preparing some coffee, he decided. But as he pushed back his chair he noticed that someone had filled his empty water glass with wine. Laura, probably. Or maybe Richard. Dougie stared at it. Around him the merriment continued, no one seeming to have noticed his lack of participation. The wine was a rich, enticing red, as innocent as cordial. It was Richard's liquid contribution to the evening, he knew, a Sangiovese, from Tuscany, a grape and region with which he was familiar and of which he was very fond. It would be light on the tongue, then heavy in the swallow, the flavours spreading like warmth.

Dougie glanced away, but found his eyes drawn back to the wine. One drink and he would forget being tired. One drink and the hash of his past, all the worries about his future, about Stevie, would dissolve. One drink and he would have fun, like the rest of them.

He cupped the glass, his pulse quickening, but in the same instant there was a thunderous crash against the wall beside them. All five of them froze, like characters in some stage play. Another crash followed, just as loud. A picture, an enlarged photograph Dougie had taken of a Cornwall sunset, swung on its hook. Dougie released the wine glass and got up to turn off the music.

'Bloody hell,' said Simon, wiping the sweat from his forehead with a handkerchief as he dropped back into his seat. 'What kind of a wife-beater is caged up behind there?'

'She lives alone, a librarian.' Dougie recalled Nina's sad pallid face. A flicker of neighbourly concern was quickly expunged by the much stronger impulse not to get involved. 'I think she's a bit of a loner.'

'Loners commit murder,' said Gary.

'Or get murdered,' whispered Laura, who had curled up on her chair and was hugging her knees, all the fight and feistiness gone out of her.

'Noise pollution,' announced Richard, with some authority, 'that's what it is. They've got a special council department for it, these days. You should give them a call.'

'It's gone quiet, though,' Gary pointed out. They all listened, cocking their heads.

'Or has it?' Laura gasped, her saucer-eyes popping with horror as a new spine-chilling wail broke the silence. 'What the fuck is that?'

'That,' said Gary, grimly, getting up from his chair, 'is Lois.' He glanced at his watch, swearing softly. 'Christ, how did it get so late? Ruth will kill me.'

Dougie saw them out, it having been agreed that they would head off in search of taxis. Back inside he found Laura hunched up on the sitting-room sofa, looking like a punctured ball. 'The noises have started up here now,' she whimpered, pointing at the wall. 'I'm scared, Doug. I mean, what *is* going on?' As she spoke there was a series of muffled thumps, faster than the early ones, but not nearly so loud.

'I suppose I'd better check it out,' Dougie conceded, although all he really wanted to do was to crawl upstairs to bed, preferably that minute, preferably alone. He took his house keys and stepped outside. A dilapidated low wire fence divided his and Nina Carmichael's front gardens. He took a big step over it and rang the bell, only then thinking to stand back, by way of a precautionary measure against murderous relatives or boyfriends.

The door was opened at once by his neighbour, wearing an innocuous candlewick dressing-gown but looking faintly murderous, thanks to the expression of hostility on her pale, blotchy face and the fact that she was clasping a large stiff-bristled broom. Most shocking of all, however – though Dougie managed resolutely to look as if he hadn't noticed it – was her head, which was round and bald, and so smooth it shone like a polished stone under the dim wattage of her hall light.

'I assume you've come to apologize.'

'I beg your pardon?' Dougie laughed uncertainly. 'Apologize? For what?'

'For that fucking noise, that's what.'

'Look here –'

'No, you look. Music, screaming, howling dogs – I need to sleep, okay? I *need* to . . .' She clutched her head, digging her fingers so fiercely into the bare skin that Dougie found himself flinching.

'I'm sorry, I –'

'Okay. Done. Goodnight.' She slammed the door.

When he returned Laura was waiting for him by the door, looking more composed and faintly sheepish. 'I've ordered a taxi,' she said. 'I hope you don't mind. Just couldn't face the early start – getting home for my things before work. Call me, yeah?'

'Yeah,' Dougie echoed, trying to hide his relief.

After she had gone he dragged himself downstairs to break the habit of a lifetime and clear up. The way his diary was looking, he couldn't afford not to. In the next three days alone he had numerous bookings, not just of classes but catering for a birthday dinner and canapés for a marquee summer party. He needed to get to the market early, stay within his budgets, keep on his toes. Dougie worked robotically, his mind wavering between awareness of his drained state and guilt about his neighbour. She had made such a sorry spectacle. Alopecia or chemotherapy – either way it was a cruel blow for one clearly not much blessed in the looks stakes anyway.

By the time Dougie had finished it was gone one o'clock. With the dishwasher on, the sides swabbed and the drainer loaded into a precarious mountain, he was about to turn out the light when he noticed a plate of left-over vanilla biscuits, perched on the window sill. Thinking of Nina, he carefully wrapped them in tinfoil and scrib-bled a note of apology, putting both in a plastic bag, which he left on her doorstep before going up to bed. Sleep came at him, like the embrace of a lost friend. But on the brink of it he was assailed by images of one of the street's many foraging foxes, tearing the bag and its contents to shreds.

Drugged with fatigue, close to sleep-walking, he pulled on his jeans and stumbled downstairs to make his third sortie of the evening to Nina's doorstep, where he picked up the bag and tied the handles to the door knocker instead, to keep it safe. Back in bed, sleep was waiting for him still: a plunge pool this time. He dived in head first, joyfully rubber-necking the untouched glass of wine as he went, much as a grateful driver accelerates past the scene of someone else's accident.

Chapter Eight

As they drove away, Janine kept her eyes fixed on the rear-view mirror. For a few seconds the pair of them were as neatly framed as a photograph, Dougie swinging Stevie's holdall onto his back, checking the road was clear as they crossed, Stevie clopping behind him in the new wedge-heel platform sandals she had bought with birthday money from Janine's parents, her arms full of all the last-minute things that hadn't made it into her suitcase. The birthday itself had been celebrated the previous evening – a cinema and pizza outing with friends from which she had, once again, returned well past an agreed curfew, reeking of smoke and alcohol. With the morning farewell imminent, Janine had let it pass, persuading Mike to do likewise.

Mike slid his near hand off the steering-wheel and onto her knee. 'That seemed to go well.'

'Yes, it did.'

'A trial run.'

'Exactly. That's *exactly* what I was thinking.' Janine squeezed his fingers gratefully. He knew her, that was the joyous thing. He knew her and never seemed to tire of demonstrating the fact.

'On all fronts.'

'On all fronts,' she echoed, while her mind drifted back to the expression on Dougie's face as she had given Stevie a final hug goodbye, the curious flexing of sadness and hope. Something inside her had twisted to see it, like the throb of an old wound. He was to be in full parental charge for the week, while she and Mike went on a final reconnaissance trip to Stockholm, to sort out details about the Lidingö house and generally get their bearings. Stevie, now fully informed of the plan for moving abroad, had taken full advantage of the advice not to rush into responding to it. There had been none of the histrionics Janine had feared, no tears, no sniping comments, indeed barely any questions. She would think about it, she had declared archly, then get back to them. Since when she had hardly referred to the subject, not even during their recent trip *à deux* to see Janine's parents, which had been somewhat emotional since they ran a busy garden centre in Keswick and rarely had time for weekends off, let alone trips to Scandinavia.

'She'll make her mind up about coming with us in her own good time,' Mike said, managing yet again to read her thoughts. 'It's a lot for her to take in.'

'Yes, it is.'

'And if she stays with . . .' he balked as usual at saying Dougie's name '. . . in London, it'll only be for a couple of years, during the course of which there'll be loads of trips home for you, as well – obviously – as visits for her to us.'

'Yes, loads. And today . . .' Janine turned to look out of her window, wondering idly whether she would miss the English countryside, that day a galaxy of gold and blue rolling along behind the borders of the M11. Since the final week of Stevie's exams the early summer warmth had segued into a record-breaking heatwave. The colours were blinding, surreal, shimmering like wet paint. She had been so pumped up about the handover to Dougie that morning, so wary of the huge next step ahead, yet in the end it had been easy. Stevie had been phlegmatic to the point of distant, while her own thoughts had been popping with excitement at the trip – seeing the house on the island, buying furniture, a car. Pieces were falling into place on all sides: she had handed in her notice at work, triggering a string of tearful, bosomy hugs from Donna; she had found tenants for her house, starting in September; she had even booked packers for the first week in July. It was all starting to come together, to feel real. Dougie was the only one who had looked forlorn, Janine reflected, seeing again the expression on his face and deciding that most of it was sheer exhaustion. There had been that pinched look round his eyes, the one he always got when he wasn't sleeping well.

Mike steered his silver Mercedes smoothly into a sliproad off the motorway. He had found a private buyer for the car and was taking even more care of it than usual. 'Today?' he prompted, as her silence continued.

'Just the saying goodbye,' Janine explained, quickly banishing Dougie from her thoughts. 'It wasn't nearly as bad as I was expecting. It made me realize that so long as Stevie is okay then I'm okay and – Hang on . . .' She peered at a signpost. 'This turning's too early for Stansted. Do we need petrol?'

'Nope.' Mike set his lips together, looking pleased with himself. 'There's something I want to do first.'

'Really?' Janine glanced at her watch.

He stroked her arm. 'Don't worry, it won't take long and we've heaps of time. Bear with me, okay?'

'Okay.' She sat back in her seat.

'You trust me, don't you?'

'Oh, yes.' She sighed happily. 'I trust you.'

Ten minutes later he pulled into a lay-by on a country lane. 'I don't know if this is the exact place, but it looks pretty close to what came up when I Googled the post-code. A forest, a public footpath, a place to sit down –'

'A forest . . . a place to sit down? You're mad,' Janine cried, laughing as she got out of the car, catching her breath a little at the heat, which was a smothering blanket after the icy cocoon of the Mercedes' air-conditioning. She watched with mounting curiosity as Mike opened the boot and lifted out a small black holdall, the smallest he possessed in a matching set of three.

'Come on.' He held out his hand.

She let him lead her along the path into the wood, where the canopy of foliage offered immediate relief from the belting midday sun. Between the trees the domes of bracken grew thick and high, like a sea of tents in some vast natural campsite. 'Mike, we really haven't got that long –'

'Here. This'll do.' He let go of her hand and moved off the path to stamp down a relatively tame patch of under-growth. Unzipping the black bag, he pulled out a tartan blanket, which he shook out onto the ground with a flour-ish. 'If Madam would like to take a seat?'

'She would.' Janine giggled, dropping obediently onto the rug, her imagination running wild with possibilities. They had been together for nearly a year, after all. Her heart bounced.

'To toast us on our way,' Mike announced next, produc-ing two plastic beakers and a half-bottle of champagne from the wrapping of dampened newspaper that had served to keep it chilled. 'We're like a ship, you and I. We're being launched. On a new journey. To us, babe.'

'To us,' Janine echoed, as they touched beakers. They drank and then kissed, pulling apart as an elderly couple walked by with a spaniel that got a scolding for nosing at their legs. 'Nothing more in that bag of yours, then?' she teased, poking it with her foot. And when he said no, she was glad. Steady Mike, taking it steady. One step at a time. It was everything she loved about him; everything she needed.

A hundred miles further south, in a field of wild flowers, under a thin straggle of branches that did little to shield them from the grilling sun, Victoria and Simon sat on canvas stools at opposite ends of their easy-fold picnic table. Victoria was wearing a wide-brimmed straw hat, which did not exactly match her blue silk dress, but made her feel closer to the elegance expected of Glyndebourne, while at the same time saving her from the certainty of a heat-headache. The bottle of white wine they had brought was warming as fast as they could drink it. Sodden with condensation, its once handsome, gold-embossed label hung limply, like a strip of wallpaper abandoned halfway through gluing. They had china plates and proper cutlery, but were mostly picking with their forks straight out of the Tupperware boxes into which she had loaded the food: fillets of salmon, poached in dill and wine, a walnut salad, sun-dried tomatoes and several torn hunks of ciabatta, which had already developed rocky edges in the heat.

They were there for *Don Giovanni*, a version set in the

Mafia world of Sicily about which the critics had been unanimously ungenerous. Simon, reading out one of the reviews over breakfast that morning, had jokingly asked why they were bothering. But the tickets had been a gift from her father, handed over for the very sad reason that her mother was now ensconced in her Scottish 'residence', and Victoria was determined to use them.

'Cheers.' She raised her glass at Simon, who had given up on the picnic and was tipping his chair back in a precarious reclining position, which she had been doing her utmost not to remark on. The toast was just a way of securing his attention. Time was slipping by and she wanted to launch into all of the matters she had been preparing in her head in the car, some of which were going to be tricky. Very tricky. But she would begin with the decidedly un-tricky business of coming clean about his birthday surprise, she decided, sitting forwards and pushing the brim of her hat up out of her eyes. 'We should do this sort of thing more, like we used to. Don't you think? We've become so lazy.'

Simon squinted at her, knitting his eyebrows against the glare of the afternoon. He had embarked on a new effort with contact lenses and they were hurting. 'Lazy is good. Lazy means happy. Silly girl. You're the workaholic, remember?'

'So I am.' Victoria smiled, experiencing the usual swell of grateful affection at how innately relaxed he was about everything compared to her. 'Simon, I've got something to tell you.' Her smile deepened with the pleasurable anticipation of one on the verge of delivering a surprise. 'Oh, no, not that,' she cried quickly, the smile dying, as

Simon rocked his chair upright, his face frozen with the readiness to be astounded. 'Not *that* sort of big news.' Victoria laughed, awkwardly now. 'At least, I don't think so – I mean, I haven't done a test for a while because we haven't . . .'

'You mean, because there's been so little need?' Simon fumbled for his sunglasses and pushed them onto his face.

'Something like that,' Victoria admitted quietly, hating this new fragility between them and her powerlessness in the face of it. To broach the subject of sex – or, rather, the lack of it – had indeed been part of her conversation-hatching plan, but not so clumsily, so impossibly. It had been many weeks now. So many she had stopped counting.

They both let their gazes drift, as if the undeniable beauty of their surroundings might help them through the moment. Victoria thought of all the nights she had spent lying awake in the dark, torn between wanting to touch her husband and not wanting to put pressure on him. Concluding that all the manuals and thermometers had to be the turn-off – shouting their presence even though she had long since stopped referring to them – she had picked a quiet moment that week to stow the whole lot at the back of the spare-room wardrobe. On her knees, however, fumbling in the dusty dark, behind shoes she no longer wore and fallen misshapen coat hangers, her hands had alighted upon a box she did not recognize – a quite heavy box, full, as it turned out, of men's magazines, fifty of them at least, some old, some very new.

Victoria had sat back on her heels, more surprised than anything. The most recent was just a month old and contained, between occasional articles about cars and computers, and readers' letters describing fantasies, the most lurid sexual images she had ever seen: girl on girl, man on girl, men on girl, men on girls – chain after chain of improbable copulation involving every orifice the human body had to offer and a great variety of props. Shocked, and even, rather to her surprise, faintly aroused, Victoria had flicked through several before heaving the box back into the bottom of the cupboard.

The light was softening around them now, casting a faintly blue tinge over the soft Sussex stone of the Glynde-bourne manor house and darkening the healthy green glow of its hedged gardens and rolling lawns. There was birdsong and the faint murmur of other picnickers, camped at their own tables or on rugs, the men splendid in black tie, the women self-conscious of the effort they had made in their high heels and flowing summer gowns.

'So, come on, then, what's this big news of yours?' Simon prompted gruffly.

Victoria kept her gaze averted. 'It won't seem big now.'

'Go on, dummy. Yes, it will.'

'It's for your birthday –'

'Aha,' he cut in gloomily. 'I can guess that one. It's a gun. You've bought me a gun to shoot myself. Forty. Bloody hell. Leave me now, Vic. Find a toy-boy. I'm use-less. I know I'm useless.'

'You're not useless, and I don't want to leave you, Simon. But maybe we should talk about . . .' He was look-ing at her in a way that made it hard to go on.

He left his chair and came to crouch next to her, taking off the sunglasses and stroking her cheek with the backs of his fingers. 'Don't be sad, bunny. Or cross. Don't be cross with me.'

'I'm not cross.'

'We'll make a baby, I promise. Just give us – me – time. Okay?'

He touched the tip of her nose with his and she smiled at him, her eyes flooding with tears, whether from being sad or happy she couldn't really have said. It was the tenderness in his voice that moved her more than anything, the reminder of how deeply he cared. 'That's sweet, Simon, thank you. And I believe you. But it's not just that, it's . . . well . . . lately . . .' Her mind blazed with an image from one of the magazines: a girl on her knees in a cowboy hat, her rear bared to the camera, her suitor poised, leering, with the handle of a riding crop. '. . . I've begun to wonder how well I really know you.'

'Don't be a goon. Of course you know me.' Simon nudged her nose again. One of their special Eskimo kisses. 'I'm the Hopeless Case you married twelve years ago. The one who loves you . . .'

'Do you? Do you love me, Simon?'

'Victoria, stop. What is this? Of course I love you. And if my knees weren't seizing up I'd stay down here longer to make sure you never questioned the fact again. As it is . . .' He pulled a comical long-suffering face as he got to his feet, shaking a hanky out of his pocket and dabbing it across his forehead. 'This heat. Maybe it's driving us mad.'

'Yes, it's baking, isn't it?' Victoria closed her eyes. The image of the cowgirl came at her again and she decided this time not to be afraid of it. Pornography was no big deal; indeed, it was commonplace, especially with the

Internet. Simon probably visited sites there, too, although she had resisted the urge to check. The fact remained that her husband had never been especially libidinous. So if he sought a little private help now and then, was this really the right moment to be fretting about it? When they were supposedly trying for a child? The poor man could use all the help he bloody well needed. Indeed, some women in her shoes, Victoria decided – the truly liberated women, the ones with greater sexual confidence – would probably be scouring lingerie racks or organizing fitting sessions at a good fancy-dress shop.

Simon had come to stand behind her. He put his hands on her shoulders and began gently kneading the muscles at the base of her neck with his thumbs. 'I'm so sorry, my darling Vic. You had a surprise to tell me and I've completely ruined it. Can you tell me now? Can you give me a second chance?'

Victoria released a long breath, letting her shoulders drop. The massaging felt good. There were deep knots and his fingers were finding them.

'We'd got as far as my birthday, I think . . .'

'Yes, your birthday.' She dropped her head forward so he could rub the tender patch at the base of her skull. He had asked for time and she would give it to him. It was obviously pressure from her that had been the problem. She needed to back off, give him space. Sex was never as straightforward as people liked to make out: it could be a delicate business; all kinds of healthy love flourished without its dominance. Simon was right, they would get there – become parents – but it was only fair that it should be at a pace that suited both of them, rather than just her.

'The big surprise,' she went on, once Simon had deposited a parting kiss on the top of her head and flopped back into his chair, 'is that I've arranged for us to spend your birthday in Spain, at Dougie's place, a long weekend. Dougie will be our chef, of course – his very bestest meals ever. I've been working up some menus – all the things you love. I've asked Gary and Ruth to come too. Keep it small, I thought. I did suggest Dougie bring someone – I thought it was only fair – but he said he didn't want to, apart from Stevie, who's apparently going to be at the end of some school trip to Valencia and so might join us on the Sunday. On the Monday I've booked flights from Alicante to Seville and organized a hire car so we can spend a week exploring down there – Granada, Córdoba, all those incredible Moorish cities. Si, what do you think? Are you pleased? You haven't said a word.'

Simon laughed. 'That's because I'm speechless.'

'Because if not, I can still cancel.'

'Bloody hell, are you mad?' He reached across the table for her hand.

'Or if you want more people – Danny and Heather, Paul and Trish, we haven't seen them in ages. Or that Richard guy you met at Dougie's and said you liked . . .'

'No, I don't think so – at least, I'll think about it.' He grinned, giving her hand one of his vice-squeezes and then kissing it. 'It's a wonderful surprise. Thank you, Vic, so much. I'd been feeling low about this bloody birthday, but not any more.'

'And I've been plotting behind your back for weeks,' she confessed, laughing now, 'wondering when to tell you. It was after you mentioned Dougie was struggling to rent the place that I first had the idea. And now he says he might be selling, which is really sad because it's such a lovely villa, isn't it? Do you remember, Si, when we went there before, how lovely it was? All that skinny dipping we did before breakfast . . .'

'I certainly do. How could I ever forget?' They looked at each other, the last wisps of tension floating away. 'Christ, I'm lucky to have you, Vic. Never let me forget that, will you, how lucky I am? Spain will be wonderful. You're a genius for thinking of it.'

The critics were wrong, they agreed, driving back to London some four hours later, picking over the best bits, Victoria's nose still a little red from crying in the final scene, which had moved her not with sorrow – the ruthless, phil-andering Don Giovanni deserved everything he got – but because of the sheer resilience of the man's sinning spirit, defiant to the very end, even as the flames of eternal dam-nation sucked him down through the stage's trapdoor. Opera didn't exaggerate the human condition, she decided, as its opponents liked to complain: it simply showed what went on underneath, the storms most people spent a life-time trying to hide, the blood and bones laid bare.

Chapter Nine

Dougie and Stevie stopped at the first free table and slid into the window seats opposite each other. The train was half empty and had the stale morning-after smell of a party. They were on the fourth day of the week granted by Janine and Mike's preparatory trip to Stockholm, a hot, airless Wednesday. At Wimbledon the previous afternoon, a pretty young Russian had been stretchered off a brown and balding Centre Court with sunstroke. A photograph of her, sprawled on the grass next to her racket, dominated the front page of Dougie's paper, advertising both the drama and her famously long, tanned legs, visible to the glorious frilly edges of her underwear. Dougie studied the picture, mulling over whether it was exploitative or not and deciding it wasn't. The tennis player would be pleased at the publicity, he decided; there would be more offers of lingerie endorsements, more money.

He put the paper down and let his gaze drift to the messy hinterland of south London – the power station, warehouses, waste dumps – even the ugliest of it claiming some sort of glory that morning, thanks to the illuminating ebullience of the sun, converting old brick to burnished gold and making even the scrappiest metal glint like silver. They were going to Tonbridge to visit his father, a venture prompted – much to Dougie's shame – by the old man himself, phoning to complain that he never saw his granddaughter. Dougie had spent the morning doing his best, both to look forward to the visit and not to bring up the subject of Sweden as they travelled. He had slept well for once, but it had left him feeling dopey and leaden. In the train window he could make out the faint reflection of his face, and Stevie's, even more indistinct, next to him, bent over her blessed iPhone, as it had been for virtually every minute since they had walked out of the Camden Carphone Warehouse on Monday afternoon. It was the best birthday present she had ever had, she had informed him solemnly, causing Dougie such a burst of joy that he had already stuffed a fresh twenty into the empty savings jar by way of an advance towards any further such treats or necessities in the future.

The window reflections disappeared suddenly. Dougie turned to sneak a proper look at his daughter instead, drinking in her familiar features with the new greed that had come from the fear of losing her. What was she really thinking? What was she going to decide? *When?*

'Sweden might be cool,' she had remarked, in the first flurry of conversation that had followed the drop-off by Mike and Janine at the weekend.

'Of *course* Sweden would be cool,' Dougie had yelped, wondering that she couldn't hear the snap of his heart, pondering what an excellent job Janine must have done of presenting the new situation and her right to make choices within it. No pressure, that was what they had agreed; a plea that Dougie had read again in the look Janine threw at him as she hugged Stevie goodbye. He had nodded back to show he understood, painfully aware of the watchful gaze of Mike, hanging over the open door of his fancy car like a sloth. What on earth did she see in the man anyway, he had wondered viciously. Kindness? A big dick? Sobriety?

That morning he had seen Laura Munro off for good. She had done her usual trick of arriving unannounced the previous evening, when the hour was late and his defences down. Sweden would be the making of his daughter, she had informed him blithely, when the sex was done with and they were falling asleep. She had gone on to explain what a brilliant place Stockholm was for teenagers – shopping, outdoor sports, a fantastic night-life. Stevie wouldn't want to come back to London, she had claimed, demonstrating a bluntness so devoid of empathy or interest in his own mind-set that Dougie had found it easy to see out his plan of bringing things to a dignified end. 'It's been fun, a lot of fun,' he ventured over their morning coffee, 'but the fact is Stevie arrives later today and then I'm going to Spain, and so –'

'Okay, I get it.' There had been no sign of perturbation in her cool grey eyes; indeed, no sign of anything very much. 'We'd probably run our course anyway. Yeah . . . fun, like you say.' She had kissed him lightly and skipped off without a backward glance, leaving Dougie feeling almost rebuffed, which had led him to ponder, more clearly than he ever had before, the pointlessness of phys-ical gratification without the moorings of emotion.

The sun was now streaming through the glass of the train window, burning the side of his face and arm. Dougie shifted position so his shoulders bore the brunt of it. 'Okay, these exams of yours, young lady – when do we get the results?'

Stevie squinted, as if it took considerable effort to bring him into focus. 'August.'

'I see. Any chance of knowing on which of its thirty-one days that might be?'

'Uh-uh.'

'Good. Glad you are so clued up – most encouraging.'

'Look, Dad, I'm sure I've done fine in the subjects that matter. Okay?'

'No, not okay. Put that thing down a minute and talk to me. I know it's partly my fault for working so hard, but we've been under the same roof for three days and I've barely seen you.'

She dropped the mobile with a clatter onto the table and folded her arms. She crossed her legs, too, clad that day in shorts as tight as underpants and a strappy pink top fringed with yellow lace. 'So what do you want to talk about, then? Apart from *exams*.' She had some gum in her mouth which she tore at with her teeth.

Dougie summoned patience, recalling the difficulties Janine had mentioned. Given the imminent upheaval, the uncertainty, it was hardly surprising if Stevie decided to act up with him, too. He was determined to take that into account, but had no intention of being walked over either. 'Doh . . . let me see. What could there possibly be for you and me to talk about?' He screwed up his face in the manner of one trying to retrieve a vital fact, summoning and resisting the temptation to use the opportunity to quiz her about Sweden. 'Maybe we could begin with your imminent language-improvement excursion to Valencia. Or whether you're happy about the plan of coming on to the *finca* afterwards, where I'll be running the birthday show for Simon. Or what you really think about Mike –'

'Ah,' she butted in, wagging a finger and tossing her long hair, that morning assembled into a straggly bird's nest with glittering clips, 'you're not getting me there. It's obvious you want me to hate Mike, but I don't *actually*.'

Dougie grinned. 'Good. This is called a "conversation", my love. Fun, isn't it?' He gave her a playful thwack with his newspaper. 'I'm glad you don't hate Mike. The guy can't help how he looks . . .'

'Dad – shut *up*.'

'And if you hadn't stayed out so late drinking and smoking with your pals on Monday night, or were capable of getting out of bed before lunch, we might – even with me being busy – not need a train journey to catch up on news.'

She released a squeal of outrage, so high-pitched that a baby snoozing in its mother's lap at the next table blinked its eyes open and stared at her. Stevie stared back, momentarily transported to a memory of the tiny dark-eyed sibling with whom she had briefly shared her parents' attention five years ago. On the day before his death he had looked at her properly for the first time, falling for the trick of sucking her little finger. Until then, she had been suspicious of him more than anything, the time he took up, the noise he made, which was a lot.

'Who says we were drinking and smoking?' she challenged carefully, returning her attention to her father, her thoughts flicking to the bench on Hampstead Heath where she had partied with her girlfriends on Monday night – vodka, fags, the usual things – while two boys with pimply faces circled them on skateboards, firing sarky comments and asking for their phone numbers. 'Anyway,' she blurted, on a rush of courage, 'it's not like you can really talk when it comes to that stuff, can you, Dad?'

Dougie tried not to look surprised. He held her gaze, noting its undercurrent of insolence, deciding that the real surprise was that she hadn't said anything similar before. While never openly discussed, the subject of his over-indulgence in alcohol, both during and after its stranglehold, was unequivocal and known. Janine had made sure of that. For Stevie's protection, she said, so that she never felt afraid or culpable. She claimed, rather to his relief, to have been a little more circumspect about his infidelities, releasing as much information as was needed, she said, as much as Stevie could handle, and then only when everything was over and because she had asked.

'Oh, but that's where you're wrong, my love,' he countered softly. 'I can talk. For two reasons. One, I know what I am talking *about*, and two, it's a parent's job to tell their kids the right way to live, no matter what mistakes they've made themselves.' He paused. Stevie's attention was already drifting, to the window – an expanse of emerald playing-fields now, dotted with schoolboy cricketers – then to the dark-eyed baby, who had fallen back to sleep, mouth slack, chin on chest like an old man. 'Booze and fags,' Dougie pressed on, laying equal emphasis on both words, trying to reel her back in, 'are bad for you. Period. Addictive, destructive –'

'Yeah, right. But then there's that woman who lives next to you, isn't there? Having cancer when she says she's never done anything unhealthy in her life.'

'And what kind of cancer does my neighbour have?' Dougie exclaimed, astonished.

'It was in her lymph nodes.'

'Really?' He laughed, impressed. 'And how did you come by that information, may I ask?' Since the night of the broom-bashing, he hadn't even seen Nina Carmichael, let alone talked to her. If the vanilla biscuits had restored any goodwill, there had been no indication of it.

Stevie shrugged. Her father's interest made her wary. She had been crouching in a corner of the garden smoking furtively when the neighbour had appeared, a black cat weaving between her knees. The sight of the woman's head appearing over the top of the fence, shining and hairless, like a rising moon, had made her jump. But then they had got talking in a way that had been quite nice, covering various things before getting to the fact of her having been ill.

Stevie gnashed at her gum, which had grown stiff and tasteless. 'It was yesterday – I was sunbathing and she said hi.' She hesitated, weighing up the lie. It was true she had been sitting in the sun, but only so she could smoke. 'She said she had just finished some treatment and was through the worst, but really annoyed she'd lost her eyelashes. She said with the heatwave she didn't wear a headscarf except for going out. She said she had an expensive wig but that was even hotter *and* itchy.'

'Christ, poor creature . . .'

'Can we stop talking now?'

'Nearly. Tell me first, Valencia – are you looking forward to it? It's a great city – by the sea, lots going on. You'll have a brilliant time, you lucky girl.'

Stevie pulled a face. Now that it was almost upon her – just a couple of weeks away – she couldn't imagine what had possessed her to agree to spend seven days of her precious summer holidays with some random Spanish family. It was part of a new placement programme that her school had pushed really hard at all pupils who were going on with languages into the sixth form. The family had a daughter her age called Maria who, judging from their brief Facebook contact, was pretty babyish and not into any of the same things. Even more daunting was the prospect of having to use her stumbling Spanish for so long in front of total strangers. 'I suppose I have to go, do I?'

'Of course you have to go. Why wouldn't you want to? You'll be jabbering like a true Spaniard by the end of it – think what a head-start that will give you on the A-level front. And, by the way, this thing –' Dougie tapped the iPhone '– is for emergencies only while you're out there. Got it? Emergencies. It'll cost the earth otherwise. And coming to the *finca* afterwards is all sorted,' he added, more kindly. 'We'll get you a train ticket to Alicante on the Sunday and I'll pick you up. Simon and Co leave on the Monday. You and I will fly back to London on the Tuesday, after I've had a chance to close the place up properly. Okay?'

She nodded glumly.

'Are you worried about this Sweden business, sweetheart?' Dougie blurted, breaking his promise to himself, his innards churning, as they always did when she was sad. 'Is that what the matter is?'

'A bit.'

'Of course you're worried. Take your time, okay? Think it through. Don't worry about hurting Mum's or my feelings or anything like that. It's your feelings that count. Whether you're with me or with Mum and Mike, you'll be fine. It's just making the choice that's hard. Once you've done it, the rest will fall into place.' Pleased with this, at how measured and firm it sounded, how well it masked his own terrors, Dougie left the conversation there and shook out his newspaper.

Stevie returned her attention to her birthday gift. She had downloaded lots of her favourite music onto it already and was now picking through the pictures from her birthday night out, trying to decide which ones to load onto her Facebook page. She slid her fingers back and forth across the little screen, scrolling, zooming, deleting, relishing the concentration required, the way it shut out the world. She had been so happy when her GCSEs ended but then, all too soon, life had flooded with things to dread: visiting grandparents. Spain. Sweden . . . There was no way she was going to live there. No way. Mike full-time? Some new foreign school? Losing her friends? She wasn't an idiot. She would stay with her dad. It would be weird, but cool. And yet something had stopped her saying as much out loud; an empty feeling deep inside; a feeling to do with her mum not being there, not even to piss her off.

'Hey, Gramps.'

'Goodness, but how you've grown. Quite the young woman, these days, isn't she, Doug?'

Lenny Easton winked at his son, but Dougie pretended

not to see, feeling for Stevie having to endure such platitudes and not liking the oblique un-grandfatherly reference to his stepdaughter's blossoming figure. A minute across the threshold and he was already, as usual, fighting the urge to bolt. The place smelt for one thing, of stale fish tinged with detergent. And there was a faint griminess too, of objects not moved for years, of surfaces cleaned for too long by a cursory hand and in the shadows of failing eyesight. It wasn't that the old man couldn't afford domestic help, he just preferred not to have it.

'How are things, then, Dad?'

'Can't complain.'

'Why not?'

'Pardon?'

Dougie exhaled slowly. Stevie had gone upstairs to the bathroom. They were in the kitchen where Lenny, amid much sighing, had prepared three glasses of orange squash. 'I just mean you *can* complain, Dad – it's not against the law.' Dougie sipped his drink, which was too sweet and lukewarm.

'Well, I don't, do I? That's how we were brought up, my generation. None of the moaning that goes on these days . . .'

While Lenny talked, Dougie let his gaze drift to the photo of his mother, Hilary, who had died, quickly and unexpectedly, of ovarian cancer thirty years before. It had sat on the window sill for as long as he could remember, the glass freckled with age. It was a glamorous black-and-white studio picture, with her posing like a film star in an off-the-shoulder dress and a pearl necklace. In the aftermath of her death Lenny had seen fit to use a maturing life policy to send Dougie away to prep school, a fact that Janine, once upon a time, in her fonder moments, had liked to blame for the roots of his manifold failings. Yet the truth was Dougie had loved the little school. It had been run in an old manor house by a pair of childless eccentrics who had encouraged the recitation of Latin verbs as well as adventurous spirits, while at the same time providing hefty meals from a well-stocked kitchen garden. He had only happy memories of the place. It was going home he had grown to dread, the tightness between his brother and his father, the sense of exclusion.

Lenny, as was his wont after any allusion to the theme of his own stoicism, had moved on to the subject of the war. He had been nine when it started, he told Stevie, now returned from the bathroom, her hair in a new style – up on one side and down on the other, like a lop-sided curtain. Nine to fourteen, he went on, recounting the evacuation to a farm in Sussex, the roaring black skies of the assault on London during the Blitz, the gnaw of hunger left by rationing.

Dougie, who had heard it all before, scores of times, watched Stevie with pride. She appeared transfixed, gripping her orange squash and asking a string of pertinent questions. She did the same when they got to the pub for lunch and the conversation moved, with equal predictability, to the subject of his younger brother James: she widened her eyes at the familiar stories of her uncle's exploits in the arena of battle, the medal for bravery in Afghanistan, the close shaves, and prompted the old man if he seemed in danger of running out of steam.

'He's quite a man, your uncle, Stephanie,' Lenny

declared, pushing away the plate he had so carefully wiped clean of the gravy from his steak and kidney pie – a dish that Dougie would have refused to eat for its smell alone. He and Stevie had gone for the much safer option of chicken and chips. 'It's just a shame your father can't see it.'

'I have nothing but admiration for James, Dad, as you well know,' Dougie replied calmly, casting Stevie a reassuring smile. 'My little brother's courage and talents are jaw-dropping. They always have been. I couldn't be happier that he's currently treading a safer path in Germany. Our lives our pretty separate, that's all. I've tried to see a bit of him over the years, but he's never been that interested.' Dougie signalled to a waiter for the bill.

'The words "chalk" and "cheese" spring to mind,' continued Lenny, dourly, stifling a burp. 'Chalk-and-bloody-cheese.'

'You mean they were good at different things?' Stevie piped up, looking from her father to her grandfather, sensing that the conversation, of which she had secretly grown very bored, was entering new, and possibly interesting, territory.

'You could say that, I suppose.' Lenny belched again, this time into his paper napkin.

'Like what?'

'Like Jamie making a go of things,' Dougie explained, breaking the silence before it grew awkward, 'wowing them at Sandhurst, while I was busy dropping out of uni, wasting the money spent on my education. Oh, yes, and there was that Chelsea talent scout after him for a while, wasn't there, Dad?' He turned back to Stevie. 'Chelsea

Football Academy, turned down in favour of the army –
not many boys would do that, would they?'

'And there was that business with the girl,' Lenny muttered, swiping the napkin across his upper lip, then
inspecting it.

'Blimey, Dad –' Dougie stopped, aware that his calm
was in danger of deserting him. There were always gibes,
he reminded himself. The trick was to ignore them. Without engagement no battle could take place. The girl referred
to was by no means an edifying memory, but it had been
years ago: a one-night stand, during a rare visit home after
he had abandoned the course at Exeter. Ione Watkin. She
had been a gauche, elfin creature – not his type at all – who
had revealed practically everything about herself during
their night in her lumpy single bed, apart from the signal
information that she was going out with his brother;
secretly engaged, as it transpired, although it had clearly
been a farce of an arrangement since they were both only
eighteen.

Lenny balled up his napkin and dropped it onto his
plate. He was sucking in his lower jaw, looking emotional.
'I've not got long, you know, Douglas . . . You'll be shot
of me soon – you and James.'

Dougie glanced at Stevie, who was visibly disconcerted
now, fiddling with one of the coloured braids tied round
her slim wrist. 'Don't start getting morose, Dad. You've a
few decades left in you yet.' The waiter arrived and Dougie
quickly settled the bill with cash.

A few minutes later they were making their way back
along the road, Stevie busy on her phone, Lenny hobbling
because of his bad hip. Dougie walked slowly beside him

sucking hungrily on a cigarette, grateful that the roar of passing traffic drowned the need for any further conversation.

As soon as they got inside he ordered a taxi to get back to the station and then made tea, which Lenny drank noisily in front of the television, his feet resting on the scuffed side table that he used as a foot stool. 'Never get old, Stephanie child, you hear me?' he croaked, flecks of spittle flying to the corners of his mouth.

Stevie smiled sweetly, showing her dimples, before hurrying out into the garden, on the pretext of needing to make a phone call. Dougie watched with envy as the door closed behind her. 'My new business is going well, Dad.'

'What business is that, then?'

'Cooking – private parties, classes, remember? I told you on the phone? I have a website and –'

'Oh, yes. That. And weren't you writing a book, you said? Now *there*'s an occupation – writing. That would be a fine thing, don't you think, to have a book on a shelf with your name on it? None of this digital nonsense.'

'Indeed it would,' Dougie admitted hollowly. As a busy widower with young sons, Lenny's idea of cooking hadn't moved much beyond tins and the virtues of long-life bread. Three restaurants, the acclaim – the star – for the Black Hen, all the years of grind, might just as well not have happened.

'So have you got good contacts in the publishing world?' Lenny barked. 'All those famous people you know, you must have, eh? I only ask because I've been doing a spot of writing myself.' His broad, grizzled face split into a rare grin. 'I've been writing,' he repeated proudly.

'Writing?' Genuine surprise cut through Dougie's gloom. 'About what?'

'This and that. Memoirs, I suppose you'd call it. I was hoping you might be able to put in me in touch with a publisher . . . .one of those fancy friends of yours.'

The doorbell rang, heralding the arrival of the taxi. 'Fancy friends?' Dougie echoed weakly, getting to his feet. 'Well, obviously, if I think of someone, but . . . to be honest, Dad, it's unlikely. Publishing, it's not really my bag.'

Lenny laboured out of his chair, making a big show of lifting the leg connected to his bad hip. A hip replacement had been recommended by his GP several times, but he had refused, saying he preferred to take his own bones to the grave.

At a rap on the window, Stevie trotted in from the garden, smelling of smoke. A few minutes later she and Dougie were sprawling in the air-conditioned cool on the back seat of the cab, in a state of mutual and silent relief.

'Well done, sweetheart,' Dougie murmured at length. 'You were fantastic.'

Stevie frowned, licking her finger and rubbing at something on her precious phone screen. 'He's just so *old* now, isn't he? And grumpy, like a bear.' She took a couple of clips out of the pinned-up side of her hair and put them back in again. 'And I'd never sort of noticed it before but . . .' she turned to him, her face creased with sympathy '. . . I'm not sure Gramps actually likes you that much, Dad, does he?'

'No, I don't think he does,' Dougie conceded, with a sad smile, wondering if he had ever loved her more. 'He and Jamie always got on better.'

She snorted. 'No wonder you're not that keen on *him*, then.'

'Oh, your uncle's fine, really. We're just different. Gone separate ways and so on. And, as Dad was so keen to remind me at lunch, I did nick a girlfriend of his once, which I shouldn't have done. I've tried to say sorry but . . .' He shrugged, looking out of the window. A moment later he felt Stevie's hand arrive in his.

'But I like you, Dad. Heaps and heaps.'

'Do you? That's good.'

'And I'd like to stay with you, if that's still okay. The whole Sweden thing . . .' She sighed heavily. 'I'll spend some time there this holidays, like Mum suggested, but then come back and live with you. It's not Mike that's the problem – though the guy is a total douche-bag – it's more that I don't want to leave my friends or have to go to a weird new school. Better to stick it out at St Margaret's, get some A levels and all that crap.'

'All that crap . . . absolutely.' Dougie swallowed, breathless at the power of her, how little she was aware of it. 'Well, that sounds a good plan to me. We must make sure we tell Mum, okay? Just as soon as they get back from their house-hunting. She . . .' He hesitated, thinking how Janine would take the news, knowing that for all her bravery, it would be a body blow. 'She'll need time to take it in.'

Stevie's phone buzzed and she released his hand. Dougie stared ahead, focusing on the small cardboard tree air-freshener dangling from the rear-view mirror. He took several slow, deep breaths, wondering that the scent of cheap vanilla could smell so good.

PART TWO

Chapter Ten

Gary watched Ruth do her lengths, the shadows of the nearest olive tree dancing across the paunch of his stomach. Ten on her side, ten on her front, ten on her back – she had been going through the same routine religiously several times a day, putting the rest of them to shame. But she hadn't stayed up nearly as late as they had – all three nights it had been gone two in the morning by the time he, Dougie and Simon had crept to their rooms. The night before – Simon's actual birthday – even Victoria had hung on until gone one.

She was quite a sight, his wife, Gary acknowledged happily, in her electric yellow bikini, her breasts full almost to indecency, her belly as smooth and protuberant as a Henry Moore sculpture. If he hadn't seen the scan, he – as so many others had freely commented, strangers in the street some of them – would have guessed it was twins. And yet she was still under seven months. When she had peeled off her sundress on the first afternoon, he had spotted Victoria doing a double-take before quickly exclaiming how fabulous Ruth looked to cover it. Simon and Dougie had made a big, typically male show of not staring, then sneaked glances later on. It had made Gary proud and also unbelievably horny, which had been something of an inconvenience at the time. He had stayed lying on his stomach till the urge passed, using the time to size up Victoria's contrastingly boyish thin frame from behind his sunglasses, deciding that there was a lot to be said for flesh on a female, something to get hold of. He had cast a critical eye over Simon and Dougie while he was at it, reluctantly acknowledging that, when it came to the tedious challenge of trying to hang on to one's youthful body-shape, both his old friends were beating him hands down. Simon had an athletic, compact figure, but it was Dougie Gary might have been jealous of, if he'd had a mind to be: a misspent past of no mean dimensions and yet, even in his baggy Bermudas, it was clear the guy still had the sort of physique men far younger sought through hours of exorbitantly priced sweating in city gyms. As far as Gary knew, Dougie still did nothing but a spot of cycling, and then only when the bastard absolutely had to.

Ruth padded back to their encampment on the far side of the pool, grinning at him as she squeezed out the wet ends of her hair. 'Is that any good?'

Gary lowered the book, a biography of an American advertising guru, which she had bought him especially for the trip. 'It's brilliant. You should read it too.'

'Maybe.' Ruth scowled as a reminder that she preferred her reading matter rather more fictional and escapist. 'Are you sure you've got enough cream on? You look a little red.'

'No, I'm fine.'

'Do you mind doing me, then? I can feel my back burning. And that brown thing on my tummy has gone so dark – look, isn't it amazing?' She pointed at the muddy line that had appeared down the middle of her lower abdomen a few weeks before, like a vertical fissure in an egg on the verge of cracking. 'It makes me feel sort of marked out. *Chosen.*' She giggled, handing him the sun cream, then carefully lowered herself onto the edge of his sun-bed with her back to him, her belly resting on her knees.

Gary squirted some cream onto his palms and rubbed it into her skin in slow circles, pressing hard with his fingertips, the way he knew she liked.

'God, this is bliss. This is bliss,' Ruth repeated, then raised her voice to Simon and Victoria across the pool: 'Simon! Victoria! This is bliss. Thank you so much. When's Dougie back, by the way? Did he say? Poor man, all that shopping and cooking – and now with that daughter of his to pick up, too. And yet he seems to have been enjoying himself, don't you think?'

'He's getting *paid*,' Simon reminded her.

'What's the daughter like?'

Victoria and Simon exchanged glances. They had subsequently decided that Stevie joining the party on its last day was far from ideal. As friends, they had been briefed on and understood the situation, but as fee-paying guests, they would have far preferred her to stay away.

'What with all the trouble between Dougie and Janine, we haven't seen Stevie for a few years,' Victoria explained diplomatically, 'but I'm sure she'll be fine. She was always sweet enough, wasn't she, Si?'

'Yes, she was splendid. Not originally his kid, you know – Janine was pregnant when they met, by some Ozzie beach-bum who disappeared back down under.'

'Wow. Gary never told me.' Ruth poked Gary's leg. 'Why didn't you tell me that?'

Gary gave a little shrug and carried on reading.

Simon sauntered to the poolside. In the polished glass doors of their bedroom he could see a loose-edged reflection of them all, their white-pink skin smudgy, their sunglasses glinting like the eyes of giant insects. At the sides of the glass doors, behind the folded wooden shutters, the long muslin bedroom curtains stirred, as if tweaked by invisible fingers. Dougie had insisted he and Victoria have this, the finest of the *finca*'s four bedrooms, positioned right at the edge of the pool and with the clearest view of the valley, where the orange trees marked the undulations of its slopes like lines of marching soldiers. It was normally the one Dougie requisitioned for himself, but birthday boys deserved the best, he had teased, especially those coping with the trauma of arriving at such an advanced age.

Simon slid into the pool. He lay on his back, gently paddling his hands to stay afloat, letting the water fill his ears and drown the women's voices as they started up a fresh conversation. It was good to be quiet, to have his head cool, seeing off the last traces of his headache from the excesses of the night before. Not that he had gone mad. But with a couple of vodka martinis before the meal and all the fabulous wines Victoria and Dougie had picked, not to mention a tot or two of the fine malt he had brought, some semblance of a hangover had been unavoidable.

During the entire three days they had eaten like kings – lobster, crab, crayfish, prawns, beef fillet, loin of lamb; Victoria's choices, not to mention Dougie's cooking, had been impeccable. For the approaching final night, it was to be paella – another pet love of Simon's – although Dougie, with his new sober straightforwardness, had explained that it was mainly a way of using up leftovers.

Simon arched his back, letting the water slosh over his forehead and sunglasses. The flawless sky looked different through wet lenses – blurred, darker, altogether more interesting. Dougie was being a little distant, which he didn't like much, but knew to forgive. The man had had an awful lot to do and Victoria could be a hard taskmaster, as Simon was only too well aware. Otherwise the whole weekend – the company, the food – had been amazing, impossible to fault. Simon righted himself to take off the glasses, placing them carefully, lenses up, on the poolside, wishing he could shake off the niggle of dissatisfaction that had persisted through the weekend. It seemed to hover with such maddening readiness, these days, no matter where he was. *Is this your life?* cawed a voice inside his head. *Is this your life? Is this your life?*

The question stayed with Simon as he plunged into the water. He had taken easy options, that was the thing, followed the path of least resistance; allowed Victoria to steer a course and trotted along behind. And yet he had been happy to do that, happy to fiddle at a career while enjoying the luxuries that having a wealthy wife afforded. The energy of real ambition had never seized him. Could one really regret something one had never *felt*? Or was it the baby business that was bothering him? Simon took a moment to ponder the bulldozing effect Victoria's determination on the subject seemed to have had on his libido.

The more likely and immediate problem was turning forty and having a headache, he scolded himself, surfacing to breathe, then blowing out air until he was sitting on the bottom of the pool. He let his body go heavy, watching his swimming shorts balloon round his thin thighs. The week in Andalucía – seeing the Moorish glories of Seville, Córdoba and Granada – would be wonderful; further spoiling after he had already been spoilt. As well as Dougie's five-star hospitality, he had been showered with gifts: a pair of slipper-soft buckskin loafers from Victoria (along with the promise that an even better present awaited him at home); from Dougie there had been a book listing places to visit before he died, while Ruth and Gary had presented him with a state-of the-art kitchen knife, made by a famously exclusive Japanese company out of Damascus steel. Dougie had asked to look at it at once, turning the blade carefully in his hands, his voice weighted with awe as he remarked on its features.

It was to encourage Simon in his cooking, Ruth and Gary had explained, exchanging looks and giggles that suggested there had been some tale-telling out of class about Simon's culinary ineptitude. And there was a penny in the box for good luck, Ruth had added, explaining that it was mandatory for the prevention of ill fortune when giving any sort of knife. The penny was duly looked for but not found. Simon, shaking the empty box, had laughed the matter off, but Ruth had been concerned enough to drop to her hands and knees and start scouring the dining terrace's hard tiled floor, comically cradling her belly, like a child with a stomach ache. 'But that's bad, Simon,' she had wailed, when persuaded at last to give up and collapsing, red-faced from her exertions, back into her chair. 'Really, if it was me, I'd freak out.'

By the time Simon clambered out of the pool, shaking the water out of his ears, the women had settled upon the idea of a shopping trip to Alicante. Not wanting to bother Dougie, who had the only hire car and wasn't expected back for an hour at least, Ruth had summoned a local taxi. They set off some twenty minutes later, having changed into sundresses and headgear, Victoria in the wide-brimmed straw boater with which she had graced Glyndebourne a few weeks earlier and Ruth opting for the funkier protection offered by a pink scarf, tied in a large off-centre bow among the spikes of her crimson-streaked hair.

After they had gone Simon lay in the sun and jotted down a few notes about a vague idea he had had for a TV script: lesbian cop falls for a prostitute, jeopardizing both her career and a long-running drugs investigation. It was embryonic but strong, he felt – especially with the right casting. He would begin with a pilot, but have back-up scripts for a full series. If he could just think where to start . . . a strong opening scene. It was hard, though, in the heat. His brain felt as if it was being slowly boiled. He put his notepad down and watched through his sunglasses as the drops of pool water on his stomach turned into rivulets of sweat. Catching Gary's eye, he mimed a drink, then went to the fridge in the pool-house to fetch a couple of beers. By the time Dougie and Stevie arrived, a little over an hour later, they were on their third refill and too embroiled in a game of table tennis to hear the car.

It was good, both women agreed, to be away from the intense heat of the poolside. The taxi was rough and ready, without air-conditioning, but they didn't mind, winding the windows right down instead, trailing their arms out of the car and letting the warm breeze dry the sweat on their faces. For miles the road was lined by the endless sentinels of orange trees. They were thicker close to and verdant – lush green leaves – bulging with electric-coloured fruit, each something of a miracle given the parched dusty land from which they grew.

As they left the *finca* and the scattered hillside village behind, Victoria became aware of a weight lifting. The birthday weekend – her grand plan – was almost done with. And it had gone well. The food – Dougie's catering – had been unbelievable. Calm, generous, capable, he had got on with the job like the professional he was, while at the same time managing, effortlessly, it seemed, to fill the sometimes demanding role of being Simon's best friend. A cheque, albeit for several thousand pounds, felt dimly inadequate for the rewarding of such a feat.

And Ruth had been a pleasing revelation too. Indeed, it had been the unexpected bonus of an already wonderful weekend to find that, beneath the rather strident, socialist front with which Victoria had come to associate Gary's wife, there lurked real warmth, as well as a refreshing line in humorous self-deprecation.

'By the way,' she announced now, tapping Victoria's knee to wrest her attention from the window, 'all that stuff last night about not wanting to know the sex of the baby was total bollocks. I do know. It's a girl. I just haven't told Gary. I've bought all these dear little things in pink and hidden them in a bag under the stairs, where Gary never ventures for fear of coming face to face with the Hoover. Is that awful of me?'

Victoria laughed. 'Yes. Terrible.'

'Oh, but Gary's such a soppy tool, wanting the thrill of being surprised and all that blah. Whereas I'm, like, no way – if this thing's going to pop out and ruin our lives, the very least I need is to be properly prepared. We agreed on yellow for the nursery – Gary finished painting it last weekend – but I've got this beautiful cheesy frieze of pink fairies, which I'm going to stick round the walls the moment we bring her home.' She slapped a hand to her mouth. 'Sorry. Baby talk. So boring. Not another word.'

'It's all right, I don't mind,' Victoria murmured, wondering what Ruth would say if she confessed to her own mounting desperation to produce a child. Her and Simon's talk at Glyndebourne had helped enormously to clear the air, but even so they had made love only once since, and then on a day that Victoria had worked out was hopeless for her cycle. So far, being at the villa hadn't give the situation a boost either: Simon was certainly enjoying himself, but falling into bed each night too full of food and wine to do anything but sleep solidly until the middle of the morning.

'Well, I mind,' Ruth rattled on. 'I bore myself stupid, in fact. Now let's make sure this sweetheart knows where we're going.' She levered herself forward and began gabbling in expert Spanish to their wizened, moustachioed driver. She sat back a few minutes later to report that there was a market he recommended, in the old part of town, near a marina and lots of great waterfront cafés.

'I've always wanted to learn Spanish,' said Victoria, admiringly. 'Ever since reading Hemingway in my teens.'

Ruth grimaced. 'All that fishing and bull-fighting and absinthe – not my cup of tea at all. I'm more a P. D. James girl myself, or Ian Rankin – I love Ian Rankin. Hey, you should join our book club. You have to wade through a bit of crap sometimes, but basically it's great fun. Gary thinks it's just girls' gossip, but actually he's wrong. We discuss the books for a bit and *then* gossip.' She let out a hoot of laughter. 'I'll ask Katie – she started the club so she's kind of in charge. She's the other half of Richard – you know, the third guy in their cooking classes . . . not to be continued, apparently, which is a shame. Christ, but he's good, Dougie, isn't he? That lamb last night – oh, and the seafood starter. I thought I'd gone to heaven. Though I paid for it afterwards, I have to confess – indigestion half the night, fucking agony . . . In fact,' she pulled a face 'I'm getting something similar now. Bad baby.' She wagged a finger at her stomach and then sat back, blowing air out of her mouth in short, heavy bursts, the tan on her face draining to grey.

'Ruth?'

She shook her head, motioning with her hand against the need for interference. A few moments later she was grinning, the pink back in her cheeks as she ferreted in her purse for euros to pay the driver.

Stevie was quite good at table tennis. There had been a club at school when she was much younger and then for a couple of summers she and Merryl had had a sort of craze for the game, spending hours playing on an outdoor table with Merryl's two elder brothers. So when Gary, out of politeness, asked if she wanted to take on the winner between him and Simon, she didn't hesitate. It turned out to be Simon, who beat her easily, but then her father was persuaded to join in and they had a long, tight, thrilling three-set game of doubles, swapping partners so that she ended up having to hold her own alongside all three of them.

The table-tennis table was parked in a patch of shade between the pool-house and the barbecue, but even so it provided little protection from the heat, which, by mid-afternoon, had soared into the forties. When their mini-tournament ended the men, dripping in perspiration, took running jumps into the pool, while Stevie hastily unzipped her suitcase and rummaged for her bikini. She slipped into the pool-house to put it on, struggling to pull its small stringy pieces over her damp skin. When she emerged her dad had disappeared, and Gary and Simon were hurling a tennis ball across the water at each other, lunging around like kids. Seeing her hesitate on the pool steps, they suggested she join them for a throwing and catching game called Donkey, which allowed six chances to drop the ball before disqualification, instructing her to stay in the shallow end to give her a better chance. Stevie still lost, but only after a decent length of time.

She then plugged herself into the music on her iPhone and lay on one of the spare sun-beds, watching through half-closed eyes as the glow of her body deepened. Thanks to many hours spent on the beach in Valencia, her tan was already pretty advanced – a bonus of a week, which, while proving far less of an ordeal than she had expected, had not been exactly thrilling either. Maria had lived up to all her fears, the kind of girl her mother would have described as 'sweet': big-toothed, earnest, bashful. On the wall in her bedroom she had a poster of a dorky Spanish boy pop star, which she had kissed reverentially every night before getting into bed. Whenever Stevie leant out of the window to smoke she would squeal in disapproval and leap across the room to guard the door, standing with her back to it, batting the air with her hands like a fussing old granny.

Under instruction from Maria's mother, a fierce, squat woman who delivered sentences like machine-gun fire, in unintelligible bursts, they had spent the mornings taking buses to see various sights round the city, the old town, the cathedral, the aquarium and – the highlight, in Stevie's opinion – a large, deliciously air-conditioned shopping centre, called Corte Inglés. The afternoons they had been allowed to spend on the beach, where a gaggle of Maria's equally babyish schoolfriends would invariably join them, chattering too fast for Stevie to follow, even when they thought they were slowing down. They treated Stevie as if she was a visitor from another planet, cooing over the rings in her belly-button and taking it in turns to bestow admiring strokes to her long, thick hair, which did its usual thing of producing copper highlights the moment the sun hit it. Whenever she decided to overlook her tight finances and buy something cheap and alcoholic from the beach-side bar, they begged for sips, rolling their eyes at their own daring.

'So what was Valencia like, then? *Hablas bueno español?*'

Simon was standing next to her, holding a fresh bottle of beer and dabbing his face with the towel that was draped round his shoulders. Stevie pulled out one ear-piece. 'Nope.'

'Good time, though?'

'Yeah, okay, I guess.' She scowled, trying to think of something interesting to add. She couldn't have been happier to see her dad, waving from the barrier at the station in Alicante, just like he'd promised. But then in the car they had had a horrible row. She had said Valencia hadn't been much fun and he had accused her of being negative, saying a free week in Spain was something any sixteen-year-old should be grateful for rather than immediately looking for ways to trash it in the telling. If he didn't want her barging in on his friends' party he should have told her, Stevie had retorted. In fact, why didn't he just turn the car round and drop her back at the station. Dougie had snorted dismissively and put his foot down on the accelerator. There had been a pulse going in his temple that Stevie had never seen before, like a tiny worm trying to wriggle its way out of his head. It had made her afraid for some reason, about what was going on inside him, whether he really did want her with him.

'The house was cool,' she told Simon, 'really old and dark, down the end of this cobbled street, with a beautiful courtyard thing right in the middle of it, full of plants and stuff. But then there was this church nearby that bonged its bells every fifteen minutes – literally, even through the night. Nearly drove me mental.'

'Christ, how horrible. Must feel nice and quiet here, then.' Simon let his gaze drift to the battalions of orange trees. The tick of dissatisfaction – boredom, whatever it was – had vanished. In fact, since the beers, the table tennis and the idiotic pool games he was suddenly having a thoroughly brilliant time. It was a relief, like rediscovering something treasured that one had feared lost for good. He nodded at the iPhone, which lay next to Stevie's hip, its wire caught in the jumble of the side-ties of her bikini. 'What music are you lot into these days, then?'

'Oh, the usual. Here, have a listen, if you like.'

He parked his beer bottle between his feet and sat on the end of the sun-bed. Stevie offered him the free ear-piece, keeping the other in place so that he was forced to shuffle closer. He did it carefully, so as not to come into contact with her legs, which were the colour of dark honey and faintly freckled round the knees. She had to have grown two foot at least since he had last seen her. Her waist had undergone a transformation, too, the twelve-year-old roundness he remembered replaced by neat indentations above the hips and a hard, smooth stomach, flat but for the two rings hooked into its centre. With regard to her chest, the very opposite process had taken place: roundness where there had once been a scrubbing board, the sort of roundness that, even with studied lack of close examination, summoned clichéd images of ripening fruit, more than filling the two brief nylon triangles responsible for containing it.

'That's quite a tan you've got going there.' The music was pulsing in his ear, tinny and throbbing, utterly pointless. He jigged his head to the beat, pulling a funny face by way of feigning enjoyment.

'Thanks. I always go that colour, maybe because of my Australian heritage.'

Simon sat up, pulling the wire out of his ear. 'So you know all about that, then?'

'Of course I do. I can't remember not knowing.'

'And do you think you'll want to meet the guy one day?'

'God, no. What would be the point? He was clearly a dick.' She picked up the ear-piece he had used, giving it a discreet wipe before popping it back in.

Impressed, taking the hint, Simon stood up. 'Did it hurt having those things put in, by the way?' He nodded at her stomach.

Stevie squinted at the two rings. 'Nah . . . A bit. Not much. I mean, pain doesn't matter, does it, when you want something badly enough?'

He smiled, surprised again. 'No, I suppose it doesn't.'

'Simon, give the girl some peace, can't you?' called Gary amiably. 'I'm off to catch forty.' He pressed his hands together and put them against his cheek in an imitation of sleep.

'No stamina, boy,' Simon quipped, retrieving his beer bottle and wandering back to his own sun-bed on the other side of the pool.

A moment later Dougie appeared on the balcony above them. 'All well?'

'Great.' They waved.

'I'm going to the village – I forgot bread. Stevie, move that thing, please,' he added, in a much harsher voice, gesturing at her suitcase, still half open and blocking the doorway to the pool-house.

'In a minute.'

'Not in a minute. Now. Someone will trip over it there.'

'*Okay.*' She groaned, not moving, aware of Simon

listening behind the notepad in which he had been writing something.

Dougie hovered on the balcony. 'Now.' He pointed at the suitcase. 'Now.' He shouted it this time. 'Christ, Stevie, it's not much to ask, is it?'

'All right, I'm *going*.' She swung her legs off the sun-bed and sat up. But the moment Dougie disappeared from view she lay down again, her heart pumping with hurt and dismay. He had been nice during the table tennis but it was all gone again. Now she was just an inconvenience.

After the sound of the engine had died away, the silence felt heavier, the heat thicker. The pool water was mirror-still, apart from an occasional whisper of a breeze ruffling its surface. Stevie put her phone away and swam a few lengths, taking care with her style in case Simon was watching. She wasn't really a natural swimmer, but could make a show of being so for short bursts. She finished with a few strokes of butterfly, experiencing a surge of elation at having the whole Valencia thing behind her – all that strain of having to be nice, to pay attention, to strangers, all the indignity of being treated like a child and having to pretend not to mind.

'I don't suppose I could have a beer, could I?' She stood so that her shadow fell across the page of Simon's notebook.

Simon burst out laughing. 'Take a pew. I was going to get another for myself anyway.' He got off his sun-bed and padded to the pool-house, scampering the last few steps as the hot stone seared the soles of his feet. 'Do you want this in your room?' He scooped up the suitcase before she could answer and set off up the steps to the main terrace.

'Omigod, thanks so much . . .' Stevie watched his receding back, popping with muscles thanks to the weight of her case, which he was carrying in his arms instead of using the handle. Its heaviness had been yet another recent bone of contention with her father. A kilo over the weight allowance, easyJet had insisted on some extra money. Dougie had turned to Stevie to ask curtly if there was anything she could possibly take out, and she had said no. It had added an unwelcome edge to their farewells.

It was almost as if her agreeing to live with him had changed something, Stevie decided, dropping onto Simon's sun-bed , pondering why this might be so and, in the mystifying battle of trying to grow up, how hard one had to fight to be treated right, how the simplest things could feel so stupidly complicated.

Simon reappeared a couple of minutes later with two bottles of beer. He handed one over and settled himself on Victoria's sun-bed.

Stevie took a long swig. She didn't much like beer as a rule, but it tasted good for being fizzy and ice-cold. 'This is great – thanks. Just what I needed after a week of lame Spanish fifteen-year-olds.'

'That bad, were they?'

'You can't imagine.'

'You're a London girl, that's why – more sophisticated.'

Stevie grinned, enjoying both the compliment and a sudden memory of Simon from when she was a little girl, always breezing through the house in her father's wake, making excuses the moment her mum appeared, occasionally ruffling Stevie's hair as he flew in or out of the door. 'Hang on.' She skipped over to her handbag, stowed out of the heat in the lee of one of the large shrubs bordering the pool, and returned with a lit cigarette. 'I might go to Australia one day, I suppose, in spite of what I said before.' She looked at the valley, bracing herself for the inevitable comment about smoking, but it never came. 'Check out my roots and all that.' She exhaled as she spoke, careful to steer the plume away from Simon's face, delighted he had remained silent. In truth, she had never given the notion of going to Australia any serious thought. The remark had just slipped out, reflecting nothing more than a dim, lingering anger with her father and the sense that it might somehow impress her companion.

'Sounds reasonable to me,' observed Simon, coolly. 'That's why I asked about it – Hang on . . . there goes my phone.' He cocked his head towards the open bedroom door, from where a tinny version of Bach's Toccata and Fugue in D minor was burbling.

'Aren't you going to answer it?'

'Nope.' He grinned, settling more deeply into the sunbed, pillowing his hands under his head and crossing his legs.

A moment later Stevie's phone was ringing. She trotted round the pool to retrieve it, pulling faces at the screen as she made her way back. 'Oh, God, it's Dad . . . Hey, Dad, how's it going? I moved the case.' She eye-rolled Simon, who winked. 'You tried to call Simon, did you? . . . No, he obviously didn't hear it . . .' She caught Simon's eye again, then quickly swung away, slapping her hand to her chest. 'She what? You're joking.'

Simon sat up, alerted by the shock in her voice.

Stevie turned back to him, her hand still pressing her

chest, her blue eyes huge. 'Oh, blimey – right, will do. Okay. No worries. Ten minutes. Yes, I'll get Simon to do it. Is she going to be okay, do you think? . . . No, I see . . . Yes, yes, straight away.'

'Get Simon to do what?'

'It's Ruth,' Stevie explained breathlessly. 'She's gone into labour or something – they're not sure. She collapsed in a café loo but she's on her way to hospital and she wants Gary there – obviously – so Dad's coming back to get him. He's been trying to call Gary as well as you, he said, but not getting any answer.'

'Bloody hell.' Simon was already off his sun-bed, hopping comically as he tried to get his feet into his deck shoes. 'I'm on my way . . . That is not good, not good. I mean, I'm no expert but – shit!' He had knocked over his bottle, which broke into three neat pieces, spewing beer. A thin grey lizard, sunning itself at the poolside, darted down a crack.

'I'll see to that. You wake Gary.' Stevie picked up the segments of glass and scampered ahead of him towards the main house, her long legs taking the steps two at a time, the tassels on her tiny bikini flapping. Simon paused to watch, before turning left along the path that offered the shortest route to Gary's bedroom.

Within ten minutes Dougie had swept his hired Ford Focus into the *finca*'s gated drive, pressed a bag of fresh bread rolls into Stevie's hands and swept out again, Gary sitting bolt upright in the seat next to him, both hands gripping the dashboard.

'Wow. Poor Ruth,' murmured Stevie, as the car sped away.

'Poor Ruth indeed,' Simon agreed.

'And Gary.'

'And Gary.'

'Where shall I put these?' She dangled the bag of bread rolls off one finger.

'Fridge, I should think – they go stale otherwise.'

'I feel sort of bad, just going back to the pool, not doing anything.'

'So do I. But the fact is we *can't* do anything, so there's no point in beating ourselves up about it. I've texted Vic to give me news the instant she has any. In the meantime, we're the Home Guard, my dear Stevie – vital in any campaign – and a very *thirsty* Home Guard, speaking for myself.' Simon plucked two fresh bottles of beer out of the kitchen fridge and chinked them together. 'It could be a long afternoon. And this might be a good idea, too, young lady,' he added, seizing an empty ashtray as they crossed the terrace and headed back down to the pool.

Chapter Eleven

Hams hang from long hooks in the ceiling of the bar, scores of them, their flesh wine-red from curing. In front of him sits a glass of Coca-Cola, half drunk, a melting pebble of ice floating at its centre. Victoria has opted for sherry, medium sweet, which has arrived in a tall flute and from which she is taking furtive sips, barely wetting her lips. She looks as drawn as he has ever seen her, the bones of her face pressing through her skin, the lines framing her mouth deep as cuts.

Dougie stirred as the image shimmered. He was conscious enough to know he was asleep, but reluctant to wake up. The dream was holding him down, taking him back through all that had happened, as if something needed confronting before his mind could relax and release him.

'She had this spell in the taxi . . . then in a café . . .' Victoria's voice comes in and out of reach, ebbing and flowing. They are alone. Gary is in the hospital with Ruth. Victoria's left hand is under his, the solitaire diamond of her engagement ring scraping his palm. 'For a moment I thought she was dead,' she says. Dougie's innards contract. From wanting to smoke, yes, that's it. Then and now. He wants to smoke. Victoria's voice is back in his head: 'You've given up? Well done, you.' She displays the grin that shows her back teeth, instilling in him a brief suffusion of pleasure at having his no-nicotine ordeal noticed, congratulated. Day Four. Day Four, and it is hell. 'Because of Stevie? To set an example?' Victoria's mouth blurs to a gash. 'She must mean a lot to you.'

Dougie's limbs jerked, threatening to wake him. It was taking something like willpower to stay under now, along with the dim sense that the balance of the dream had shifted, that he was trying to avoid something rather than track it down.

The slideshow in his head shoots forwards, to Ruth hooked up to bags of liquid, Gary in a chair at her bedside, his head in his hands, his hair sprouting in clumps between his fingers; a nurse glides between them, checking screens and clipboards. He sees all this but he is in the corridor outside, alone again with Victoria, as they sip water from triangular paper cups. Next to them a water machine bubbles. Victoria leans back against the wall, her arms crushing the life out of her big straw hat. 'Simon and I have been trying for a child.' She downs the water and balls the paper cup to a pulp in her fist. 'But I don't think it's going to happen. I'm not sure Simon wants it.' She shakes her head from side to side. 'Does Simon want it? Does Simon want it, Dougie? Does he? Does he?'

Then suddenly he is in another hospital room, Janine breaking the bones in his hand as she labours, toothmarks in her lips, her eyes bloodshot from pushing. And for a glorious moment it seems to Dougie that the churning images have found their point at last: Stevie, of course – that was what he wanted to think about. Stevie, who emitted such a bloodcurdling cry of pure outrage as she slithered from the warm tethers of her mother into the cold bright world that even through his tears – of joy, of relief – he had feared for her, feared for her suffering.

In his sleep Dougie's eyelids fluttered. He had been too tough on Stevie, that was the thing, too critical, taken out his stress, not given her enough space, not shown enough of his love. That was it. He had to put it right at once, make amends.

He surfaced properly at last, in a lather of sweat, the hot Spanish light streaming through the slits in his bedroom shutters, a headache punching his temples. Such a headache. Monumental. As bad as a . . . Dougie tried to block the thought, but there was no escaping it. He had a hangover. A very bad one. It accounted for the intense remembering-dream: alcohol had always tended to do that as the oblivion wore off. Disbelieving, disgusted, Dougie pressed his knuckles into his temples and levered himself into a sitting position against the headboard. It turned out Ruth had merely been ill, he remembered suddenly: gastroenteritis not childbirth, though the former could trigger the latter, apparently, if they had understood the broken English of the doctor correctly.

For a moment hope cut through Dougie's grogginess. Maybe he, too, had simply fallen sick? Eaten a bad prawn, as they had decided must have happened to Ruth. Yet the pain drilling up through his neck and skull told him otherwise. The pulsing behind his eyeballs, the rotting taste furring his mouth and throat: it was so familiar. And the desire for another drink was there too, strong as a heartbeat.

Dougie crooned expletives, hugging his pillows as he forced his brain, consciously this time, into reverse. There had been the bottle of vodka, he remembered grimly. It had been sitting out on the sideboard when he and Victoria had finally got back from the hospital, a good third of it left. He had noticed it and dismissed it. The *finca* had been swimming in booze all weekend. It hadn't seemed a big deal. He and Victoria had entered on tiptoe because of the late hour, talking in whispers about their relief for Ruth and the baby, about their concern for Gary, who had insisted on staying at the hospital until she was discharged. Dougie had leant on the sideboard to remove his loafers, not just for quietness' sake but to enjoy the cool of the villa tiles under his bare feet. He had swung a shoe in each hand as he and Victoria had said their goodnights, agreeing for the umpteenth time what a mad, worrying few hours it had been, how happy they were at the outcome. There had been a trace of awkwardness, of intimacy, Dougie remembered, something to do with the hush of the night around them, the shared dramas of the evening. I could kiss her, he had realized with some astonishment; I could kiss her and she wouldn't resist. The moment had passed and they had turned for their respective bedrooms.

It was only when he reached the end of his corridor that Dougie had halted, dropping his forehead onto the cool wood of his bedroom door. What a day it had been. What a night. What a weekend. Ruth's food poisoning notwithstanding, it had gone well. Simon – all of them – had had a great time. Dougie had kept his head against the door, contemplating the fact of having worked his bollocks off for four straight days through yet another bout of insomnia. Exhausted, watching black lighten to grey through the gaps in his shutters, his stress levels rising, he had tossed under his thin sheet every night, the desire for nicotine clawing at his innards.

It was the thought of repeating this for a fifth night that had tipped the balance. A drink – one drink, a nightcap – would help him unwind in the way he so badly needed. And what harm could one drink do now? He was so much stronger than he used to be, so much more in control. The hard work had ended and he deserved a reward, Dougie reasoned. One drink. To loosen him up. One drink, because Ruth and the baby were going to be okay, because Stevie was going to live with him, because the grand birthday weekend had been a triumph, because his money worries had eased. One drink, because he could, because no one would see; one drink, because privately, through the thirteen months of abstinence, he had clung to the hope that eventually he would return to being a creature who could manage the simple challenge of moderation, a normal creature, capable of enjoying a glass or two when the occasion warranted.

He had put his shoes down with meticulous care, Dougie recalled suddenly. He had made them tidy, in exact alignment with the wall, taking his time, as if giving himself a final chance to change his mind.

Once in the kitchen he had moved with contrasting speed, pouring a single shot of vodka into a favourite old glass and sitting out on the terrace to savour it, tipping his head up to the glittering velvet Spanish sky, just as beautiful and huge as he had remembered it from the vantage-point of his scrubby north London garden. And then – perhaps inevitably – to complete the pleasure of this self-reward, he had lit a cigarette. It hadn't taken much rummaging to find a few in an old packet, tucked into a bottom drawer. A second of both – a smoke, a drink – had followed, because it could do no harm. And then a third. And so on, until the vodka was done with and he was launching into Simon's precious malt and riffling through old jacket pockets for more cigarettes. When his hand grew sufficiently unsteady to slop the drink into his glass, the voices in his head still cheered him on, pointing out that if he was going to have a lapse, better make it a big one; better bloody well *enjoy* it.

Dougie pushed his face into his pillow, as the final, regrettable images of the night returned, in the form of Victoria, floating like some ghostly apparition onto the terrace, clutching the flimsy wings of a white silk kimono across her chest. 'Simon's snoring,' she had said softly, by way of announcing herself.

Dougie had nodded, not trusting himself to speak, not sure he even could.

'What a day.' She had lowered herself into the chair next to his with a sigh, her silky dressing-gown falling off her long, slim legs as she crossed them. It was only then that she had registered the near-empty bottle, the glass, the pile of cigarette butts round his chair. 'Oh, no, Dougie . . .'

'Fuck off,' he had growled. 'Fuck off and leave me alone.'

Dougie levered himself onto one elbow and felt along the wall for the air-conditioning switch. The heat in his room was unbearable. He could smell the alcohol coming off his skin, acrid-sweet, mixed with sweat. He wanted to know the time but for some reason his watch wasn't on his wrist. There was a plastic water bottle next to the bed but it was empty. Somehow, he got his feet onto the floor and staggered into the bathroom, where he ran his face under the cold tap, taking greedy gulps between allowing the water to jet into his eyes. As he straightened, blinking, he spotted his watch, hanging from the tooth-mug holder. He had no recollection of putting it there. No recollection of coming to bed. Victoria was his last clear memory, her white back, shrinking into the pre-dawn pitch dark, her shoulders hunched in disappointment.

Dougie fumbled the watch onto his wrist, the hairs catching in the links. It appeared to say half past twelve, which had to mean he had put it on upside down. Six o'clock in the morning was more like it – time to get himself washed, presentable, fix a decent breakfast going for everyone, put a call through to Gary and see how things were progressing at the hospital. He jabbed his toothbrush at his teeth, trying not to look at himself in the mirror, but seeing anyway the red rims of his eyes, the puffed ruddiness of his face, the flattened lank hair. He brushed to the point of derangement, until rivers of peppermint foam were bubbling over his lips and down his chin. He wanted a drink, that was the thing. A cigarette would have tasted like crap but he wanted that too, the arse-kick of it, hot on the heels of the alcohol.

Back in the bedroom, he hoisted the shutters, blinding himself. The sun was high in the sky, setting fire to the tree line. He hurried along the corridor, glancing again, in disbelief now, at his watch. It wasn't on the wrong way up. It wasn't six fifteen in the morning: it was a quarter to one in the afternoon. In the kitchen an envelope was propped against the kettle, addressed to him in Simon's trademark careful handwriting.

Bloody BRILLIANT weekend, mate. Didn't want to wake you – figured you'd earned some extra kip. Flights to catch etc. Vic had sorted transport. Keep us posted on R and G. Love S and V Ps cheque enclosed (I wasn't allowed to look!)

The cheque, in Victoria's much looser, larger handwriting, was for a whopping eight thousand pounds. Dougie whistled softly. A piece of paper was folded round it.

Don't say it's too much, you earned every penny. As to the other business, if you need help getting help, please ask. Vx

Dougie screwed up the message with a wince of shame and dropped it into the kitchen bin. He stowed the cheque in the back pocket of his jeans and filled the kettle. Catching sight of his phone on a chair, flashing a low-battery light, he found a missed call and a message from Gary: *Ruth doing great. Back this afternoon. Changed our flights to first thing tomorrow.*

Dougie got some coffee on and dropped a heap of smoked ham rashers into a pan, guessing that the enticing smell would rouse Stevie from her bed down the corridor. It brought the saliva to his mouth, too. He worked on for a few moments, tearing the bread into chunks setting plates and cutlery on the kitchen table, finding eggs, orange juice and butter in the fridge – aware of the need to keep busy. When the ham was crisp he went to the start of the corridor and yelled, 'Brunch, sleepyhead! Now!' cupping his hands round his mouth to ensure the sound carried as far as her door. He took the pan off the heat to do the eggs, dropping them into the fat so the yolks would stay soft and the whites would sizzle without burning. Hollow now with hunger, his head exploding, Dougie slapped generous slabs of butter and a bunch of the ham rashers into a roll and stuck it into his mouth as he strode down the passage to Stevie's bedroom door.

'Hey, in there.' He raised his fist and then, remembering the dream, the fierce joy of her birth, the resolve to treat her more gently, knocked softly. 'Hey, sweetheart – grub's up out here.' He pressed the last of the rough sandwich into his mouth, licking the grease off his fingers, before knocking again. 'Eggs and bacon, Spanish style.' When there was still no response, he opened the door a crack and peered inside. To his surprise, the bed was not only empty but made, the sheet drawn up over the pillows. After a precautionary knock, he put his head round the bathroom door, but there was nothing there either: no used cotton-wool balls or tubes of cream or hair clips; no hairbrush or earrings or palettes of eye-shadow. No wash-bag even. Dougie hurried back into the main room, trying to focus through his throbbing head. The entire place was empty – not a bra, not a magazine, not a shoe. No suit-case, either. In desperation he dropped to the floor and looked under the bed. But there was nothing there either, except a penny piece, very shiny, as if it had rolled there straight from the Mint.

By mid-afternoon Victoria and Simon had checked into their palatial hotel, once the sumptuous town residence of Alfonso XIII, and were bumping along on the lumpy leather back seat of an open horse-drawn carriage, seeing the sights of Seville. In spite of the heat, Simon was sitting very close to her, one arm protectively across the back of the seat, where it made a welcome headrest for the many occasions they lurched round corners or across cobbles. He was having the greatest time, he had declared more than once, reinforcing the fact with uncharacteristically physical zeal, planting kisses on her cheek and the crown of her head. He looked good, too, fresh as a flower in his loose pale blue shorts and lemon T-shirt, his wraparound sunglasses tight against his temples, his skin shining with its usual ruddy tan after a few days in the sun. In his spare hand he held the guide book, from which he read occasional extracts, making her giggle by inserting ludicrous details as he went along.

'Alfonso the Forty-fourth sat on that very bench,' he chanted, as they bounced through the large formal park in the centre of the city, an oasis of greenery and gravelled paths, away from the hubbub of traffic and tourists. 'In fact, rumour-mongers at court declared it was here, on these very wooden slats, that little Alfonso the Forty-fifth was conceived, on a cool autumn day, when Mrs Alfonso was wearing a particularly voluminous skirt.' He stood up to salute the bench, causing consternation to their driver, who thought he was trying to climb out.

'Behave, Si,' Victoria hissed, doing her best not to laugh. 'The poor man thinks you want to escape, that you aren't enjoying yourself.'

'But I am,' he cried, '*so* much.'

'I know that, of course, but he just thinks you're an insane Brit.' When he sat down she dropped her head onto his shoulder, keeping it there even when the ridge of his collarbone started to make the position uncomfortable. It was wonderful to see him so happy and, better still, to feel that the holiday she had organized was responsible. At the villa things between them had been good – more relaxed, anyway – but now the elusive chemistry-closeness seemed to be asserting itself and she wanted to capitalize on every second.

Victoria shut her eyes, giving in to her tiredness for a few moments instead of fighting it. Flying anywhere was always exhausting, let alone on the back of a hospital vigil and three hours' sleep. Thanks to Dougie, it had been a fitful sleep too, broken by images of him sprawled on the terrace chair in the moonlight, so much the picture of a man at ease with himself, dozing under the caress of the cool night air, that it had been a horrible shock to realize he wasn't sprawled so much as slumped, soaked with booze to a point beyond coherence. Turning back for her room, Victoria had found herself choking with sadness and sheer incomprehension. They had been so close that night, riding out Ruth's crisis. She had glimpsed the Dougie she had almost forgotten existed, the one she had first met fifteen years before; a man of good sense and energy, of infinite potential; a man on whom one could lean. Simon rapped her head lightly with his knuckles. 'Okay in there?'

'Yup. Hot.' Victoria sat up and wiped some of the clamminess off her face with a tissue. So far she hadn't mentioned Dougie's relapse. She still felt too emotional about it, too baffled. Part of her feared that Simon might choose to pooh-pooh the incident, saying that was Dougie, and what did she expect, making light of it in that dry, dismissive way he had sometimes, not understanding the awfulness for her of seeing him like that again: the old-man sag of his head, the floating, unfocused eyes, the clumsy efforts to sit up, to speak. It made no sense either, after the happy outcome of the evening's dramas. What sort of person would choose such a moment to hit the bottle? The question had nagged at Victoria for what little remained of the night, taking her right back to Miles – all the lies of an addict, all their helplessness, leading nowhere.

She buried the damp tissue in the bottom of her bag. 'Great news about Ruth, isn't it?'

Simon laughed. 'You mean that Dougie poisoned her with a prawn? Yes – fabulous.'

'Oh, that's not fair,' Victoria cried. 'Everyone knows how dodgy shellfish can be. It certainly wasn't Dougie's fault. The rest of us had the same starter and were fine.'

'I say . . .' He had been distracted by a glimpse of their palatial hotel across the busy roundabout of traffic. 'Do you think we could persuade this chap to drop us there instead of back at the cathedral?'

'I shouldn't think so. That road's so busy – the horse won't like it.'

Simon ignored her and tapped the driver on the shoulder, shouting his request over the clack of hoofs and wheels, a serious deterrent to conversation now that they had left the park and were back on tarmac. A considerable debate ensued, much of it in sign language. 'The gist is, yes, but only if he still gets full payment . . . at least, I think that's the gist.' Simon flopped back onto the seat while their chauffeur, radiating disaffection, brought his charge to a halt in a taxi rank opposite the busy road ringing their hotel.

A few minutes later they were safely back in their opulent room. Since they had checked in and deposited their suitcases, a basket of fresh fruit had appeared, along with a card welcoming them, in stilted, formal English, to Seville. After nibbling a few grapes and pinning up her hair, Victoria left Simon channel-flicking on the flat-screen television and ran herself a bath of mountainous scented foam. She sank into it with something akin to ecstasy, letting her arms float on the bubbles, observing how even her fair skin looked attractively tanned against the frothing cushions of so much white.

'Alfonso the Fiftieth would like to know if ze madam would like her back scrubbed?'

Simon was in the doorway, smiling at her and waggling his hands like a surgeon with evil intentions.

'Madam certainly wouldn't, not with that look on his face.'

'Aw . . . please?' He switched to a boyish grin.

Victoria pulled her knees up to her chest, causing a drift of foam to spill over the edge. She smiled enticingly. 'It's a big bath. Always room for two . . .'

Simon grinned. 'Okay. Hang on, I'll be right back. Don't go anywhere, will you?'

Victoria sank lower into the water. He would lay each item of clothing carefully on the back of a chair as he removed it, she knew, one of the repeated patterns of tidiness that ran through what was in other ways a thoroughly disorganized life. She hugged herself, loving that she knew such a thing, loving that she loved him for it.

They had needed a holiday, that was all; such a cliché, but powerful for that.

The ensuing attempt at an intimate sojourn in the bath did not last long. Defeated by a combination of water-slopping and discomfort, they soon transferred their lovemaking to the wide bed instead, among an encampment of damp towels. It was enjoyable until Victoria suddenly found herself thinking of the women in Simon's magazines and almost losing heart. Those brazen, big-busted creatures would have managed the erotic aquatics, she was sure, adopted wild poses, made it feel sexy instead of awkward. She had to make a conscious effort to get through the moment, reminding herself that such lurid images were the product of mercenary commerce, using jobbing actors, nothing to do with real life, real people, real feelings. She sought refuge finally, with a sudden vicious intensity, in the notion of making a baby, pulling Simon to her with such force that his eyes flew open, shooting her a look of pained surprise.

Afterwards Victoria lay very still, keeping her hips tilted, willing the sperm to go about their business. Remembering a recent article on the power of visualization to achieve goals, she tried that, too, picturing swarming microscopic tadpoles tail-wiggling their way up her Fallopian tubes. She reached for Simon's hand, thinking how especially focused he had seemed once they'd got going, as if for him, too, there really was now a very definite, cherished goal beyond the pull of his own climax.

Simon fetched the two luxury bathrobes off the back of the bathroom door and they lay side by side on their grand bed, Victoria reading a biography of Van Gogh that she had waited for months to come out in paperback but had not wanted to risk spattering with oil at the villa, and Simon watching a rain-drenched golf tournament he had managed to track down on the telly. When his phone launched into its thin rendition of Bach's Toccata they both groaned.

'Dougie.' He frowned. 'Wonder what he wants.'

Victoria returned her gaze to her book, listening hard. Dougie might mention the drinking himself. Yes, that would be good, she decided. Dougie would tell Simon and then the whole thing – Dougie's drunkenness, her strange nostalgic mood – would be off her conscience. She flicked her eyes to her husband, who had launched into a thank-you for the weekend, then stopped abruptly, looking grave.

'Really? No, mate, no . . . No, we didn't . . . Not a thing, no . . . Hang on.' He put his hand over the phone. 'Dougie says Stevie's gone AWOL and did we see her before we left this morning. We didn't, did we?'

Victoria put her book down. 'No, we didn't. AWOL? What sort of AWOL? Here, shall I talk to him?'

Simon pressed the phone back to his ear, widening his eyes in mild irritation at this suggestion of wifely distrust in his ability to follow through on the conversation. 'Our taxi came at seven and we got straight into it . . . No, no, there was no sign of her . . . Yes, which I guess means she could have been gone by then. Or maybe not.' He mimed regretful despair at Victoria. 'Yesterday afternoon? No . . . nothing . . . She seemed fine . . . Look, it's a pain, but I'm sure there's nothing to worry about. She'll just be trying to show you who's boss, I expect. By her age we were hitching across Europe, weren't we? Beer festivals, sleeping on beaches ... What? Yeah, obviously ... Well, I know that, Doug, I just meant try to calm down, okay? Of course ... Yes.'

He clicked off the phone, shaking his head gloomily. 'Bloody girl.'

Victoria laughed, a little shocked. 'Simon, that's not very nice.'

'Well, I don't think it's very *nice* of her to do a vanishing act and get Dougie so stirred up that he's got half the Spanish constabulary combing the countryside for forensic evidence of her murder.'

'Oh, God, he hasn't, has he?'

'Not yet. But he's going to soon, he says, if he doesn't hear anything.'

'I suppose he's tried her phone ...'

'One would assume so.'

'And yesterday afternoon, when you were with her, how did she seem?'

'Yesterday? Fine. Why?'

'Well, I just thought maybe –'

'She was fine. Totally normal ... in so far as I can be expected to pass judgement on the mental state of someone I barely know. She's a young woman, for Christ's sake, her mother's bolted to Finland –'

'Sweden.'

'Maybe she's not too keen on Janine dumping her with Dougie. He's not her *real* father, remember that, Vic. Maybe something about the situation suddenly got to her.' Simon shrugged, turning the volume of the TV back up. 'It's anybody's guess what's going through her mind.'

Victoria gathered up the towels and retreated to the bathroom where she showered, this time giving up on the challenge of trying to keep her hair dry and letting the water pummel her head. She felt desperately sorry for Dougie, but also for the hapless Stevie, clearly behaving selfishly, as all teenagers were inclined to, but also messed up, no doubt, thanks to all the comings and goings of her parents. Victoria squirted the courtesy shampoo and conditioner into her hair and rubbed till her scalp burnt. Simon was right, of course – the child would almost certainly turn up, like the proverbial bad penny, probably with little clue as to what she had put her father through, but it didn't detract from the stress of worry in the meantime. Just when Dougie could really do without it.

Back in the room, Simon's earlier bubbly mood seemed well and truly gone. He had turned off the television and was studying the hotel information pack. 'They offer fine dining at its most *exquisite*,' he read out loud. 'I'm not sure I can face that – not after the last four days.' He slapped his stomach, which looked as it always did – not toned but not remotely protuberant. 'It's bad enough getting old without getting obese to go with it. What about a snack up here instead? We could check out the DVD list – eat off our laps?'

They ordered plates of what turned out to be limp, over-salty tuna salad and sipped glasses of indifferent white wine. The film list had contained many promising options but at the last minute Simon pleaded to be allowed to watch the end of his golf tournament instead. Victoria withdrew to the delights of her book – a total make-over for Van Gogh: not the screw-up history had made him out to be, apparently, but a warm, rounded, compassion-ate man. It made her feel outrage on the painter's behalf that such a genius should have so little power over how the world chose to see him, but also glad that he – that every human – could remain an enigma. She eyed Simon round the side of her book: he was clearly a little happier once again, glued to his men sheltering under dripping brollies, wiping the rain out of their eyes and the mud clods off their clubs, firing balls into trajectories one could barely follow. If anyone resisted straightforward translation it was her husband. Their closeness was gone and she didn't know why. Although he did that, with-drew emotionally, after sex sometimes, she reminded herself. She had read somewhere that a lot of men did, as if the act temporarily emptied them of love as well as lust.

She was almost asleep when her thoughts drifted back to Stevie. There had been no word and it was gone nine o'clock. Simon had manoeuvred himself under the duvet with his back to her and was snoring softly. Careful not to wake him, Victoria eased herself off the bed and went to find her phone.

Still no news? You must be sick with worry. But stay strong – she's bound to be fine. Victoria wrestled with the wording of the text for several minutes, deleting and rewriting, aware that she was losing the point of messaging, which was intended to be swift and simple. *Stay strong* meant *Don't drink.* He would know that, surely. She wanted him to know it. Yet she also wanted to strike the right balance, make it clear, but not spell it out; be supportive rather than critical.

'What are you doing?'

She spun round. 'Dougie.' She waggled her phone. 'I'm asking him if there's been any news.'

'He said he'd let me know if there was.'

'Yes, but I just thought I'd check –'

'Can we turn the light out now? I know it's early but I'm bushed.'

'Yes, me too, but, Si, he must be so worried. Aren't you worried too – *for* him? I mean, the stories one reads, these days, the stuff that can happen to young girls –'

Simon rolled onto his side, pulling one of their many pillows into his chest, saying sleepily, 'Hey, Vic, don't start telling me what I should and shouldn't feel about my oldest friend, okay? Of course Dougie must be going through it – I know that. But I also reckon Stevie has a very good idea how to take care of herself. The girl will be running rings round him. She always has. And I have no desire to let that ruin the rest of *our* holiday, okay?' He reached above the headboard and turned off his bedside light.

Victoria sighed. Something was in danger of feeling ruined anyway, something she couldn't put her finger on. 'Okay. But I'm leaving my phone on, too, just in case.' She pressed 'send', then put her ring-tone into silent mode before placing it on her bedside table. She turned off her own light and lay in the dark, trying to keep her eyes open, watching for the screen to light up.

By mid-afternoon Dougie had abandoned his new pledge and was chain-smoking. After discovering Stevie's empty bedroom, he had gone on a knee-jerk reaction drive to look for her, taking the opportunity to stock up with several packets. He had kept all the windows down, alternately trying her phone and shouting her name uselessly into the orange orchards and olive groves. Rounding each bend, he fully expected to see her, stomping whatever anger was surging in her heart into the hot road, yanking her ridiculously heavy suitcase along behind her like a recalcitrant pet. But the road – the entire landscape – had remained empty, barren to the point of cruelty. It was the time of day when the heat reached its crescendo. The locals had retreated behind their shuttered houses to eat and sleep. To find cigarettes Dougie had had to drive as far as the garage two villages away. Apart from a couple of cars, the only signs of life he saw on the entire trip were a thin old man on a rusty bike and a goat, clearly broken free of its tether, snacking on some scrawny roadside grass.

He had been back an hour when a horn sounded in the drive. Dougie ran out eagerly, his hopes soaring and then dying at the sight of his property agent, Xavier, hopping with his usual energy out of a small dusty black car. 'Douglas, *como estas*?' He took Dougie's entire arm in both hands to shake it, pronouncing his name in two heavy syllables – Dog-lass. 'Is beautiful, no?' He swept an arm at the scenery. 'Spain is beautiful.'

'Yes. Very,' Dougie murmured, loath to drag his thoughts away from his daughter, gone now for somewhere between two hours and ten – the uncertainty of that alone was crushing. He had completely forgotten about the meeting he had arranged with Xavier, forgotten everything, it felt like.

Blessed with a squat body and short legs, the agent had to trot to keep up with his client's much longer stride as they made their way round to the terrace, where Dougie left him to fetch a bottle of sparkling water and two glasses.

'You good time here?' he pressed, when Dougie reappeared, adopting his customary manner of the proud host, in love with his country and eager for converts.

'Very good time, thank you,' Dougie replied briskly, adjusting the sun umbrella to shield the table as he sat down, resolved to get their business talk over with as quickly as possible. He gripped the bottle hard in order to pour the water, but still managed a couple of splashes as he filled the glasses. He pushed the least wet one towards his guest. 'Okay. So, tell me . . .' he flattened his hands on top of his thighs to stop them twitching '. . . how things are looking, what the chance is – the realistic chance – of selling this place by the end of the summer?'

The Spaniard shook his head. 'We get good price maybe two years, maybe three – not now. Now bad for everyone. Rent – sell – it is, how you say? Una *pesadilla* –'

'Nightmare.'

'Yes, nightmare. Only buying is good. Prices very cheap. *Baratissimo.*'

'Xavier, I can't afford to wait three years. I need the money now,' Dougie explained heavily, in too ragged a frame of mind for circumvention or niceties.

'Okay, okay. *Vale!* We try harder, yes? We make price twenty thousand less, okay?'

Dougie nodded, so glumly that the agent squeezed his arm, genuine concern flashing across his wily rodent face. 'There are plenty Germans coming – always the Germans, eh?' He rubbed his fingertips together to indicate ready cash. 'New low price now, yes?' He clapped his hands, clearly pleased with the plan. 'So, how your holiday here with your friends?' He grinned encouragingly. 'Good time?'

'Very good,' Dougie repeated wearily, 'except . . .' He hesitated, his wretchedness deepening as he glimpsed his watch. Half past four. Half past four and still no word. Instead of improving, his hangover was unfurling like some vast, invisible bruise, burning with new colours, firing pain into every nerve-ending in his body. The hateful thirst was growing too – a dry glueyness in his throat, which he knew no amount of juice or coffee or water was ever going to assuage. One proper drink and it would go. One slug and he would have the sharpness back that he so badly needed, the ability to make decisions, to know what he should do. Dougie threw the last drops of his water down his throat. 'How's your family, Xavier?'

The agent whistled, shaking his head, his deep-set dark eyes twinkling. 'They good, Dog-lass, very good. My boy, he play football all the time – *all* the time. I say to him, if you study so hard, you be *professor*!'

'And your daughter, how old is she now?' prompted Dougie, softly, a great envious sorrow washing through him. Questions about his family always made the Spaniard glow.

'Ana, she thirteen.' He rolled his eyes. 'Oh, boy, oh, boy, I am telling you, Dog-lass, she like a *lady* now and talking all the time.' He mimicked a phone, putting his hand to his ear with the thumb and little finger splayed. 'Same for my wife!' He broke off to laugh at his own joke, pressing one hand to his small barrel of a belly and shaking his head. 'These women, eh, Dog-lass? What to do with them?'

It was another possible cue to mention Stevie's

vanishing act, but Dougie didn't feel up to it. The agent's bubble of happiness was too bright – too innocent and inviolate, impossible to burst. His own feelings, meanwhile, continued to ricochet from hope to despair to self-recrimination. Stevie was sixteen, after all, half grown-up. He had been tetchy and critical and she had got the hump. Millions of teenagers all over the globe played out such storming pranks every day. Alternatively, he reflected grimly, she might have seen him on the terrace, slouched in his chair, the empty bottles next to his glass; maybe that was what had driven her away.

In the evening Gary came and went, packing up his and Ruth's stuff. The hospital had decided to keep her in until their early start for the airport the following day, he explained, and he had found a hotel nearby. He offered Dougie what consolation he could, while making it plain that he had too much on his own plate to engage with the situation fully. With one foot in his taxi, his suitcases loaded into the boot and a final round of apologies and thank-yous between them done with, he said, perhaps driven by the dazed expression on Dougie's normally animated face, 'Look, mate, we're not exactly talking child kidnap, are we? She packed her own bags and left. So try not to worry. I bet you she'll be in touch any minute.'

As the evening wore on, Dougie sought distraction in some clearing and packing up of the villa, gritting his teeth against the urge to tear the cork from the half-empty bottle of wine sitting in the fridge door and avoiding the sideboard, where he knew a few millimetres of sherry glistened in the bottom of an old decanter, tucked away in a cupboard behind four chipped crystal tumblers,

survivors from a handsome set of eight that someone had given him and Janine a decade and a lifetime
before. Between chores, he checked and rechecked his
phone for messages, now cursing his early warnings to
Stevie about not overusing her birthday gift abroad. It
would be just like her, he consoled himself, just like any
surly teenager, to produce that as an excuse for not making contact.

He had let another hour go by before deciding to call
Simon in Seville, but then rather wished he hadn't. There
was no useful information to be gleaned, and something
about his friend's easy reassurances dragged his spirits even
lower than they were already. The man was on a luxury holiday with his wife, Dougie reminded himself. Deciding he
might be ready to become a father himself was no preparation for the emotional body-blow of the real thing. Simon
couldn't know what he was going through and it wasn't fair
to expect him to.

Out of sheer desperation, Dougie then braved a call to
the family with whom Stevie had stayed in Valencia. He
was defeated by the mother's rapid staccato Spanish, so
the daughter, Maria, came on the line to spell out shyly, in
breathy grammar-book English, that they hadn't heard
from Stevie since they'd taken her to the station the previous morning. 'She is well, yes?'

'Oh, very well,' Dougie replied, with as much breezi-
ness as he could manage. 'Just a misunderstanding. Thank
you. And to your parents. She had a great week.'

Next, aware of the panic, which was now ready to
throttle him if he let it, Dougie riffled through some
booklets of local services and called the police. After

a couple of false starts, not aided by his limited command of the language, an impressively fluent English speaker was asking a few brief questions. 'I am her *father* and I couldn't be more worried,' Dougie gasped, when the conversation appeared to be zigzagging nowhere. He was told that the authorities at Alicante airport would be alerted, but that in such situations they normally gave the truant twenty-four hours' grace.

'Don't you at least want a photograph?' Dougie cried, desperation getting the better of him. He was duly given an email address to which he could send a picture, a task he fell on the instant the call was over, scrolling through his phone to a snap he had taken just a couple of weeks before – on the day Stevie had officially moved in with him in Kentish Town. She was standing in the kitchen next to the sink, her arms folded and her head cocked in affectionate tolerance at having been asked to pose. Dougie stared at the image, swallowing hard, the worry back in all its dizzying force. She already looked so different. Even at sixteen she was still changing every day – her hair, the shape of her face, the poise: she was like a sculpture still only half chiselled from its stone.

As darkness fell, Dougie got into the car to go on another search but then sat there uselessly, the keys dangling from his hand. Stevie had taken her suitcase. She had left him. To expect to find her anywhere in the vicinity was insane. And yet the thought of closing up the *finca* – of going back to England without her – was simply inconceivable. He got out of the car and slammed the door hard. The darkness seemed very thick suddenly, very quiet. The crickets had stopped. Through the cherry trees to his right something rustled. Dougie spun round, thinking of the wild boar the locals liked to talk about, shy but brutal, with tusks like skewers. She might have gone voluntarily, but she was still barely sixteen, still a child.

His heart pounding, he lit a cigarette and made his way down the side of the house to the pool. In the dark, without its under-lights, the water glinted like liquid jet. He slumped on the sun-bed that Stevie had used and closed his eyes, willing coherent thought. His hangover was lifting at last, one of the tight head-bolts loosening. He had been too harsh on her, he told himself, rerunning the events of the last twenty-four hours for the umpteenth time. That was all it was. He had been too preoccupied with his other duties, stressed from cutting out the fags. He had been surly and she had decided to teach him a lesson. Gary, Simon, the police person – everyone's efforts at reassurance were right: at sixteen kids did stuff like that. It was no big deal. She was probably camped at the airport, asleep across a few seats, waiting for a sheepish reunion when he turned up there the following morning.

Dougie stretched out on the sun-bed, fighting the long-suppressed, abhorrent idea that it might be time to call Janine. But, then, was it fair to worry her when he had no firm answers? When everything might yet be okay? He shut his eyes as the other, truer, darker reasons for his reluctance to contact his ex-wife surged inside, reasons dating back to the time that, even five years on, he could still hardly bring himself to contemplate. And if he mentioned the drinking Janine might make the same connections; make them and not refer to them. That was how she was. Peace-maker, burier of bitter truths, even though they soured her heart.

He only realized he had been dozing when his phone beeped. Terrified, hopeful, his fingers jigging madly, Dougie looked at the message, snorting with disappointment when he saw it was from Victoria. *Stay strong . . .* He deleted it at once, and then, cursing softly, accepting that the time had come, dialled Janine's mobile number. He leant back as it rang, squeezing his thumb and forefinger round the bridge of his nose, trying to imagine how the conversation would go. Even saying he had slept late, cutting out the part his comatose sleep had played in Stevie's easy escape from the villa, would make Janine suspicious. He was a habitual early riser and she knew it: never once had she seen him lounge around in bed, not even on a lazy Sunday, not even during one of his phases of not sleeping . . . Janine *knew* these things. She knew him. That was the trouble.

When the phone cut to her answering message, Dougie released his nose, breathing heavily. A large lizard, fluorescent green, darted up the nearest wall and disappeared under the lip of the roof tiles. Two more followed, smaller, and such a light green that the white paint seemed to shine through their bodies. She was probably asleep, Dougie reasoned, checking his watch, struggling through his exhaustion to work out what the time difference might be between Spain and Stockholm. Instead he found himself imagining what the bedroom might be like on her new island home, Mike a hazy lump under the bedclothes and her curled away from him on her side in that tidy, asymmetrical way she had of sleeping, one arm up under the pillow, the other draped over her hip, one leg under the duvet, one on top. Her mobile would be on her bedside table, next to her watch, which she always took off at night, and whatever book she was reading, one of those heart-wrenching relationship tangles probably, the ones he couldn't stomach; next to that would be her glass of water, from which she always took one final sip before closing her eyes, and next to that a box of tissues, one of those small fancy ones, lightly scented, in floral packaging.

When his phone rang, Dougie slapped it to his ear with a groan. 'Janine?' Her name seemed to stick between his lips. For all the difficulties, there was no one else he wanted to talk to, he realized; no one else who would truly understand. The ache for her was pure reflex, visceral.

'Sorry, no. I'm phoning about your daughter, Stevie.' The tone was female, business-like, official, but with a hint of sympathy.

Dougie tried to speak but his tongue seemed to have swollen, pressing against his throat, snagging on his back teeth. This was it, then, the bad news. The thing so dreaded. Lightning wasn't supposed to strike twice, but that didn't mean it couldn't. For one mad instant he almost switched off his phone. 'Is she . . . ?'

'She's in a bit of a state, but she's fine.'

A noise came out of Dougie that he didn't recognize: a low moan. 'Where is she?'

'London.'

'*London?* Hang on, who is this?'

'Sorry, it's Nina. Nina Carmichael, your neighbour. I heard a noise and thought you were being burgled. You were, but it turned out it was your daughter, trying to break a window. She had keys but couldn't find them, she said. So I invited her in, seeing as it was so late and I'm not up to cat-burgling, these days. First she said you knew where she was, but she seemed all over the place and I didn't believe her. I used to be quite a consummate liar at her age so I thought I'd better phone you and check. Had to wheedle your number out of her, mind you.'

Dougie wondered if joy, too, could break a heart. 'Oh, Nina, thank you – thank you – thank God for you. I can't tell you how happy I am that you rang. You brilliant woman –' He broke off, laughing. 'Christ, she had me going, the minx. This time she really had me going.'

'She's asleep now, but she seemed pretty upset,' Nina said, in a voice that suggested she found his mirth inappropriate.

'Yes, yes, and I think I know why . . . well, some of it anyway.' Dougie ran his hand over his face, trying to compose himself. The white walls of the villa shimmered through his fingers. 'It's . . . never mind. I'm back tomorrow – she knows that. If you could hang on to her until then, that would be fantastic. Tell her I'm not cross. Tell her I'm sorry. Tell her I love her to bits.'

'Or you could do that yourself.'

'Oh, believe me, I will.'

Much to Dougie's own disgust, the urge for a drink surged the moment he came off the phone. Misery, celebration – the sly voice in his head always found some damned excuse. He walked slowly round the pool and up the terrace steps, placing his feet carefully within the frame of each tile, the path clear, thanks to the faint flare of the garden night-lights. Instinct told him to delay his re-entry into the house, to be totally in control of what he might do. In the kitchen doorway he paused, keeping his eyes off the sideboard, off the fridge. Maybe Victoria had been right. Maybe it was time to swallow his pride and get outside help.

He focused on his fatigue. He had been running on adrenalin for days, weeks. Sleep, that was what he needed; what he would now allow himself. Moving heavily, deliberately keeping his eyes half closed to shut out full engagement with his actions, he removed both the wine and the sherry bottles from their quarters and emptied them down the sink. He then shuffled up and down the corridors, locking outside doors, cleaned his teeth and crawled into bed.

Stevie fine, he texted, sending the message to Simon, Victoria and Gary. To Janine he wrote nothing. If she phoned back he would find some other pretext for discussion. Stevie was safe, that was all that mattered. And so was their worst darkness, their *rock bottom*; briefly disturbed, an echo of old pain, it could now sink back into the depths where it belonged.

Chapter Twelve

'So you're busy because of this TV script?' Dougie said, for a second time. He had called Simon to arrange when they might next meet up but didn't seem to be getting anywhere. 'The lesbian cop idea you mentioned in Spain?' He tucked the phone between chin and shoulder, unlocking the back door and propping it open with a brick to let in what the garden stairwell allowed of the late July midday sun. It was eight days since his and Stevie's somewhat staggered return from Spain and the heat-wave was showing no sign of abating. The news that morning had been full of a forest fire that had devastated parts of Devon, including a campsite, injuring scores of people and killing two unfortunate dogs chained to a post.

'Yup, that's the one − feeding the viewing public's never-ending hunger for grime and gore.'

Stevie had drifted down into the kitchen. She was in cropped pyjama bottoms and a T-shirt, her hair tangled, her eyes guarded and sleepy. Dougie tried to get her attention, but she went straight to the fridge and tugged open its heavy door, idly scratching her stomach as she pondered its contents.

'And this has come together thanks to Danny?' Dougie prompted, returning his focus to the phone call.

'Thanks to a friend of a friend of his who works for a script production company.'

'So it's a commission, then?'

'As good as. I've pitched the idea and it's been accepted. But you know what these things are like — one step down a very long and bumpy road, everybody having their say, writing by committee if you're not careful.'

'And what with that, plus going to Scotland to visit Victoria's mother, you're going to be too busy to meet up for a while?' Out of the corner of his eye Dougie saw Stevie pluck out the boxes of leftover Chinese she had persuaded him to buy the night before, making a pagoda of them in her arms. She kicked the fridge door shut, but then opened it again to take out a carton of chocolate milk, which she managed to tuck under her elbow before heading back up the stairs.

'Hang on a minute, Simon.' Dougie put his hand over the receiver. 'Where are you planning to eat that lot, may I ask?'

'Sitting room,' she threw over her shoulder, not looking back.

'A good-morning would be nice,' Dougie called after her, 'or perhaps a good-afternoon.' He cocked his head, hearing no response beyond the light patter of bare feet on the hall floor. 'Blimey — haven't got any hot tips for difficult teenagers, have you?' he growled, slumping into a chair with the telephone.

'None whatsoever. Except to leave them alone.'

'I thought you just said you didn't have any.'

'Yeah, well, everyone knows that one. Don't you remember wanting your parents to get off your back?'

Dougie pictured his father and his brother, the sensation of being a stranger in his own home. 'Not really, no.'

'Wishing she'd done a proper runner in Spain after all, eh?'

'Of course I bloody don't.'

'Lighten up, mate.'

'Sorry, but that's just not very funny.'

'No, you're right,' Simon conceded quickly. 'I didn't think. I'm sorry she's still playing up. It must be very hard.'

'It is,' Dougie admitted, with some energy, 'though I suppose not exactly unexpected. She's a teenager, after all. Besides which, she must be missing her mother. She doesn't *say* it, but I know she is. And I'm trying not to smoke,' he added glumly, 'which probably doesn't help.'

'Well, smoke, then, for fuck's sake. You've given up every other vice in the book. You'll be joining a monastery next.'

'Do you know,' Dougie confessed, with a dry laugh, 'the frightening thing is that there's even some appeal in that thought? Silent contemplation of the world instead of wrestling with it, no material possessions, no emotional complications, just nurturing vegetables between prayers.'

Simon chuckled. 'You need help.'

'You're right, I do.' Dougie felt for the nicotine patch on his arm, pressing it more firmly into place. 'So tell me, before you rush back to your desk, did you and Vic enjoy your jaunt round southern Spain?'

'Fabuloso. We stayed in palaces, including one that was part of the Alhambra – Vic had pulled all the stops out. It was pretty bloody special. But now it's back to reality and some hard work –'

'On this script commission.'

'Exactly. It could be the kick up the arse I've been

waiting for, Doug. I've been cruising for so long. I've got to give it my best shot. I mean, I'm fucking forty, for Christ's sake – time, surely, to give up or get serious.'

'Of course,' replied Dougie, unable to quell a stab of childish hurt at the sensation of being sidelined. 'And I wish you well with it,' he went on carefully. 'Just don't forget your old mates when Hollywood or whatever comes knocking . . . Hang on, it's not Victoria, is it?' he blurted, as the doubts, the dim sense that Simon was not being quite himself, got the better of him. He remembered his meltdown on the terrace in the same instant, recalling again, with a gust of shame, the disappointed hunch of Victoria's shoulders. Who knew what she might have said to Simon? 'You would tell me, wouldn't you, pal, if your wife had finally decided it was time her beloved had a break from the pernicious influence of his oldest friend?'

'Doug, since Spain Vic has done nothing but sing your praises. And deservedly so. Apart from poisoning Ruth, you were a marvel,' Simon said playfully. 'Those of us not poisoned had a bloody brilliant time.'

'For which I was rewarded pretty brilliantly,' Dougie countered, before faltering again at having raised the unavoidably thorny subject of money. Maybe that was what had been making the whole conversation feel somewhat off-kilter. Perhaps Simon had glimpsed Victoria's hefty payment for his services and finally decided that enough was enough, that the days of their Dougie Easton Charity Fund were over. 'Vic was bloody generous, Si,' he said fervently. 'You know I'm grateful. In fact, thanks to that, and a very full in-box on my return, I appear to be in danger of getting back on a financial even keel.'

'That's fantastic, mate. Fantastic.'

'And I've told you, haven't I, that one day I'm going to settle *all* my debts?'

'Doug –'

'You've been bloody generous,' Dougie persisted, sensing how badly Simon wanted the subject closed, but needing, for his own sake, to make the position clear, 'and I couldn't be more appreciative.'

'Good. Okay. And now . . .'

'And now you've got to go,' Dougie finished for him. 'I hope Scotland is welcoming. And best of luck with the writing. Get in touch when you're ready.' He dropped the phone on the table, irritated by how patchy his life still felt, how devoid, still, of any true equilibrium. He had come back to England in such a positive frame of mind too, relishing the prospect of having Stevie to forgive and look after, not to mention the new wherewithal to straighten out his finances. And yet, from the moment he had charged up to Nina Carmichael's door to retrieve his daughter, nothing had quite been falling into place.

'Thanks, but I'm still a bit delicate for that,' Nina had protested, in response to his impulsive and clumsy effort at an embrace of neighbourly gratitude. She had stepped back to usher him into the hallway, one hand tweaking nervously at the paisley headscarf clamped over her scalp.

'Thanks . . . sorry,' Dougie mumbled, embarrassed, appalled at his own thoughtlessness. 'I'm just a bit –'

'Of course you are. No wonder. She's in there.' Nina nodded in the direction of her front room, smiling shyly. 'I felt silly not having keys or something. Next-door neighbours should have each other's keys, shouldn't they?'

'They should. They absolutely should. We must sort that soon,' Dougie agreed, pushing open the door and finding himself in a room that, like the hall, was painted entirely in white and decorated in the most minimal fashion – an armchair, a chubby sofa, a rug, a television, two small black-framed still-life prints on the walls. The only visual, obviously feminine, extravagance was a tall vase in the fireplace filled with exotic flowers – purple, blood-red, tangerine – their stalks fat as rhubarb, their petals splayed like swatches of thick velvet. Stevie was seated to one side of this display in the two-seater sofa, her feet planted squarely on the floor, a glazed expression on her face. Her suitcase was parked at her feet, as if she was in a public waiting room.

'Hey, Dad.'

'Hey, you.'

'Sorry.'

'I should bloody well think so.' He grinned, pushing a thatch of hair from his eyes so he could see her properly, resisting the urge to bear-hug her till she squealed. 'So you sweet-talked the easyJet people into changing your ticket, did you?'

'Yup.'

'And you did it because I had been arsy with you and you were pissed off. Is that it?'

She nodded.

'Nothing else?'

'Nope.'

Dougie hesitated, wishing she would look at him properly. 'I had a drink that night when I shouldn't have . . .'

'So?'

'I wondered if you had seen . . . if you . . .'

'No. And I wouldn't care if I had.'

'Right. Good.' Dougie glanced round for Nina, who had tactfully disappeared. 'How did you get to the airport, out of interest?'

'There was this guy with a truck full of cherries. I hitched.'

'Cherries, eh?' Dougie whistled softly. He dropped onto the sofa next to her. 'I see. Resourceful, anyway.' He ruffled her hair and beamed at Nina, who had reappeared in the doorway. She looked older than he remembered, her face more papery, the puffiness gone. It had left small deep lines, like lino-cuts, under her eyes and across her forehead. She was thinner, too, or perhaps merely showing more of herself than he had seen before, in a vest T-shirt and loose cotton shorts, no doubt driven out of her tent dresses and tracksuit bottoms by the sweltering midsummer heat. There was no muscle on her, Dougie could see now, and not much flesh. Indeed, were it not for her head – the alert, pale blue lashless eyes, the small slightly pointed nose, the feathery pendant earrings dangling from under the headscarf – she could have passed for an underfed young man. 'Nina, I don't know how to thank you.'

'More home-made biscuits would be nice.' Her face broke into a broad grin, the first he had ever seen. Her teeth were even and solid, oddly robust in comparison to the rest of her.

Dougie laughed, liking her directness. 'Well, that's easily done.' He sprang to his feet, rubbing his hands together. 'Stevie can help me, can't you, Stevie? We'll get to it this afternoon.' He offered his daughter a hand for a pull-up off the sofa, but she ignored it.

He picked up her suitcase instead, babbling more thanks to Nina, who waited until they were back on the doorstep before saying, 'And maybe a trip to the cinema? I'd quite like that too. If you had the time. Something funny. No guns. I'll Google what's on.'

Even in his state of heart-bursting gratitude Dougie had been astonished. Yet, given the circumstances, there had seemed no option but to agree. She suggested the following Friday, ten days away, saying she would be in touch nearer the time, and Dougie had replied that that would be fine, saving his snorts of nonplussed derision for when he and Stevie were safely back behind their own front door. It had taken him a few moments to realize he was enjoying the joke alone.

'Hey, come on – it's a bit of a cheek, you've got to admit. It's like she's *using* the situation, press-ganging me into a date when it's the last thing I –'

'Because she's ugly.'

'No, Stevie, that's not fair. I just felt . . . *cornered*, that's all. You saw it for yourself,' Dougie exclaimed, both amazed and disappointed that his daughter should not be taking his side. 'She's just done me this massive favour, I agree, so I offer to do a spot of cooking in return and then she throws *that* at me. Even if she was Kate bloomin' Moss I'd have thought it was a cheek.'

'No, you wouldn't. If it was Kate Moss, you would have seen it as the chance of a shag.'

For a moment Dougie was speechless. There was an element of indisputable truth in what she had said, but the words sounded so ugly, falling from her young mouth. 'OK, maybe . . . once upon a time,' he conceded, 'in my wild youth, perhaps . . .' He stopped, aware of the absurdity of being called upon to justify something so ridiculous, and to someone who, by rights, should have been on her knees at his feet, pleading for his mercy. Instead, she was already heading up to her bedroom, bumping her suitcase noisily over the edges of the stairs, scraping through what was left of the threadbare carpet.

'Stevie, wait.'

'I can't. This is heavy, remember?'

'I said wait, young lady.' Dougie strode up the stairs and swung the suitcase onto his shoulders. He threw it up onto the landing and turned to face her. 'You have behaved abominably – disappearing like that from the villa without a word.'

'I came home, didn't I? And I've said sorry, for fuck's sake.'

'Do not talk to me like that. If you had *any* idea what you've put me through – how worried I was – how –'

'You sound like Mum.'

'I am like Mum,' he shouted, some new, deeper part of him exploding. 'I am your father and I –'

'But you're not, are you? Not really.'

A silence followed, long and dark.

'I am your father,' Dougie repeated hoarsely. 'And I love you.'

'Good. Then we're all clear, aren't we? We all love each other so we'll all be fine.' She pushed past him and slammed her bedroom door.

Dougie sat down on the top stair, his head in his hands,

breathing hard. He had never been so naïve as to think his big shot at full-time parenthood would be plain-sailing, but it had never occurred to him that it would fail so quickly and catastrophically either. It took something like courage to get himself back to her bedroom door, to knock and then go in when there wasn't an answer.

She was lying on her bed facing the wall. 'Sorry,' she said at once, not moving. 'For just now – what I said – and for running off like I did. I'll never do it again.'

'Good. Right. Thank you.'

'Just don't expect me to be happy all the time, Dad, okay? Because I can't be.'

'No. That's reasonable.' Dougie looked round the room, seeking inspiration. She had put a couple of posters on the walls, one of a man with a guitar, one of a small island – white sands, palm trees – surrounded by an azure sea. The small dressing-table mirror was so heavily draped with necklaces and scarves that only a porthole of glass remained free. A couple of photos of school-friends pulling funny faces and poses were tucked into the side of the larger wall mirror. The room smelt of her, the mix of whatever scent or shampoo she used – so distinct that Dougie could have picked her out blindfold in a crowded room. It wasn't the most promising space, yet she had commandeered it, made it her own. 'You've done well in here. It looks cool. That picture – the island – I like that especially. It just makes you want to go there, doesn't it? Away from all the crap.'

'Uh-huh.'

'I'm going to make those biscuits for Nina now. Do you want to help?'

'In a minute.'

'Right. I'll get started. Cup cakes as well, I thought – they always were a winner, weren't they?'

She had made a sound suggesting agreement, but without lifting her head from the pillow.

'Chocolate or vanilla or both?'

'Both.'

She came downstairs eventually, when the baking trays were already in the oven and Dougie was finishing the washing-up.

'I thought we wouldn't tell Mum about your disappearing act. What do you think?'

'Okay. That would be good.' She shot him a glance that showed she knew she was being bargained with.

'And you can take that lot round to Nina once they've cooled. Give her those house keys while you're at it.' He pointed at the wall hook where he had kept his spares.

'Okay.' She picked a leftover blob of cake mix off the table and licked her finger.

'And when you visit Mum in a couple of weeks . . .' She tensed visibly, clamping her mouth round the finger, turning her face away. 'When you go to Stockholm in August,' Dougie pressed on, 'it's still okay to change your mind and decide you want to stay there. Stevie, look at me – this is important.'

She swivelled her head slowly, keeping her eyes pinned to something above his left shoulder. 'It's important that you understand. You can still change your mind. It's not too late. It will never be too late. And if you decide you want to start tracking down your biological father one day, that's fine, too,' he said quietly. 'It won't stop me being your father as well. And it won't stop me loving you.' Dougie paused, aware of the adrenalin thumping in his head.

Stevie was flinching – whether from horror, pain or impatience, it was impossible to tell. She opened the oven door to cover up for it, releasing the rich smell of vanilla sponge into the kitchen. 'Are these done?'

'Fifteen more minutes,' Dougie replied steadily, returning his attention to the washing-up.

An atmosphere of tense calm had prevailed ever since; a sense of hostilities suspended rather than resolved. Each day Dougie had vowed to break through it, only to climb into bed at night with the heavy certainty that he had failed. Stevie didn't want to talk to him, no matter what tack he tried. A day trip to the London Eye, Tate Modern – efforts to take her out of herself, to make the most of his now limited free time – only made the strain between them so glaring that it was a relief to get home.

The sole dim consolation was that she didn't appear to want to talk to anyone else much either. Her friends were all away, she said, and when they got back she would be in Sweden, so there was no point. As a result she had barely left the house, not even – from what Dougie could make out, surreptitiously observing her from behind half-open doors, despising his own desperation – to smoke. All she seemed to want to do was sleep, watch TV, play on her phone or laptop, and eat. After years of pickiness at mealtimes this, at least, was a matter worthy of celebration.

Yet cold Chinese for brunch was hardly nourishing, Dougie reflected darkly, slotting the phone back into its wall-bracket after the call from Simon and reaching for the folder of recipes he had started compiling for his book – a laborious task, since he had always prided himself on never cooking from written notes, preferring to leave the door open for improvising as he went along.

He riffled, with mounting disconsolation, through the sheaves of papers, thinking of all the chefs with much stronger profiles and credentials already ahead of the game. Yet he couldn't let the idea of the book go completely, he just couldn't. Victoria's cheque might have eased his position substantially (he had gritted his teeth and used it to pay off his credit cards), but with the future of the *finca* still hanging in the balance, a project offering some longer-term financial security remained vital. What he needed was a different angle, Dougie decided, angrily tearing his way to a fresh page in his pad, something eye-catching and original; maybe even a how-not-to-be-a-failed-restaurateur approach. He pondered the idea for a few moments before picking up a biro and writing: *So You Want To Run a Restaurant?*

Twenty minutes later, enjoying the old-fashioned solidity of pen and paper, he had drafted several chapter headings – The Concept, Start-up Costs, Suppliers, Public Relations, Staying Afloat – and was in a full flow on an introduction:

> *Running a restaurant is the favourite choice of second career for the nation. We love food, we love preparing food, so as a business what could be more enjoyable? And yet a staggering 80 per cent of all independent restaurants fail within the first three years . . .*

At the trill of the doorbell, Dougie paused to flex his fingers, listening hopefully for the thud of Stevie's

footsteps overhead. When none came, he launched himself up the stairs, cursing. Nina was on his doorstep,
holding the chipped oval serving plate on which Stevie
had transported their baked thank-yous the previous
week. Dougie had to struggle to stop his face falling. Their
'date', he realized, was just two days away.

'Thanks, they were delicious . . .' She blinked her big-
lidded eyes, half smiling, looking nervous, keeping hold
of the plate. 'And I've put the keys in a safe place. So no
worries next time you lock yourself out or whatever. I'll
remember to get some of mine cut for you.'

'Great. Thanks.' She had on a different headscarf,
Dougie noticed, of pea-green cotton, which suited her
better, and a sleeveless maxi dress, so long that its hem
was dusty and frayed from trailing on the ground.

'And, look, about Friday,' she said, talking now at great
speed, 'the whole cinema thing – don't worry. It was a
bloody cheek, just a whim – spur-of-the-moment nonsense. I haven't been out much recently and sometimes it
drives me a little stir-crazy.' She raised one hand in a sort
of clawing mime of a caged animal, but then seemed to
lose conviction. 'There's nothing on anyway,' she continued, talking even faster, 'except *Shrek Four*, or it could
be *Five*, and Jennifer Aniston, who's more rubbish with
each film. I bet she thought *Friends* was the start of a great
career trajectory – I bet they all did – but instead it looks
like that was as good as it was going to get. But life's
funny like that, isn't it, tricking you about its high and low
points? It's only right at the end, looking back, that you
can truly know that stuff. Ta-ra, then.' She spun on her
heel. 'Nice to talk.'

'Hang on,' Dougie stammered. 'I mean, we could still do Friday. If there's nothing at the flicks we could have a bite to eat instead, if you like? Always nice to have a break from my own kitchen . . .' He summoned a stiff smile, aware that he was being propelled by the Kate Moss conversation with Stevie and marvelling at the lengths to which he was prepared to go for daughterly approval. 'There's supposed to be a good tapas place on Thurlow Road, La Santa, which I've never tried.'

'Okay. That would be nice . . .' She studied him for a moment, distrust flashing across her face. 'Thanks.'

'I'll book a table, for, say, eight o'clock?'

'Could it be earlier? Seven? I tend to be flagging a bit by eight.'

'Seven. Fine. I'll knock on your door . . . and, look,' Dougie muttered, 'about you being ill, can I just say —'

'Nothing. Say nothing, thanks, if you don't mind.' Her translucent eyes flared wide with warning. 'I *was* ill, but now I'm getting better. End of. How's Stevie, by the way? Has she . . . is she okay?'

'Yes . . . At least . . .' Dougie frowned, reluctant to confess to the trouble he was having. 'Why? Has she said something to you?'

'No.' The guarded expression was back. 'I haven't seen her. I was just worried . . . I mean, to run away like that so dramatically, I figured she had to be pretty upset about something.' She plucked at her dress. 'And that night she stayed . . .'

'Go on.' Dougie folded his arms, trying to hide his eagerness for information, hating that she might know something he didn't.

'Well, when I was up in the night – which I tend to be – I thought I heard her crying. But then it stopped and it didn't seem right to barge in.'

'Crying? Really? Oh dear . . .' Dougie held his pose, inwardly squirming under what felt like a new revelation of his failure as a father. 'I suppose that sort of figures. Her mother has gone abroad recently, you see, leaving me in full charge . . . I'm doing the best I can.'

'I'm sure you are.' She smiled kindly, the glare in her eyes gone. 'Here. I nearly forgot.' She handed him the plate.

'Thanks. And see you Friday.' Dougie kept his cheerful face in place until she had scurried over their unravelling boundary fence. A panel of her dress caught on one of the loose wire spokes, but she pulled at it without a backward glance, not even when the material ripped.

Back in the house, he put his head round the sitting-room door. Stevie had made a bed of the sofa cushions on the floor and was watching something on her laptop while nodding to music piping into her ears from her iPhone. 'My Friday date is still on,' he announced, having signed at her to remove an ear-piece. She had emptied all the food cartons, he noticed, and stacked them neatly on the table. 'Nina tried to bale out but I held firm. We're just going for a meal now. No cinema. Come too, if you like.'

'Nah.'

'Don't want to cramp your father's style, is that it?' He tried a goofy grin but it was half-hearted and her gaze had drifted back to the computer.

Chapter Thirteen

That evening Ruth asked Gary if he would mind driving her to her book club. She felt unsafe now, behind the wheel of a car, not just because she had to slide the seat so far back to accommodate her belly (her hands barely reached the steering-wheel), but because she was increasingly aware that she was in a state of permanent distraction, at one remove from whatever was going on around her. Pedestrians, cyclists, trucks, bollards – all the hazards of London driving – were obstacles she dared not risk, appearing like pinpricks down the wrong end of a telescope. Her own body was her world now: the baby in her huge heaving stomach paddling to get out – or so it felt – and in the process dictating all the basic needs over which Ruth had once exercised unthinking control: sleeping, eating, visits to the bathroom. She had mood swings – crying one minute, laughing the next. Lately, even her breathing had changed. She wheezed like an old woman, the baby's occupancy apparently having extended up behind her rib-cage, crushing her lungs into a space too cramped for proper inflation.

Strangest of all, though, was how little these inconveniences bothered her. After Spain – the panic, the relief that had followed – nothing had seemed to matter much except keeping herself and the baby safe. Maternity leave – once such a feared milestone – had been fine too.

More than fine, in fact: joyous. Saying goodbye to all her colleagues on the fifth floor, having negotiated an earlier date to go than originally planned, Ruth would have skipped along the corridor if her great ship of a body could have managed it. Going down in the lift, she had found herself standing next to a tall, lithe media planner who, she remembered, had been pregnant a couple of years before; a woman she had never paid much attention to. But that afternoon she had started up a conversation, asking questions about the progress of the child, marvelling that she had once deemed something so momentous not worth a second thought.

'It was a boy called Anton and he's at nursery,' she told Gary, who was waiting patiently with the engine running while she wrestled with her seatbelt. 'And it was four years ago, not two. Isn't that incredible? *Four.*'

Gary agreed that it was indeed astonishing, and they waved at Lois, who had taken up her usual valedictory position in the front room as they pulled away, paws on the sill, head at the window, panting with her customary despair at being abandoned.

'I'm not really in the mood for this thing tonight, if I'm honest.'

Gary, half out of the parking space, put his foot on the brake. 'Well, why the hell are you going, then?'

'Because it'll be my last for ages. I won't have time to read books for months and months – everybody says so. And I feel bad for Katie because numbers are down with everyone being on holiday. Victoria said she was coming but then pulled out as they've gone to Scotland. I'll enjoy it when I get there, I know I will. And you should be carrying on with your cooking lessons,' she added brightly, 'for the same reason.'

Gary shook his head, checking his mirrors carefully as he turned into the high street, where the traffic was busy but moving fast. 'No, they really are done with. Simon had already pulled out and Richard wasn't fussed. But now Dougie says he's too busy anyway and wants to keep free what evenings he can because of Stevie. I'm not sorry, to be honest.' He turned briefly and grinned at his wife. 'Spain was fun – until your little problem, of course – but by the end I was really starting to feel like I'd moved on from the whole Dougie-Simon scene, that *we* had moved on.'

'How sweet, Gary. I like that.' Ruth threaded her fingers through her husband's curly bush of hair. 'Hmm, this needs a snip, even for you.'

'And you'll probably think I'm losing it when I say this, but . . .' Gary paused, slowing for a flashing amber light, letting a woman finish pushing an elderly man in a wheelchair back up onto the pavement. It was seven thirty in the evening and the sun, though low in the sky, was still glossy and huge. Momentarily blinded, he tugged down the visor above his windscreen before moving off. 'But,' he continued, 'what with you getting sick and that thoughtless girl of Dougie's taking off as she did, putting him through it, I began to feel like there was some really bad vibe going on over there – that the only safe thing was to get away and stay away.'

Ruth chuckled. 'You're right, that is insane. Poor

gorgeous Dougie, he doesn't deserve such insinuations. He's just one of those people with a messed-up life. They never change.'

'Gorgeous?' Gary shot her a look.

'Yes, but not remotely my type,' Ruth teased, delighted that the overblown state of her body wasn't enough to stop the knee-jerk reaction of manly jealousy. 'If there was a "bad vibe", as you put it, I'd be far more inclined to blame the penny that went missing from Simon's knife box. I *know* I put it in there.' She shivered, changing to a sideways position as the baby kicked.

Gary laughed. 'And I'm worried about being insane? Anyway, according to your crazy logic, shouldn't that mean Simon is the one experiencing the bad luck, instead of getting script commissions and swanning off on extended holidays?' A bus in front of them was slowing down. Gary indicated and pulled out, accelerating, the sun fierce in his eyes. From nowhere, it seemed, a van appeared in the opposite lane. Seeing a large truck hot on his tail, Gary kept going, certain the driver would read the scene and wait.

'Scotland isn't just holiday. It's to see Victoria's moth –' Ruth never finished her sentence because the van didn't wait. Its owner was on his mobile and in a hurry. Gary was in his lane, his space. At the last minute Gary tried to swerve. Behind him the truck's brakes screeched. The van also tried to turn, but there was nowhere for it to go other than a line of parked cars. Their bonnets collided with a thud that was astonishing for its softness, the ease with which the metal of the vehicles seemed to give way. Behind them the truck's brakes screamed as it hit their bumper, shunting them another ten yards. Ruth's seatbelt, which hadn't caught properly, unspooled smoothly and quickly, releasing her towards the dashboard.

In the evening light the midges danced like dust motes over the glassy surface of the loch. Above them the sun was a flaming palette of bloody orange. It had been sinking fast, shifting the colours on the nearest stretch of water from turquoise to silvery blue and emerald. Further away, in the advancing shadow, great swathes of the lake had turned to slicks of oily black. The mountains had darkened, too, looking more like smoking volcanoes as the sun-reddened cloud swirled round their peaks. On their lower slopes, the forests, such a rich ivy green in the afternoon sun, had shrunk to a dark blur, indistinguishable from the barer, rockier ground marking the approach to the lakeside. Along the bank from where Victoria was sitting, a lone spindly tree, frothy with foliage, leant out over the water, as if poised in a perpetual effort to catch a glimpse of its reflection. It made Victoria think of a Strindberg painting she particularly liked, one of several she had recently been researching for an autumn exhibition by the Tate. The painting was called *The Lonely One* and depicted a solitary rowan, set against the backdrop of the artist's beloved archipelago. '. . . *so solitary yet, in the absence of competitors, so unusually strong, as if it was better able to defy storm, salt and cold than the scramble of envious equals for the bits of earth . . .*' Or something. Victoria wished she could remember it better. It had been a revelation to discover that Strindberg could be as masterful with words as he was with paint.

She hugged her knees closer to her chest, releasing a sigh of pure wonder as she returned her gaze to the lake. It was her first visit to Scotland – not embarked upon for the happiest of reasons – and she had somehow expected brutal landscapes, cold, alienation. She had never imagined the heat-wave playing out so far north, with such beauty, such stillness. Even the air was different – creamy, each inhalation as enriching as a mouthful of good food. After the bustle of London, and the whistle-stop tour of Andalucían cities the week before, the peace of the place – the absence of noise, of population – was like a dose of medicine she hadn't known she needed. During the entire walk that afternoon, she and Simon had seen no one but a solitary hiker, a leathery-faced creature with wild, gingery hair and a plastic map round his neck, who had saluted like a general as he strode past.

Their hotel, the Country Lodge, was more like a guesthouse, with a homely communal dining room and just a handful of bedrooms. It was set a few hundred yards back from the edge of the lake, at the end of a lane that spiralled down through woodland from the main road. Victoria had chosen the place purely for its geographical convenience, led there online after punching in the postcode of Rosemount, her mother's 'residence'. The website had been quaint and amateurish, its clutch of old photographs no preparation for the magnificence of the setting. It was only during the drive in their hire-car from Glasgow airport that the sheer scale and serenity of the landscape they were entering had begun to dawn. Victoria had stopped commenting after a while and merely gawped. The possibility of actually enjoying the trip had started to dawn then, too, along with the notion that her father, in posting her mother to such a place, might after all have made a good decision.

Victoria stood up and walked down to the very edge of the water, crouching to trail her fingers in its icy cool, while using her other hand to scratch an ankle. She had sprayed herself with repellent but the midges were getting at her anyway, in her hair and ears, inside the edges of her socks. Simon, who was always more of a target, had turned back for the lodge, conceding defeat, ten minutes before. He had tried to persuade her to give up, too, commanding her with gruff affection to take care when she refused, then issuing the order a second time at the top of his voice before disappearing round the curve in the lakeside. Since Spain he had been a little moody, so she had been nothing short of delighted at his ready enthusiasm to accompany her on the trip north to spend time with her mother. He had broken the news of the script commission in the same breath, saying he couldn't think of a better environment in which to focus on some serious work.

Victoria had issued a private prayer of thanks for his project both then and many times subsequently. Simon had needed a nudge, she realized. Having to work hard at something had made him much more alert, on his toes, as if he was *engaging* with the world again, instead of letting it pass him by. With her deep into the copy for the Strindberg catalogue – the pair of them tapping away on their laptops – fond memories had resurfaced of their early days together, in the pre-marital London flat, head to head at their respective desks, her slaving over the endlessly extended brute of a thesis on Byzantine art while Simon churned out countless articles and short stories, happy to get into print with whoever would have him.

Victoria pulled her water bottle out of her knapsack and drank deeply, watching the necklace of mountains, smoky purple now, shimmer through the plastic. The little tree on the bank rustled, exposing the white underside of its leaves as a faint breeze blew up its skirts. Victoria eyed it fondly, thinking again of the Strindberg painting and her own predilection for falling a little in love with which-ever subject required her concentration. Painter, botanist, alchemist, experimental photographer, depressive – she couldn't imagine anyone not being smitten by such eclec-tic and troubled genius.

But it was time to go back. Her scalp, especially, was on fire with bites. In desperation she smeared some of the repellent on her fingers and ran them through her hair before setting off. She could feel her stomach cramping, too, reminding her that before long she would need the bathroom. Her period had arrived that morning, just before they had left for the airport. It had seemed a cruel blow at the time, but now, in this glorious place, it didn't seem to matter so much. There would be other months, other cycles. For all his moodiness, she and Simon were making love regularly again, that was the main thing. As he himself had said, several times now, they would con-coct a child soon enough, in their own good time.

She found her husband behind a newspaper in a deep, wide-winged leather armchair in the lodge's cosy oak-beamed sitting room. Above him a stag's head protruded from a shield on the wall, sporting an impressive set of antlers and an expression of haughty resignation. 'Ah, there you are – good. I was getting worried.' Simon got up at once, folding the newspaper neatly away. 'Dinner for everyone is at eight on the dot, apparently. No stragglers or else. Oh, yes, and I've got directions for getting to Rosemount tomorrow morning,' he added, with something like pride. 'They all seemed to know the place, said it was very fine. I thought I might come, too, if you'd like me to.'

'Oh, Simon . . .' They had set off along the carpeted corridor towards their room. Victoria stopped, catching his arm so she could look at him properly and he could see how touched she was. 'That's very dear of you, really, but I think I'll stick to the plan of making the first visit on my own. Don't worry,' she added, reading a trace of disappointment in his expression. 'I'm sure my flagging daughterly affections will need the boost of your support later in the week. You stay and work. Those script people, what were they called again?'

'Beaumont Productions.'

'That's it. I keep forgetting. Clever Danny pulling off such a networking feat. Maybe we should have him round when we get back, him and Heather, say a proper thank-you.'

'Maybe. But I think they go to their Dordogne place in the summer – for weeks and weeks. And the script will probably stay in the pipeline for an eternity anyway – there'll be rewrite after rewrite. It's a crazy business.'

'But they are sending you a proper contract?' They were at their door, Victoria waiting out of habit for Simon to produce a key.

'Oh, yes. At least, it's in the pipeline, too . . . but that's also par for the course.' He reached past her and turned the handle. 'No keys here, remember?'

'I forgot,' she exclaimed, laughing. 'Imagine that in London!'

'Bonkers, if you ask me. Our laptops alone are worth two grand. Add another eight hundred for our phones. There's absolutely no signal, by the way – I've tried everywhere. The girl at Reception said it depended on your network. Do you want to try yours?'

'Not really. I rather like being "off the hook" . . . being just the two of us.' She shot him an impish grin before disappearing into the bathroom.

'Hey, don't be long,' Simon called, 'or we'll get our knuckles rapped for being late into dinner.'

They weren't late and the meal was delicious: a succulent beef stew, followed by apricot crumble. Afterwards the waitress suggested they take their coffee outside. A couple of their fellow diners – of whom there were only a handful – did the same, sitting on the big wooden benches positioned with the best view of the loch. Simon and Victoria stayed on their feet, quickly finishing their coffee and moving nearer the water to savour the moonlit view on their own. In the dimness it was a sheet of black ice, the moon a yellow bore-hole at its heart, the stars a scattering of frost.

'Strindberg took photographs of the night sky,' Victoria murmured, '"celestographs", he called them.'

'Did he now? A man of many talents.'

'Yes, and he did it without a lens or even a camera, just using photographic plates exposed to the sky. The result was a series of dark pictures speckled with dots of light. Strindberg believed the dots were the stars, but the truth is they could just as well have been dust particles.'

Simon laughed. 'Oh dear, that's rather sad.'

'Do you think so? I think it's fantastic – that he tried, that he believed in his results. I mean, it's the *believing* in something that matters, isn't it, rather than any fixed idea of a so-called "truth"?'

'Hey, you're shivering. Take this.' Simon slipped off his jacket and put it over her shoulders. He stayed standing behind her, slipping his arms round her waist and nestling his head under her right ear. 'There, is that better?'

'So much, thank you.' Victoria tightened her to jaw to stop her teeth rattling. 'Oh, Simon, I thought Spain was wonderful, but this – which I was so apprehensive about – is even better. I can't thank you enough for coming. I was so sure you'd want to stay in London alone, hanging out with Dougie and so on.' She sighed happily. 'It's like we've started *doing* things together, like we used to. Have you noticed that? Let's not ever lose it again, okay?'

'Okay.' He nuzzled her neck.

'You're the one who's freezing,' she cried. 'Your nose is like an icicle. We should go inside.'

'No, a few more minutes. Let's go a bit nearer the water.' He kept hold of her, propelling her legs forwards with his, pushing his knees into the back of hers, until they were inches from the edge of the loch. She laughed, squirming.

'Not afraid, are you?' he teased, tightening his grip.

'Happy-afraid,' she gasped, gripping with her toes inside her shoes and pushing back as hard as she could. 'Happy-afraid, but I've had enough.'

'This bit's not deep and I'd fish you out.'

'Simon, that's enough, okay?'

'I'd rescue you, Vic, that's what I'm saying.' He loosened his grip and turned her to face him. 'Would you rescue me?'

'Of course,' she whispered, kissing his cheek.

'Even in that icy cold? Even if you had to grope for my hand in the murky dark?'

'Even then, silly. Hey, are you trying to tell me something?' She laughed uncertainly.

'Only that I love you.'

'And I love you.'

They rubbed their frozen noses together, one of their special Eskimo kisses, before turning to walk back up the path. The lodge, its windows lit, glowed on the crest of the slope above them, like a Chinese lantern. They moved towards it slowly, fingers linked, their arms swinging.

Later, when their lights were out and they were cocooned in their creaky four-poster, the thick soft pillows cushioning their faces, their bodies touching but not entwined (Victoria's cycle had put paid to that), Victoria raised the subject she had privately sworn never to raise, saying softly that, baby or no baby, she loved him wanting to have sex with her and always would, and if he had ways of getting turned on that he hadn't shared with her, then that was fine too.

In the silence that followed Victoria could have sworn she heard the drumming of his heart, a counterpoint to hers. She thought she heard the magic between them snap, too, as surely as a dry stick under her foot.

'And what am I supposed to take from that?' He was rigid, facing away from her.

Victoria stared at his back, pushing a finger into her mouth, feeling for a nail to tear with her teeth, cursing her courage. But it was too late to pull back. 'Those magazines, the top-shelf stuff . . . Si, I found them by accident a little while ago now and I just want to say –'

His bark of scornful laughter stopped her going any further. He rolled onto his back, raising his arms high, then dropping them with a thwack onto the duvet in a gesture of amused despair. 'Magazines . . . You mean that box in the spare-room wardrobe? Oh, that's good, that's really good.'

Victoria was tempted to put the light on. She needed to see his face. She couldn't read where he was coming from, what his mood was, whether she had done a sensible thing or a stupid one. 'Simon, I understand, really I do –'

'They're Dougie's, you nincompoop.'

'Dougie's?'

'Yes, he asked me to store them, as a favour, when he got the nod about Stevie moving in. He said he didn't think he should have them lying around the house. I should have told you.'

'No – I mean, it's hardly a big deal. Oh, God, sorry. Now I feel a perfect twit.'

Simon chuckled. 'No, I'm the twit. I should have told you. Poor Vic, all that angst.' He picked up her hand and kissed her fingers. 'You're all I need, okay?'

'Okay. Sorry, Si.' Victoria turned on her side and closed her eyes, sticking one leg out of the duvet because the room suddenly felt too warm. Before sinking into sleep, she allowed herself one long, slow exhalation of relief. It wasn't a big deal, but she was still glad. Dougie. Of course it was Dougie. It made so much more sense that she was almost surprised she hadn't worked out the explanation for herself.

Chapter Fourteen

Nina opened the door so quickly that Dougie was certain she must have been standing immediately on the other side of it, spying on his approach up the path through the mottled panel of glass, one eye on her watch because he was so late. For the first time since he had known her she was wearing makeup – heavy blue on her eyelids and a faint pink on her lips. There was colour in her cheeks, a bit too cherry-red given the alabaster shade of the rest of her, but it flattered the sculpture of her face. She was dressed in the most feminine way he had yet seen, a loose-fitting, sleeveless calf-length white dress, flecked with green sequins, and gold flip-flops. Her feet, he noticed, were large and bone-white, the second toe so markedly longer than the first that it stuck out a little over the end of the sandal. Most eye-catching of all, however – so eye-catching indeed that he didn't dare inspect it – was the hair on her head. A wig; presumably the one Stevie had mentioned. The effect was no less than transforming – somehow not *faux*-looking (it had to have cost the earth), long, dusty fair hair streaked with sandy brown. She had tied a green silk ribbon through part of it, allowing the rest to float around her shoulders.

'This is not a date, by the way,' she said at once, blinking her big unprotected eyes. 'I just wanted to make that clear, in case you –'

'No, that's fine. I mean, I didn't think . . .' Dougie dropped his gaze to the floor, fearing his expression had already betrayed the reluctance with which he had arrived on her doorstep. Looking forward to the dinner had never really been a possibility, but to make matters worse Gary had phoned just as he was leaving the house to report in a deathly voice that Ruth and the baby had had yet another close shave – in an accident involving a white van this time, with him driving. 'They're okay – we're all okay – but they're keeping Ruth in for another night because she's so many months gone and a bit concussed. Jesus, it's beginning to feel like we've got a marked card or something.'

Dougie, seeing a possible, and truly decent, route out of his dinner-date, had offered to come round but Gary had turned him down. 'Thanks, Doug, but no, I'm fine, just a bit shaken up. Look, I was really calling to find out when Simon's getting back – wherever he's gone it appears to be completely under the radar.'

'Inverness-shire. But I'm not sure for how long.'

'Right. It's just that Ruth's now got a bee in her bonnet that I've got to send him some money – a coin. She's decided there's some kind of bad karma going round because of that bloody knife we gave him.'

'Blimey.'

'I know, I know, but I can't let Ruth have a bee in her bonnet about anything at the moment – she's pretty close to the edge – and, frankly, I'm starting to wonder whether she hasn't got a point.'

'I could deal with that for you,' Dougie offered, glad to see some way of being useful. 'Tell Ruth I think I found the actual lost penny, that I'll sort it. Okay?'

'That's good of you, Doug, I appreciate it.'

'And call if you want, Gary, any time. Being on your own at home,' Dougie had concluded thickly, 'I know how rough that can be.'

Nina had locked her front door and was giving him a penetrating look, as if, indeed, she knew all about his unwillingness to be there. 'Which isn't to say I don't think you're attractive,' she said sharply. 'You are – very, as it happens. But I promise – hand on heart – that I have no current hopes, romantically, *vis-à-vis* you or any other male on the planet. Is that clear?'

'Perfectly.'

'And if this is making things more awkward, I'm sorry. It looks like it might be.'

'No, you're doing fine.'

'Good. Thanks. I just thought clarity was the way for-ward.' She grinned suddenly, the big teeth lighting up her face. 'Do you mind if we go in my car? I know it's not far but my energy levels are crappy. It means you can drink if you want.'

'I don't drink.'

'Oh, yes, I remember. It said in that article . . . Good. Right. Well, that makes two of us. There's no air-con, I'm afraid,' she warned brightly, manually unlocking a black Mini across the street, which Dougie had noticed many times but not known was hers. 'Not that the heat's quite so bad by this time of day, is it? And you're in trousers so at least a boiling plastic seat won't burn your bum . . .

'I do like men, by the way,' she continued, once they were manoeuvring nimbly through the evening traffic, 'in case you're wondering. I even had a husband once.

Trevor . . . Mind you, with a name like that I should have known he'd turn out to be flaky.'

'What sort of flaky?' Dougie prompted gloomily, wondering what they would talk about if the life-story was done with before they'd seen a menu.

'Cancer and husbands.' She changed gear energetically. 'Not always a good mix. Trevor baled out, using the time-honoured sneaky route of being a total bastard so that I was the one who brought things to an end. It was only afterwards that I found out he'd had someone else for two years. Two *years*. Which rather neatly equated to the month I got my first diagnosis: wife gets sick, acquire bit on the side – it's a well-worn path, apparently, for certain types of men. Is a single yellow still okay after six thirty? I never know.' Without waiting for an answer, she backed swiftly and neatly onto a yellow line in a space only a couple of feet longer than her small car. Tugging up the handbrake, she turned to look at him.

'I'm not going to spend all evening moaning about my ex either, if that's what's worrying you.'

'It's not –'

'Nor do I want to talk through the gory details of my condition.'

'Fine. Good.'

'Like I told you, I've been ill. I've finished the treatment. I'm to have regular checks but have basically been given the all-clear. I'm just trying to get back to something like a normal life.'

'Fine.'

'So you can stop looking so worried.'

'Why do you keep saying I'm worried? I'm not.'

She eyed him steadily. 'You're also a liar.'

Once they were sitting down she asked, much more warmly, 'Anyway, how's Stevie?'. The waiter had shown them to a quiet corner at the back of the room, next to an open window overlooking the street. The table, with a vase containing a single fresh rose, was wooden and small, and wobbled badly under any pressure from their elbows.

'Stevie is still not as cheerful as I would like,' Dougie admitted cautiously. 'But I keep reminding myself she's a teenager. And she's going to visit her mother in Stockholm in a couple of days, so I'm hoping that might help . . . make her more certain of what she wants.' He set his phone down on his side plate as he talked, simultaneously making a couple of unsuccessful efforts to shift their table onto more even floor. 'She might just be worried about her GCSE results, of course.' He moved the table again, knocking the vase but catching it just in time. 'I fear, though, that the real problem is she's just dying to get away from me.'

'Oh, I doubt that. She adores you.'

Dougie glanced up in surprise. They had both been given menus – long, hand-written, barely legible lists on crumpled pieces of recycled brown paper.

Nina kept her eyes on the page. 'She's terrified of letting you down.'

'Really?'

'I ate in that Notting Hill restaurant of yours once, you know.' She put down the menu and folded her arms, her pale face full of merriment.

'You mean the Black Hen. Well, there's a coincidence. I hope you liked it.'

Her eyes shone. 'It was fantastic. I was with Trevor. We'd just got engaged and were about as happy as we ever got. I ate like a horse in those days,' she added wistfully. 'Now it's bits here and there. All the treatments, they don't just play hell with your appetite, I swear they change your taste-buds too. And with tapas I never know what to order anyway.' She pushed her menu further away. 'I'll have what you're having. Follow the expert.'

'Oh, blimey. Is there anything I should avoid in that case?'

'Celery. Offal. Yoghurt.'

'Right . . . that shouldn't be too difficult.' Dougie caught the waiter's eye and ordered quickly, making sure his choices covered fish and meat, as well as vegetables.

'So tell me,' Nina said next, dipping a tiny crust of the bread they had been brought into a saucer of oil, 'what was it like being famous? Did you enjoy it?'

'I never was famous,' Dougie protested stiffly, even less keen on this particular conversational route than any other she had picked so far. He altered the position of his phone, aligning it more exactly with his side plate, while the dark thought unfurled that maybe his dining companion's eagerness to help in the library all those weeks before hadn't been quite so innocent as she had made out, that she had in fact been the loner-stalker type all along, waiting for her chance to pounce. The notion was replaced by a disproportionately fond memory of Laura Munro. The journalist had been energetic, hungry, exciting, far more the sort of creature on whom he should have been lavishing his still very precious funds. Laura had at least helped him forget things. Nina was just making him feel worse.

'It was the place rather than me that attracted the head-lines,' he explained, forcing out a friendly tone, fiddling again with the position of his phone. 'And even then it was more tabloid stuff – who was partying there – rather than because of the Michelin star I managed to acquire in the process. But, to answer your question,' he smiled wearily, 'no, fame didn't seem much fun. *Getting* there was okay, I suppose – the struggle for recognition, et cetera. But after that, as I believe you know, I sort of blew it anyway.'

'Yes, I do know that.' She narrowed her eyes. 'I also know that if you look at that damn mobile of yours one more time I'm going to walk out. Leave you to trough through all that food you've ordered on your own.'

Dougie stared at her, stupefied.

'I know you're only here because I asked,' she bowled on, 'but, honestly, I just wanted an evening out – *time* out – with someone who's not connected to all the rubbishy things I've had to deal with over the last couple of years. Someone with whom I have no *history*. Conversation. A laugh. Someone who, unlike my lovely well-intentioned friends and family, won't treat me as a total invalid. For your information, I really liked being able to help you out with Stevie – being *useful*. It's a long time since I felt that. Especially since I had to give up work –'

'You've given up the library?' Dougie interjected weakly.

'I've done my best to take the pressure off,' she galloped on, dots of real colour in her pale cheeks now, 'to make it clear to you that I'm not a bunny-boiler – not trying for a mercy shag – that all I wanted was a bit of friendly conversation over some nice food, but I can see now that that was absurdly naïve. So . . .' She picked up her paper napkin, roughly folded it into a tight wad and, in one swift, deft movement, bent down and slipped it under the wobbly table-leg. She then stood up, dusting her hands. 'I'm going to take myself off – put you out of your evident misery.'

'Please sit down,' Dougie said quietly, glaring at a woman staring at them from another table. 'I'm sorry about the phone. I didn't mean to be rude. I've been keeping an eye on it in case a friend rang. I told him he could call if he wanted. He phoned me just as I was coming round to yours tonight – he's been in a car accident and his wife, who's heavily pregnant, is still in hospital.' Dougie could feel a muscle fluttering in his cheek, deep under the lower ledge of his left eye socket. 'She's fine apparently – concussion – but it's not the first thing that's gone wrong for them lately and he sounded pretty cut up.'

Nina had sat down again, her eyes liquid with sympathy. 'Bollocks. Sorry. You should have said . . . should have cancelled. You idiot.'

'I thought you'd think I was wriggling out.' Dougie shot her an apologetic grimace.

She cast her eyes skyward, shaking her head. 'Well, you could have explained I was wrong, couldn't you?' The head movement somehow showed up the artifice of the wig, the long hair seeming not quite to swing in time with her face. 'I may be single-minded, but I'm not stupid – I'd have understood. Look, we can still call it a day – all we've had is some bread and two glasses of tap water.' The words were barely out of her mouth when their waiter appeared, hands and arms laden with their order. They caught each other's eye and laughed, moving condiments to make room for the dishes.

'It's the randomness that gets me as much as anything,' Dougie confessed, helping himself to the food, which his expert eye had realized at a glance was good – fresh, authentic, beautifully presented, smelling excellent. Nina made more indecisive inroads, her fork hovering, picking off morsels here and there. While they ate he described Ruth's health scare on the day before Stevie had bolted back to England. 'So then you think, right, mother and baby safe, panic over. All back on course to live happily ever after. The last thing you imagine is she's going to get driven into by a van in a north London high street . . .'

The more he talked, the more Dougie realized how badly he had been in need of the release of adult conversation. What with Simon's withdrawal, his new onslaught of work commitments and the wall Stevie seemed to have erected around herself, a wall that appeared to thicken under every fresh effort of his to break it down, it had been a gruelling ten days. That morning he had even, guiltily, caught himself wondering if it wouldn't be a relief to post her onto the plane to Stockholm. Rebellion, flouncing, attitude, bad behaviour he could have coped with, but not the punishing silence to which he had been subjected ever since her decampment from Spain. None of his usual tricks got through to her now – teasing, spoiling, bad jokes; he was lucky if he could trigger a monosyllable, let alone a smile.

'And I feel like it's my fault,' Dougie confided, having arrived, with what felt like inevitability, at the subject of his daughter. 'When she first agreed to live with me I tried too hard, you see, pushed her . . .' He stared at the forkful of food he had been about to put into his mouth – aubergine, smoked pork, a sliver of red pepper – and slowly lowered it back to his plate. 'Life's so frigging tricky, don't you find?' he said huskily. 'Sort one thing out and another ten pop up in its place. At least, that's how it's felt since . . .'

'Since?' Nina laid her cutlery down, two neat bridges across all the small islands of her untouched food.

'I'm not in the business of dishing up my sorry life-history,' Dougie mumbled.

'Well, thank God for that. I might fall asleep. And I snore.'

'Ah . . . I'll be extra careful in that case.' He managed a smile, but the bleakness was moving through him, unstoppable, like a cold wind. 'I had a good life,' he muttered, 'but I screwed it up . . . as you know.' He looked away, the openness of her pale blue eyes suddenly too much to take. 'From that newspaper you so kindly showed me in the library all those weeks ago. I drank too much. I threw away good fortune, a good wife . . .'

'Janine, who sang.'

'Yes. Janine. Who sang.' Dougie put the pork and pepper into his mouth, tasting nothing but his own saliva. He ground the food between his teeth, his thoughts suddenly transported back to the call he had made from the poolside to Stockholm when Stevie had run away, the terror in his heart, the need to hear the voice that never came. Finding the food in a clump at his throat, he swallowed.

There was no question of smiling now. It was all he could do to speak. 'But you know, Nina, what's really been getting me down lately is that now, when I've genuinely been trying for months and months to do things right, *not* to screw things up, to stay in control –' He broke off.

Nina had gone very still. 'Go on.'

'I – no – nothing.'

'I have no idea what you're talking about, but I do want to know – really I do.' She leant across the small table, saying in a soft, urgent voice, 'What was it you were going to tell me just now? There was something else, wasn't there?'

Dougie flinched, looking away.

'That bad, eh?'

'Yeah, that bad,' he grunted, keeping his eyes averted. The walls of the restaurant had started spinning, melting the posters of flamenco dancers and matadors into streams of colour.

'But, actually, nothing really is that bad in the end, not once it's been said.'

'Is that so?' Dougie had to speak loudly to keep the words firm, to quell the up-rush of what felt like disintegration. Within this monumental effort lay mortification: for allowing such feelings to ambush him, emasculate him, in company. Sadness wasn't a thing he did publicly, ever, not even during his drinking days, apart from the one memorably terrible time in the wine-bar with Janine. 'I might seek out the Gents . . . if you'll excuse me.' The screech of his chair on the floor was piercing. Dougie walked slowly, the blood pounding in his ears. The room was full of obstacles – people, chairs, tables. The sign for the toilets came in and out of focus. He kept his eyes on it, walking slowly and unsteadily, each tread feeling like a stepping-stone across a torrent.

A skinny man in his twenties was at the furthest of the three urinals. Dougie went to a basin and kept an eye on him in the mirror, playing for time by washing his hands, willing him to hurry up and finish. He seemed to take an age, doing up his fly, running his fingers under both taps, drying them on two squares of paper, remoulding his quiff, tugging at his jaw. For appearance's sake, Dougie moved to the urinal, but nothing came out. When the door swung shut, leaving him alone at last, he zipped up his trousers and fell with both fists against the hard, tiled wall. He breathed hard, closing his eyes, counting to ten, then twenty, then thirty.

On entering the dining area a few minutes later, he found their table empty. He looked round to see Nina waving by the main door. He went to join her, feeling dazed still, almost punch-drunk. 'What about the bill?'

'All sorted. My treat. And don't quibble because that's always embarrassing. Now, then, my place or yours? Er . . . that was a joke, by the way,' she added, eyeing him uncertainly as they stepped out into the street. 'That said, I do tend to hit the herbal tea pretty hard about this time of day and you're welcome to join me. To be honest, you look like you need . . . something.'

Dougie nodded, offering a thin smile. 'What I'd really like is a cigarette. But they're also *verboten* these days.' He was aware of having to clench his teeth to speak. Something inside – some vital, tight, important part of him – was still shaking, a rope untethered, flapping. He wanted to go home but the thought of Stevie's coldness, the hum of her laptop behind her closed bedroom door, made it hard to breathe. 'Not tea, but maybe a coffee, if you've got it?'

Inside the car Nina pulled off the wig and tossed it onto the back seat. 'I'm sorry, but the fucker itches like hell.'

'Don't ever wear it, then,' said Dougie. 'Never wear it. Not if it's for other people's sake rather than your own.' He spoke harshly, firing the words out like a reprimand. To have minded what this good, kind, suffering woman looked like struck him now as the remote, ridiculous reaction of a simpleton – laughable, had it not been heinously offensive. The world was as fragile, precipitous, hostile as it had ever been. He had thought he could take it on but he couldn't.

'Stop at the next off-licence, would you? I feel a change of tactic coming on.'

'No need,' she said smoothly. 'I've got most things. Wine, gin, whisky, brandy, vodka –'

Dougie jammed his hands together in his lap. 'I'll probably go for the whisky in that case. Thanks.' He kept his eyes on the road, willing her to leave it at that, not to ruin things with any meaningful questions or clever comments.

The whiteness inside her house felt dazzling this time. It was unsettling, Dougie decided, like being shouted at in the same loud voice over and over again. He walked looking at his feet, shutting it out, wanting to think only of the thirst, raging, now that it was so close to being assuaged. It filled not just his mouth but his throat and chest and stomach; even the tips of his fingers tingled.

Her kitchen, a basement conversion like his, was less

white, more homely. It had a scruffy pine table, wicker chairs and a deep, wide-armed sofa filled with loose cushions. Nina opened the back door and gestured at the sofa, which was positioned alongside. 'Sit. Relax. I won't be a moment.'

Dougie did as he was told. Through the open door he could see a tumble of honeysuckle that was invisible from his side of the garden fence, so flower-heavy it leant towards him, its tentacle branches quivering, their snowy loads glowing softly in the dark. He breathed deeply, smelling the sweetness of the flowers in the cooling night air.

Nina reappeared at his side with a tray. 'One coffee – instant, I'm afraid. And one whisky. Five-year malt, or something – an old one of Trevor's. I'm not what you'd call an expert.' She set both drinks down on the wide arm of the sofa next to him and drew up one of the wicker chairs for herself, positioning it in the path of the open door, blocking his view of the garden. 'I'm not without good friends, by the way. Well, I've got one. And you only need one, really, don't you?' She blew at the steam rising off her mug of herbal tea. 'She's called Linda. Annoyingly, she fell in love with a New Zealander and now farms sheep in Auckland. We Skype. A lot. She totally gets me, funny stuff, bad stuff – she's my favourite person in the world. I'd hoped to find something similar with Trevor, but sex got in the way. I miss him, though. He had a way of laughing that I used to really like – a rumble that started in his tummy and came out in a big boom through his mouth and nose. And you miss Janine, I've noticed that. The way you said her name, I saw it then.'

Dougie was watching the whisky in the glass. She had

given him a good two inches. It looked beautiful: light, honey-gold. Next to it, the instant coffee was as appetizing as thin mud. The thirst seemed to have swollen his tongue now: it filled his mouth, pressing against his teeth, blocking his throat. Yet somehow he deferred the moment of starting, the inevitability of what would surely follow – the freefall, the consequences – producing a sort of suspenseful joy. He blinked at Nina, sitting with her thin arms wrapped round her legs, her mug resting on her knees, the smooth dome of her head outlined against the backdrop of the night sky. She had said things about friends, about Janine; good, true things. She was talking again, with shining eyes, about the girl in New Zealand, how they had met at primary school. Now, he thought. Now.

He turned for the whisky. It was still there, amber and solid. Another moment then; he would wait another moment. Instead of lifting the glass, he nudged it more into the middle of the sturdy sofa arm. *To a place of greater safety*, he thought, wondering where he had heard the phrase and liking it for its dark ironies. Looking up, he spotted a deep pockmark in the wall behind the sofa – a gash in the white paint, centred by a hole of pink, crumbling plaster. He swivelled further round, noticing several similar patches scattered across the wall.

'Er . . . yes, those,' Nina said mildly, following the line of his gaze. 'That was the night I flipped out at you and your wild party. A mallet, I'm afraid. Not my finest hour. The broom I used upstairs was a much better idea, in terms of damage limitation. It had been a bad day. Sorry.' She stretched out her legs, resting her feet on the sofa.

'No, don't be sorry.' Dougie carried on looking at the

wall, seeing not the fiasco of the cooking class that night but the full wine glass next to his plate. He had been reaching for it when Nina's hammering had started. With all the ensuing distraction, the temptation had passed, as temptation could, if ignored for long enough. Dougie tensed, aware that he was digging very deep inside himself, searching for something to hang on to. The point was he hadn't drunk the wine and he had been glad of it. Very glad. Yes, that was the point.

He turned back to face Nina. Setting his jaw, he reached across her feet for the mug of sludgy coffee, hooking his fingers tightly through the handle. It tasted as muddy as it looked. Time seemed to have slowed right down. He was aware of Nina watching him, as if she knew the difficulty of the choice he had made. It felt wonderful that she knew. It spread warmth inside him, a sense of true safety. She knew the world had dark places. She knew because she had visited them. And yet here she was still, strong, funny, warm-hearted, willing him on.

'Stevie had a little brother once,' he said, his voice a monotone. 'He died when he was five weeks old. A cot death, they said. But his blanket was half over his face, like he had burrowed under it. So he must have cried, fighting for breath. I'm sure he must have cried. But I didn't hear it. I was in charge and I didn't hear it. I told Janine to get some sleep in the spare room – said I'd do the night-feed, give her a break. Normally I'm a light sleeper, you see, except . . .' The tic was back behind his cheekbone, fluttering. '. . . except when I drink. And that night I drank. So I slept through . . . Janine was the one to find him.'

'Cot deaths are horribly common –'

'I slept through. I didn't hear him.'

'The heart just stops.'

'But if he did cry I wouldn't have heard.'

'It wasn't your fault.'

'So everyone said. But we'll never know, not really.'

Her wall clock filled the silence that followed – an old round mahogany-rimmed one with roman numerals. It reminded him of Sunday evenings in the kitchen at home, when *Songs of Praise* meant there wasn't even an excuse to have the telly on.

'What was he called?'

'Ross.' Dougie looked past her, towards the thicket of white flowers. 'And then in Spain, when Stevie ran away, I might have had a chance of hearing her but I'd had a drink, a skinful, and slept late. And I thought it had happened again, do you see? I thought it had happened again.'

'But it hadn't.'

Dougie nodded, swallowing spittle. 'No, but the way she's been ever since – it's like I've lost her anyway.'

'Oh, you poor love.' Nina pulled in her legs and dropped to a crouching position at his feet, where she picked up both his hands, sandwiching them between hers. She had small fingers, thin and bony, but he could feel the strength in them. After a moment she got up and returned to her chair.

Dougie pointed at the whisky, saying, in a muffled voice, 'Could you take that away, do you think?' He went and stood in the open door so that he didn't have to watch her empty the glass down the sink. One sip and he would have needed to smoke, but that felt a little easier too now, if only by a fraction. Outside, the temperature had dropped. Swatches of ragged cloud covered the moon. The honey-suckle flowers had turned grey. Dougie rubbed his bare arms and stepped back inside. Nina was standing closer than he expected – right behind him – with a look on her face that made him wonder, briefly, if, after all, she had expectations of him beyond what she claimed.

He hesitated, a trace of his old apprehension returning. He liked this woman. But he didn't want to have sex with her. It was a new combination; faintly exhilarating. He had told her of the blackest moments in his life and she had soaked it all up, contained it, made it seem not quite so unbearable. The sense of intimacy this had created, the hope, was still coursing through him, healing, a sort of unc-tion. To find that she wanted intimacy of a different kind in return would have been nothing short of heartbreaking.

'I think I'd better get going.'

'No, wait.' She put a palm on his chest, pushing him back down onto the sofa. 'Since we seem to be trading confessions, there's something I've decided to tell you. But you have to promise you won't go berserk.'

'And why would I do that?' Dougie replied, eyeing her with even more alarm.

She met his gaze coolly, her pupils huge and solemn. 'I swore to Stevie that I wouldn't say anything, you see. And I'm not in the habit of breaking oaths. But, here's the thing . . . It might be to do with why she ran away.'

Dougie crossed his arms so he could grip his elbows. 'Go on.'

'She had sex with someone in Spain.'

Dougie laughed, a reflex of shock quickly giving way to relief. 'Well, I suppose that's hardly so surprising –'

'Agreed. But they didn't use protection – idiot children – so there's a chance that –'

He was already shaking his head. 'Oh, Jesus, don't tell me she's –'

'That night she stayed it was still too early to know, of course. She wasn't sure, just afraid, and that's why she was crying . . . Yes, I *did* go in to see what was up. I couldn't not. It took a while but I got it out of her. She swore me to secrecy – said she'd get back to me if she needed my help. I can't tell you how terrified she was that you would find out. It made me think that maybe you were some kind of ogre after all, that there was some side to you I hadn't seen – but you're not,' Nina concluded simply, 'so that's why I'm telling you. And because, from what you've been saying tonight, it sounds like she might not be okay after all.'

'Right. I see. Well . . . thanks.' Dougie's head was spinning with all that had been going on at home, how it made sense. The thread of relief was still there. It was terrible, but it made sense. Having unprotected sex was one of the dumb things teenagers did; whatever transpired, it could be dealt with.

Nina had hurried across the room and was rummaging in a drawer. 'I bought one of these – in case. I told her to get one. I even offered money because they're not cheap, but she refused. So I got one anyway, as back-up. I've been loitering like mad, hoping she'd give me an update, but to no avail. Here. Take it. It's supposed to be a hundred per cent reliable.' She pressed the small oblong pregnancy testing kit into his hands.

Dougie got up from the sofa, still shaking his head. 'I'd better go,' he muttered.

'Er . . .' Nina hovered by the sofa, wringing her hands. 'Is this you going berserk? Tell me, Dougie, please, what's going on in that handsome head of yours. You're too tall for me to eyeball you properly, and if you give me the silent treatment I might start to wonder if you just think I'm a conniving –'

Dougie shut her up with a hug, squeezing as hard as he dared because of her delicate frame. 'You've been amazing, Nina – dinner, paying, which you shouldn't have done, thank you, and then afterwards, here . . . now . . . how you've been, what you've said, how you've listened. I can't tell you how much I appreciate it.' He waved the pregnancy testing kit, which rattled. 'And for this too. I'll report back. Okay? For female advice if nothing else,' he added grimly. 'In a little over twenty-four hours Stevie gets on a plane to visit her mother and if we don't know the score by then – and have a plan for dealing with it – the stuff will really hit the fan.'

Chapter Fifteen

Lidingö didn't feel like an island – at least, not in the slightly romantic way Janine had imagined it might. It was as solid and built-up as any other part of the city, and connected to the mainland via a long, sturdy, four-lane bridge. The house Mike's company had found for them, and which they had checked out during the course of their reconnaissance trip back in June, was only a five-minute walk from the nearest shore, on an attractive rocky outlook that faced the Baltic, a stretch of water busy with liners and cargo ships steaming in and out of Stockholm's main harbour; Janine found that she needed to remind herself of that sometimes, since any sightline, even from their top floor, was blocked by neighbouring houses occupying higher ground, and the endless pine trees that grew between them all, as tall as church steeples. A couple of times, when Mike was working late and the evening sunlight thinning, Janine – settled on the decking, glass of wine in hand, the scent of pine thick in her nostrils – had caught herself feeling almost hemmed in.

On the day Stevie was scheduled to arrive, she woke early, her chest so tight with anticipation she half wondered if she was falling ill. At the construction site in the next street the workers had already started – she could hear the drilling and, every so often, the dull vibrations of the explosives they used to tunnel foundations into the island's solid rock ground. They were building two more houses, two storeys, three bedrooms – identical to theirs. Next to her, Mike lay on his back, both arms neatly at his sides, pinning the duvet round him like a tight sleeping-bag. His capacity for deep sleep was astonishing, prodigious, maddening.

Janine slipped out of bed and padded down the hall to the bathroom. It was pine-walled, like the entire house, and with a small adjoining sauna – a cause of huge excitement when they had first arrived, but now filled with still-packed boxes, which Janine suspected might never be removed. Another early cause of excitement had been a lake on the island called Kottla, a blue jewel surrounded by pinewoods and fringed with slabs of smooth rock ideal for sunbathing and picnicking. During the first couple of weeks, when Mike was still on between-jobs leave, they had been there almost every afternoon, taking a hamper of cold meats and cheeses, along with bread and a cooler of wine, leaving their car in the roadside car park and picking their way to the waterside through the forest.

Janine tugged at her face in the mirror, baring her teeth. She couldn't wait to show Stevie around, to enjoy all over again the fun of discovery that she had shared with Mike. She rubbed the sleep from her eyes and splashed water on her face. But with her nose in the towel, she paused. Three weeks and then it would be over. Stevie would go back to England. The dread of it filled her slowly. With clumsy fingers she threaded the towel back onto the rail. Missing her daughter had not been part of the plan; missing her a bit, yes, but not as she had lately, with a sense of choking terror behind the pain, a terror of perhaps having taken

240

an irrevocable wrong turn, the point at which it had been made receding beyond reach.

Mike, who had lived in various countries, said it would get better, that there were peaks and troughs to settling in, that it took time. And although Janine knew this had to be true, she also couldn't help thinking that for Mike, with an office to go to – a familiar construct, with desks and meetings and people and routines and targets – it would always be a lot easier than for her, alone all day in a strange place, daunted by every humdrum thing, whether it was tracking down a dry-cleaner, understanding traffic systems, or finding her way round an alien supermarket, with prices that swam before her eyes and products she had to guess how to cook. A one-hour weekly language lesson had provided her with a friend of sorts, Esther, the Dutch wife of an English diplomat, who spoke impeccable English, but so far they had only exchanged pleasantries over a couple of coffees. There was a near neighbour who had also caught her attention, a handsome blonde woman with flinty blue eyes who always found the time to shoot her a smile as she herded her four white-haired elfin offspring in and out of a people-carrier. There was friendship there too, Janine was sure, if she could pluck up the courage to seek it.

'Hey, babe, up early.' Mike shuffled into the bathroom behind her and peed with his usual immodesty, carefully wiping a square of lavatory roll round the rim afterwards. 'I've decided to take the day off – come with you to Arlanda airport. I know you were worried about the drive, weren't you?' He reached round her to wash his hands. 'Getting through Stockholm and out the other side – could be tricky.'

'Yes . . . I . . . Thanks Mike, that's sweet.'

'You're sexy in the mornings, have I told you that?' He slid a hand under the curve of her buttocks. 'I hope you were planning on coming back to bed.'

'I'm going to make tea, then yes . . .'

'I can wait as far as the tea's concerned.'

'I can't.' She eased herself out of his arms, blowing a kiss through the banisters as she headed down to the kitchen. 'Back in five.' Out of earshot, Janine banged and clanged the kettle and crockery, venting anger at the wrecked prospect of meeting Stevie by herself and her own despicable ingratitude.

As things turned out, it was Mike, who – doubting her directions – took a wrong turn off the city ring road, almost making them late. Stevie appeared minutes after they had entered the arrivals hall, wearing an unattractive grey shell-suit Janine didn't recognize and dragging her huge suitcase on its two little wheels. She looked about her anxiously as she walked, her hair swinging across her face. Janine let out a shriek and charged towards her, checking herself at the last moment only because Stevie stopped, staring at her with wide eyes and a frozen face.

'Darling?' She was plumper, Janine noticed, with some surprise, and exhausted. Unless it was some new washed-out chic look she was trying for with smudged eye-shadow.

'Mum.' The word emerged as a sort of bleat. Then she fell against Janine, bursting into tears. Mike hung back, waiting for the hugging and crying to end, and when it didn't, he busied himself with the suitcase, leading the way back out to the car park. When the two women didn't follow, ducking into the Ladies instead, Janine throwing him a what-can-you-do glance, he called work and said it looked like he'd be coming in after all.

For the journey back to Stockholm Janine did most of the talking, describing things, sketching plans for the days ahead, asking about Spain and London. She was careful to include Mike in all that she said, turning to address Stevie on the back seat, but constantly saying 'didn't we?' and 'wasn't it?' and touching Mike's arm. When he pulled over near a convenient underground station for getting to his office, she kissed him on the lips before slipping behind the wheel. 'I thought we'd barbecue tonight,' she adjusted the car seat as she talked, 'get some sausages and steak. Hey, don't you want to get into the front now Mike's gone? No? Okay. Suit yourself. Swedish taxi driver at your service, madam.' Janine shifted her concentration to the traffic instead, which was heavy and fast-moving until they were safely on the Lidingö bridge.

'Not quite north London, is it?' She searched the rear-view mirror for her daughter's face, glimpsing only a bird's nest of hair. 'There are islands all over the place. One of them is called Skansen – it's, like, especially for tourists, with funfairs and shops and things – worth a trip, everyone says. I've been saving it to do with you. And then there's the old bit of the city – Gamla Stan. It's really beautiful. Mike and I had dinner there a couple of weeks ago – all cobbled streets and little boutiques.' As they passed the turning to Kottla, she explained about the lake, saying how hot the weather had been and how the forecast was for it to continue.

Once they were home, Janine carried on in the same determinedly enthusiastic vein, conducting a guided tour of the house – the box-filled sauna included – before letting Stevie retreat to her room to unpack. She then made herself a coffee and went to sit on the shady part of the decking, telling herself it was far too early for disappointment. Stevie was clearly exhausted, which was normal for a sixteen-year-old, even if it did make the mother in her want to get on the phone and interrogate Dougie as to exactly what brand of ridiculous, loose-reined parenting he had been pursuing for the last few weeks. Between sips of her coffee she kept an eye on the kitchen, willing Stevie to emerge with a smile on her face, and fending off darker, guilt-driven fears about the resentment her daughter might still be harbouring towards her for turning their lives upside-down.

'So, how's it been with Dad?' she prompted, when Stevie appeared at last, no smile in evidence and having changed from the shell-suit into a pair of tight denim shorts and a vest T-shirt that made it even more obvious that she had put on some weight. With her height she carried it off – just – but soon wouldn't, Janine realized, again thinking that a consultation with Dougie was required so that she could point out gently that there were pitfalls to a couch-potato teenager having an accomplished cook for a father.

'Dad's been great,' Stevie muttered, leaning against the wooden railing and flicking open the tab of the can of Fanta she had found in the fridge. She drank from it greedily, making small smacking noises. Watching, Janine found herself remembering the energetic thirst Stevie had always shown as a baby, how her throat and mouth had worked like a little double-piston at teats and beakers, not pausing to breathe till she choked.

'When's lunch?'

'Soon. It's just help-yourself salad and stuff . . . but, hey, what do you think of the house, your room . . . *Sweden*?'

Stevie peered over the balustrade of the decking at the garden – a small balding lawn fringed by rocks and a few hardy plants. 'Can I have some crisps now? I saw some in the cupboard.'

Janine looked at her watch even though she knew the time. 'Sure, if you can't wait. We'll be eating in half an hour or so. Then I thought we could go for a walk – there's a place only five minutes away where you get a really great view and can pick your way right down to the water. Though you'll need trainers,' she added, casting a doubtful look at Stevie's bare feet, the toenails ugly with the chipped remains of some black varnish.

'I'm not sure I'm in the mood for a walk.'

'Well, you might be after lunch. And there's no point in being here if you're not prepared to explore, is there?' Janine laughed quickly, trying to retract some of the harshness in her tone.

Stevie scowled. 'And I suppose I'm not allowed to smoke either.'

'Of course you're not allowed to smoke. What is this?'

'This, Mum . . .' she took a few steps towards Janine, viciously gouging her index finger into her chest '. . . is *me*. Remember ME, your annoying *child*?' She dropped the can of Fanta, which clanked down the steps onto the lawn, and ran back inside. A moment later the slam of her bedroom door reverberated through the patio doors.

Janine sat very still, gripping her empty mug, fighting

yet another violent urge to phone Dougie, not just to get a fuller picture but to hear his voice, hear his comfort. Inside her the guilt surged. Stevie was clearly unhappier than ever and it was her fault. She had left her daughter in England, dared selfishly to put her own needs first, and was now paying the price. And yet she had worked hard at factoring in Stevie's needs as well, Janine reminded herself, given her the chance to choose, helped her understand that the physical geography of their lives was a small and finite part of the immediate future, without the power to change anything long-term. Yes, Janine pondered miserably, she had tried to do it right. And so, to his credit, had Dougie. In fact, through the whole business he could not have been more supportive, of Stevie, of her. Yes, Dougie had been wonderful. Amid all her other churning emotions Janine found herself pausing to examine this realization, holding it up to the light as if it were a precious stone, seeing the depths of its beauty for the first time.

In her room, Stevie sat on the end of her bed, breathing hard. It was a double and very springy. Inlaid into the door was a full-length mirror. From where she was sitting her new belly-roll of flesh was clearly visible, sticking out between the bottom of her T-shirt and the top of her jeans – so disgusting that she had stopped wearing the rings in her belly-button for fear of drawing even more attention to it. She had thought she was pregnant. What a joke: 'eating for two' when in fact she was just a greedy pig.

Raising her head, Stevie studied her reflection squarely, her face flexed into an expression of pure revulsion. It had been easy to say Dougie had been great. He *had* been, and sort of hilarious, too, with his embarrassment and his Predictor kit and telling her about a hundred times that even if it was positive it would be okay, that they would work things out, that he still loved her just the same. He had even reminded her of how her own creation hadn't been exactly planned, but still remained the best thing that had ever happened to him and Janine. While Stevie had gone into the bathroom to do the business, peeing most of it on her hands because they were shaking so much, he had sat outside on the floor in the corridor, like some worried would-be dad, his back against the wall, his hands clasped round his long legs, his head bent, like he was praying. 'We'll look together, okay?' he'd commanded, before she went in. 'Bring it straight out here. I'm not having you waiting the full three minutes on your own.'

And when, even after five minutes, there had been only one pink window and not two, he had said, 'Bloody brilliant!' punched the air, then almost cracked her ribs he hugged her so hard. For a few wonderful moments Stevie had felt nothing but the relief too – a sort of ecstasy at being let off the hook. But then he had said he hoped that whoever it had been in Valencia knew what he had put her through and would she be seeing him again and did she want to go on the pill, and all the happiness had curdled.

The door to her bedroom opened slowly, removing her reflection and replacing it with the figure of her mother. She didn't look angry now, but soft-faced with shining eyes. She tapped her phone. 'I've just been speaking to Dad. He told me . . . about the pregnancy scare. He said he'd agreed to let you tell me in your own good time, if you wanted . . . but I'm afraid I wore him down.' She smiled, looking a little bit sorry, but mostly very pleased. 'You poor sweetheart, going through all that worry. The boy in Valencia, are you still in touch?'

Stevie shook her head, biting her lip, looking out of the window. Some things were unsayable, no matter how much you wanted to let them out. Her bedroom was at the back of the house, with a view onto the patch of forest that separated them from the neighbours in the next street over. On a balcony an old woman with prune skin and silver hair sat on an upright chair, knitting. The needles flashed in the sun. Her mother was talking again, about contraception, STDs and relationships, the words pouring out of her, as if she had been dying for years to say them.

'Spain wasn't my first time, Mum,' she said, in a bid to stop this flow.

'Oh. Right, I see. Well, in that case I hope you –'

'Hope I what?'

'Nothing. Just, well . . . I think we should get you on the pill. But even with that, you need to be careful, darling, with yourself, I mean, your *feelings*. Take it steady.'

'Be in *love*, you mean?' Stevie sneered.

Janine sighed and came to sit next to her on the bed, her weight on the soft mattress tipping them towards one another. She slipped both hands under her thighs and nodded wisely before responding. 'Not necessarily. Look, sex is about exploring, of course . . .'

Her mother's voice had shrunk to its most gentle timbre, spongy soft in its effort to communicate a capacity for limitless womanly understanding. Linked over the years to many 'difficult' conversations – bad news, parental edicts, the divorce – it was a tone that, for Stevie, had gradually come to have the opposite effect of its soothing intentions. 'There wasn't a boy in Valencia,' she snapped, before she could stop herself. 'It was after that.' She looked through the window for the knitting needles but the woman had gone. She let her gaze rest on a boulder of smooth grey rock instead, inwardly weighing up the truth of her claim about it not having been her first time. Like most of her girlfriends, sex had been on the agenda for a while, but in her case the full thing had only happened once, against a wall at Merryl's sixteenth birthday party. Both she and the boy in question had been quite drunk. The position had been awkward and he had come so quickly she wasn't even sure he had been inside her properly.

'But after Valencia, you . . .' There was a shadow of doubt across her mother's face now, as if the capacity for understanding might not be so limitless after all.

Observing this, Stevie felt almost sorry for her. She knew it wasn't yet too late, that she could still steer the conversation in any direction she chose, but for some reason she pressed on. She wondered many times afterwards why this was so. There was the bursting need to get it off her chest – the little-girl part of her wanting to confess – but something else was going on too, some ugly urge to blast the last trace of Oprah-Winfrey-I'm-listening smugness off her mother's face. And the view from the window – that had helped, too – the foreignness of it, which had engendered a sudden and unexpected sense of absolute protection, as if she was reporting on an incident in a parallel world.

'It was when I was with Dad. At the *finca*.'

'At the *finca*?'

'Actually, it was Simon.'

Janine seemed to pin her eyes to something on the skirting-board before slowly swivelling her head. '*Simon? As in Victoria and Simon?*'

Stevie felt afraid suddenly. She stood up and dug her cigarettes out of her handbag, lighting one with a shaky hand. 'Look, it wasn't like . . . I mean, it was totally . . . I mean, it was just stupid.' There was no relief, no good feelings at all. Her mother was looking as if a bomb inside her was exploding slowly, but worse than that was how saying it out loud had made it real again, taken her back to the long, hot afternoon and evening round the pool with Simon, drinking, first more beer, then vodka, supposedly waiting for news from the hospital, but actually not giving Ruth, or anyone else, a second thought. It *had* been stupid, but also — at least to begin with — a lot of fun. They had ended up trying to play table tennis, her so giggly she could hardly hold the bat, let alone hit a ball back. Simon had said did she need a beginner's lesson and come round behind her, taking her hands, like he was some kind of ping-pong maestro. It had seemed so funny. And even when he pulled out the bows on her bikini, she had found it hilarious, doubling over in a hopeless attempt to cover her modesty.

It was only when he backed her into the pool-house that she had stopped laughing, aware that things had skidded onto a new level. Half flattered, half curious, thinking a bit of kissing could do no harm, she had responded as she knew he expected her to, but suddenly the way he was touching her had got more urgent, much harder to extricate herself from, even if she had wanted to.

'Okay?' he had whispered, pulling back a little and stroking her arms, as if he sensed her doubt and cared about it.

'Okay,' she had answered, somewhat surprised at the clarity of her own voice, its ring of purpose. She had stood back and watched while he kicked together a make-shift bed of swimming towels and then, without any hesitation, stretched herself out on top of them.

'*Simon?*' Janine said the name with such sharpness this time that Stevie backed against the wall. 'When, for God's sake? How?'

'Look, Mum, I feel terrible, but it just sort of happened –'

'Just sort of happened?' she echoed, aghast. 'Did he . . . I mean, did you . . . ?'

'No one else was around . . . Both of us had had a lot to drink,' Stevie faltered, remembering how detached being drunk had made her, how she had felt as if she was watching Simon touch her rather than actually experiencing it. Even when he was on her – in her – it had never got to the point of feeling sexy or particularly *real*, not until it hurt and that was when he was finishing so it hadn't lasted long. Afterwards, back in her room, there had been a few spots of blood in her bikini bottoms, which explained the pain and confirmed her doubts about the thoroughness of her encounter during Merryl's party.

The business of feeling bad had only kicked in gradually, filling her like nausea as Simon had bundled the towels into the bottom of the laundry basket, then patted her stomach, saying in an uncertain voice how lovely it had been and that the thing about proper grown-ups was that they knew how to keep secrets.

'I feel sick about it,' Stevie told Janine, in a choking voice. 'In fact it wouldn't be possible to feel worse.' She tried to take a drag of her cigarette, but found herself gagging on the smoke. 'And you're not to tell Dad,' she sobbed. 'I need you to promise that, Mum. To *promise*, or I swear I'll . . .'

Janine stood up, looking dazed. Ignoring the lit cigarette, she gently cupped her palm round one side of Stevie's face, stroking her chin with her thumb. 'This matters, okay, sweetheart?' she said softly. 'It matters. And the thing with sex, unless it's forced . . . Stevie, was it forced?'

She shook her head miserably, the tears now streaming down her face. 'No. I – I agreed. It was my fault.'

Janine hesitated a moment before continuing, her voice strained but calm. 'The thing about sex – consensual sex, at least – is that it's always two people's fault. And when one of those two people is a girl, barely turned sixteen, and the other is a grown married man, not to mention your father's best . . .' She left the sentence hanging, lunged at the window to tug it open and pushed her head out into the warm afternoon air. She took several deep breaths, hunching and dropping her shoulders. 'You should have known better,' she gasped, 'but, dear God, so should he.'

Chapter Sixteen

'They've run out of paddle-boats – we should come back later.'

'We'll get a rowing-boat, then.'

'But you'll have to do all the rowing – I'm still too feeble.'

'I like rowing.'

'Have you even done it before?'

Dougie stood up to his full height, planting his hands squarely on his hips in a show of righteous indignation. 'Yes, I have, as a matter of fact, on holiday with my brother when I was eight, an oar each, which is harder. I seem to recall going round in a lot of circles.'

Nina laughed, nudging him to move as the queue for the ticket booth shuffled forwards. The heat-wave had reached its hottest temperature yet and the park was packed. One more couple and it would be their turn. 'Where was that, then, this circular rowing?'

'A river somewhere in Kent about a hundred years ago.'

'A brother, eh? Well, you've kept very quiet about him during the course of all our little chats, I must say. Is he younger or older, this brother?'

'Younger.'

'Mmm, even better.'

'And a pain in the arse.'

'That's a sibling's prerogative, isn't it? To be a pain in

the arse? Personally, I think I should have liked that far more than enduring the spotlight of being the Only Child, focus of all love and expectation. Bear that in mind for poor Stevie, won't you? Especially given that, for a brief period of her short life, she *wasn't* the only one.'

Dougie widened his eyes, inwardly marvelling at how Nina seemed to get away with saying things no one else could, still uncertain whether it was a gift she had or sheer bloody-mindedness.

'What does he do now, this brother?' she went on evenly.

'Shoots at people. Iraq, Afghanistan, Germany.'

Nina squinted up at him from under the rim of the yellow baseball cap she was wearing. 'Bloody hell, Dougie, what a worry. Sorry, I had no idea.'

'Don't go all dramatic on me,' he muttered. 'I suppose a part of me does worry – sort of – like a hum in the background, but to be honest, we don't really keep in touch.'

'What? Not even emails?'

'Not even emails.' They had reached the booth at last. Dougie disregarded Nina's attempts to pay and secured the hire of a rowing-boat for one hour. A young boy with pockmarked skin then delivered some over-rehearsed stale patter about health and safety before handing over two life-jackets and pointing out a free vessel.

'God, the seat's sopping,' Nina squealed, jumping up and then quickly sitting back down as the boat rocked.

'Steady,' Dougie warned, laughing as he tried to get to grips with the oars, aware that the ready audience of the queue was enjoying the spectacle. 'If we're going to capsize – which might even be nice on a day like this – could we make sure it's somewhere a little less *public*?'

Nina saluted. 'Aye-aye, Captain. By the way, I can't swim.'

Dougie whistled. 'Now she tells me. Well, you'd better do your bloody jacket up tightly in that case, hadn't you? Saving lives not being my forte,' he grunted, wrestling next with the rowlocks, which were very loose. The boat, meanwhile, drifted away from the queue and came to a halt against a flat bank of mud where several sunbathing Canada geese started to unfold themselves, eyeing them warily. 'Ruining lives, now, yes. There I have a skill.'

Nina pushed up the rim of her cap and sat forwards. 'Janine being the primary case in point, I suppose.'

'Yes, clever clogs. Though there are others.' Dougie kept his attention on the rowlock screws, which were resisting his efforts to tighten them.

'Well, from what I've managed to whittle out of you over the last few days, I would say Janine doesn't sound remotely ruined,' Nina replied lightly, scooping some water into her hand and flinging what she could of it at Dougie. 'Quite the opposite, in fact. She has a lovely new man, with whom she's enjoying a lovely new life, a fabulous – happily *un*-pregnant daughter – and, by way of the icing on the proverbial cake, her ex-husband still in her thrall. All in all, I would say that lady has got it *made*.'

'I am *not* in her thrall,' Dougie scoffed, giving up on the screws and starting to row. 'And you've got a bloody cheek, twisting things I might have said and hurling them back at me. I'll think twice next time.'

Nina grinned. 'No hurling intended, I promise. We've done some talking, that's all, and talking is *always* good.' She sat back in the front V of the boat, looking smug, trailing both hands in the water on either side of her. She was wearing huge bug-like sunglasses, which, in combination with the yellow baseball cap, made her pale skin look a drained greyish-white. Her bare legs, visible between the hem of a voluminous pair of denim dungaree-shorts and grey ankle socks tucked into thick-soled hiking boots, were also pitifully chalky and as thin as her arms, more like the limbs of a prepubescent girl than a woman in her thirties. Dougie understood (because she had been at pains to explain it more than once now) that the slightness of her was a temporary thing, arising out of the havoc the chemo had played with her appetite, but it was still a sight that pained him. So much so that he had found himself undertaking the small, private challenge of rectifying the situation, a decision that had been largely responsible for the recent blossoming of their acquaintance.

'You are what you eat,' he had scolded, presenting himself on her doorstep with a stack of Tupperware boxes on the day after he had posted Stevie off to Sweden, having spent several hours conjuring various dishes that he hoped would be light and tasty enough to satisfy his neighbour's picky needs. 'So I hope these appeal,' he had added, bashful suddenly as he handed over the boxes, which contained a smoothie of berries, mint and honey; a tomato and Gruyère tart, the pastry handmade and flavoured with Dijon mustard; a fast-melting mango sorbet; and a fresh batch of the wafer-thin vanilla biscuits of which she had declared herself so fond.

Nina had been so visibly stunned that Dougie had been glad he could divert her from his offerings with the happy news of Stevie's negative pregnancy test. In subsequent days, he had enjoyed thinking up new dishes to please her – hopping over the front fence with more plastic boxes – between his classes and catering commitments. Sometimes he stayed for coffee and one of their talks, but the real pleasure continued to be Nina's nonplussed delight; she was running out of fresh expostulations of gratitude at his presentation of each new dish.

'So, when are you going to stop stuffing me with food?' she had enquired lazily that afternoon, during the course of the picnic that had preceded joining the queue for the boats. She had eaten so much of his beetroot and goat's cheese salad that she was lying flat on her back in the grass, rubbing her stomach and cheerfully bemoaning her gluttony.

'When you're fully better.'

She giggled. 'Silly Billy, don't you realize that will just make me malinger? Talk about creating a rod for your own back. Besides, you might make me fat.'

'No chance.'

'Hey, is that why Janine left?' she teased. 'Did you make her fat too?'

'I did not.' Dougie, who was also lying on his back, had turned and squinted at her. 'Janine could never get fat – she's too tall, and one of those types who burn a lot of energy.'

'So what made her leave?'

'Let me see now.' Dougie propped himself up on his elbow, plucking a grass stem and chewing it while he pretended to think hard. 'It could have had something to do with the fact that I was a lying, cheating bastard.'

'Sounds a reasonable assumption.'

'And a drunk.'

Nina swatted her hands to dismiss the subject. 'I get the picture. Let's go back to discussing how long you're prepared to commit to pampering my damaged taste-buds.'

Dougie rolled onto his back. He was glad Nina had backed down. Her interest in Janine unsettled him, mostly because of the things he found himself saying in response to her comments. The truth was he had been thinking more and more about his ex-wife in recent weeks, almost as if the geographical distance between them had forced on him some paradoxical need to focus on what had gone wrong; on what had been lost. 'Okay, back to those pesky taste-buds it is.' He kept his face to the sky, narrowing his eyes until it reduced to a thin blue line. 'Let's say, assuming work doesn't go mental, because obviously I shall always put my bank manager's, not to mention my landlord's, happiness before yours –'

'Obviously.'

'Then let's say I shall continue the meals-on-wheels service until your hair has all grown back.'

'Will you? Wow. But to how many inches? That's the question.'

'Three, maybe four . . . five at a pinch.'

'Whoopee.' She sat up and slapped her thighs. 'That could take months. Although it's made a start. Look.' She took off her cap and leant nearer, blocking out the sky. A fine layer of sandy fuzz was now sprinkled like gold-dust across her scalp. 'Apparently it can be curly when it re-grows. I've always wanted curls. What do you think? Is there any sign of bendiness in my follicles?'

Dougie squinted. 'Bendiness in the follicles, eh? It all appears pretty un-bendy to me. But it's early days. Hang on in there.' He kissed her head and levered himself into a sitting position. 'Hey, when will you go back to work, do you think?'

'Not sure.' She plucked a cherry from one of the picnic boxes.

'Presumably they're keeping the job for you, though.'

'Yeah, I've got a while yet.'

'And have you always wanted to be a librarian?'

She laughed, throwing the cherry at him. 'You think it's a lame career, don't you?'

'No, I don't.'

'Yes, you do.' She threw another cherry, which Dougie caught nimbly in his mouth. 'I did too, once,' Nina admitted, 'until I started it, which was after I got sick. It was local, part-time, not too taxing, dealing with books, DVDs – I *love* books and DVDs. It was perfect. Before that, during the Trevor days, I was an events organizer, so there. Very high-powered, buzzy and stressy, just what an emancipated girl is supposed to dream of. I loathed every moment.'

'Do you think that might have contributed to you getting ill?' Dougie ventured, cautious as ever on the subject she was always instructing him to avoid.

Nina had frowned, keeping her attention fixed on a small hole she had started gouging in the earth with a twig. 'I think that *not* doing it has definitely helped me get better. I also think we should pack up this lot and hire a paddle-boat.'

By now Dougie had rowed the length of the boating

lake, his shoulders were stiff and he was sweating hard. His palms were starting to hurt too, sprouting red lumps that, with only a little more exertion, were clearly going to turn into blisters. Steering into a bird-free section of bank, safely out of the way of other boats, he shipped his oars, shook off the life-jacket and peeled off his shirt. 'Apologies. Needs must. Christ, it's hotter than bloody Alicante.'

'Don't apologize,' Nina murmured, her expression inscrutable behind the beetle lenses. She settled deeper into her V seat, pulling the peak of her cap down over her face and folding her arms across her chest. 'Time for a snooze, I think.'

Dougie splashed a couple of handfuls of lake water over his face and flicked some at her legs.

'Bugger off,' she growled, not moving. 'By the way, that pregnant friend of yours who had the car accident, how's she doing?'

'Great. She's had the baby – early, so they're keeping her in, but Gary says they're both doing fine. It's a girl. Polly.'

'That's brilliant.'

'Yes, isn't it, after all they've been through?' Dougie hesitated, remembering his promise about delivering the coin to Simon and feeling bad. He had decided to do it in person but Simon and Victoria still appeared to be away, either because of some new jaunt or because the week in Scotland had been extended. He had sent a couple of texts but heard nothing.

'That brother of yours,' Nina said next, her voice muffled from under her hat, 'you should make it up with him.'

'I've tried.' Dougie couldn't help bristling at the sudden

change of tack, which had been abrupt even for Nina. 'Not recently. But I've tried. He's the one who doesn't want contact with me.'

'And why's that?'

'Stupid ancient history, that's why. He and my father always had a bit of a mutual-admiration thing going . . . Believe me, it was no fun. Then I nicked one of his girl-friends . . . well, fiancée, actually, but I didn't know it at the time and they were both still in their teens.' He paused, giving time for the inevitable sarky come-back. 'Then I started making a lot of money,' he went on, when Nina remained silent, 'getting talked about, and I think maybe he got jealous.'

She peered at him over her sunglasses. 'Well, that, at least, wouldn't be a problem now, would it?'

'How kind of you to remind me.' Dougie smiled in spite of himself. 'Though it might interest you to know that I am almost debt-free, these days. As of this morn-ing, I've even paid the friend of the friend who designed my website.'

'You should make up with him, Dougie,' she cut in, ignoring this attempt at deflection. 'He might die any day – one of those roadside bombs – then you'd feel shitty about it for the rest of your life. Crap happens. Look at Ruth and Gary, and they were in north London, not Afghanistan.'

'Yeah, well, they're fine, aren't they? And James isn't in Afghanistan at the moment, he's in Germany. Just outside Münster, to be precise. He's been there for nearly two years.'

'I don't care where he is. You should still make it up. We're a long time dead et cetera.'

'Are you familiar with the phrase "Mind your own business"?' Dougie countered, an edge of real irritation in his tone.

'Yes, boss.' She settled back in her seat, unruffled as always, then grew so still under the protective peak of her baseball cap that Dougie assumed she really was having one of her sleeps.

A pleasant, sturdy breeze was picking up, rippling the water and bobbing the boat against the bank. Chilled suddenly, Dougie slipped his shirt back on, did a few shoulder rolls and flexed his hands. He was steeling himself to pick up the oars again when his mobile rang.

'Dougie, it's me.'

'Hey there. Did it go all right after we spoke the other day? Is *she* all right? I've been resisting getting in touch – assuming no news is good news – giving the pair of you *space*. Worth some Brownie points or what?' From out of the shrubbery on the bank next to him, two little black coots appeared, bouncing at each other and shrieking.

'What is that? Where are you?'

'Er . . . at this exact moment, I'm on a boat in Regent's Park. But don't worry. I'm parked – and with a life-jacket to hand.'

'So, not alone, in that case.'

Dougie looked across the water towards the footbridge. Behind it, over the tops of the trees, he could see the zigzag netting top of the Snowdon Aviary at London Zoo. Above it, the sky, a solid Wedgwood blue for so many weeks that he had come to take it for granted, had turned a gun-metal black. 'Not alone, no.' From her prone position under her hat, Nina slowly raised one hand and waved.

'Oh, you're with the journalist.'

'No, Janine, I am *not* with the journalist – and who the hell told you about her anyway?'

'Oh, I hear things.'

'Well, for your information, I'm with my neighbour. Stevie might have mentioned her . . .' Dougie hesitated. If Nina hadn't been within earshot, he would have had a stab at explaining the situation better; to boast how he seemed to have made a new friend – a real friend, who happened to be female and rather frail; who was honest and funny and undemanding and supportive, all the things, in fact, that he had only experienced with one person in his life before, but then managed to trample on and throw away.

'No, Stevie has not mentioned your neighbour,' Janine replied tartly, crushing any desire in him to explain anything.

Nina was sitting up properly and staring at the plate of black cloud, rolling towards them now, like some giant sliding roof. The wind was starting to whisk up the water with serious force, beating it into little eddies. Along the paths and across the grass people everywhere were hurrying to get away, gathering up blankets, deck-chairs, balls, papers, food, pets and children.

'Look, Janine,' Dougie murmured, 'if it's not urgent –'

'Oh, no,' she cried, hurt and breezy, 'not urgent. Sorry to disturb. Perhaps you could give me a call back when you're not so busy.'

'I'm in a frigging rowing-boat, Janine, with the heavens about to open and someone who is not in the peak of health. I'll call you as soon as I get home.' Dougie grimaced at Nina, who had been watching him, her expression neutral. He picked up the oars, glad of having them to squeeze. Even the pain in his palms felt good. He pulled hard against the choppy water, hauling the boat bumpily back across the lake.

The rain started, gently. Nina took off her cap and sunglasses and tipped her face to catch the drops. 'Trevor found someone else, so it was easy.'

'Well, Janine has found someone else, but it's not remotely easy. It's never fucking easy. Because we have Stevie. And because Janine's a nice person. Really nice. Every bad thing about her, she learnt from me.' To his surprise, Nina burst out laughing.

'Whoa now. You're not blooming Atlas – the world on your back. Lighten up. Let others take their share. The saintly Janine will have had nasty stuff inside her, too, right from the start. Everybody does. It's how it balances out that counts, how you keep it in its place.' As she spoke the rain began to pelt with real ferocity, drenching them in seconds, spattering off the boat, drilling the water.

Nina threw down her cap and leapt to her feet, making the boat lurch. 'God, don't you love this? I love it,' she shrieked, spreading her arms, perhaps for balance, though she looked as if she would embrace the whole storm if she could.

Dougie set his shoulders into the task of pulling the oars, a real labour now in the wind and the rain. Nina stayed upright, swaying stiffly, like some proud carved figurehead on a mighty vessel, much to the consternation of the life-jacket helper, who stood on the jetty signalling reprimands, the edges of his long orange cagoule dripping.

Simon sat in the car, playing solitaire on his phone and listening to a local radio station. It was their last day, the extended second week done with. They had checked out of the little lodge of a hotel and had stopped by Rosemount so that Victoria could say goodbye to her mother. Simon had done his bit, putting his head round the door to offer a cheery farewell before leaving her to it. He had also sat with the old bird a couple of times during the course of their stay, managing a show of merriment and some mind-numbingly dull conversation, while privately vowing that he would cut his wrists long before he ever allowed himself to be parked in an armchair among other lost souls, watching television. He didn't care about all the things that were supposed to be so great and soothing – the things that Victoria now raved about: the view of the purple-heathered mountains, the excellent organic food, or the quality of the psychiatric care. In Simon's view the place was Hell in a flimsy disguise – a way, he couldn't help suspecting, for Charles to get his wife of forty years off his hands, probably allowing easier access to some mistress he kept in London. Victoria's mother had always been a bit of a gloomy goat, so who could blame him?

Simon knew better than to share such subversive thoughts with his wife. She would, naturally, have been appalled, loving her father as she did, assuming him to be a gentleman of honour. She valued old-fashioned things like honour, did Victoria; it had always been one of the most appealing and daunting things about her. Simon had no desire to shatter such illusions, or to jeopardize the new understanding that the trip seemed to have wrought between her and her mother; a sort of peace, Victoria described it, not, as far as Simon understood, from any 'miracle' cure or sudden improbable filial bonding, but simply because the combination of drugs and therapy seemed to be working against the depression.

'And Miles probably had it too,' Victoria had reported elatedly, after one of her talks with the doctors. 'It's why he couldn't cope with life, why it all ended the way it did. I think maybe Mum always knew it, that she may even have felt guilty for having passed it on. That's why she finds it so hard to speak about him.'

Privately Simon doubted so easy a retrospective appraisal of his wife's tricky family. He had once got on quite well with Miles and could recall little sign of a depressive nature: he had been a laugh, his brother-in-law, game for anything, but also a spoilt public-schoolboy with more money than sense. By his early twenties he had fallen in with the wrong crowd and not had the strength of character to haul himself out of it. That was how Simon had always viewed the tragedy. When the addiction had asserted the truly ugly side of its stranglehold – the stealing and lying, the disappearing acts followed by begging phone calls, usually to Victoria, usually in the small hours – Simon had been one of the first to lose patience, and hope. Indeed, the inevitable fatal overdose had come almost as a relief – the only solution for putting everyone out of their misery.

But that wasn't something he was going to own up to either, Simon mused, smiling and waving as Victoria appeared at the top of the steps of Rosemount's grand front entrance. He had agreed with the depression theory and would continue to do so. Keep life sweet: that was his motto now more than it had ever been. Do not look for problems: there were enough trip-wires scattered around without the need to go hunting for any extras.

As his wife approached the car, Simon was aware of his smile freezing slightly. Stevie, giggly and tipsy in her tasselled bikini at the *finca* poolside, had been a trip-wire, of the most explosive kind. Having spotted it, Simon knew he should have backed off, stepped over or round the damn thing. And yet, try as he might, it was hard to regret the encounter. She had been taut-soft to touch, like a just-ripe peach; absurdly young, of course – but in spite of that wonderfully *knowing* somehow, as well as irrefutably, irresistibly compliant. Oh, no, it was hard to regret. There had been guilt at first, inevitably. Truckloads. He had found himself being extra nice to Victoria on account of it. But as the days in southern Spain had unspooled this had given way to the sharp fear of being found out. Maintaining some distance between him and Dougie had felt like the only – albeit desperate – measure to take. The Scotland trip had been a blessed help.

But now, after fourteen days' seclusion at their lakeside retreat, Simon's anxieties on that score had receded pleasantly. Dougie was the very last person Stevie was likely to open up to on such a subject, he reasoned. The odd schoolmate, maybe, but not her father. The girl was too independent, too feisty. Which was precisely why what had happened had happened.

And he was a *good* husband, he reminded himself, leaning across the passenger seat to open the car door for his wife. Lately Victoria had told him so, many times. And if she believed in him, what else mattered? It took more than one self-indulgent misdemeanour to make a 'bad' man.

'Okay?'

'Ish.' Victoria got into the passenger seat quickly and closed the door. 'She was sad I was leaving, I could tell.'

She pulled a tissue out of her cardigan sleeve and blew her nose.

'Hey, cheer up. She'll be fine.'

'I know.'

'She's in the best place – you said.'

'Yes, she is.'

'And you've had some good talks, even about Miles.'

'Good talks, yes.'

'And whenever she wants she can go home.'

Her lips trembled. 'God, Simon, I think I'm the one who needs drugs and therapy. I've spent so much of my life not really liking her, blaming her, and now I realize it's so much more complicated than that. Do you know, I think she must always have been a bit jealous of me and Dad – the way we get on, how protective he is of me? Can you imagine how difficult that would be as a *wife*? Especially if you felt like you needed protecting yourself.'

'Absolutely.'

'I mean, for a mother to envy her daughter and her husband . . .' She shuddered. 'You'd better make sure that never happens to us.' She reached across the gear-stick and nestled against him. 'I mean, if we have a little girl, you'll always want to look after me, won't you?'

'Always,' Simon echoed thickly, while inside a tendril of the old worry snaked its way back up through his peace of mind. Being cocooned by a Scottish lake was one thing, but who knew what awaited them in the outside world? He even felt an ache of longing for the tick of boredom that had been haunting him in the run-up to Spain. There was a lot to be said for dullness, he mused, if it had the tag of security attached to it.

Driving slowly, with needless obedience, he followed the white exit arrows directing them out of the almost empty car park. He let the steering-wheel slide loosely between his hands, at the same time undertaking the private challenge of trying to summon a clear picture of Stevie's face and immediately feeling better when he couldn't. Nearly a month had passed, after all. He might never be able to regret it, but the incident certainly needed to be left behind. It was reassuring to find that his memory was already complying with this necessity, confirming the happy truth that all difficult memories could be forgotten eventually, if left alone – given distance – for long enough.

'To boldly go to Glasgow,' he declared, feeling much more cheerful as he edged out of the gates at last and accelerated up the narrow lane.

Thirty minutes later, emerging out of the winding valley onto the main road, their phones began chiming and buzzing with messages.

'Talk about a welcome back to the big bad world,' Victoria exclaimed, laughing, as she started to scroll through her inbox. 'Phew, nothing here that can't wait. Do you want me to check yours? In case there's anything urgent – like with the TV people or something?'

'Nah, I'll take a look later.' Simon tucked his phone between his thighs.

Within minutes it started to rain hard. Caught behind a truck, its wheels sloshing water, Simon was forced to slow right down and put the windscreen wipers on at their full manic speed. On the roof the water drummed like the fingers of some giant impatient hand.

'Back to reality, I suppose,' said Victoria, a little bleakly this time, using her tissue to wipe a smeary porthole in the steam on her window.

'If I can get past this fucking lorry, that is. Ah . . . here we go.' The road suddenly widened into a stretch of dual carriageway. Simon changed down a gear and shifted lanes, giving the truck driver a wave as they swept past.

At the airport he did a speedy and covert check of his phone's inbox while they waited to load their bags, but there was nothing to fuel his fears. Dougie had clearly tried to get in touch a few times, but left a couple of straightforward texts, asking him to call on his return. There were also attempts at contact from Gary, and two messages, one saying he had managed to prang the car in a nasty dust-up with a van but that both he and Ruth were fine, the second reporting the early but safe arrival of their baby. Simon broke the news to Victoria, who hugged him, her eyes moist and shining.

'Polly? How sweet. How absolutely *sweet.*'

The cabin crew were demonstrating safety techniques when Simon's phone beeped with the arrival of a fresh text from Dougie. A jaunty steward, his face smooth and spray-tanned, leant over their seats, chirruping, 'All electronic goods switched off now, please, sir.'

Simon read the message quickly before obeying.

'Everything okay?' Victoria asked, through a yawn, dropping her head onto his shoulder.

'Yup, fine.' Simon turned to look out of the window, glad to have a view to study while a fresh, irksome ripple of unease played itself out. *Call me asap bastard,* Dougie had written. Dougie always called him names, didn't he? Simon's eyes glazed as the concrete airport buildings sped past and the plane gathered speed. *Bastard.* Yes, that was an endearment he and Dougie used with each other all the time. It expressed the rough, sparring nature of their friendship.

Next to him Victoria righted herself with a contented sigh. As the plane heaved itself off the runway, nosing towards the sky, she found his hand. 'A great holiday,' she whispered. 'The best.'

Simon nodded, keeping his eyes on the fog of grey cloud filling his window as an unexpected and uncharacteristic nausea swelled inside his gut. He wouldn't be sick. He was never sick. It was like anything else in life: mind over matter. Saliva flooded his mouth but he swallowed it. Travelling on an empty stomach, that was the trouble. It was hours since they had had breakfast. A British Airways sandwich and he would be himself again.

Chapter Seventeen

Gary opened the door, his normally jovial face sallow, his eyes red-rimmed, his big square head brutally exposed by a fierce haircut that had reduced his trademark curls to tight waves. 'Victoria. Simon. Nice of you to come.' He delivered the greeting in a dry, flat way that immediately made Victoria wonder if she hadn't pushed him too hard on the phone. It was the day after their return from Scotland and she had called to ask if they might make an early-afternoon visit, persisting through Gary's hints of reluctance and the news that Ruth was with Polly, having some sort of check-up at the hospital.

'We won't stay long,' she exclaimed, kissing him, trying to make up for it. 'We just wanted to see *one* of you – didn't we, Si? – and to say well done and thank goodness, after the time you've had, and to give you these.' She handed him two small parcels of pink tissue paper trailing pink ribbons; one contained a soft grey elephant, the other a pair of socks so small they would have fallen off her thumbs.

'Ruth's still at the hospital,' Gary said, hugging Simon with a fervour that seemed to catch Simon by surprise, then ushering them inside. 'I don't know how long they'll be.'

'Yes, you said on the phone. That's fine.'

Gary ran a hand over his newly shorn head, looking dazed. 'It's been great having Polly home, but she's seems

very unsettled, crying all the time, and Ruth's being struggling with the feeding –' He broke off to introduce a
stocky man with a ruddy complexion and short, peppery
hair who appeared at the end of the passageway. 'Ian, this
is Simon and Victoria – I think you might all have met at
our wedding. And they were in Spain with us. Remember
we told you?'

'Hello.' The man hung back, giving them a wave. 'Val's
making tea. I'll see if she needs a hand.' He ducked through
a doorway, managing to catch his foot on Lois, who was
slumped along the skirting-board just outside it. The dog
yelped, and got up to follow Gary as he led the way into
the front room.

'In-laws,' Gary mouthed, rolling his eyes and looking
much more like his usual self. 'Driving us *mad*, but what
can you do? And with all the toing and froing from the
hospital, they have been useful,' he admitted, sinking into
a chair with a sigh, 'especially with this princess.' He stuck
out a foot and pummelled Lois's belly. The dog panted at
him, pleased. 'Thanks for these.' He indicated Victoria's
tissue parcels, which he had put on the coffee-table. 'I'll
save them for Ruthie.'

'And you're suing that bloody van, I hope,' said Simon,
with some energy. He had taken up a stance by the mantelpiece where he was fiddling with the array of 'New
Arrival' cards.

'Probably not,' replied Gary, wearily. 'It was one of
those accidents where it's not exactly clear who's at fault –'

'The main thing is that nobody was hurt,' Victoria
interjected, shooting Simon a look. 'And, Gary, if there's
any day-to-day stuff that *we* could help with . . .'

'God, no, thanks, Vic, we're swimming in help.'

As if on cue, his mother-in-law sailed into the room bearing a tray of mugs. 'Here we are,' she sang, 'tea all round. I'm Valerie, by the way, Ruth's mum. Though I think we have met, haven't we? At the wedding? Help yourself to sugar. I gave you both milk – I hope that was right.' She bustled between them, taking command in a shrill voice that made Victoria careful not to catch Simon's eye. She did indeed remember Valerie from Ruth and Gary's wedding, mostly on account of the dress she had worn, which had been fuchsia, with an extravagant fascinator to match. She was dressed strikingly now, her barrel-waisted figure squeezed into close-fitting black jeans and a pink T-shirt sprinkled with sequins. Her hair was long and lavishly coloured honey gold, shaped into artful flicks and curls that drew attention away from the heavy age-lines of someone clearly well into their sixties. With the image of her own mother's frailty – white-haired, stick thin, sunken-eyed – still so vivid, Victoria found herself drinking in the details with some wonderment.

'They'll want to see the pics, Gary,' Valerie announced, dropping to her knees to riffle through a pile of papers on the coffee-table. 'Ah, here we are.' She plucked a fat envelope out of the pile and made her way on all fours to Victoria's chair. 'You have to see – she's such a poppet.' She handed over each photograph individually, although they were all more or else identical. 'These are the very early ones. I took them on my phone and printed them off on Gary's computer. Isn't technology wonderful?'

'Yes,' Victoria whispered, aware that the snaps of the pixie-faced little Polly during her first hours appeared to be making her feel queasy. Or maybe it was the new grand-mother's perfume, which was pungent and overpowering. 'Gosh. Lovely. So small. Heavens.' She looked to Simon for support, but he had slipped from the mantelpiece to talk to Gary on the sofa.

'God, that was grim,' Simon muttered, once they had hurried through the rain to their car some ten minutes later, an escape he had taken it upon himself to engineer with talk of his work commitments.

'What do you mean "grim"?' Victoria said crossly, not sorry to be out of the stuffy sitting room, but wishing they could have hung on longer for Ruth and the baby. Simon had produced the leave-taking excuses without so much as catching her eye. 'They've found true love, survived a load of last-minute scares, had a child – I'd call that pretty wonderful.'

'Yes, yes, yes. Gary, Ruth, baby, wonderful,' Simon replied testily, 'but, Jesus, those parents of hers.'

'They're thrilled and just trying to help,' Victoria muttered, aware that her emotions were crackling out of control, stirring the vague urge – the first in months – to pick a fight.

'Well, obviously.'

They drove the rest of the way in a tense silence and were right outside their block, a free permit-holder's slot in sight, when Simon suddenly pulled over to the opposite side of the road. He told her to jump out and go up to the flat without him as he had thought of a couple of things he needed from the stationery shop. 'Paper, print cartridges.'

Victoria laughed, a little scornfully. 'But that's round the corner. You don't want to take the car, surely.'

'Yes, yes – I mean, I might as well. I'm out of everything and need to stock up. There's always a parking space round there and I have no desire to get drenched.' He peered gloomily through the windscreen, which was a lot clearer than it had been when they had started out, the rain having reduced to a drizzle. The wipers, squeaking with every swipe, had been doing little to alleviate Victoria's irritation.

'If you want to be on your own, Simon, just say so.'

He slapped the steering-wheel. 'Of course I don't want to be on my own. I want to spend every waking – and sleeping – hour of the rest of my life with you. Okay? Even,' he added, exhaling, and speaking much more gently, 'when you're being weird, like today.'

'*I*'m being weird?

Behind them a bus was snorting fumes, unable to pass.

'Okay, see you in a minute, then,' Victoria said curtly, getting out of the car and offering a wave of apology to the bus driver as she crossed the road.

On the steps of their block she noticed a large old-fashioned bicycle chained to the railings with a plastic bag over its seat, but didn't equate it with its owner until she was through the main door and staring at Dougie, halfway up the first flight of stairs in a sodden brown jacket and blue jeans darkened with water.

He turned quickly, looking surprised and faintly guilty. 'Hi, Vic. I was just going up to try your door. Someone was coming out as I arrived so I didn't bother with the intercom. Is Simon upstairs?' He had made his way down the stairwell towards her, but then stopped on the bottom step, clutching the newel post and pushing self-consciously at his hair, which was sticking in wet clumps to his forehead.

'Hi, Doug. No, were you expecting him to be?'

'Well, no, I was just passing and . . . Never mind. Another time.' He pushed off the banister and deposited such a cursory, awkward kiss on her cheek that, for one painful, fleeting moment, Victoria even thought he might be drunk, doing the thing drunks did of behaving with exaggerated normality in the hope of covering up the fact.

'Come on up for a coffee,' she said warmly, starting up the stairs. 'He won't be long. He's just nipped round the corner to the computer shop. He'd be annoyed to miss you.'

'Would he?'

She laughed. 'Of course. We only got back from Scotland yesterday.'

'How was that?'

'Fantastic, thanks. And today we've just been to see Gary. He looked happy, but pretty frayed. Are you coming or what? I always walk it.'

'Okay, then, thanks.'

Once they were in the flat she took his sodden jacket from him, holding it at arm's length. 'I might hang that in the bathroom if you don't mind. Tea or coffee?'

'Just water, please.'

'Water? Are you sure?'

Victoria returned from the bathroom with a large, freshly laundered towel, which she placed on one of the sitting-room armchairs. 'Here, sit on that . . . if you want to sit, that is . . .' Dougie had taken himself over to the windows and was staring out across the balcony into the grey, scratchy expanse of rain. 'Because your trousers are also rather wet,' she ventured, fearing he might have taken offence at the instruction about the towel. 'I'd offer you some of Simon's, but a pair of his wouldn't reach much further than your knees. Er . . . I've got a brolly,' she added tentatively, when Dougie continued to stare out of the window, 'if you were wanting to smoke.'

He swung round stiffly, arms pinned behind his back. 'No, thanks. Packed it in. For good this time.'

'Gosh.'

'*And* the other stuff, before you ask.'

'I wasn't going to.'

'Yes, you were. Which is totally understandable, given the state I was in the last time you saw me. Sorry about that. It's called falling off the wagon. Happens to the best. I was letting off steam . . . or something. For what it's worth, I don't intend to let that happen again either. I just hope I didn't say or do anything I should be apologizing for.'

'Of course you didn't. You were fine. I was worried for you, that's all.' Victoria went to the kitchen, disconcerted by Dougie's strangeness, willing Simon to hurry up. A few minutes later, having returned with his glass of mineral water and a small cafetière for herself, she exclaimed, 'Spain seems a long time ago now. Thank you, again, so much, Doug, for all your hard work. Simon had a fabulous time. So did I. A shame it ended somewhat dramatically . . . but, goodness, doesn't that all seem ages ago and pretty irrelevant now?'

Dougie nodded, clearly back in a state of not-listening. He had shifted his attention from the washed-out view to a bookcase, and run his fingers through his hair so many times it was chopped and wild – a look that rather suited him, Victoria decided, her bafflement mounting as to why the encounter was still feeling like such hard work. The final night at the villa had got awkward, certainly, but that was over with, apologized for. Reflecting on the evening herself, as she had many times, she had forced herself to recognize that there had been elements to Dougie's relapse which had been decidedly fortunate. She had been in a funny mood herself that night; a dangerous mood, even, thanks to the intensity of the time they had spent together. Nostalgia had been threatening, a nostalgia for times that could never be revisited. If Dougie hadn't been drunk, who knew what embarrassment she might have caused herself?

'This is one of yours, presumably?' He had pulled out one of the now completed Hopper catalogues and was riffling through its pages. 'I really should get to art galleries more – feed my soul or whatever. Hopper is all those people in American diners, isn't he? No one talking or looking at each other . . . Human disconnection.' He slid the catalogue back into its place, shaking his head.

'Yes, among other things,' Victoria murmured, sparing a glancing thought for the naked woman in the sunbeam she so loved. 'I've been working on Strindberg since then. Now there's a –'

'Will Simon be much longer, do you think?' He stood squarely with his back to the window to deliver the question, as if the release of it had taken courage and effort.

Behind him the north London skyline resembled a great grey tanker, sinking in a white-grey sea.

'I don't think so. I could call him if you like . . . Look, Dougie, was there something urgent, because you seem . . . ?'

'No, no, I'm working soon, that's all. Five o'clock. A birthday group of eleven-year-olds. I'll give it a few more minutes. Finish this.' He raised his glass, as if a couple of inches of tap water warranted savouring.

'Eleven-year-olds! Goodness. How do you know where to start? In this weather you can't even throw them out into the garden.'

'Mango hedgehogs – I often kick off with those to keep them quiet. At least, I call them hedgehogs. It's basically just a way of cutting the flesh into bite-size pieces.' He demonstrated, criss-crossing his hands. 'Kids like the simplest things,' he added, with a sudden burst of boyish eagerness. 'Baking bread has also proved a real winner. And eating meals straight off the table – no cutlery, no plates, just tucking in with their bare hands – that works a treat too. I swear with that tactic I can get them to try almost anything. Even broccoli. The mothers never believe me, but it's true. I'm thinking of giving Heston's worms a go next.'

'Worms?' Victoria echoed, intrigued.

'Deep fried, injected with ketchup – I was reading about it the other day. I'll need to practise first.' He chuckled and then stopped abruptly, the humour and enthusiasm draining from his face as if someone had pulled a plug inside.

'So work's going okay,' Victoria urged, trying to stoke

some of it back again. 'I'm glad, Dougie. You deserve it. You're so talented. Truly.'

He had sunk into a chair, not the one where she had placed the towel. 'Thanks, Vic.' He threw her a half-smile. 'You deserve good things, too.'

She was baffled by the heaviness in his voice. 'And you should be running cooking courses from that *finca* of yours,' she declared, the thought arriving in her head from nowhere as her best ideas often did, 'not selling it. Advertise it on that website you've got – target all those well-heeled middle-class banker types who've been booking you to give their little darlings cooking lessons. Five-star accommodation and five-star food under a Mediterranean sun, like you did for me and Simon, but conducting lessons while you're at it – getting them to do the donkey work. All that lobster boiling and chopping onions.'

Dougie was staring at her with an expression of mild amazement. 'Do you know? That's not a bad idea.'

She offered a little head-bow of acknowledgement. 'Thank you. Can I tempt you to some tea or coffee on the back of it? I really can't think where Simon's got to. He can't be long now.'

'No, thanks. I'd better go.' He sprang up from his seat, tugging his wet jeans free of his legs. 'I'll get my jacket from the bathroom.'

Victoria followed him into the hall, apologizing for the couple of boxes parked in his way. 'They're waiting to be put in the loft – I need Simon for that. Can't manage getting up the ladder on my own. Some of it's yours anyway, of course,' she couldn't resist adding, nodding at the one she had got out of the bottom of the wardrobe.

'Mine? Why?'

Victoria could feel herself blushing. 'Hmm . . . Shall we call them "adult" magazines? Look, it's no big deal,' she rushed on, regretting having opened her mouth. 'Simon explained that you asked him to take charge of them because of Stevie.'

Dougie had paused in the doorway of the bathroom. 'Simon said *what*?'

'That you . . .' she faltered, her blush deepening.

Dougie slapped the wall, shaking his head. 'Well, with apologies to you, Vic, that husband of yours is talking total bollocks or muddling me with someone else. Personally, I've always preferred the real thing,' he growled, reappearing with his jacket a moment later and hoisting his long legs carefully over the box in the manner of one trying to avoid contamination.

'And how is Stevie?' Victoria asked, with a final brittle effort at brightness once they were at the door, the embarrassment about the stupid magazines still upon her. She was now so keen to be rid of Dougie she could have kicked him down the stairs. She stepped onto the landing and peered over the balcony into the stairwell, still half hoping to see Simon. 'Have you forgiven her for giving you the run-around like that in Spain?'

'Of course I've *forgiven* her,' Dougie retorted. 'She ran away because she was upset. *Very* upset.'

Victoria spun round. 'Dougie, I'm sorry. I didn't mean . . . I never meant . . .' She was close to tears, she realized suddenly. A day that should have been good had somehow turned bad and she didn't understand why. She didn't understand anything.

Dougie patted her arm, his expression softening. 'I know you didn't . . . I know. Forgive me, Vic, I'm not myself today. I've been dreadful company. I should never have come up and bothered you.'

'So what had upset Stevie?' Victoria asked miserably, dimly sensing, in spite of his apologies, that there was some need to make amends, something she had got badly wrong.

'It doesn't matter. She's fine now – having a great time with Janine in Sweden. Here.' He fished inside his jeans pocket and pulled out a coin, a shiny new penny piece. 'I almost forgot. This is for Simon. It's to go with that birth-day knife of his.' He dropped it into her palm. 'I found it when I was packing up the villa, so it might even be the one Ruth originally put in the box. Anyway, I promised Gary I'd give it to you – after that accident of theirs Ruth's apparently been freaking out about bad luck. Ridiculous, of course, but no harm either.'

'No harm indeed. Blimey . . . Okay.' Victoria closed her fingers round the coin. 'I'm not superstitious but I'll give it to Simon, of course.'

In spite of the rain, which was thickening to stair-rods, Dougie took his time unclamping his bike and removing the plastic bag from the saddle. The bag had a rip in it so the saddle was drenched anyway. He loitered for a good five minutes after that, balancing with the help of a lamp-post, squinting through the downpour for any sign of Simon at either end of the road before giving up and ped-alling home.

Once back in his own street, he felt sufficiently dispirited to go straight to Nina's front door, now certain enough of her affection to know that she would welcome a dripping bike into her hallway, not to mention a soaked cyclist in a sour mood. But there was no answer, so Dougie retreated, feeling even more battle-weary, to his own side of the fence. He brought the bike in out of the rain, driving a dirty tyre mark over a white envelope on the door mat before he noticed it.

Dear Dougie,

I have gone to visit parents – duty call. Back in a few days. Could you feed Sam? Food under sink.

Hugs, N xxx

PS Key under big stone by the dead geranium (can't believe I never gave you a set!).

The eleven-year-olds were rowdy, a group of six rather than five, as had been agreed, meaning Dougie had to wring more money out of the tense-faced father despatched to pick them up. After they had gone, he left the washing-up and phoned Laura Munro instead.

'That daughter of mine is away.'

'Well, that's interesting.'

'Yes.' Dougie cleared his throat. 'I should warn you, I only want sex.'

'Sounds perfect. Give me an hour.'

She arrived fifty-five minutes later in a haze of musky scent, a short, close-fitting skirt and her trademark boots, which she locked with bruising tightness across Dougie's hips, having demanded a piggy-back upstairs.

They made love with the briskest efficiency they had yet managed, after which she quickly showered and put her clothes back on. 'By the way, I'm engaged,' she announced lightly, sitting on the bed and clipping her earrings back into place. 'So I won't be doing this again. That was, like, for old times' sake.'

Dougie raised himself on his elbow, shaking his head in admiration at her candour. 'Well, I'm honoured, in that case. Might I be allowed to enquire who this fortunate fiancé is and where he sprang from?'

'An old friend from France – kindergarten, actually. We've been on-off for years. I always knew we'd end up together.'

'Congratulations.'

'Thanks.'

'So you'll stick to the marital bed from now on?' Dougie clicked his fingers. 'Just like that?'

She grinned. 'Just like that. I'm not saying I won't want other people. Of course I will, sometimes. I just won't do anything about it.' She pulled a brush out of her bag and swept it through her mane of blonde hair, first one side, then the other, picking the hairs that fell loose off her chest and shoulders and shaking them onto the floor. 'It's just about choice in the end, isn't it? Deciding what you want and sticking to it.'

'Yes, I suppose it is,' Dougie murmured, impressed at such steely simplicity, finding he had no doubt at her capacity to see it through. 'Anyway, thanks. For everything. And this evening especially. I kind of needed it.'

She flashed him an impish smile. 'Yeah, I kind of got that impression. But thanks to you too. You were fun . . . for an *old* guy, that is.'

Her heavy soles clumped down the stairs and then the door slammed. Dougie stayed in bed, watching the darkness thicken through the gap in his bedroom curtains, wondering if the house – the world – had ever felt emptier.

Chapter Eighteen

That Saturday, with thirty minutes to kick-off, all entrances to the Emirates Stadium were flooded with people. Simon stood outside Gate Three, as he and Dougie had agreed, scanning the crowds but keeping his back to the wall so there was no chance of being taken by surprise. He was more than ready to see his old friend – thoroughly looking forward to it, in fact – but very much wanted the encounter to be on his terms. It was for exactly that reason that he had bolted at the sight of Dougie's bike on Wednesday afternoon, having spotted it chained to the railing outside the flat after his and Victoria's visit to Gary. It had been an act of pure, self-defensive instinct. If there was any air to be cleared – and Simon couldn't shake off a lingering uncertainty that there might be – he certainly hadn't wanted it to happen via a doorstep confrontation, with Victoria hovering, her ears flapping.

The bolting itself had been deeply unpleasant: parked at the end of the street, crouching on the back seat of his own car like some lowlife, waiting for Dougie to emerge and pedal off, which he took his time doing, the bugger. And then having to bluff it out with Victoria, who had been in an even worse mood than when he had left her, tetchy and inquisitive about his modest bag of stationery purchases, waving the birthday knife and its newly bestowed lucky penny around, saying sole management of Dougie in a bad mood wasn't her idea of fun, not on a day when she was stressed out and cranky anyway. Simon had resorted to a story about having bumped into Danny – fresh back from the Dordogne, he claimed – to account for the length of time he had been away. Victoria had still exacted what felt like revenge by getting him to scurry up and down the loft ladder like a monkey for the rest of the afternoon, stowing things away.

By the evening, however, they had been back on an even keel, side by side on the sofa, enjoying a good bottle of wine and some telly. At which point a certain degree of sheepishness had crept over Simon about the drama he had made of the afternoon. Back during the distant school years of being picked on, he had never been one to run away. And now, aged forty, there was nothing to run away *from*, except an old friend, who was understandably pissed off and mystified to be kept at arm's length. Even bumping into Stevie wasn't an issue for the time being, since the girl was in Sweden, Victoria had said, spending time with her mother.

And he missed Dougie, Simon had realized, with a jolt, sitting thigh to thigh with his wife that night, watching a grisly and improbable series of village murders undertaken with fishing tackle. Their friendship had been shifting during the course of the year, not always easily, thanks to the need to accommodate Dougie's straitened circumstances and sober, darker moods, but there was still no one else with whom Simon felt he could relax in quite the same easy, non-judgemental way, no one, essentially, who knew him so well and so acceptingly. Even before Gary had gone under the radar with Ruth and fatherhood, he had always been a poor alternative. And Victoria was such a tight package of intensity that Simon needed to get away from her from time to time. Dougie had always understood that, too, like no one else ever would or could.

So when Gary had phoned later that evening to offer the football tickets for Arsenal's opening game, his voice breathless with regret at having to surrender such treasure, Simon had accepted at once, saying he would recruit Dougie to enjoy the treat with him. Football was such an uncomplicated pleasure. It was just what they needed, Simon had seen suddenly, to get things back on the old footing, before all the somewhat muddied waters of recent weeks. He had called Dougie straight away and found him equally, reassuringly, enthusiastic, with no trace of the glowering mood Victoria had mentioned. He would have to shift one of his classes, Dougie had explained cheerily, and added how honoured he was that Simon could now squeeze him into his own busy work schedule. The stay in Scotland had lasted so long, he joked, that he was surprised Simon and Victoria hadn't returned with their own tartan. All very jolly. All very Dougie.

Simon checked his watch, wondering if the class had got in the way after all. With only ten minutes until kick-off, the crowds streaming through the turnstiles were starting to thin out. An air of desertion was descending on the concourse, the litter showing, stragglers running. Near him a fat man, looking irredeemably idiotic with the nylon of his team shirt stretched tight over his beer paunch, was shouting into his phone, while his small son looked on forlornly, his own matching strip hanging like a dress round his knees.

'Hey, you bastard – given up on me?'

Simon spun round from watching the father and son, for all his precautions caught off guard. 'Almost. Where the hell have you been, Doug? We said two thirty. But, hey, it's bloody good to see you.' They clamped each other in their usual bear-hug, Simon hanging on for a second longer than usual, wanting Dougie to know he really meant it.

Dougie punched him lightly on the arm as he pulled away. 'Yeah, sorry. Got late. Took a bus. Shall we get on with it? If you've managed to remember the tickets, that is, what with being so *busy*.'

'Yeah, yeah,' Simon countered, happier than he could have put into words at the easy banter between them, the sense of everything being unchanged and okay. 'So I've been away and working hard. Get over it. And now, thanks to you, we've no time to get food or drink, which means the delight of joining the bun-fight for sustenance at half-time.'

By the time they took their seats, the players were trooping onto the pitch, holding the hands of small children wearing the team strip and clutching mascots. A few minutes later the match was in full swing, the crowd roaring in early eagerness at every touch of the ball. The run of play was even until a star Arsenal striker made his first serious rush on goal, enticing a swallow-dive tackle of such determination from the Chelsea keeper that the ref blew for an Arsenal penalty. It looked like a mis-kick from the striker but then the ball bounced at an awkward angle and flew past the goalie's outstretched hands into the back of the net, whereupon every home supporter – Dougie and Simon included – leapt to their feet in a human tidal wave of celebration.

'Was it really a penalty, though?' Dougie shouted. 'I think he was going for the ball.'

Simon looked about them, laughing. 'Keep your voice down, mate, unless you want to get us lynched.' Catching the eye of a burly man in the row behind, he nodded vigorously to indicate that they shared his joy. In front of them, meanwhile, four youths with tattooed necks and shaved heads were chanting the striker's name and air-punching their fists.

'By the way, your wife's given me a good business idea,' Dougie said, as the game settled into a quieter spell.

'Has she? Good old Vic. What was it?'

'Cooking courses in the sun – a way of using the *finca*. She threw it at me when I came by on Wednesday.'

'Wednesday? Oh, yes, sorry I missed you . . . Blimey, did you see that?' Simon pointed at the pitch where a Chelsea midfielder had been felled by a vicious sliding tackle. 'That's the third in a row.' Dougie said something else, but Simon couldn't make it out in the hubbub. He said it again, just as the youths in front of them embarked on a fresh round of chanting.

'Sorry, Doug, still didn't catch it.' Simon leant sideways, putting his head next to Dougie's, keeping his eye on the game. The Chelsea player had got to his feet but was making a meal of it, hobbling, looking for the free kick and a red card. The ref flashed a yellow and the game spun on. 'What did you say?'

'Congratulations.' Dougie roared it this time. He turned, forcing Simon to look at him, so close, their noses were almost touching. 'On soon becoming a father.'

Simon started to laugh and then stopped, blinking at Dougie, aware as he did so of his contact lenses shifting, with their usual slight discomfort, between his lids. 'What?' He began a smile, but found he couldn't see it through. 'What?' he repeated, unease stirring, along with the prickling sensation of the loser who has misheard a punch-line.

'Victoria said you'd been trying,' Dougie shouted.

'Did she?' Simon's face flushed, the unease ceding to hurt. 'Victoria told you that? What – when you came round on Wednesday?'

'Oh, no, long before Wednesday. In Spain. I've always liked Victoria, by the way. On the neurotic side, of course, but a big heart . . . Yes, I've always liked that about her. In fact, you are, to coin a phrase, a lucky man. And talking of luck . . .' The crowd started some competitive singing, blocks of home and away supporters doing their best to drown each other out. 'Talking of luck,' Dougie yelled, 'did you get that coin okay, the one that –'

'Yes, I got the fucking penny . . . Dougie, what the fuck are you on about? What are you *on*?'

'It's just that you might be needing it . . . some luck, that is. Every prospective father does. Believe me, it's a minefield. You never know what problems you're going to have to deal with.' Dougie swung back to watch the game, cupping his hands round his mouth and hollering, 'Come on, you Gunners.'

Simon leant over and put his face so close to Dougie's

he could see the individual hairs pushing through from his morning shave. 'What the hell are you telling me, Doug? That Victoria's pregnant? That she told *you* before *me*?'

'Oh, no, not Victoria.' Dougie turned again to look at his friend, their faces now barely an inch apart. 'No, that's the irony of the whole thing,' he hissed. 'It's not Victoria who's expecting, it's Stevie.' He enunciated his daughter's name with exaggerated care, his blue eyes blazing as they held Simon's. 'Yes, I know, I can't believe it either. And how must you feel – still firing blanks with your dear wife and then, bingo, one crack at Stevie and she's up the –'

Simon's punch landed squarely on Dougie's left jaw, shutting off the sentence. He had stood up to deliver it, using his right hand. Dougie was still reeling when he delivered another higher up his head. In the midst of all his other feelings, as he deposited this second blow, Simon was able to acknowledge a certain visceral satisfaction, a connection perhaps to all the playground fear that had haunted his childhood, the sheer relish of physically standing up for himself successfully, to Dougie of all people, when it really mattered. Dougie tried to swing back, heaving himself to his feet, but was too dazed to get his balance right. Behind, the burly man and his companions were yelling at them to sit down and get a grip, while the four youths were whooping and hollering encouragement. Within seconds, it seemed, a couple of solidly built stewards in reflector bibs had pushed their way along the row and were hauling them out of the stand. They were manhandled to the nearest exit and pushed out of the stadium compound, with warnings about not getting such an easy ride the next time.

'I need a fucking drink,' Simon growled, sticking a finger at the stadium and marching off down the street.

Dougie gingerly touched his lip, which felt numb. His eye socket was hurting, too, right at the point where it met his cheekbone. Janine would tell him off – would be appalled, in fact, that he was playing such games, at such a time – but to exact a little punishment, make Simon sweat a bit, had seemed more than fair in the circumstances. He let him march off, then followed him down the street and into one of the large, soulless pubs a few hundred yards from the ground, empty because all its recent clientele had left to watch the game. By sprinting the last few yards, he managed to get to the bar first. 'A pint of lemonade, please.'

'Have a drink, Doug, for fuck's sake,' Simon snarled. 'Have a *fucking* drink.'

'And a pint of special and a whisky chaser for my friend here, thank you,' said Dougie, steadily, keeping his eyes on the barman. 'Go and sit down, Simon. I'll bring them over.'

Simon huddled in the corner of the velveteen bench seat, not talking, even when Dougie arrived with the drinks. He drank the whisky in one, slamming the glass down. 'I'll pay, of course . . . you know, a termination.'

'Oh, good. Splendid. That's all right, then. I'll tell Stevie.' Dougie folded his arms, sitting up straighter in his chair. 'But what I really want to know – old friend – is why, when the planet is teeming with females, you had to screw my sixteen-year-old daughter.'

Simon muttered something under his breath.

'What did you say?'

'I said stepdaughter,' he growled. 'Let's get the facts straight, at least. She's not *yours*, is she? She is the progeny of an Australian surf-boarder. And if you want to know why I did it, I'll tell you. Because she was *up* for it, that's why – she *wanted* it. It takes two, Doug, as you, with your impressive track record, should know.' He sat forwards, pressing his lips together in the way he did before saying something serious, his eyes flinty with the intent of one prepared to do what it took to defend himself. 'In fact, I wouldn't be surprised if it hadn't crossed your mind at least once, Dougie, old mate . . . *step*father. A looker like that, it would be only natural.' He sat back, signalling at a boy wiping tables to bring him another chaser.

Dougie did not move. He had imagined many scenarios for the conversation but not this. Since a phone call from Janine on Tuesday evening, breaking the news that Simon, rather than some Spanish boy, had been the architect of Stevie's pregnancy scare, he had thought of little else, playing out what to say, how to say it. He had been shocked – deeply disappointed – but ready to try to understand, telling himself that sex happened (as he did indeed know only too well), that Stevie was a consenting adult. During the phone call he had calmed Janine down, with talk of perspective and lessons learnt and no lasting damage done. On Wednesday, after he had sent Simon a deliberately provocative text and received no reply, he had cycled to the flat through the rain merely to establish whether they were back yet, with vague plans of a private man-to-man somewhere, so he could tell Simon what a dick he was and be done with it.

But at the sight of Victoria's pale, innocent, questioning face in the apartment hall, something in Dougie had shifted, almost as if twenty-four hours of post-shock numbness had worn off. He had seen, with sudden and fierce lucidity, that quite apart from any moral arguments, Simon had done a despicable thing, to his wife, to Stevie, not to mention to him and their friendship, a precious, fragile balance of connections that once destroyed could not easily be reassembled. Dougie hadn't been able to think straight after that. Every word he had spoken to Victoria had felt stiff and remote, so alert was he for the sound of Simon's key in the door. The small twist over the porn stash had been the final straw. The existence of the material was no revelation to Dougie and he couldn't have cared less. But he wasn't taking the rap for it. Not after everything else.

And now there had been this insinuation that he might be capable of sexual feelings towards his own daughter. Dougie studied his friend's face as the fresh shock of this, the disgust, sank in. If Simon could think such a thing, even for a second, then he knew nothing, Dougie realized. Nothing about what mattered; nothing about love; and certainly nothing about why it had been possible to stick at the long, never-ending grind of trying to keep himself clean and clear-headed. Because when all was said and done, all the crap stripped away, the effort behind that was about Stevie. She was the one thing he hadn't yet made a total mess of; the one true thing in his life, truer than any purpose he had yet found for himself. Stevie was his daughter, in the fullest possible sense. And because of that, Dougie understood, to the point of pain some-times – pain at his own helplessness – that she was still fragile, half formed; still young enough to need caring for; still not always up to knowing when she had been taken advantage of.

Dougie inhaled deeply, aware of the hunger to smoke, and breathing out slowly. If Simon, after twenty-four years of friendship, did not know these things, then he wasn't worth the effort of having them explained to him. He took a sip of his lemonade. 'Stevie had only just turned sixteen,' he said softly, observing Simon accept his second whisky, which he downed in one, smacking his lips. There had always been gaps in his friend's make-up, he knew, more dark and shade than most people, holes where things didn't join up, like loose knitting. It had made him interesting, easy to forgive and like. But now Dougie found himself remembering what Janine had said about Simon's less appealing 'small-man' traits, how Dougie himself had always been too close to see them properly, too much part of the equation. 'Girls that age, they don't always know what . . . effect they have.'

Simon barked a laugh. 'Oh yes they fucking do. And since when have you become Mother Teresa on such a subject, anyway? Dougie Easton, the shagging chef – wasn't that one of the old headlines? You worked your way through a few young ones in the process, if I recall. Or should I check that with Janine?'

Dougie slowly set his glass down, warning himself, as he had learnt to do with his irascible father, to remain calm. He was witnessing the hostility of an animal cornered, he knew, one on whom he had once taken pity for exactly the same behaviour. 'Yes, you're right, Simon. But my repertoire, even during my worst excesses, did not, to the best of my knowledge, ever include a just-*sixteen*-year-old girl, let alone the child of my oldest friend, let alone adding the lazy audacity of not *bothering* to use a condom. I don't care how much she supposedly begged for it, Simon, you should have said no. She could have sat on your face for all I care – you should still have known to say *no*.' Dougie paused as a gasp of anger escaped him – an up-rush from deep inside, like the opposite of breathing. 'Because . . .' he went on desperately, the anger fusing with the chill of real sadness – this was Simon, after all, *Simon*, the one person he'd thought he knew and could read, whose default position he had expected, at the very least, to be regret or penitence '. . . because surely,' Dougie croaked, 'surely, Simon, one of the very few consolations of growing older has to be the *growing up* that can and should go along with it. Otherwise we're just like animals, nothing ever making sense.'

Simon threw the last of his beer down his throat and pushed his glass away. 'Well, you sanctimonious prick.'

'Maybe,' Dougie conceded in a lifeless voice, the sound of two and a half decades of friendship crashing about his ears, 'maybe I am. But you could have apologized, you know. Today. Here. Now. There was always that option. Or at least paused to consider Stevie's welfare – that was a possibility too, instead of just waving that fat wallet of yours.' Dougie threw his head back and stretched his legs out under the table, fighting again to compose himself, thankful that circumstances had given him time to prepare. 'She's not pregnant, as it happens,' he said quietly.

'What?' Simon looked as if he had been electrocuted.

Dougie shrugged, taking his time, surveying the room. 'She thought she was, but she wasn't. It was horrible for her. She fell apart. She's with Janine now, much better, thank God – having a good time, in fact.'

Simon levered himself to his feet and planted a hand on either side of his beer glass. 'You bastard,' he hissed, leaning across the table. 'You total fucking bastard.'

'Are you going to hit me again? Go ahead. I bet you're pleased, though, aren't you? Off the hook – that must feel good.'

'I don't know you any more, Dougie – I just don't know you,' Simon cried, slumping back onto the bench, a timbre of real despair in his voice. 'Look, I'm not saying what happened with Stevie was a good idea – I'm not stupid – and I'm sorry, obviously, that it happened, that she had a scare, but, Jesus, is there really the need for you to be so holier-than-thou about it? After the things you've got up to in your life, Jesus, I would have thought you of all people would understand.' He spun his empty shot glass between his hands. 'You really used to be more fun, mate, do you know that?'

And maybe it was as simple as that, Dougie marvelled, recalling some of Simon's sourness in recent months, the thread of snide comments, the faint undercurrents he hadn't understood. Maybe it hadn't suited Simon to see his old friend getting his act together, keeping off the booze, trying to start again at the bottom of a business ladder. Maybe he had preferred the rollercoaster years, when Dougie's life had hurtled between collisions and he had had a ringside seat. That must indeed have been more 'fun', more exciting, perhaps even a sure-fire way of feeling better about himself. In which case Janine's diagnosis of the small-man thing barely scratched the surface, Dougie reflected grimly. A chippy desire to be noticed was one thing, but vicarious pleasure in a friend's strife was quite another.

'So this is where you threaten to tell Victoria, I suppose,' Simon said, crossing his legs, switching suddenly to a smooth, casual, man-of-the-world tone, as if they were discussing the final score in the football or where to go for dinner.

Dougie hesitated, not persuaded by the show of nonchalance, but not certain of what lay behind it either. He studied Simon's neat, narrow face, shocked still at the extent to which he had misread him. A part of him did indeed want to inform Victoria of her husband's crass infidelity, all the worse, somehow, for occurring at a time when they were supposedly pulling together to have a child. He had meant what he said to Simon about Victoria: she was a good – a decent – woman; he liked her now more than he ever had. But there were different ways for someone to be emotionally hurt, and who was he to decide which it should be for her? And even he could see that there would be an element of hypocrisy, given his personal history, to take on the role of whistle-blower. 'No, Simon, I won't say anything to Victoria,' he said heavily. 'At least, not if you promise to stay away from Stevie.'

'From you in that case.' Simon looked away.

'I guess I am saying that, yes.' For all that had happened, the words were a wrench.

'How did you find out, anyway?' He stood up. 'Did Stevie tell you?'

'No. She doesn't know I know. But she did tell Janine.'

'Ah, Janine . . .' Simon released the name slowly, as if the mere mention of Dougie's ex-wife held all sorts of explanations for the point they had reached. 'I'm going to the Gents, then I'll find a cab. What do we do? Shake hands?'

'I don't think that would feel right, do you?'

'Fuck knows,' Simon snapped, turning on his heel and walking away.

Dougie took his time getting home, slipping down side streets to avoid the crowds, now spilling out of the stadium gates and thronging towards the tube, not caring particularly which direction they took him in. Stopping under the lee of a shop canopy, he phoned Janine's mobile, the well of emptiness inside him deepening when she did not reply. No one else in the world would understand the enormity of what had happened, he reflected bleakly. Simon, gone – with good riddance but such a sense of loss too, of betrayal. He dialled the number again, this time leaving a brief muted message, explaining how the confrontation had unravelled. He then tried Nina, who didn't pick up either. So he left her a message as well, asking, with fake, cheery sarcasm, if she could find time in the midst of the no doubt exacting demands of her parents to give him a call.

He got on a bus eventually, hunching down on a back

seat on the upper level, aware that he was absorbing the trauma of having excised not just Simon from his life but what felt like a core part of himself, a part he wasn't even certain he was ready to let go. Because Simon, for all the snarling and nasty insinuations, had been right about one thing: the old devil-may-care Dougie Easton *had* been more fun. The creature who had been zigzagging along the straight and narrow for more than a year now was mind-numbingly dull in comparison, lousy company both for himself and those around him. He might have been out of debt but he was still pretty skint. His bad moods followed him around like a sour smell. And what was the point of all the effort, Dougie asked himself bitterly, if it had brought nothing better than the prospect of returning alone, friendless, to an empty house on a dank Saturday afternoon?

He tunnelled deeper into his seat, pulling his jacket collar up around his ears. The man sitting directly in front of him was obviously trying not to fall asleep, his lank-haired head lolling and quickly righting itself; the woman next to him was curling more tightly against the window, clearly fearful of having her shoulder used as a pillow. Dougie found his thoughts drifting back to Victoria's Hopper catalogue, the pictures of people in ill-lit spaces, side by side but not touching, their gazes fixed in different directions. That was how the world worked, how it was: ugly, disconnected. If it wasn't for Stevie . . . Dougie groped for his phone like a man fumbling for a lifeline, needing to see his daughter's latest message from Scandinavia, though he knew it by heart anyway: *Such cool time – lake again with P, H & D – rlly good friends now. Miss ya x.*

Who were P, H and D? Dougie couldn't remember. He stared at the screen till the back light faded. She wouldn't come back to live with him. The realization was like a slap across the face – so brutally obvious, he felt a dope. He had told her there was no pressure to return to London and she would take him at his word. Because what was there for her to come back to anyway? The dingy house, him, Simon . . . No, there was nothing she could possibly want in England.

He rang Nina's bell en route to his front door, thumping it with irritation when the sound echoed back at him through the letterbox. Once inside his hall, he punched his answering-machine button with similar force, releasing a groan of disappointment when his father's voice burst into the silence of the hall: 'Doug, are you there? I've found what they call a vanity publisher.'

Dougie tucked the phone between neck and chin and slid down the wall till he was sitting on the floor.

'They're in Brighton and I'm meeting them on Monday,' Lenny shouted, talking in the loud, affected way he always did when leaving messages. 'And before you say anything, no, I haven't agreed to pay them any money yet. I'm not an idiot. I'm going to meet them first, to discuss terms. But the real news . . .'

Dougie shifted the phone to the other side of his neck and loosened the laces in his trainers. His socks were damp and clinging to his feet. He peeled them off and rubbed the numb ends of his toes.

'. . . is that brother of yours, getting married – I assume you've had the same invitation, gold edges and confetti, a bloody *Schloss* for the guests. I don't know who this

Katarina girl is, but she must be minted. Mind you, Germany in November . . .'

Dougie glanced back at the doormat, knowing already that there was no missed envelope. He turned off the answering machine and threw his socks at the wall.

When Nina finally returned his call, he was picking at a plate of spaghetti, the desolation steadily filling him, like thickening fog, suffocating the hunger. 'How long is this parental visit going to take?' he asked hoarsely. 'I need to talk to you. My life is a fuck-up.'

'What, again?'

Dougie hesitated. She didn't know about the Simon-Stevie thing because she hadn't been around to tell. Even his new best friend wasn't there when he needed her and he was in no mood to broach the subject on the phone. 'When are you coming back? I need you back. I need someone.'

It was her turn to be silent for a moment. 'It'll be a few days yet, I'm afraid.'

'But tomorrow's Sunday. All parental visits should end by a Sunday.'

'I can't come tomorrow. They . . . they need me here.'

'Tell them I need you.'

A raspberry reverberated out of the phone and Dougie blew a half-hearted one back. 'How are those curls coming along, by the way?' he teased, mining some level of himself he hadn't known he had for cheerfulness. 'I've been meaning to tell you, cabbage is the thing for ringlets – and bread crusts. That's what my gran always used to say. At least, I think it was my gran – we are going back a bit.'

'Cabbage and crusts.' She chuckled. 'Brilliant. Thanks

for the hot tip. I'll adjust my diet forthwith. And what else have you been up to other than remembering old wives' tales from your dodgy childhood?'

'My dad's got some sort of memoirs thing on the boil,' Dougie gabbled, seizing on the easiest subject he could. 'It's made me think that if the old duffer can string together a manuscript then surely I should be able to write a cookbook.'

'Christ, you're so competitive – it's pathetic.'

'Yup, I am. Oh, yes, and that brother of mine you're so keen on is getting married to some German girl and hasn't invited me to the wedding.'

'Well, ask him to ask you, then.'

'No way.'

'Ask him to ask you.'

'You just said that.'

'Ask him to ask you.'

'For fuck's sake, Nina!' Dougie shouted. 'What is it with my bloody brother? You never fucking give it a rest.' He clamped his mouth shut, flinging his head back against the wall, making sure it was hard, wanting to punish himself. 'Shit, sorry, that came out worse than I meant.'

'No, it's okay,' she said mildly. 'You're right, I am a meddlesome cow. Look, Doug, sorry . . .' he heard her yawn '. . . but I'd better go. It's long past my bedtime. Take lots of care . . . and hang on in there, wrestling with all those demons of yours.' The sleepiness was making every word an effort. 'By the way . . . all that looking after me . . . have I said thank you?'

'About a million times.'

'Yeah, well, you've been a good friend.'

After the call Dougie sat at the kitchen table staring at his hands, working hands: long-fingered, big knuckles, muscled, they were like kitchen implements in themselves. Darkness fell as he sat there, the last of the late-August light draining from the sky. His hands could do many things besides prepare food, Dougie told himself. They could, for instance, compose an email to his brother, offering congratulations, begging to be included in his nuptials. Or they could sift through the shambles of his faltering book project, make more notes under his chapter headings. Or they could open a bottle and pour a drink. Dougie trembled at the thought, not with fear, but with desire.

Outside it had started raining again. The drops made small slaps and thuds as they fell through the metal stairs into the concrete dug-out of a patio. A light needed turning on, but there seemed little point. Instead, Dougie stayed where he was, watching the pale glow of his skin grow fainter. When he stood up at last, his body felt stiff and heavy. Moving through the gloom, using the banisters, he made his way upstairs and into his bedroom, coming to a stop by the jar of money that lived on the mantelpiece. His Stevie jar.

He shook out the notes and coins and counted them slowly, doggedly, straining his eyes in the dark, making tidy piles on the mantelpiece. It was at just over eighty quid. A good haul. Enough for his purposes anyway. He looked at his watch, astonished to see that it was past midnight. But somewhere would be open, a place he could go. There always was, if one looked hard enough. And a drink was a friend, the kind with whom you knew where you were, the kind who never let you down, not after one year, ten years or an entire bloody century. He stuffed the money into his jacket pocket and headed down the stairs, fast this time, taking three with each stride, wanting to get out of the door before he changed his mind.

Chapter Nineteen

Stevie half opened her eyes, studying the pointy tops of the pines through the grille of her wet lashes. The slab of rock was like a smooth warm hotplate under her towel. She could hear the faint lap of the water at its edges, water that was inky black and so ice-cold that for the first few seconds of every swim her head ached from the shock of it. On each visit to the lake she had made herself plunge in several times, loving it when the shock wore off and she could start to enjoy swimming in something that was half a mile long, under an umbrella of cloudless blue skies and with Hansel and Gretel forests all around. Paul, her new best friend, lying beside her on the rock, had told her that in the winter holidays he came with local friends to this same lake to skate and play ice-hockey, that there could be up to five or six games going on at once, that safety scouts patrolled the perimeter, checking the thickness of the ice, but that even so they had scares sometimes, when a group of them were gathered on one spot and the frozen water under their feet started pinging and zinging, as bubbles of trapped air went mad.

Paul was the son of a British diplomat and had lived on Lidingö for two years. His Dutch mother, Esther, was Janine's friend from language classes. He and Stevie had met when Janine dropped round to borrow a DVD, leaving Stevie in the car and promising to be back in a few minutes. Stevie had been hanging out of her open door when Paul appeared in the doorway of the house, rubbing sleep and thickets of hair out of his eyes. He didn't ask Stevie inside, but picked his way down the steps to the driveway, gingerly, because the gravel was hot and sharp and he wore no shoes. He had a big soft red mouth, huge teeth and startled green eyes, and looked about her age, although he turned out to be couple of years older. He was at the start of a gap year between finishing his A levels and going to university.

'Hot, isn't it?' He had flashed the equine smile, pulling a pouch of tobacco and some papers from his shorts pocket. 'Would you like one?'

Stevie had glanced at the open front door, shaking her head regretfully. After the one in her bedroom on her fraught first day, her mother had reintroduced the ban.

'I get it. Maybe another time, then.' He winked. 'Mine are both chimneys so they leave me alone.' While he assembled the roll-up he told her a bit about his plans for the year – how he would be visiting London in October, then travelling round South America. 'It gets kind of mental here in the winter to be honest – two hours' daylight for months on end. My mum goes stir-crazy but Dad doesn't mind. Are you doing A levels and all that shit?'

Stevie had said she was, but then admitted she had only just got her GCSE results.

'No, really? You look way ahead of that. Go on, then.' He grinned encouragingly. 'Tell me what you got.'

When she confessed to the clutch of As and A stars, relayed to her over the phone by an excited teacher a few days before, he looked genuinely impressed, making

Stevie even happier about her results than she was already. By the time Janine came out of the house, ostentatiously waving a DVD entitled *Teach Yourself Swedish*, they were deep in conversation.

'We could go to Kottla one afternoon, if you like,' he said, without any trace of self-consciousness as her mother approached. 'I get to use Mum's car if I ask nicely enough. I'll swing by and pick you up. Give me your number. I'll get some others along too.'

That had been a week ago, since when they had got into a bit of a routine, spending afternoons on towels, with snack picnics and cigarettes and music, invariably with a local friend of Paul's called Håkan and sometimes a girl called Daisy, whose father was a military attaché at the embassy, whatever that meant. Daisy and Paul appeared to know each other from England, too, because their boarding schools had been in the same county, they said, but Stevie suspected there was more history there than they were prepared to admit to. They were all older than her, but made her feel welcome in a way that was fantastically unfussy. Håkan was the most aloof, tall and un-Swedish-looking with pale skin and short black hair. He spoke perfect English and clearly fancied himself as something of an intellectual, engaging Paul in arguments about things like the meaning of art and whether the Americans were the most hated nation on the planet. He was the only one of them who didn't smoke – because he had had bad asthma as a kid, he said. He kept to the shade, while the rest of them fried themselves, and often disappeared into the lake for long swims, his lithe white body shimmying through the translucent water, like an eel.

That afternoon neither Håkan nor Daisy had been able to come. Paul was lying on his back next to Stevie, tapping his fingers on the rock in time to something on his iPod. Stevie rolled onto her front, putting up with the discomfort of the stone digging against her hip bones, because it was a nice reminder that she was slimming down again. It had happened naturally, through the swimming and not having time to graze between meals. Her body was starting to feel normal again, *hers*. As if she had reclaimed it after the hiatus earlier in the summer. 'What?' Paul was looking at her.

'Nothing. I thought you said something.'

'Nah.' She propped herself on her elbows, watching an ant trying to hoist itself onto her towel. They were huge, the forest ants, and capable of biting, Paul had warned. Stevie flicked it away, wishing thoughts – especially those about what had happened with Simon – were as easy to banish. For most of the holiday she had done a good job of not remembering, but that afternoon, with her holiday near its end, images had been flooding back; images like the expression on Simon's face when they had been in the pool-house, hesitant but greedy, and sort of surprised – yes, that had been a part of it, Stevie remembered suddenly. And the *not* enjoying it: she had found herself thinking about that, too. She hadn't liked it, but she hadn't stopped it. What had that been about?

Stevie rolled over onto her back, closing her eyes. Her mother had tried to extract more details, but she had resisted the temptation to give any. Consent was the thing and, for whatever inexplicable reason, she knew she had given it. In fact, it was clear in her mind that she had led

Simon on. She had led him on and seen through the consequences. Because men reached a point where they couldn't stop – every girl knew that.

Brushing a knuckle accidentally against Paul's arm, Stevie flinched, her mind still hovering in the poolhouse. But then Paul picked up her hand and pressed her fingers to his lips. He kissed each one lightly, keeping his eyes closed, between mouthing the words of whatever song he was listening to. Stevie sneaked a glance at his face and quickly looked away. It was so unexpected and yet it felt so good, so gentle, like it didn't have to mean anything; like it was possibly the start of something, possibly not. When he got to her little finger he started again, delivering another peck to each fingertip. Then they just stayed lying on the hot rock, like two stranded starfish, holding hands.

Later that evening, in the car, after a rush to get ready for going out, Janine asked brightly if she had had an enjoyable afternoon. Stevie would have liked to answer properly but Mike was with them. They were booked into an expensive restaurant in Gamla Stan – a treat for her last weekend. Two days, and she would be heading back to England. As the afternoon by the lake had worn on, the dread of this prospect had built with sudden unstoppable speed, like some deep barrier inside her had given way. She kept trying to think how nice it would be to see her London friends but it wasn't helping. So much had happened that they didn't know about. And she had been in such poor contact throughout the summer that they were starting to drop jokey comments about it on their Facebook pages between posting new photos of recent reunions and clearly having the same old laughs even though she wasn't there.

Mike was driving, his shorn head set in the solid, obstinate way that Stevie couldn't like no matter how hard she tried. She was so glad he knew nothing; nothing about anything, Janine had assured her several times, smiling like it was nice that they had a secret from him, even such a horrible one. In fact, once the first terrible day of the holiday was done with, Stevie didn't think she had ever loved her mother more. It had been almost like having a sister sometimes, with all the excursions they had made together, sightseeing and shopping, and one double-visit to the hairdresser where they'd got the giggles because the man in charge spoke such incomprehensible English. They had managed to emerge with decent trims and highlights, but at such expense that later that night she had heard Mike raising his voice about it from behind their closed bedroom door.

In recent days, though, Stevie had become aware of a certain heaviness behind Janine's smiles when they were hanging out together, like she was going through the motions of having a good time rather than actually having one. She kept talking up England – how nice it would be once Stevie got back into the swing of things – but it was plain she was going through exactly the same ordeal as her daughter, sharing the same dread. And it was pretty non-sensical, Stevie reasoned, staring at the flames of the sun setting fire to the Baltic as they sped towards the mainland, having to say goodbye just when they were getting on so well. Quite apart from the wrench of having to leave Paul and her other lake friends, none of whom had to suffer the ignominy of going back to school, let alone in grey old England.

But by far the sharpest focus of Stevie's misgivings, emerging like the front runner in some hateful, invisible race, was Simon. Returning to England was bound to mean coming across him. Janine said it wouldn't, insisting that Dougie claimed they hardly saw each other, these days, that lately the two men's lives had really diverged, but Stevie couldn't quite believe it. Simon was her father's oldest friend, after all; that was why she had sworn her mother to secrecy on the shameful truth about what had happened at the *finca*. No matter how busy he and her dad were, it was just a question of time before she and Simon ran into each other. Or maybe he would simply call round – catch her off-guard. And then what would happen? Would he ignore her? Or would he wink, or pinch her bum, or corner her behind a door, whispering some of the dirty words he had used in Spain, telling her he wanted more of the same? She had given in once, after all. Might he not expect her to again? The uncertainty of that alone was starting to make her feel sick.

'Wine, Stevie?' Mike picked the bottle out of the ice bucket with a waiter-like flourish, drying its glistening bottom with his napkin. He had had two beers while they waited for their food and his cheeks were showing a flush through his tan. 'We're going to miss you, aren't we, Jans? Very much indeed.' He dug the bottle back among the ice cubes, then squeezed his knuckles in the way he liked to, making the joints click. 'But you'll come and see us over Christmas, I expect. They do it splendidly here, by all accounts – candle-lit processions, snow and sleigh bells, midnight skating and so forth.'

It dawned on Stevie that what he was really happy about was that she was leaving: then he would have her mum to himself again. Before she knew it, the realization had merged with all her other fears. 'I'm having second thoughts, actually,' she blurted. 'In fact . . . that international school you mentioned once. I was wondering . . . would it be too late for me to take a look at it?'

Mike fired a look of total exasperation across the table. 'Well, I –'

Her mother's face was harder to read, but her voice sounded full, as if something was blocking her throat. She gripped Stevie's hand, casting fluttering, anxious glances at Mike. 'I'm sure . . . I mean, if you're sure, then . . .'

'Well, yes, I expect it could be arranged,' Mike barked, looking like someone being forced to suck lemons, all his sunniness gone. He tugged his chin, where a dark triangle of evening stubble had formed. 'If that's what you want.'

'Yes, it is. Yes, please.' Stevie lowered her gaze to her plate, swamped by her own confusion, feeling closer to six than sixteen. 'I've had such a great time, you see,' she faltered, 'the best, in fact. So I'd just like to take a look at the school . . . re-consider my options,' she concluded meekly, steering her fork through her food, hating herself but relieved to have got the dreadful confession done with.

Chapter Twenty

Crossing the courtyard of Burlington House on her way to an editorial meeting at the Royal Academy, Victoria heard her name called. She turned to see a woman signalling with a crutch from the bench in front of Sir Joshua Reynolds. It took her a few moments to recognize Danny Crane's wife, Heather.

'Victoria – long time no see. How are you?'

'Very well, thank you. Gosh,' Victoria frowned sympathetically at the crutch, 'what on earth happened?'

'A pavement edge, if you can believe anything so stupid. Just misjudged it and went over. The perils of becoming an old crone. But life's obviously treating you well. You look fantastic . . . *really* well.'

'Thanks.' Victoria beamed at the older woman, sorry for her, not just on account of the sprained ankle but because the few years since they had met had so clearly taken their toll. Flyaway grey hair, a thickening waist, loose folds of skin under the sharp brown eyes – ageing was the cruellest sport. 'Sadly, I can't chat, I'm on my way to a meeting. But please say thank you to Danny, won't you, on my behalf?' She started to walk away but then, seeing Heather struggling to her feet, felt compelled to wait. They set off towards the entrance together, very slowly.

'It's the arms that really start to hurt,' Heather muttered, placing the crutches gingerly on the cobbles before each swing. 'But why am I saying thank you to Danny? What's he done?'

'Oh, he didn't tell you? Well, it was some string-pulling for Simon – helping get a script thing off the ground. He set up a meeting with some TV production company and it snowballed from there. It's been brilliant – Si had been drifting a bit, to be honest.'

Heather had taken a breather from her hobbling and was eyeing Victoria doubtfully. 'What TV production company? I wasn't aware Danny knew any.'

'Oh, goodness, what was it called? . . . Beauchamp Productions. No, that wasn't it, but something like that.'

'Danny certainly hasn't mentioned it. And since he was made redundant –'

'Redundant?'

Heather laughed wryly. 'What are husbands like? Not telling us girls anything. Yes, I'm afraid it had been on the cards for a while but finally happened in June. His poor old dad's cancer hit the terminal stage round about the same time, so he's had a hell of a summer, mostly down in Newport, keeping an eye on the poor dear, getting power of attorney and trying to sort out the junk in his house – you know how these situations are. He's been there for the last two weeks solid – terrified of leaving in case the old man gives up the ghost.' She prattled on, negotiating the steps up to the entrance, confessing to worries about having two children not yet through university and whether Danny, at fifty-two, would be able to find another job. 'A script commission for Simon?' she ended, her thoughts coming full circle, once she had successfully reached the top step. 'I'm surprised he didn't mention that, I must say.'

Victoria sneaked a look at her watch and saw that she had already missed the start of the meeting. It was about the plans for a retrospective on the Spanish sculptor, Juan Muñoz. She had spent most of the weekend on the Internet, swotting up. 'So you haven't been in the Dordogne recently, then?'

'Heavens, no. We sold the house a while back, when the kids stopped wanting to come –' She broke off, pointing with her right crutch. 'Oh, lawks, swing doors – I might need a hand here.'

Victoria took her arm and they shuffled through together.

'And now I need the Ladies. I tell you, the inconveniences of decrepitude never end. Do you know where it is?'

Victoria indicated the passageway on the right of the stairs. 'Can you manage?'

'Oh, yes.'

'Because I'm sorry but I've really got to dash. Are you sure you'll be all right?'

'Yes, yes. I'm early as usual, meeting a friend.'

'Oh, good. Lovely to see you. Love to Danny. I hope his dad . . .' Victoria let the sentence hang, as she hurried away, not able to think what to wish for the old man other than a good death, which didn't seem right.

The meeting room was overheated. Juan Muñoz had a passion for balconies and staircases, which Victoria didn't think she could ever share. One of her colleagues, a French woman with a thick accent, was in full flow, virtually incomprehensible at times in her desire to show her knowledge and enthusiasm. Victoria steered clear of the coffee and sipped a plastic cup of tepid water instead, hoping to see off the headache that was starting to skewer her temples. It was clear the retrospective was going to be as much a feat of organization and co-ordination as some of the far larger exhibitions she had been involved with. Lots of the works would be coming from private collections scattered across the United States and Western Europe, and many were both cumbersome and delicate. Someone else picked up on this point, launching into a horror story about shipment damage and under-insurance.

Victoria's attention drifted to the images spread out in the middle of the meeting-room table. Uppermost was a photograph of the Muñoz famous rotating *Hanging Figures*, two clothed people suspended by ropes round their necks. From her research she knew about the celebrated ambiguity of the work: were the pair circus acrobats – echoing Degas' *Mlle La La at the Circus*, which Muñoz was known to have visited frequently during his time as a student in London, or were they torture victims, resonating with the themes depicted by his beloved Goya? Tragedy or comedy? That was the question. Happy or sad? Good or bad? Victoria felt her head spinning. What was truth, anyway – what was it *worth* – if it couldn't be pinned down? Simon had lied once, maybe several times, that was the thing. But did it matter?

Why was the room so hot? What was the heating doing on when it was still only September? Victoria threw a despairing look at the radiator, weighing up the unwelcome disruption of leaving her seat to try to turn it down.

A breather in the corridor seemed a better option. There was a Staff Only toilet there. She could get some cold water to drink, dig around in her bag for some analgesics. 'Excuse me, but I need to –' She stood up as she spoke, only to find the room going black. She tried to grab the table edge but pitched sideways, past the French woman's chair.

When she came round they were crouched around her, fanning her with leaflets and pieces of paper, their faces contorted in various caricatures of concern. Someone put a hand under her head and her paper cup of tepid water was pressed to her lips. The exhibition curator, a slim, earnest man with large tortoiseshell spectacles then took charge and lifted her into a chair, where someone else gently pushed her head in the direction of her knees. There was talk of ambulances, which she managed to wave away. Instead, although it was still against her wishes, Simon was summoned. He arrived very efficiently, and somewhat dramatically, forty minutes later, having taken a taxi all the way from north London and made it wait while he tore inside. By which time Victoria was seated on a sofa in another private room, sipping tea and feeling fine.

'We should get you checked out,' he said, once they were in the taxi.

'It was so stuffy in there, that's all.'

'But you fainted, Vic. You never faint.'

'There's a first time for everything.'

'Even so, I'm taking you to the GP. In fact we'll go

now – they always see extra people at the end of the morning session.'

'I'm not going to the GP.'

'Right. A and E, then.'

'Don't be ridiculous.'

'I'm assuming it's your swoon that's making you stroppy. Husband flies to the rescue. Husband gets his head bitten off.'

'I bumped into Heather Crane this morning. Danny's wife.'

'Ah, and how is she?'

'She looked terrible, since you ask. About a hundred years old. With a sprained ankle – I felt really sorry for her. Danny has spent most of the summer in Wales, looking after his dying father.'

'Has he now? Poor bloke.'

Simon had turned to look out of the window. He appeared relaxed, Victoria noticed, sitting forwards, his hands hanging loosely off his knees. It was the most relaxed she had seen him in days. Indeed, it was such a perfect, crafted position, it almost looked false. The cabbie had cut down to Marble Arch and they were crawling up solid traffic in Edgware Road, where the first dry day of the week had drawn swarms of people onto the pavements, most in flowing Arabic clothes.

'Why didn't you mention that?'

Simon let out a cry of disbelief. 'Because I didn't know.'

'And a few months ago Danny lost his job –'

'Yes, a bad do, that.'

'So you knew about it, then?'

Simon sighed heavily. 'Yes.'

'Well, why didn't you tell me?'

He flung his arms wide in a show of frustration, the relaxed pose done with. 'What is this? An inquisition? In fact, I think I did mention it —'

'Yes, this is an inquisition and, no, Simon, you did not mention it. And what's more Heather had never heard about this script deal of yours. Nothing. *Nada.*'

'Why should she, for Heaven's sake?'

'And their place in the Dordogne,' Victoria snapped, having been saving this trump card. 'They sold it. Years ago.'

'I only said I *thought* they'd been there . . . Jesus, we're definitely consulting a doctor because something has most certainly happened to your head.'

Victoria folded her arms and crossed her legs, turning away from him. His explanations did not quite add up. Since Scotland he had definitely been acting strangely – moodier than she had ever known him, quick to take offence – more like a man in need of a holiday rather than one who had just returned from one. And after he had bumped into Danny the other day, she was sure he had specifically said the Cranes were just back from the Dordogne . . . hadn't he? Or had she misheard? 'Put on your seatbelt, for God's sake,' she muttered, thinking she'd be doubting her own name next.

'I'm not sure I want to, thanks,' Simon said, in a muffled voice. 'My premature death is looking like an appealing option right now – to *you*, I suspect, anyway.'

'That's just stupid, stupid and sick.'

For a few long seconds they both looked out of their windows. Through the taxi partition came the faint sound of the cabbie's radio, tuned to a talk show.

'I spoke to Gary,' said Simon at length, in a strained, friendly tone. 'She really did have something wrong with her, by the way.'

'Who?'

'Polly.' He flopped back in his seat and clipped in his seatbelt. 'You know how worried they were, with her non-stop crying. Turns out there was something after all, some trouble in her gut, but they've got medicine and she'll be fine so long as Ruth keeps off dairy.'

'That's fantastic,' Victoria replied tightly, marvelling that he should have such a deflective trump card of his own at such a time. And on a subject so certain of winning her round. If it was a performance, there was certainly something to admire in it.

'And now we're most definitely going to the GP,' he declared, pulling the seatbelt to its full capacity and tapping the partition window to give the driver the new address.

Victoria stared at the advert on the folded seat in front of her, listening to the strong, familiar, genial tones of her husband in conversation with the cabbie and wondering if she really was losing her mind. For months now, it seemed, they had been struggling to find some sort of equilibrium, up one minute, down the next, getting close to being happy but never quite sustaining it. On the outside, things looked normal. But Simon was good at the outside things. It was the inner stuff that always kept her guessing. 'Truth matters, Simon.'

He turned to her, scornfully raising his eyes skyward. 'Doh. Thanks for reminding me.'

'If there's someone else –'

'Someone else?' The mockery left his face. 'For fuck's sake, Vic.' He clamped his mouth shut, looking genuinely distraught.

Victoria summoned her courage and pressed on. His denials still didn't ring true and, having got this far, she couldn't let it go. Something wasn't right. Ambiguity was all very well for sculptors hedging their bets, trying for a show of 'depth', but it wouldn't do for her. 'If you are seeing someone else – using Danny as some sort of cover – for God's sake, just tell me,' she blurted. 'Tell me now. Get it over with. I'm not a child. I'll be able to take it . . . deal with it.'

'You are amazing, you know that?' His voice was muted with wonderment. 'I am *not* seeing anybody else. I swear on my life. But, yes, there are a couple of things I haven't told you . . . or, rather, that I haven't been exactly straight about recently.'

Victoria braced herself, her thoughts flitting to the box of dirty magazines – the ridiculous magazines. Simon had stuck to his guns about them being Dougie's and she still didn't know if she believed him. They were now safely stowed away in their loft and she was fed up of thinking about them. They had never mattered in themselves: it was the discovery that she might be living with someone who had secrets that had mattered. She shifted in the taxi seat so she was facing Simon. Whatever was coming, she wanted to receive it full-on. Tablets had seen off the headache but she could feel her temples pulsing.

Simon grimaced. 'No need to look like that. All I was going to say was that the script project has hit a glitch that I didn't want to tell you about just yet. It's been put on hold for the time being, a funding issue . . . no big deal in the face of world peace, et cetera, but obviously I'm disappointed.'

'Beaumont Productions.' The correct name dropped back into her brain.

'Yes.'

'The company Danny put your way.'

'Yes.'

'They've pulled the plug.'

'For the time being, yes.'

'Oh dear. I'm sorry, of course, but . . . is that it?'

He was twisting his hands in his lap. They had reached St John's Wood and were about to turn right towards Regent's Park. 'No, it isn't.' He pushed nervously with his finger at the ridge on his nose that had once supported his glasses. 'The truth is, as you seem to have worked out, I didn't actually run into Danny the other day, after Gary's. What you guessed at the time was right. I was pissed off . . . just needed some time on my own. Sorry, Vic, I should have said. I can be a miserable sod, I know I can.'

Victoria stared in amazement at her husband's suddenly stricken face. His irises were big and glassy behind his lenses, as if he might actually be on the verge of tears. She had never seen Simon cry. Ever. The prospect frightened her. It seemed such an inappropriately huge response to what he had told her but, then, who was she to judge what could or couldn't get under someone else's skin?

'God, you nit. Come here.' She unclipped her belt and

huddled against him, stroking his shirt front. 'That's too bad about the script – no wonder you've not been yourself, keeping that under wraps. I didn't mean to make matters worse, I really didn't. And it's okay that you were pissed off after Gary's. I was too. Nothing felt right that day, and after Scotland being so brilliant it seemed especially awful somehow. But you know what?' She nestled closer, picking her words carefully, wanting them to make a real difference. 'We don't share enough with each other, Simon, we keep too much back and we've got to put that right, get better at telling each other how we really feel ...' She left the sentence hanging because, while Simon's eyes had remained dry, hers were streaming.

'Hey, hey.' He pulled her closer. 'No need for that, Vic. Everything's fine. We're fine.'

Much to their surprise the surgery was almost empty. A large woman sat turning the pages of a book for a toddler with scarlet cheeks and a running nose, while an old man in a tweed cap fidgeted with a set of keys. Victoria was seen after only ten minutes, a consultation that encompassed various tests, including taking blood and supplying a urine sample. She pulled a funny face at Simon as she tripped back down the corridor from the surgery toilet clutching her plastic beaker, only to emerge white-faced a few minutes later with the news that she was apparently a couple of weeks pregnant.

They staggered, leaning against each other, to the nearest coffee shop, where Simon had a double espresso and Victoria an apple juice, followed by a large cinnamon pastry. 'God, this makes sense of everything, doesn't it? I've been feeling off – not myself – for days and didn't know why. Oh, and now I'm starving,' she cried joyfully, biting into the Danish. 'Oh, God, I'm *starving.*'

'I think we should leave London,' said Simon, solemnly.

'Really? Oh, God – okay. Anything! I feel I – we – could do *anything.*'

'I mean, you used to want to, didn't you, aeons ago? You went on and on about it.'

She nodded, her mouth bulging. 'You were the one who didn't want to.'

'But now I do. I mean, you'll want time off anyway, and it's not like we need the money, and both of us do so much of our work via computers. And this is like a new phase of our life, isn't it? A new phase – a new start. We could go somewhere back where we started – Devon, say, or Cornwall.'

Victoria shook her head, dabbing at the pastry flakes on her lips. They were gabbling like new lovers – anything possible, the world their oyster – and it felt wonderful. 'Cornwall's too far.'

'Devon or Somerset, then. Somewhere with a big garden for the –'

'Baby,' she finished for him, her eyes welling all over again. 'But, no, it would have to be somewhere much nearer London, like Buckinghamshire, an easy commute. I'm not giving up my job – I love my work. And not a word yet to anyone, okay? Not till three months at least. So much can go wrong – oh, God, remember Janine? And that was after –'

'Nothing's going to go wrong. Do you hear me? Not to

us. Other people's tragedies are other people's tragedies. We are going to be *fine*. You getting pregnant was meant to be. I told you it would happen if it was supposed to. I love you.'

'I love you too.'

'And I'm sorry how I've been keeping stuff to myself. I was just –'

Victoria cut him off, pressing her index finger against his lips. 'It's okay. I know you don't spill things out like me. You're different. You find it harder. You keep things in. I just forget sometimes and put too much pressure on you, which isn't fair.'

That night she was supposed to be attending her first session of Katie's book club, but Simon offered to phone and get her out of it, saying she was delicate and beautiful and he would take charge of supper and her entire life from now on, if she would let him. He commanded her to lie on their little kitchen sofa while he prepared soup, handing her a property supplement that fell out of the paper as he cleared the table.

'Might as well start looking. The sooner we leave London the better, as far as I'm concerned.'

'Really?' Victoria peered over the top of the magazine, which, with the curiously reassuring synchronicity that life managed sometimes, contained a special feature on country houses in Buckinghamshire. The vehemence of his tone had surprised her. 'I know there's this,' she gave a fond pat to her stomach, flat as ever under the buckle of her jeans, 'but why are you suddenly *so* keen to leave London?'

Simon shrugged, busy with pans and tin openers, making a palaver of the soup preparations, as she had known he would. 'A gut thing. The sense of it being time to move on.'

'Dougie will miss you.' Victoria dropped her gaze back to the magazine, privately acknowledging that it would feel decidedly odd for her, too, not having Dougie Easton in the immediate background of their lives, to talk over or wonder about or be annoyed at. 'Hey, this one looks nice – five bedrooms, three acres, a tennis court, a stable conversion . . .'

'Dougie won't miss me,' Simon countered firmly. He had moved to the hob and was stirring the soup so hard Victoria didn't have to look to know it was slopping over the sides of the pan. 'In fact . . .' he glanced over his shoulder to check he had her full attention '. . . that's something else that's been on my mind a bit lately. Dougie and I, it's kind of feeling like we might have outgrown each other.'

'No way . . .' Victoria started to scoff, then saw he was serious. She lowered her magazine onto her lap and crossed her arms. 'Outgrown each other *how*?'

'Dunno . . . hard to explain. We're just not getting on like we used to. Take that football match last weekend. We kind of got on each other's nerves. Badly. I know he was as relieved as I was to get away.'

Victoria was shaking her head in disbelief. She recalled only too well Simon's air of distraction after the match the previous Saturday and had put it down to the smell of beer on his breath and the terse account of it having been a bad game. 'But he would miss you,' she burst out, recalling Dougie's evident desperation on the Wednesday when she and Simon had argued, how obviously he had been in need of his friend. 'In fact, let's get him over here for a meal.' She swung herself off the sofa and tugged open the cutlery drawer, which lived under the rim of the table. 'Sort out whatever funny business has gone on between the two of you. We can have that daughter of his, too, if she's back – which she must be by now.'

'No.'

'No?' Victoria paused, her fingers hooked under the handle of the drawer. 'Just like that?'

'Just like that.' Simon was back at the oven, trying to extract a French stick without using mitts. Behind him the soup saucepan was billowing steam, being boiled to within an inch of its life in the way the instructions on the carton warned against.

Victoria turned her back on the mayhem and took her time laying the table, puzzling over Simon's intransigence, but also slightly wary of her own eagerness on the subject of Dougie, knowing better than to draw attention to it.

'Apart from anything else,' Simon continued softly, once they were seated in front of two overfilled steaming bowls of Waitrose chicken broth, 'I would quite like my wife to myself for the time being, *if* that's acceptable to her.'

'Of course . . . I only meant . . . It just seems a shame if you two have fallen out.'

'Oh, God, we haven't *fallen out*,' Simon cried, now using his new birthday knife to slice through the baguette he had heated, a little too thoroughly, on the top shelf of the oven. 'Nothing like that. Just wheels turning rather more . . . separately. Shall we listen to something nice while we eat? A spot of Vivaldi or Mozart? Aren't the classics supposed to encourage foetal well-being and cerebral development?'

Victoria giggled, sniffing the soup, which smelt appetizing in spite of its maltreatment. 'Or whale-song. I've heard that works well.'

'Let's become real baby-bores,' called Simon, gleefully, hopping to his pagoda of CDs in the sitting room and picking out some Chopin preludes. 'Buy birthing books, go to classes – the works.'

They sipped their scalding meal gingerly, blowing hard at their spoons. The piano music wove in from the sitting room, removing the effort of conversation, melodious but with the usual Chopin timbre of melancholy that always made Victoria want to choose something else. 'You'll be a good dad, Simon,' she said, on a burst of tender sincerity. 'I know you've had your doubts, but you will be good.'

'That's a lovely thing to say. Thanks, Vic.' Simon reached round the table and gently touched her stomach. 'I can feel it in there, you know,' he whispered, holding her gaze with his soft green eyes. 'Our future, in the palm of my hand.'

They started the dinner party outside on the decking, with canapés of gravadlax, smoked reindeer and smoked eel, served to the accompaniment of a champagne so costly that Janine feared Mike might kick up a fuss when he found out about it, in spite of the justification for such extravagance being his own birthday. But the September evening chill soon drove them inside, the women leading the way with cries of relief, their limbs goose-bumped in their skimpy summer cocktail dresses and flimsy wraps. Janine went last, scooping up the discarded plates and paper napkins, thinking how odd it felt to entertain a bunch of guests who were virtual strangers. They were mostly English, all English-speaking, all from Mike's work. She had left the inviting to him, since there was no one she knew well enough to ask, except Esther, who hadn't been able to come.

Once they were all inside, Janine surveyed her sitting room with some desperation. She was kneeling on the floor because they didn't have enough chairs, and could feel pins and needles gathering in her toes and ankles. Mike had told her who everyone was and their places in the company, but she kept getting them muddled. Twelve people were a lot. A couple of names had stuck but the rest were a blur. In the kitchen her beef stew simmered in two casserole dishes; she wasn't sure of the tenderness of the meat so was giving it an extra half-hour, which had meant putting the rice on hold. At home she used easy-cook, but Mike liked basmati, so she was giving that a whirl. The rinsing off of the starch, the exactness of the water for so many mouths – it had been a worry.

Janine wished Esther was there because then she could have talked about Stevie. Her daughter had left for England the day before, a decision largely engineered by Janine herself after a harrowing last forty-eight hours of indecision. Missing her had started long before that – a week at least – and built to a pain now so intense that Janine felt as if a physical weight had been hung around her heart, that she had to make a conscious effort to hold herself upright to accommodate it. Esther, she knew, would understand what she was going through. The last time they had met, her new friend had talked movingly about the misery of having to send her children away to boarding school. A posting to Pakistan had meant that Paul, her youngest, had gone when he was just eight. It had been like having a limb torn from its socket, Esther had said, easing only gradually after weeks and weeks. She had spoilt him ever since to make up for it, she had joked happily – blindly, wickedly and devotedly. He was her baby, after all. The pain eventually went because they always came back, she had concluded, with a sigh, each homecoming all the sweeter for the separation. And Janine had nodded as if she understood, resisting the urge to add that sometimes they didn't come back, that sometimes a child could be lost for good.

'Your Scandinavian winter sounds daunting,' she ventured, to the man nearest her, whom she thought was called Benkt but wasn't sure enough to say. When he had arrived, she had presumed he was on a similar work-level with Mike but had subsequently changed her mind. There was something innately authoritative about him, an aura of self-importance. He had put his arm across Mike's back for several hushed conversational asides, and clearly enjoyed cutting across the bows of anyone trying to lead the conversation. Next to him was an Englishwoman called Melissa, who was some sort of PA and looked as glamorously blonde as any Swede. 'What does everyone do to get through it?'

'We skate. Do you skate?' Melissa responded.

Janine shook her head.

'Okay. Well, there's cross-country skiing. Are you a skier?'

'Not yet,' she confessed, feeling feeble.

'Oh, well, there's always the other thing,' Melissa went on cheerily, exchanging a conspiratorial look with Benkt, 'and that's hitting the bottle.'

'Oh, yes, there's always that,' Benkt agreed, laughing with her.

'There are these wild vodka and crayfish parties,' Melissa explained, turning back to Janine. 'We'll have to get you and Mike along to one – a shot between every mouthful. It takes some stamina, I can tell you. No surprise that Stockholm has one of the highest rates of alcoholics *per capita* of any city in Europe.'

'Gosh, does it?' Janine murmured, and escaped to the kitchen to poke at her rice.

Mike appeared a moment later. He patted her backside as he opened the fridge to get out a fresh bottle of white wine. 'You're doing great, babe, just great.'

'I feel like I don't know anyone.'

'Yeah, but you will – it takes time.' He shot her a reassuring grin and disappeared back into the sitting room. Janine was about to follow when her phone buzzed in her handbag.

Hey Mum, sorry for bad mood when I left. U
no I didn't want to go. Was such a gr8 hol.
All ok here so far. Ams came round and dad
cooked amzing duck thing. We meeting 4
bus ride in tomoz – she being rlly nice x

Janine read the message greedily, using the inside of her sleeve to dab away the inevitable tear, careful not to disturb her makeup. Her nose poured anyway, requiring further swabbing with a tea-towel. Aware that her pots of stew were looking dangerously sticky, she set about composing a hasty reply only to find the phone ringing halfway through.

'Dougie. Not a good moment.'

'Dare I ask why?'

'A dinner party.'

'Ooh, la la.'

'Shut up. It's Mike's birthday. I'm doing a stew which is already overcooked –'

'What sort of stew?'

'Beef, but honestly I can't talk now –'

'Add red wine and mustard if it needs reviving –'

'I know that –'

'And a chicken stock cube –'

'*Chicken?*'

'Any meat, it works best as a short cut for flavour. What are you having with it?'

'Basmati –'

'Doesn't sound like you. The trick is to treat it gently – don't stir it, just a fork at the end. And a wedge of butter. Loads of pepper.'

'I *know.*' Through the doorway behind her Janine could see some of her guests, all deep in lively conversation. She shifted out of view, turning her back. 'What's the matter anyway?'

'Nothing's the matter.'

'Why have you called, then? You sound odd. Is Stevie okay? She just sent me a text.'

'Yes, Stevie's fine.' He hesitated, for so long that had it been anyone else, other than Stevie, Janine would have brought the conversation to an end. 'I wanted to thank you,' he said at last, , 'for not keeping her there. I thought she wouldn't come back, you see . . .' His voice had shrunk so much she could hardly hear it. 'I'd convinced myself and it nearly . . . I nearly . . . I got in a state, Janine, a real state . . .' There was what sounded like a choke before he burst out, 'Fuck, I just know how you must miss her.'

'Do you?' Her eyes were streaming again. She had half a tissue up her nose now, the other half shoring up her lower eyelids in a bid to afford some protection to her mascara. 'Oh, God, Dougie, I can't talk now, I just can't.'

'And whatever you did over there, it's worked wonders,' he went on, talking exuberantly now. 'She looks bloody great, she seems so happy, she –'

'Good, good,' Janine gasped, loving the comfort of what he was saying, but needing him to stop because it was unravelling her.

'She's almost herself again.'

'The Simon thing – remember she doesn't know you know,' Janine cut in, sniffing back her tears, glad to be able to switch to a subject that made her angry rather than sad. 'She was adamant about it.'

'I won't forget, don't worry.'

'Good. Hang on a minute.' Janine put the phone down, blew her nose properly, then shifted out of view of the open kitchen door. 'What you put Simon through, by the way – scaring him like that – well done. He deserved it. That bloody man, he's always been so . . .'

'So what?'

'Nothing. Never mind.'

'Another time, then, eh?'

'Dougie –'

'I promised Simon I wouldn't tell Victoria – did I mention that?'

'No.' Janine closed her eyes and pushed shut the kitchen door, wishing she could close out the imminent demands of her dinner party as easily. 'Poor Victoria,' she murmured, adding in a strained voice, 'But wives are always the last to know these things, aren't they?' On the other side of the door there was a muted gale of laughter. She held her breath, listening to Dougie's pause, the faint sound of him breathing.

'But it wasn't that that broke us,' he said eventually.

'Oh, really? Is that so?' Janine could feel her heart, in all its heaviness, thudding inside her sternum.

'You know it wasn't.'

The door burst open, knocking into her. Mike's head appeared round the side of it, his expression cheerful but his eyes leaping with challenge as they registered the phone.

'Look, Doug, I can't talk now,' Janine said evenly, keeping her eyes on Mike's as she dropped the mobile back into her bag.

'Can I help, babe? I think everyone's starving.'

'Sorry.' She kicked her handbag under the kitchen table. 'I know it's all got late. Five more minutes, okay?' Janine started bustling round the kitchen, peering under saucepan lids and opening drawers, but stopped the moment Mike had gone. She was shaking, she realized, her whole body running with tiny pulses, like minute electric shocks. It wasn't just from what Dougie had said, the subject he had dared to broach: it was from the way he had said it, the softness in his voice. All this time, all the things that had happened, and still he had that effect on her. How? Why?

It happened when he was kind, she reminded herself briskly. That was when Dougie had always got to her, when he was *kind*. She threw herself into the final preparations for the meal, doing all the things Dougie had recommended – the mustard, the wine, the chicken stock cubes, the butter, the pepper, the fluffing with a fork – remembering to check her makeup for smudges before calling out that dinner was served. Fifteen minutes later the stew, presented buffet-style from the dining-room table, was being declared a triumph. After it she produced a shop-bought birthday cake, studded with lit candles, which Mike blew out like an eager child, and an easy lemon tart of Dougie's from the early days, which she had done so many times she could have thrown it together with her eyes closed. After the meal the women stopped drinking and the men had liqueurs. It was close to two o'clock before she and Mike closed their bedroom door.

'Hmm, don't take those off . . . not just yet.'

Janine paused, the hold-up stocking halfway down her leg. 'I don't think so, Mike. I'm tired.'

'But I'm the birthday boy. Birthday boys get what they want, don't they?'

Janine pretended to consider the matter, checking her watch. 'Yes, but the birthday is officially over. Carriages back to pumpkins. Cinderella to rags. And, anyway, this particular princess is bushed.' She continued peeling the hold-up down her leg.

'Don't do that.' Mike sat forwards, gripped her ankle. 'Please, babe.'

'No, Mike. I said no. And can you not call me "babe" so much? I don't like it.' Janine got off the bed and hopped to a bedroom chair. 'You're too pissed anyway.'

'Well, you should be used to that.'

'I beg your pardon?'

He screwed up his face, sticking his tongue out in an ugly imitation of a begging dog. 'Dougie-Dougie-Dougie.' He whined and panted the words, then stopped suddenly, staring at a fixed spot on the wall, his expression glazed and forlorn. 'Look,' he mumbled, 'all I am saying is that for an ex your *Douglas* is still very much on the scene. You're always on the phone to him. Always.'

Janine sat bolt upright on the chair, her stockings in pools round her feet. He had had too much to drink, she reminded herself. He didn't do it often. It wasn't some sinister backsliding, it was part of modern social life. It didn't make him a bad man. It didn't mean she shouldn't love him. And if there were undercurrents of jealousy about Dougie she should be glad. Love contained such dark eddies: she knew that more than anyone: the fear of loss, the desire to possess, it could swallow you. 'I think I might sleep in the spare room.'

Mike slapped his thigh, laughing hollowly. 'Oh, yes, she runs away . . . She *runs away.*'

Janine shook the stockings off her feet and stood up. 'It's late. You're drunk. And I'm upset –'

'Upset? Why? Because your partner wants to screw you? Because he calls you "babe"? Oh, dearie me, what a tragedy.'

Janine slowly put on her dressing-gown, using the moments to compose herself. 'I am upset,' she said quietly, 'because my daughter has gone back to England and I won't see her for another ten weeks at least, maybe fourteen if she decides not to come out at half-term. I am upset because I am the one who persuaded her to go, who talked down that bloody international school we visited when all I wanted to do was sign her up there and then. I did all that because I thought it was best for her. Best for us.' She tightened the belt on her dressing-gown so that it cut deeply into her waist. 'I found it hard, putting her on the plane. Talking to Dougie, staying in touch with what she's up to, how she's coping, means a lot to me. I could have done with you understanding that, Mike, you of all people. Even though it's your fucking birthday.'

Once in the corridor, Janine didn't go to the spare bedroom but put on her fleece, then slipped her feet into the fur-lined boots she had given Mike as a birthday present. In the garden she picked her way across the scrubby lawn to a low stone with a flattish top and sat down, tucking her hands under her armpits for warmth. She couldn't see the

Baltic but she could smell the wind blowing off it, damp and slightly salty. There would be the usual ships chugging in and out of Stockholm – mostly cargo, a couple of cruise liners, the more distant ones looking stock-still, the nearer ones ploughing visibly through the chop of the waves. They hooted and boomed at each other intermittently, like salutary remarks slung out between passing friends. During the day she barely noticed, but on bad nights it could keep her awake. Mike, brought up in Portsmouth, said it made him feel at home.

'What are you doing?'

'Christ – you made me jump.'

Mike was standing behind her, looking comical in flip-flops and boxers, a jumper on back to front and the too-long beanie that she liked to tease made him look like a garden gnome. 'Go back to bed. You look frozen.'

'So do you.'

'I'm in the mood to be frozen.'

'I upset you.'

'Yes, you bloody did.'

'Sorry.' He paused, pulling the woollen hat lower over his eyes. 'He's just so in your life still, it drives me mad.'

'He's only "in my life", as you put it, because of Stevie . . . *our* child.' Janine stressed the word on purpose, daring him to say what she knew he was thinking – what lots of people had thought over the years – that Dougie was only a stepfather, one removed from the real thing. She steeled herself, but he didn't say it.

'Not for much longer,' he ventured instead, making audible efforts to stop his chattering teeth.

'What do you mean?'

'Well, she's nearly grown-up. Look at what happened in Spain – nearly getting into trouble with that boy.'

Janine caught her breath, glad she had kept her promise to Stevie and only told Mike a highly edited version behind the reasons for her daughter's emotional arrival at the airport three weeks before. Betraying a similar plea for confidence with regard to Dougie had been quite a different matter – justifiable, necessary – integral to their role as parents. She stood up, hugging herself, turning her back on the sea. 'Listen, Mike, there is something you have to understand once and for all. It doesn't matter how grown-up Stevie gets. She will always be my daughter. Dougie will always be her father. Between us we will always worry for her, always want the best for her –'

Mike held up his hands. 'Okay, okay. I get it, really, I do.' She could hear the strain in his voice, the mind-over-matter effort at sobriety. 'I'm sorry if I was out of order. Can we go back to bed now? And I won't touch you, if that's what you're worried about.' He hung his head, peering miserably at her from under the rolled brim of the hateful hat. He had taken a step sideways, triggering a security light, which did nothing to improve his appearance.

Janine found herself suppressing a smile. 'You look like an escaped nutter.'

'I am,' he muttered, 'a nutter for you. A frozen nutter, with frozen nuts.'

'Come on.' She turned for the house.

He hurried after her, slinging an arm across her shoulders. 'It was such a great party. Thank you so much, ba–Janine. You were a star. A total star. I won't drink for a month.'

'Don't be silly. Your drinking is fine. I'm just feeling a bit flaky, that's all.'

'Of course you are. I should have understood more, been nicer . . .' Behind them, the timer on the security light switched off, casting the garden into darkness. Mike pulled her closer. 'You phone Stevie all you want, okay? And that bloody ex-husband of yours. Sod the bills – do what you need to do, any time of the day or night. Just don't stop loving me.'

Chapter Twenty-one

The cat followed Dougie out of his house and across to Nina's doorstep where it sat licking the inside of its left back leg while he frisked his pockets for the door keys. Since Stevie's return at the beginning of the week it had taken to sneaking upstairs late in the evening, settling itself on the highest shelf of the boiler cupboard, between the tank and some crusty old linen. The first time Dougie had tried to coax it down, only to be stared at by the blinking inscrutable yellow eyes, as if the animal already had the measure of the battle and knew who would win.

Sleeping over was one thing, but so far Dougie had resisted feeding Sam in his own kitchen and warned Stevie to do the same. Yet pushing open the door that morning, the cat scooting in ahead of him, it seemed to Dougie that Nina's strong white walls were starting to exude a distinct air of dejection at the continued absence of their owner. There was a hint of dampness, too, which he did his best to counter by poking in the under-stairs cupboard and turning up the heating thermostat to give the house a quick blast of warmth. Sam bolted past him and down the stairs to the kitchen, mewing.

Dougie followed, but then paused on the bottom step, for a moment loath to enter the place where the dreadful, difficult previous Saturday had finally ended; a day of such after-shock and grisly self-examination that he could still hardly bring himself to think about it. There was drink at Nina's he had finally realized, after pacing the streets like some feral animal, the eighty quid Stevie money heavy in his pocket, arriving at bars and all-night stores and walking past them, somehow not up to the ignominy of witnesses – fellow-drinkers, the sallow-faced youths manning the check-outs – to this latest, despicable back-sliding. Whisky, gin, vodka – Nina's drinks cupboard had 'most things', he had remembered, bitterly recalling both the words she herself had used on the night of their first surprising dinner-date and the clever, clear sight-line she had given him to her stock of booze, as if she had known all along that to betray any awareness or judgement of his wavering will-power would have been the one thing guaranteed to push him beyond the point of no return.

He would begin with wine, Dougie had decided that night, arriving finally in Nina's kitchen, footsore and sober, almost twelve hours after the miserable business of parting company with Simon in the stadium pub. Wine at least had a veneer of civility to it, the suggestion of some capacity for restraint. There had been only one bottle in the cupboard – a supermarket shiraz. He had taken it out and studied the label carefully, feeling like a ski-jumper poised for launch, blind to everything but the plunge below the tips of his skis. Maybe he would have one glass and then stop. Yes, there was that possibility too.

Dougie was forced from his reverie by Sam dancing with frustration in front of the cupboard that contained his diminishing pyramid of food, balancing on his back legs to paw the handle, thrashing his tail like a whip.

'Okay, okay.' Dougie pushed off from the step and

fetched the half-empty tin from the previous day's feed out of the fridge. He scooped the mush into a bowl and set it on the floor. The cat immediately burrowed his face into it, purring so vigorously it seemed a wonder he didn't choke as he swallowed. Dougie sank onto the sofa to watch, allowing himself a moment of quiet gratitude that the Saturday night low-point had passed, been lived through. Here he was after all, in exactly the same spot six days on, still alone maybe, like some survivor floating on a piece of driftwood, but clear-headed again, alive. Somehow the darkness of those hours had lifted. The week had brightened: Stevie had come back. Simon had stayed away. Demand for his cooking was continuing to gather pace: that morning he had taken a couple of bookings for the run-up to Christmas. And Janine had been thanked, yes, that had been a milestone too. Dougie let his thoughts hover over this achievement in particular, the phone call to Stockholm that had interrupted the beef-stew dinner party, the sense of *something* that had seemed to emerge from their conversation – perhaps just a new level of candour, perhaps something more. He wished he had Nina next to him now so he could get her take on it. She was always good on Janine.

And he had put the shiraz untouched back into the cupboard. Dougie would have liked to tell Nina about that too. In fact, he *would* bloody tell her, Dougie decided, yanking out his phone and punching in his neighbour's mobile number. He had almost spilt it out to Janine during the phone call, but then realized the moment wasn't right, and probably never would be. But Nina was different. Nina was a friend, an integral part of this new stage

346

of his life, a stage of trying harder than he ever had before and not being afraid to own up to the fact. Even the indents in her kitchen wall were starting to feel like old friends. They had played their part the previous weekend, as had the memory of Nina's many kindnesses, her faith in him. It had been excruciating nonetheless. Dougie had clung to the wine bottle before letting go, and the handle of the cupboard before closing it, feeling all the while as if he was clawing his way out of a pit, inching back up towards lost resolve, capable of losing his grip at any moment. The struggle never went away. That was the thing Dougie knew he was still battling to understand. It was as dully repetitive as it was difficult.

Nina's phone was answered by a girl with a faint Antipodean accent. 'Nina's phone – hi, Linda speaking.'

'Can I speak to Nina, please? Tell her it's Dougie.'

'Oh, right – hi there, Dougie. I'm afraid Nina's gone out. Can I take a message?'

'Yes, tell her to let me know when the hell she's coming back. Tell her Sam has adopted me. Tell her I'm going to charge for house-maintenance. Tell her that friends have needs as well as parents . . . Are you the Linda who lives in Auckland?'

'The very same. And you're Dougie, the neighbour, right? The guy who cooks?'

Dougie couldn't help chuckling. 'The guy who cooks, yes. So she's mentioned me, has she?'

There was what sounded like muffled laughter. 'Oh, she certainly has.'

'All good, I hope.'

'Not for a moment.' There was another off-stage noise.

'Are you over for a holiday?'

'Yes . . . sort of . . . A mix of things.'

Dougie detected a hint of reluctance, the withdrawal of the desire to be friendly. 'When is she coming back, do you know? Look, I'm not stalking her or anything, it's just that . . . Well, it would be useful to know for a number of reasons. She keeps fobbing me off with texts, changing the date of her return. That's the other thing you can tell her: no more fobbing me off with texts. Those exact words. Got it? And what's she going out without her phone for anyway? Tell her that's dumb too.'

'Okay.'

'She's not ill again, is she?'

'God, no.'

'Good. Okay. Well, nice talking to you, Linda.'

'And you, Dougie.'

He then sent a text, for good measure, aware that Linda might be enough of a snoop to read it:

Linda sounds nice. Going to re-set your
heating to come on for a couple of hours a
day – might stop Sam hanging out so much
at our place (so don't say you weren't
warned). Call/text when you back from
wherever you are. Dx

Stevie elbowed her way to the top deck, keeping the place next to her for Amelia. Four days into the term and it already felt routine. From her dad's house, school was eight stops away instead of three. Amelia got on at the second. They had been in the same group of friends for years but now it felt like they had a new special thing going, kick-started by Amelia inviting herself to supper within hours of Stevie's arrival back from Stockholm at the beginning of the week. They had ended up getting on really well, catching up on gossip about friends and making plans to hook up for the ride to school. Identical A-level choices meant they had spent most of every subsequent day sitting next to each other, sharing books as well as stories about their holidays, sealing the bond.

For Stevie this had meant surrendering a few guarded details about Paul. Amelia, in return, had supplied several long, breathless confessionals about her feelings for a friend of her elder brother's called Ricky, who had joined her family on holiday for a week in the summer. There had been a tennis court down the road, she explained, closing her eyes with intoxicated sighs to indicate that this was where the relationship had blossomed, though little of it, from what Stevie could later gather, through the playing of any tennis.

'Heard from Paul?' Amelia asked at once, dropping her bag onto her lap as she sat down.

Stevie shook her head glumly.

'Hey, five weeks and he'll be here anyway, remember?'

Stevie pulled a face. 'Then he's going travelling for months and months. So it's hopeless.'

'You don't know that,' Amelia cried, before reporting on the equally unlikely prognosis for her own relationship, Ricky being based in south London where he was embarking on a slog at a crammer for the purposes of retaking every one of his A levels. 'He wants to do sport, really,' she explained earnestly. 'He's totally brilliant at it.'

Stevie was glad to notice that Amelia, like her, was already starting to flout the lame school rule about no heavy jewellery or makeup. She had a big silver chain round her neck and had outlined her dark, feline eyes with thick inky lines and a glossy coating of mascara. She had braided some gold thread into her lush, raven hair, too, making Stevie envy it more than usual, although Amelia herself had recently confided that its abundance was a real burden, for the low hairline that came with it, its lack of malleability and, worst of all, the depilation problems that being so hirsute was now posing on other parts of her body. During the summer, she explained miserably, in a bid to perfect her appearance for Ricky, she had taken the drastic step of waxing her arms as well as her legs. So many in-growing hairs had now resulted that she daren't wear anything but long sleeves, while her mother had been sufficiently concerned to book her an appointment with some sort of skin specialist. So, yes, for all her beauty, Amelia wasn't afraid to own up to problems. It was one of the things Stevie liked most about her.

Rain started to fleck the bus window. Down on the pavement umbrellas popped open and strides quickened. Stevie felt her heart tighten. It was such a grey, uninviting sight – so many million miles away from the pine-scented forests and big blue skies of Sweden. The warm, sun-soaked rocks, the glassy water, Paul's hand round hers: she held the image in her mind, conjuring it like a protective shield. She still couldn't believe it was over, that her grand decision to stay had come to nothing. She had thought that that was all it would take – a decision from her. Her mother hadn't wanted her to return to

England – she had known that absolutely. And yet, some-how, for reasons she was still struggling to come to terms with, her desire for Stevie to stay had not translated itself into support.

'It's not so much the school, Stevie,' Janine had said, as they drove away from the visit, 'and switching to the Bac-calaureate – I'm sure you'd manage. Making new friends, that would happen too . . . It's other things.'

'What things?' Stevie had sniped, unable to believe her ears, having expected Mike's absence from the excursion to be the trigger for a lovely discussion about how it was all going to work out, what things her dad would need to send out to her.

'Messing Dad around, for one.'

'Dad would understand. He even said it would be okay to change my mind. In fact, he was always saying it.'

Janine sighed heavily, nodding. 'Yes, well, he would.'

'So what's the problem, then?'

'Dealing with stuff, that's what. Facing up to it. Not running away. You've had a great holiday here, but life, sadly, isn't a holiday, and . . . I sort of think that's what you're hoping for. Paul and Daisy won't be around for much longer. There will be schoolwork, lots of it –'

'Mike doesn't want me around, does he? That's the reason.'

'Mike wants what I want,' she replied tersely. 'I can deal with Mike.' They had arrived home by then but were still in the car. The house, with its ugly pebble-dash walls, was above them, perched on its rocky outcrop like some great grey bird. The skies were overcast that day, but the air was still warm. Stevie wound down the window, sticking her elbow out. 'So why did we even look at that place? To *humour* me?'

'Of course not. To help you make the choice —'

'But I'm not making the choice, am I? You are. Getting rid of me.'

Janine turned to her, her expression solemn, unmoved. 'It's just gradually been dawning on me that you should stick to the plan of returning, for the time being anyway, just in case . . .' she frowned, biting her lip '. . . just in case there's a part of you that might one day look back and see you were running away.'

'Running away? From what? Simon?' she sneered.

Her mother shrugged. The lines around her mouth were tight, her eyes wide and sad. 'Him. Life.'

By the last day, the prospect of her imminent departure had hung so thickly, so suffocatingly, that it had been a relief to flee, after constrained hasty farewells, into the mind-numbing pre-flight rituals of security checks and Passport Control. A text from Paul, wishing her a good flight and reminding her to stay in touch, had buoyed her a little. They remained nothing more than good friends, but with his visit to London, who knew what might transpire? Then there had been the lovely rush of seeing her dad at Stansted, towering out of the crowd with his light-house grin, in a frayed, crumpled T-shirt and his old stone-washed jeans with the half-ripped pocket. For a moment Stevie had been dizzy with the gladness of having come back, of not having let him down. They had chatted easily all the way home, just like when he used to collect her for one of her weekend visits, back in the days before things had started to go wrong.

It was only as she was unpacking, the night darkening her bedroom window and the single central light-bulb with its ugly orange glass shade doing its usual useless job of illuminating the room, let alone the shelves in her wardrobe, that Stevie had felt the doubts creeping back in. It was almost as if a residue of the unhappiness after Spain – the panic, the binge-eating, the self-loathing – still lingered in the room, soaked like damp into its dingiest corners, behind the grimy pipe under the basin, inside the bobbling patches of wallpaper where the Blu-Tack had hardened in her absence, leaving her carefully arranged posters hanging off the wall. What had her mother been doing, sending her back to this? And her dad, clattering around downstairs, what would he do if he ever found out that the person responsible for the shameful pregnancy scare had been his *married* oldest friend? How angry, how appalled, how sickened would he be? And though she would rather sew her lips together than ever confess as much to him, Stevie had this sudden heart-stopping terror that she might cry it out in the night anyway, shrieking like some guilt-crazed creature in the middle of a bad dream. Or, even more likely, the truth would somehow reveal itself when Simon visited, as he was bound to do at some stage, in spite of her mother's reassurances.

It was into this torment that Amelia's chirpy text had arrived: *Hey, could I come round? Family driving me mental and your dad's house so close.*

Dad will say no, she had texted back. But Dougie, crashing into the room with talk of some sort of Chinese-style duck for dinner, had said yes, unwittingly opening a path for life to become bearable again, if not exactly worry-free.

Stevie had made her peace with her mother by text the same evening, missing her too much to do anything else.

Brainwashing was the only thing that would really make everything okay, Stevie reflected grimly, clomping down the narrow bus stairs after Amelia that morning, following her lead in dodging the boy who stuck his leg out, trying to trip them. One button to eradicate Spain from her memory – zap: she would have pressed it like a shot.

'Wanker!' Amelia squealed at the boy, when they were at a safe distance, the bus moving off.

Stevie stuck up a finger in support before falling into step for the final half-mile trudge to school.

'You okay?' Amelia cast her a doubtful glance.

'Yup. Good, thanks.' Stevie swung her bag onto her other shoulder. It had been easy talking about Paul. But *Simon* . . . Amelia wouldn't understand. The more time passed, the less Stevie understood it herself. Had she been insane? The thought of ever having to be in the same room as the man now – breathe the same air – made her feel ill, yet one day soon it would happen. And it was the threat of this that continued to eat away at her. He had been her dad's friend since school, in and out of their lives for as long as she could remember. Simon could play the situation just how he liked. She was the powerless one. A sitting duck. A total idiot.

'Hey, Ams, listen to this,' she blurted later that morning, when they had bunked off to Tesco Local for juice boxes and chicken fajita wraps, which they were eating sitting against a wall under the covered bit of the shopping precinct. 'What would you do if you'd got drunk and had sex with your father's best friend and were scared of seeing him? Oh, yes, and he was married.' Stevie kept her voice merry and her concentration on her wrap, feeling for a stray shred of lettuce with her tongue.

Amelia snorted. 'I'd have to be pretty messed up to do that. Anyone would.' She screwed up her face, giggling.

'Yeah, but let's just say it happened, what would you do?'

'Serious?'

'Yeah, just try and imagine it.'

'Tell my mum, probably . . . God, I don't know. What is this? What would you do? Why are you asking anyway?' Amelia was still smiling but her brown eyes had darkened with suspicion.

'It's just a game,' Stevie explained hastily, leaping to her feet. An idea had occurred to her, which she needed time to process; maybe not as good as brainwashing, but it might help make her feel better . . . less of a sitting duck anyway. Her mum, with all her talk of not running away, might just approve of it too. 'We played it a bit in Sweden,' she jabbered, improvising. 'You have to think up crazy situations and come up with honest answers as to how you would deal with them.'

Reassured, Amelia contorted her face and mimed slicing her throat. 'Kill him,' she rasped, imitating a line from the horror DVD they had recently watched, before reverting to noisy sucking on the straw of her juice box. 'What about you?'

But Stevie was already charging off down the pavement, shrieking how late they were, making a hood of her cardigan against the drizzle.

When she got home that afternoon the kitchen was full

of women in aprons, chatting and washing up and surrounded by dishes of food. Her father was standing in the middle, like a conductor who had lost control of his orchestra. Stevie pulled a face at him from the doorway and escaped upstairs. Half an hour or so later, after the slams and bangs of them all leaving, he knocked on her bedroom door. 'Not disturbing you, am I?'

'*Yes.*'

'Good.' He pulled out her desk chair and sat on it back to front, leaning on his forearms. 'Hard at work, I see.' He nodded in the direction of the bed, where she was lying propped among a clutch of extra pillows stolen from the spare room, watching a music video on her laptop.

She faked a scowl. 'Who were those women, anyway?'

'"Those women" were a lady called Miranda Charters and her yummy-mummy friends, embarking on a cordon-*blue* course to please the palates of their rich husbands. Bill-payers, in other words, our bills, yours and mine. Cooking is the new rock and roll and it's making my landlord and my bank manager very happy.'

She snorted. 'Yeah, right.'

'How was school?' As the question left his mouth Dougie was assailed by a sudden unsettling image of Simon's short, wiry body in the act of having sex with his daughter, his eyes half closed, his breath short, his narrow hips pumping. Dougie gripped the chair-back, giving the picture, the surge of anger it provoked, time to recede. Maybe it hadn't been like that. Maybe Stevie had been on top of Simon. Maybe she was an old hand at sex and he didn't know. Parents didn't know stuff: it was their lot. And she seemed okay.

'School's all right. Loads more work.'

'A levels – I should hope so, if you want a shot at university, which I believe you do.' He gave her a quizzical look.

'And how was *your* uni career, Daddy dear?'

Dougie laughed. 'I was a waste of space. We're agreed on that. You're making up for it. You're my only hope. I'm the unhealthiest of parents, living vicariously through his one and only daughter.'

'Hmm.' She looked pleased. 'Amelia's asked me to stay over next weekend – Friday *and* Saturday, if that's all right. They've got a seaside place they go to in Norfolk. Would that be okay?'

'Sure.' Dougie reached up and pushed the floating corner of one of the posters back into its bulge of hardening Blu-tack. 'Not missing Sweden too much, then? It sounds like you had such a good time. In fact, it's still a wonder to me that you came back at all . . . Boring old Dad.'

Stevie shrugged, as if there had never been any question of secret terrors or torn loyalties. 'Not always boring,' she conceded, glancing up from her screen, a flash of the old little-girl mischief in her blue eyes. 'Why don't you just start another restaurant, anyway?' she added, flipping the subject. 'Surely that would be easier than having all these people coming to our house.'

Dougie hesitated, liking the way she had said 'our' house, so nonchalantly. 'For two reasons,' he explained at length, counting them off on his fingers. 'Starting a new restaurant would take money, which I don't have. Second, it might stress me out.'

'You mean you'd start drinking again.'

She held his gaze with a new boldness that caught him

357

off-guard, more a sign of growing up, he realized, than anything she might be getting up to in her sex life. 'Something along those lines, yes. And I wouldn't see much of you, which would be a shame since I've missed out rather a lot on that score already, haven't I?' Dougie smiled, sparing a wistful thought for the recently dismantled plan to implement Victoria's idea of offering cooking courses abroad. Commuting to Europe for weeks at a time, leaving Stevie alone, was out of the question. At least, for the time being.

The door creaked open and Sam slunk in. He paused to check them out, his wary yellow eyes managing to communicate the unmistakable impression of disappointment. 'When's Nina coming back anyway?' Stevie asked, tweeting at the cat, which ignored her and slipped back out onto the landing.

'I don't know and it's beginning to piss me off.' Dougie disentangled himself from the chair. 'Dinner in ten – okay? It's fish pie – smoked haddock, boiled eggs, capers, cream, bacon, Gruyère mash, made by those posh ladies you were so rude about. And you're washing up.'

Stevie pulled a face because she knew it was expected of her. She didn't care about the washing-up, or the fish pie, come to that. She was too busy mulling over the idea she had had that lunchtime – how to see it through, whether she had the courage.

Chapter Twenty-two

Alone the following Friday evening, with Stevie on her jaunt to Norfolk, Dougie fixed upon the virtuous aim of making further headway on his book. With the *finca* plan on hold, it mattered more than ever as a long-term project for generating income, but what was just as important, Dougie knew, was keeping himself busy, fending off the inevitable loneliness that had taken him to the brink two weeks before. The house had begun to feel dangerously quiet that afternoon already, with no work booked for the weekend and an evening meal to prepare for one instead of two. For a moment he had even caught himself missing Simon, experiencing a surge of anger at what a mess the man had made of everything, the scale of what he had destroyed. Stevie seemed to have put the whole business behind her, which ultimately was all that mattered, but Dougie knew it would be a long time, if ever, before he would be able to follow suit.

He ate a plate of rejuvenated leftovers from his morning class, then settled himself at the kitchen table with a pot of coffee and a box of old files from his days at the Black Hen. He had dragged the box out from the measly storage space behind the boiler, using a step-ladder of Nina's to reach it and upsetting Sam's bed of old linen in the process. His new idea was to leave the Introduction, which had stalled, and to use the box of archives to kick-start his brain into tackling a new, much trickier chapter on the subject of start-up costs.

Bored even before he had started, Dougie ignored the box and drank all the coffee, while composing a text to Nina instead, continuing in the vein of funny headlines they had been exchanging all week: SOS: *Neglected Neighbour Considering Spit Roasting Friend's Cat – with garlic and fennel. Urgent action required. Dx*

Finally out of diversionary tactics, he then, with a groan of reluctance, tipped the contents of the box onto the table. A couple of dead spiders and a woodlouse fell out, too, along with several bulldog clips separated from the futile task of trying to keep order. The papers were badly jumbled, not just from falling out of folders but because he had never been very good at filing them. Dougie started wading through them one by one, making brave efforts to create piles. Wage sheets, rent statements, bank statements, invoices, menus, correspondence on everything from font sizes to flower deliveries: his attempts to create order spread in wider and wider circles until it seemed nothing short of a miracle that he had ever been master of such multi-layered organizational complexity.

Except, of course, he hadn't been, Dougie reminded himself, despondence setting in. That was why the Black Hen had gone under. He hadn't been master of anything. Unpaid debts, deserting staff, freeloaders, dwindling customers – it had been a long, slow, winding, grisly road. The bailiffs had come round in the end, forcing their way through his locks and bolts with crow-bars. Dougie had been waiting for them at one of his empty tables, nursing the inevitable glass and almost-empty bottle, along with dim, misguided notions of himself as some Clint East-wood-style cowboy hero, the granite-faced stoic in the saloon bar, facing the shoot-out alone. Until he had tried to stand up and realized he had pissed himself, where-upon the only route out of the situation had been a call to Janine, the most humiliating of his life, begging to be taken home.

Dougie pushed the papers out of the way feeling drained, his notepad empty. Stevie's comment had pro-voked a brief spark of hope. A foolish tendril. But it was suddenly clearer to him than ever that his success, such as it was, had been the brief pinnacle of a hit-and-miss com-bination of alchemy, energy and sheer balls. The pit-falls had been everywhere from the start, from hubris, back-handing suppliers, filching staff, to treacherous small-print. He had fallen headlong into every single one, clinging to the youthful, naïve notion of a good restaurant being like good theatre: a place where a star turn could please an audience. Instead, as he had learnt to his cost, any suc-cessful dining establishment was a complex, Machiavellian machine, requiring constant vigilance, constant adjust-ments, constant oiling. He had never been up to that, not in the long-term. He was just a man who cooked, as Nina's Kiwi friend had said, a man who *liked* to cook indeed, but with enough character failings to sink a fleet.

Dougie slapped his notebook shut and threw it across the table. A failed restaurateur offering advice on starting costs – did he want to be a laughing stock? The notebook came to rest in the biggest unsorted pile, dislodging a cream-coloured piece of paper that stood out from the rest: a formal, parchment-style material, headed with elaborate dark-inked lettering. Dougie squinted at it to make out the words, then wished he hadn't.

James Fulbright & Sons Funeral Directors.

Slowly, using one finger, he reached across the table and steered the invoice towards him through the mêlée of papers. It had to be looked at, he told himself, sorted through, sifted, like all the other scraps of his past. Only then could it be *left behind*, as people said, these days. Dougie grimaced, despising the implication that bits of a life that had gone wrong could simply be lopped off and discarded without blood-letting and pain. In front of him the columns of numbers and the items they referred to – flowers, the hearse, VAT – shifted and settled. Two thousand three hundred and forty-two pounds. It was a tiny amount, really, given the balance of what had been lost.

Dougie closed his eyes, seeing not the small white box that contained his baby son being lowered into the ground but Janine's face opposite him under her black umbrella. Her neck had been twisted to one side, her mouth open, like a straining swimmer seeking a gulp of air. Because she couldn't bear to look – at least, not downwards, into the deep pit of freshly dug earth at their feet. He hadn't been able to look there either, seeing it clearly enough in his mind's eye for all of those long moments and every one afterwards during the weeks and months ahead, each as sharp as the last, no matter how thick the prism of alcohol with which he tried to blur it.

But it occurred to Dougie now, sitting clear-headed at his kitchen table five years on, that maybe Janine's averted face had been a simple – typical – reflexive effort to protect Stevie, ten years old and self-consciously solemn on the other side of her, from seeing the full ugly force of her mother's grief: mouth wide, a dying creature trying to breathe. It had been a sight to stop a heart. It had certainly shredded Dougie, with his clear view from the other side of the grave, the drink affording no protection from that either; and he had been very drunk that day, so bad he could smell it seeping out of his skin and through his crumpled funeral clothes. It was one of the reasons he had stood where he had, head down, arms in, keeping his distance, keeping to himself in all his shame, behaving like the outsider he already was: failed, guilty, beyond the reach of his own pity, let alone anyone else's.

And that was when the last beat between them had stopped, not with all the deceitful stupidity that had preceded it, destructive though that indisputably had been, but at the graveside of their five-week-old son, Ross, their big, beautiful effort at a fresh start, gone so hideously wrong. The endgame had taken a couple more years to reach – life, the business limping on, as it tended to, unravelling until there was nothing left – but it was seeing his wife's pain through the bars of rain at the graveside that had ended it for Dougie. No sentient creature could accept responsibility for such hurt and want to stay anywhere near it. That day he had turned away from her and from all restraint for ever afterwards, or such had been his intention.

Dougie pushed back his chair and scooped all the papers up, ramming them back into the box. Until Ross's death there had been hope, that was the point. They had got something back. For almost a year they had been doing okay. He had been doing okay. In the aftermath it had been easy to forget that. And this was one of the things Dougie had suddenly found himself wanting to say to Janine on the phone: that there had been bad stuff before, most of it his fault, but that the spiralling after Ross had been different, not about running away from her so much as the sight of her suffering.

Dougie picked up the box and grabbed one of his old lighters from a pot on the window sill. Levering open the back door with his elbow, he clambered up to the garden. He chose a safe mid-point in the scrub of bramble and dirt, and held a flame to the cardboard corners until they were fully lit. He stood back to watch, tucking his hands under his armpits, his face set but resolved. It was a new, curious experience, to be down but not despairing; to be still in control. It almost felt as if disparate bits of him, floating free for years, were starting to reconnect, to make sense again. He was contemplating fetching his book notes to add to the pyre, when a flash of electric light caught his eye, sweeping across one of the dark upper windows of Nina's house. Her bedroom, if he wasn't mistaken. Dougie waited until he saw the light again, then hurried inside to fetch her door keys.

It was only when he reached the front of Nina's house that he paused, debating whether it might be wiser to call the police or one of those non-emergency numbers that arrived on the leaflets he threw away. He crouched down and peered through the letterbox. Hearing a dull thud from upstairs, he shouted, 'Oy, what's going on in there?' When a female voice shouted back, 'Hang on,' he sprang upright, feeling like an idiot, albeit a happy one. It had to be some kind of power-cut. Nina was back and the electrics were down. 'Nina? It's only me.' He put the key in the lock and stepped inside.

A torch beam appeared at the top of the stairs, illuminating two slim female legs in flared jeans. 'Nina? It's me, Dougie. Has a fuse blown? Is your power down?'

The feet moved slowly down each step, a heavy tread, clearly not Nina's, as Dougie quickly realized, but clearly not those of some desperate intruder either. 'No, the power's fine.' The voice was soft, with a familiar Antipodean twang.

Dougie flicked the hall light switch, squinting in the sudden glare that bounced off the white walls. The woman, who had wavy strawberry blonde hair and gingery freckles, blinked back at him. 'Are you Linda?'

She nodded, as if the admission depressed her. 'And I guess you're Dougie.'

'Yes, what's going on?'

She shook her head. 'Er . . . that could take a while. And possibly a drink. Do you know where she keeps it? Would you like something?'

'No, I wouldn't, thanks.'

Linda had moved towards the stairwell down to the kitchen, but Dougie stayed where he was, his skin prickling with a dull sense of impending calamity. 'Why are you here? What's with the torch? Where's Nina?'

She turned, leaning against the wall, tucking some of her feathery hair behind her ear. She had light blue eyes, which looked as if they were more used to laughter than being stern, as they were now, hard as stones. 'I was trying not to be noticed.'

'What — by me?'

She nodded glumly. 'Yes, by you.'

'Why?' Dougie would have laughed had it not been for the rigid set of her face. 'What's happened?'

'Nina is ill.'

'Some sort of relapse?' Dougie felt calm, matter-of-fact. He had half known it — known it and not known it. 'How bad?'

'Dougie, she's dying. She's in a hospice . . .' Linda's lips were twitching. 'Not long left.'

'No.' Dougie swung his head from side to side, grinning in the manner of one underlining an obvious error to a dimwit. 'Impossible. She would have told me. And you . . . *you* . . .' he pointed at Linda '. . . you told me she was fine. When I asked on the phone the other day you said she was fine. And she's been texting me all week. Look.' He held out his mobile.

Linda dropped her gaze, chewing the end of a finger. 'That was me.'

Dougie tried to laugh. 'Don't be ridiculous — those messages . . . you?'

'I'm sorry. It's what she wanted.'

Dougie clung to his phone, scrolling clumsily through his texts. 'That is just not possible. That — is — not . . .' He gave up, his fingers trembling too much to find anything. 'She wouldn't do that,' he insisted, as if it were a situation that could still be argued away. 'We were pals. We . . .' He managed a bark of a laugh, which hurt his throat. 'She . . . we told each other the truth.'

Linda was looking away, eating another finger. 'She wrote a lot of letters before she . . . There's one for you.'

'I don't want a *fucking* letter. And what do you mean *wrote* anyway? What the fuck do you mean by that? Wrote. How dare you? Is she dead or what?'

'No. But she's . . . Dougie, you're angry –'

'Too bloody right I'm angry.' The mobile somehow flipped out of his hands, bucking off the skirting-board and clattering onto the floor. It skidded, face up, to Dougie's feet, the screen criss-crossed with hairline cracks. 'And now look. Look at that,' he snarled. He picked up the phone and shook it at her, as if the damage was her fault.

'A drink –'

'I don't *fucking* drink.' He turned and barged out of the door, which seemed to have narrowed since he had come through it, snagging his elbows. He staggered on, rubbing his bruised arms, but then managed to trip, first over the pitifully obvious stone under which Nina had hidden her spare keys, and again on the sorry little spiky fence separating their house-fronts. At his own door, he stabbed his key at the lock but it didn't fit. It wasn't quite raining but the air was a cold wet sponge in his face, filling his eyes, his throat, drowning him, it felt like.

'Here let me.' Linda was at his side. She reached round him and gently took charge of the keys. 'We need to talk. I'll explain everything. She said you were great. And you are. You've helped her more than you can possibly know.'

The morning sickness came from nowhere, arriving like an unexpected punch in the solar plexus. One minute she was eating breakfast, granola, yoghurt, tea, Simon behind the newspaper across the table, and the next she was hurling herself at the lavatory bowl, not quite getting there in time.

'Blimey,' said Simon, from the doorway, sounding more impressed than sympathetic. 'Is that what I think it is?'

Victoria raised her head weakly, spittle trailing from her mouth. 'I suppose.' She sat back on her heels and began tearing off strips of loo roll in a desultory effort to wipe the mess off the floor. 'I think it was your aftershave that started it.'

'Well, that's charming, I must say. Key symptom of pregnancy: allergy to husband.'

Victoria shook her head feebly. 'I've just been noticing lately that any sort of perfumed smells seem really pungent, like in here, that air-freshener.' She clutched her throat and dropped her face over the bowl, retching again.

Simon stayed where he was, torn between offering help that would almost certainly be rejected and going back to his newspaper and toast. 'Would some water help? Decent stuff from the fridge?'

She batted an arm at him, shaking her head. 'No – thanks – go. I'll be fine.'

Simon retreated gratefully and put some fresh bread into the toaster. He liked toast only when it was still warm enough to melt butter. Cold, it reminded him of the chewy squares they had been served at school, the really hateful school, the one before he had run into Dougie. Victoria appeared a few minutes later, looking composed but very pale. 'Hey, sit down, Vic, you poor –'

'I'm sorry, Simon, but I don't think I'm going to be able to make it today. Just the thought of getting into the car . . .' She eased herself carefully into her chair, holding her stomach. 'I'm sorry. Could we refix, do you think? Or you could go alone.'

'Are you sure?' Simon folded away the paper, knowing already that he would be more than happy to keep the property-viewing appointment on his own. It was a manor house in a Buckinghamshire village, picked out not just for its stunning merits as a building – listed, refurbished, with four acres and its very own water mill – but because of its proximity to his in-laws. Not an ideal stipulation, as far as Simon was concerned, but in trying to keep Victoria's flagging enthusiasm for the house-moving project afloat, it had been the one idea she had latched on to with real conviction. Her mother was due home in a few weeks and she was full of renewed daughterly good intentions about doing her best to keep her there.

Nonetheless, she was looking at him now with a pained expression. 'I still don't quite see the rush you're in over all this.'

'It's a nice house, that's all,' Simon countered swiftly, aware that it would be impossible to explain to Victoria, of all people, his mounting sense of unease about staying in London, the imperceptible feeling that matters on several fronts were in danger of catching up with him. Geographical distance was what he sought now, from his flailing career, from Dougie, whom he missed terribly but no longer trusted, not to mention the potential awkwardness of running into his nubile siren of a daughter. Only then would he regain true peace of mind, a sense of *security* ... Yes, that was what he had lost, Simon reflected grimly, another of those subtle luxuries so easily undervalued until it was snatched away. 'The place is a *gem*,' he went on, channelling his energies away from introspection and into the immediate, much more important task of presenting a convincing case about the house-viewing, 'way ahead of anything else I've been able to find. Prices are set to go up. Everybody says so. A spring upturn, that's what the pundits are predicting – getting in now we could save ourselves hundreds of thousands.'

'Of course. Golly.' Victoria took a sip of her orange juice, wary still of triggering more nausea. If anyone had a right to claim full acquaintance with current property forecasts it was Simon. In the two weeks since the discovery that she was pregnant he had pursued the subject relentlessly – both online and off – sale prices versus purchase prices, comparing areas, the proximity of rail stations, parking facilities, commute times. It was his new pet project. The TV script, so slogged and honed and agonized over the previous month, hadn't been summoned to his laptop screen since Scotland; neither had any other writing venture emerged to replace it. He had already viewed several properties on his own and ruled them unsuitable. This was the first he had insisted they visit together. While feeling somewhat overwhelmed, Victoria knew she should be very grateful for such drive and focus. She still liked the idea of the move, but even before she'd felt ill, the gruelling process of searching and selling had held little appeal. It was wonderful to have Simon so on top of it all, precluding the awful possibility of a 'bad' decision, soaking up the stress. 'You go, then,' she urged warmly. 'If it's as good as it seems we can take a second look together, can't we?'

'Okay.' Simon hesitated. 'But you'll be all right, will you? The puking – can you take something for it?'

Victoria took a more confident swig of her juice, feeling immediately better now that the ordeal of a four-hour round trip in the car had been removed. 'Maybe, but I'd prefer to ride things out naturally. Work will take my mind off it – I've got the Strindberg to tidy up and the new stuff on the tricky Juan Muñoz to think about.'

'It's Saturday, Vic. Take a break.'

'Yes, I'll do that too. I might even visit Ruth and Gary if I feel up to it. Meet little Polly.' She beamed.

Simon waited till he had passed the last of the M4's speed-camera signs, then put his foot down. The old Jaguar took a few seconds to respond, like some trusty steed, gathering itself for a gallop. But as the engine worked its way through the automatic gear changes, Simon detected a new, throaty discord among the usual sounds, as if some deep, tiny cog wasn't quite where it was supposed to be. Irritated, deciding to drown it, he flicked through his CD options and settled on Mahler, always a safe bet for summing up life's ups and downs – music that could boost you and break you in a single line.

Simon started to hum the familiar opening but stopped as a rare catch of emotion blocked his throat. He felt as if he was living dangerously, living in fear, and he didn't like it. He was a good man who had done a bad thing . . . well, an imprudent thing anyway. He didn't deserve to suffer as Dougie had forced him to. Even now he could hardly bring himself to recall their encounter in the dingy football pub, his old friend's eagerness to climb on his moral high horse and tell him off, tell him how to live, *humiliate* him. Simon glanced in his rear-view mirror, seeing not the traffic in the lane behind but his own narrow face, pale and pinched. Dougie had made him feel small and stupid, and he could never forgive that. Ever. No matter how much he missed the man. If their friendship had meant anything to Dougie, he should have put it first. They went back more than twenty years, for God's sake. He should have put it first.

The only thoroughly good thing to happen in recent weeks was Victoria falling pregnant. In his darker moments Simon clung to this as proof that there was not only a God in charge of the world but one who was on his side. He retained many private and selfish misgivings about becoming a parent, some of which he would probably now never share with Victoria, but had still been able to recognize the pregnancy for the miracle it truly was: restoring marital harmony just when it was most needed, offering a way out, a passport to a new, secure future. Without too much effort, it was a future he could really look forward to: living in an idyllic rural retreat, writing the occasional article, doing a spot of childcare between other more enjoyable pursuits, like playing golf or shooting – he'd always wanted to have a go at that. He could picture him and Victoria becoming quite grand and 'county', like her parents. They would have house parties and go on exotic holidays. It would take some adjusting to, but it would be a fine life. And he was good at adjustments, Simon reminded himself. It was how he had always got by, learning to say and do whatever it took to fit in, to hang on to the things he wanted.

He tapped the steering-wheel to count in a surge of strings, soaring and swooping, while the darker rhythms of the music marched their warpath underneath. Beside him, the countryside streaked past, flat lines of grey and green under a monochrome sky, not far enough from London yet to be interesting. But it was still great to have the city behind him, shrinking like a bad dream. Lately, with all that had happened, he had started to feel truly out of love with the place, as if it were another old friend who had turned on him and let him down.

Victoria got out her laptop, then put it back in its case. The sun had appeared between two banks of cloud, lighting up the smears on the windows. She slid the doors open onto the balcony and went to lean on the stone balustrade, soothing her strained throat and the lingering nausea with deep breaths of air. Below her, London heaved, red buses, the green glints of office windows and patches of autumnal foliage adding colour to its landscape of concrete and tarmac. It might not be an ideal place to bring up a child, but she would certainly miss it.

When the clouds slid shut, taking the sun's warmth with them, she retreated inside and phoned Ruth, arranging to call round the following afternoon, having decided it would be much better for her and Simon to make the visit together.

After the call a sudden, drugged sleepiness overtook her. Unable to face coffee, she made tea and tried to fight it, sitting on the sofa first with one of her art books on modern Spanish sculpture and then with a couple of the property specs Simon had been amassing, one of them of the place he was seeing that lunchtime. A converted mill. Victoria peered at the photos, trying to make out what was what, but then stopped, her stomach lurching. A mill meant water, surely. With a baby to worry about? Were they out of their minds? There were enough hazards during the early years of parenting without adding to them.

She shuddered, dropping the spec to the floor and stretching out on the sofa, letting her thoughts drift to the cot death of Janine and Dougie's little boy that Simon had forbidden her to dwell on. It had to be five years ago at least; one of those random tragedies. They had been very private about it. No flowers, only family at the funeral. Seeing Janine many months later, the dark guarded look on her face, Victoria hadn't dared mention it. The baby – she couldn't even remember his name: Robbie? Russ? Ross? – had been just a few weeks old. Did that make it any easier, she wondered now. A couple of hours, a couple of weeks – was parental affection fixed from the start or did it grow with time?

Minutes later, it seemed, although Victoria realized very quickly that it was far longer, she was woken by the trill of her mobile, bouncing on the dining-room table. She rolled off the sofa, getting to it just before it cut out.

'Hey, Si . . . sorry . . . I fell asleep.' Her lips felt gummy, her head thick. 'What was the house like?'

'Fantastic. I think we should put in an offer –'

'God, really?' Victoria thought of the water, the impossibility of it, but it didn't seem the right moment to say anything.

'But there's bad news, too, I'm afraid.'

'Oh dear, what?'

'The bloody car. There was this rattling and it got worse. And then steam –'

'So where are you? It sounds like –'

'A pub. I managed to pull over in this village. Called your father.'

'Dad? But surely you need the RAC. We are members.'

'Oh, yes, them too. They're on the way – could be up to two hours, they said. But they won't be able to fix it on the spot. I know they won't. It's something bad. Big job – trust me, you should have heard it. So I've called that garage your father uses. They've been incredibly helpful, I must say. The main man there, Bill, has agreed to take a look if the RAC can get it to him. Says he'll see if he can sort it by the end of the day.'

'But what if he can't?' Victoria knew she sounded plaintive but she couldn't help it. She *felt* plaintive. The RAC could just as easily have towed the Jag back to London, that was what their policy said: one breakdown, one tow, to the destination of your choice.

'Like I said, Bill was optimistic. Apparently they open the workshop on a Sunday morning so there's really no need to worry.'

'But that would mean you having to stay over.'

'There is that chance,' Simon conceded. 'But your father has kindly said there's no problem with me staying the night, if that should prove necessary. In fact, he sounded pretty pleased that I might be calling by.'

'Did he? Good.'

There was a pause. 'He suggested golf, actually.'

Victoria looked out of the window. A group of birds was flying in formation over the Post Office Tower, like some giant pen-scrawl across the sky. 'I wouldn't have thought there was enough time left for a round of golf today, not after the car . . .'

'Yes, well, I told him maybe tomorrow – if I'm around.'

'I've just agreed we'd visit Gary, Ruth and the baby tomorrow.'

'I thought you were going to do that today.'

'I didn't feel up to it.'

There was a silence, during which Victoria wondered if she was being mean. A husband wanting to play golf with a father-in-law was hardly a crime. And it might be good for Simon to relax a little. Even since the baby news he hadn't gone back to being quite his usual carefree self – indeed, Victoria had half wondered if that was *because* of the baby news, whether he was feeling a bit panicky about it, a bit cornered. 'Look, don't worry,' she said, doing her best to sound amiable as opposed to stoical. 'I've arranged to see them at half two. If you're back in time, fine. If not, I'll go alone.'

'Okay.' Simon's voice hummed with relief. 'How's your day going? How's the puking?'

In the background Victoria could hear a swell of noise, laughter and voices. 'Everything's going all right. I don't feel sick any more, just really tired. I might try and eat something. Read a novel.'

'Good idea. I'll let you know when I have a prognosis on the car. In the meantime you look after yourself, okay?'

Victoria hurriedly set about obeying, putting on lights, the kettle, the radio, making herself some honey and toast, running a bath. She knew she was good on her own, not one of those leeching women who *needed* their men to make sense of themselves. Holding her own during the height of the Dougie times – the excesses and Simon's involvement – had taught her how to do that if nothing else.

Ten minutes later, however, in the act of pouring hot water over a sachet of fruit tea, she found tears spilling down her cheeks. Because she was pregnant, of course – hormones ricocheting: wild emotions were part of the deal. But it didn't feel like hormones. It felt like loneliness – the sort where you think you've jumped off a cliff with someone at your side, only to find you're falling alone.

Chapter Twenty-three

There were big gates, one for entry, one for exit, and between them a wide, crescent-shaped drive with room for parking, as well as vehicles passing through. The building was sturdy and of Victorian red brick, with white-painted window frames, some sporting small wrought-iron balconies, others with well-stocked window boxes of pansies, cyclamen and trailing ivy. On both sides, and extending round the back of the house, there was a great sweep of recently mown lawn, pitted with beds of roses and lavender and bordered by a hedge of tall thick privet.

Dougie wound up the window and got out of the car. He had driven in and out of the gates twice before parking. The sky was a clear deep blue. Somewhere a bird was singing and the air had the earthy autumn smell of damp leaves. In front of him there was a towering tree, its bark a soft, mossy green, its upper body a thick criss-cross of ancient boughs shrouded in verdant rust-coloured foliage. Its mighty trunk leant inwards slightly, towards the house, as if frozen in some great dance-mime of protection over its occupants. The afternoon sun was falling through its branches in broken streams of gold, casting a lattice of light across the ground. He moved closer, until he was standing in the middle of it, the sun warm on his head; a benediction, if there were such things. He tipped his chin up, shuddering.

He had not welcomed the sight of the bright skies that morning, pulling back his bedroom curtains, his eyes gritty and sore from lack of sleep. Such a burst of glorious weather had felt mocking, dropping into what had so far been the greyest of autumns like a lost beach ball, all rain-laundered and shiny new, when the world, on that day of all days, felt so dark. As he had navigated a route to the hospice, the brightness had felt even less benevolent, thickening the cloudy smears on his windscreen, casting a glow across the Kent countryside, using its trickery to create the delusion of spring warmth in a season already well into the first stride of its inexorable march towards winter.

Dougie squinted upwards, his head hot. The sun, he saw now, was indeed pouring through the boughs of the great tree, but only because of the quantity of leaves the poor thing had already lost to frost and wind, and the calamity of its own ripening. Some benediction. He took a deep breath and walked towards the heavy double front door, only to veer away at the last moment and cut through an archway in the privet hedge instead. It led onto a narrow, shaded path, which looked as if it might skirt the entire perimeter of the back garden. Dougie set off quickly along it, hopping over puddles and muddy patches, glad of the protection of the path's tunnel-high hedge walls. He would do a circuit and then he would know what to do. He hadn't wanted to come. More to the point, Nina hadn't wanted him to come. Linda, during the course of their long talk over coffee at his kitchen table the previous night, had made that very plain. He had been Nina's link to normality, she explained, the one person who saw her rather than the illness. She had wanted to keep that to the end.

On receiving this news Dougie had felt enraged – duped – yet he had also been glad. The idea of some sort of deathbed farewell, standing tongue-tied next to a wasted body, saliva dribble, pain-relief tubes and such paraphernalia, was daunting beyond words. Just not something he could ever manage or be good at. As Nina had recognized, Dougie had told himself, while he was hunting for the keys to his old Ford that morning, uncertain as to whether he really wished to find them. Beneath these doubts, the anger still heaved: at having been lied to, brazenly and consistently, for six months, used as some sort of unwitting stooge-support . . . and all in return for what? A few exchanges of confidence? Some amiable banter? What sort of *friend* did that? And as for getting Linda to write her texts . . .

Dougie stopped on the path, gripped by a fresh wave of outrage. The privet flanking the path on either side of him trembled, as if it shared his perturbation. A light breeze had started, blowing against his back, like the nudge of a guiding hand. Dougie dropped his head and walked on slowly, pondering the other thing Linda had said, the most shocking of all in many ways: Nina had found him attractive; 'gorgeous' had been Linda's choice of word. Apparently she would have slept with him if she could, if she had thought she stood a chance. The two women had enjoyed many heart-to-heart Skypes on the subject, Linda had reported, a trace of gleefulness showing through her gloom. 'She was in love with you, you see,' she had added, growing solemn again.

Dougie strode on, ploughing through mud now rather than bothering to dodge it. His old loafers were filthy anyway. He had been taken for a ride on all fronts; that was the miserable truth. He had been told nothing was wanted of him, when it was, and then it had been extracted anyway, secretly, without his permission. And now, worst of all, Nina was doing the ultimate runner, getting away with it, never having to atone or face up to it. *Dying*.

The path ended suddenly at a small clearing – a circle of grass ringed with paving stones, a weeping willow and a bench in the centre; open to the skies and yet resonating with the hush of a private chapel. Dougie slid onto the bench, deliberately not looking at the inevitable brass plaque, commemorating the inevitable dead person whose family had donated it. He studied his hands instead, which were doing their worst shaking in weeks, and the nicotine stains between his second and third fingers. They looked slightly less yellow, or was he imagining it?

'You gave her a semblance of ordinary life, Dougie,' Linda had kept saying. 'That was the greatest gift, the one she most wanted. The one she really needed.'

'She fucking lied to me,' Dougie had snarled, setting down a full coffee pot and spilling coffee as he poured. 'Lied to me and *used* me. I had a right to know she was still so ill, a bloody *right*.' He dabbed clumsily at the spilt coffee with a dishcloth. 'Tell me, did she dictate those texts you sent to me or did you make them up?'

'A bit of both. Bloody girl. Believe me, I didn't like doing it, but she was always obstinate as crap.' Linda had pulled a balled-up tissue from her sleeve and pummelled her face.

Dougie swigged coffee, burning his throat. He liked Linda. It made perfect sense that she was Nina's oldest friend – straight talking, no frills, clear-headed. 'So where is this hospice, then?' he had muttered.

'I told you she doesn't want –'

'And what were you doing in there tonight anyway – prowling round her house with that bloody torch? What were you looking for?'

Linda patted the shoulder bag she had slung over the back of her chair. 'A book, poems, I wanted to read them to her.'

'So she can't even talk?' Dougie cut in, incredulity pushing through everything else. 'She's not conscious?'

'Not for the last few –'

'Well, what does it matter if I visit her or not then?' he had pointed out viciously. 'She won't know, will she? So, what I would like to do is make my *own* mind up, if that's okay with you. I've not exactly had much of a say in any of this business so far.' He had then wrung the details out of her, an address in Kent, only a few miles from his father, so he even knew the way.

The bench was faintly damp and not comfortable for leaning back. The drooping limbs of the willow rustled, adding to the white noise inside Dougie's head. Somewhere deep beneath it he was aware of the old bargaining starting up, faint but getting stronger: endurance deserved reward, that was the gist of it. So he would go to the bloody bedside. Then he would find a pub. A pint, a whisky, a packet of fags. Dougie slapped the tops of his thighs and stood up. It was a good plan; the only one he was capable of in the circumstances. No one would know. He would sleep it off in the car, if necessary, like the old days. By the following afternoon he would be back at home, sober again, ready to face the world and Stevie, fresh from her weekend by the sea. She wouldn't guess. And apart from her, there was no one else left who cared.

The extraordinary thing about that Sunday morning, Victoria would remember later, was how refreshed she felt when she awoke, how blessed. The feeling of falling alone was quite gone, as hard to remember as the vividness of illness or pain. For the second day in a row the skies were a balmy blue, perfect for golf. Simon had stayed over with her father and the repair to the car was in hand, to be completed by the afternoon. He had sent her a text explaining it all, promising to be back early Sunday evening at the latest, saying he would pick up a takeaway from the good Thai place on the way. In a second message he instructed her to give his love to Ruth and Gary, and not to do anything but ensure she had a lovely day.

Victoria stretched among the bedclothes like a cat, intermittently dozing until the arms of her bedside clock had edged round to ten. She took her time showering and getting dressed, then ventured out to buy a fresh croissant, which she ate on the balcony table, reading bits of the paper and chasing after other bits that flew off on gusts of wind – the price both she and Simon were long accustomed to paying for any alfresco eating, no matter the season. She thought about calling Simon to tell him what she was doing, how happy she was, but then remembered golf-course etiquette forbade such indulgence and phoned her mother instead on the Rosemount main line.

'Hello, Mum, how are you?'

'Hello, darling. I'm really quite well, thank you. A lovely bright autumn day up here, what about you?'

'Yes, very sunny. Beautiful. I expect you're looking forward to getting home, aren't you?'

'So much . . . Only a week to go – I can't wait.'

'Dad must be pleased. In fact, he's playing golf with Simon today –'

'Yes, I know. He mentioned it when he rang last night. Something about the car breaking down . . . Bill at the garage will fix it – he always does.'

'Yes, Bill's great.' Victoria paused. 'Did Dad tell you why Simon was so nearby?'

'No.'

'It's big news, Mum,' she blurted. 'We've decided to move out of London. Simon was viewing a house. We're aiming for Buckinghamshire, somewhere not too far from you and Dad.' Victoria waited, aware in the silence of the thousand other silences that had followed myriad such statements over the years – about her work, her life, her opinions – the hollow disappointment when nothing was forthcoming.

'But that's wonderful,' her mother began, the unmistakable rush of real warmth in her voice, 'except, that is . . .' the warmth shrank with each word, like colour draining from a painting '. . . just so long as it's not because you think we – that I – need any sort of looking after. Because –'

'No, Mum, God forbid.' Victoria laughed, inwardly despairing at her new surging hormones as tears sprang to her eyes. Seven more months of weeping when she was happy – let alone sad; it was going to be intolerable. She wiped her nose on the back of her hand, fighting the urge to break her agreement with Simon and spill the news of her pregnancy. That would bring the colour back into her mother's reaction if nothing else did. Her father might have performed the heavy-handed badgering over the years, but there had never been any doubt that both her parents shared the bafflement as to why their only remaining child should have chosen to put off something as basic as motherhood for so long, chasing a career that offered little prospect of promotion, with earnings that were mere drops in the already substantial ocean of her private income. 'We've both had enough of London,' Victoria explained, pressing the urge away. 'We're ready for a change. I'll still need to go into work sometimes, but Buckinghamshire is perfect for commuting, and these days, so much can be done screen-to-screen anyway. You're the last thing on our minds, Mum,' she added, relishing the rare confidence of daring to tease.

'Well, I'm pleased to hear it,' her mother had retorted, still arch but sounding as if some of it was put on.

At Gary and Ruth's, the desire to confess her pregnant state proved even greater. The Moses cradle was parked centre-stage in the sitting room on a wheeled stand, its small sleeping occupant wedged between two rolled blankets, wearing a pink Baby-gro as loose as puppy skin and minuscule white anti-scratch mitts that were still twice the size of her hands. She lay on her back asleep, her eyes shifting visibly under the lids, her mouth slightly open. A milk-bubble sat on the centre point of her upper lip, as perfect as a pearl. Her eyebrows were two neat, faint, perfectly symmetrical lines. Between them ran an inch of blue vein, so close to the surface of her skin, so clear, it looked as if someone had drawn it on with a fine felt-tip pen. Victoria found herself holding her breath as she stared, part of her fighting the urge to reach out and track the course of the little vein with her fingertip, feel its power, its delicacy.

She took refuge in asking questions about Polly's stomach problems and sleep patterns, deliberately staying off the subject of the accident and marvelling at how robust Ruth looked in spite of all the ordeals; pale, much slimmer, but still her wry, jolly self, her fingers laden with big rings, her hair in its usual asymmetrical shapes, glinting with gold and red streaks. She and Gary took turns to answer the questions, behaving like some kind of rehearsed double-act, exchanging tender looks and reaching for one another's hands between sentences. When Polly started crying, Gary picked her up and laid her tenderly on Ruth's lap, fetching a support pillow and a muslin cloth in what was clearly a well-established routine for feeding. He settled next to them, casting shy, proud glances as Polly suckled, one arm protectively across the back of the sofa behind his wife, the other hand occasionally touching his daughter, as if he still couldn't quite believe she existed. Light seemed to radiate from the three of them, from their skin, their smiles; contentment, love, it was transfixing, almost as if they had stopped knowing where one of them began and the other ended.

Michelangelo could have done no better, Victoria mused, as she drove home a few minutes later, trying to conjure a similar vision of what lay in store for her and Simon, but she was too tired to manage it. By the time she parked, the new bout of fatigue was breaking over her in waves, weighing down her eyelids, pulling on her limbs. She would have liked to use the lift for once, but its doors were sealed behind a sign saying 'Urgent Repair'. Victoria turned with some reluctance for the stairs, taking them slowly, carefully, finding a moment to be grateful that there was no hint of nausea in this afternoon's version of feeling wiped out.

The stairs curved round the lift shaft and had fancy wrought-iron banisters. Usually Victoria did not give them a second glance, but that afternoon, labouring slowly upwards, she found her thoughts drifting from the ornately carved fronds beside her to all the balconies, staircases and banisters that her latest work project, Juan Muñoz, was so fond of. One of the pieces planned for the retrospective was simply a section of a staircase pinned to a wall, starting nowhere, leading nowhere, and so fragile – spindly and frail, like a broken branch. And how clever that was, Victoria realized suddenly, because a staircase was about human connection, after all, how people got from one place to another – and often they didn't know where they were going. And weren't all human relationships delicate, too? One bad blow and they could snap or swerve off course. Excited, wanting to get some of her ideas written down, she quickened rather than slowed her pace on the final flight, letting go of the railing to pump her arms, so that by the time she reached her front door she was sweating and panting hard.

She was at the kitchen tap, downing a second glass of water, when the phone rang. Simon, she thought, because landlines were so rarely used by anyone except family or pestering sales people on bad lines from call centres. But it was neither.

'Mrs Levant?' said a young, vaguely familiar female voice.

'Yes, who is it?'

'Um . . . it's . . . er, Stevie – you know, Dougie's –'

'*Stevie!* Of course I know. Why didn't you say? How are you?'

'Fine. I –'

'And your dad?' Victoria asked, with some energy, feeling in some dim way that the nonsensical rift between Dougie and Simon needed making up for.

'He's okay, thanks. Look, I was wondering if you were, like, free at the moment.'

'Free? You mean right now?' Victoria drained the last of her water. The stair-climbing had revived her somehow, making the blood charge through her veins, waking up her brain. In truth, a visit from Dougie's daughter was the last thing she wanted – not with all the new ideas she had had on the stairwell buzzing inside her. She wanted to get to her laptop, start jotting them down. But it seemed churlish to reject the child outright. 'Well, by all means pop over –'

'Actually, I was wondering if you wouldn't mind coming down to meet me – I'm only round the corner. I know it must sound odd, but I did sort of want to, er, see you on your own.'

Victoria laughed, her puzzlement mounting. 'Well, I *am*

on my own, as it happens. And will be for a couple of hours more at least. So ring the bell downstairs – flat four – and I'll let you in. Stevie, are you sure everything's okay?' But the girl had already hung up.

Victoria kicked off her shoes and put the kettle on, letting her mind skate round possible reasons why Dougie's daughter, whom she barely knew, should want a tête-à-tête with her on a Sunday afternoon. But, then, the poor creature's mother was in Sweden, she reminded herself, so maybe it was advice she sought, some kind of girls-only thing. Or perhaps it was to do with Dougie. Oh, yes, there were all sorts of possibilities there, Victoria decided, as she moved round the kitchen, rather taken with the idea of Dougie's child seeking her out as a confidante.

When the intercom buzzed she leapt at it, issuing a hurried warning about the broken lift before pressing the button to release the front-door lock. Mothering skills for struggling teenagers, she mused, preparing a big welcoming smile – who would have thought she'd be getting in some early practice? But then, she opened the door as the sound of footsteps grew nearer and saw Stevie already on the top step, one shoulder bowed under the weight of a small leather grip, her hair scraped into a tight, punishing ponytail. There was a look of such dread, such determination, etched on her face – her big blue eyes were black with it – that Victoria found her smile sticking to her teeth. This was something bad, she knew at once, something very bad indeed.

Dougie peered through slit eyes at the thin, grey, badly fitting curtains, filtering sunshine like a dirty sieve. His head had a pulse inside it, a deep, thumping drum, not painful yet, though he knew it would be soon, when he was more awake, more sober. He didn't know where he was, didn't want to know. He squeezed his lids shut again, hoping to drift off to sleep, but seeing instead the bit before the bender – the private deal with himself that had *allowed* the bender: Nina's hospice room, not a white clinical chamber of tubes and muted trauma, as he had feared, but a cosy, airy den of a bedroom decorated in yellow and white, with its own small flat-screen TV, cornflower curtains and two ebullient pot-plants, one of white African violets perched on the window sill, the other of rampant pink busy lizzies trailing down from the top of a pine bookcase. On the shelves there were scores of well-thumbed novels, a stack of DVDs, a few ornaments and a photo of Nina as a teenager with her parents on some hilltop. She sat between them on a dry-stone wall, her arms over their shoulders, a green rolling landscape falling away behind. Her face was chubby, tanned and freckled, and grinning to show crowded front teeth that must subsequently have been straightened. Her hair was so long and thick and lustrous, flying across her face, that her clear blue eyes, crinkled with smiles for the photo, were only just visible through the tangle. Dougie stared and stared, then looked away quickly, thinking ill-advisedly, irresistibly, of Stevie, now at a similar age, fresh and half burst, like an opening flower. The sweetness of life, the cruelty, it was unbearable.

He forced himself to look at the bed. He didn't have long. Ten minutes, he had said to the parents, once he had talked a nurse into performing introductions, a red-headed

Welsh girl with gaps in her teeth and dancing green eyes that he might, once upon a time, in a previous existence, a previous universe, have been tempted to see if he could coax into something like real, focused interest. A quick goodbye was what he wanted, he explained – except he hadn't called it that, either to the nurse or to Nina's family. A quick 'hello', he had called it, forcing the words out through a rictus grin, which, a few seconds into its formation, had begun to feel like a gash across his face. Her parents couldn't have been warmer. Of course, they crooned, Dougie the cooking neighbour, they had heard so much about him. Nothing bad he hoped, Dougie had quipped back, driven to pure idiocy out of desperation.

Nina lay on her back, her arms over the sheet, her chest rising and falling steadily but releasing a faint, audible crackle as it moved. Her hair had grown back remarkably, into soft, silky waves that lay flat on her head in a style that was flatteringly gamine, while bearing pitifully meagre resemblance to the lustrous mane in the photograph.

Dougie slumped into a small armchair parked near the window. The room was two storeys up, facing the front, on a level with the most verdant section of the big tree. Shards of blue sky poked through its thinning leaves.

'Bloody hell,' he growled, keeping his gaze on the window. 'Bloody hell and thanks. Thanks a bunch.' He sat in silence for a moment and then, in several quick, angry movements, got up and shoved the chair nearer the bedside. He sat back down on the very edge of it, hunching forwards with his elbows on his knees and his face buried in his palms. Through the slits in his fingers he could see Nina's arms, lying in their hateful stiff symmetry, on either side of her, scarecrow thin, the veins bulging blue tributaries into her hands. Slowly, summoning courage, Dougie reached out and touched the one nearest to him. It looked so small next to his, so in need of protection. He held the hand very gently, cradling it, even managing for a moment to relish its coolness against his own hot skin. He had to drag his gaze up to her face, not yet a death-mask but marble still. Her eyelids were closed and milky smooth, her lips slightly open and oddly dark against the pallor of her skin. Across her cheekbones the skin was stretched tight and looked thin as tissue, a mere mist of a shield for what it still protected.

'Shit. *Use* me, why don't you?' he croaked. 'I mean, feel free.' He released her hand and stood up, swinging his arms wide as if to offer his torso as a target for some invisible marksman standing on the other side of the bed. 'Help your-bloody-self. Take a piece. Everybody else has.' Dougie fell back into the chair, slamming his hand against his mouth. 'Sorry. That's not true. You didn't take anything.' He forced the words out through the clench of his fingers. 'Or at least you did, but you gave stuff back too . . . Can't quite think what now, but it felt good at the time. Anyway, you didn't want me here, I know, so this is revenge of sorts, isn't it? Hah – got you there, girl, didn't I?' He was shouting, he realized, glancing nervously at the door, half expecting footsteps. Anyone in the corridor would think he needed help, which he did, of course, just not the kind that existed.

'Jesus,' he muttered, whispering carefully now. 'I'm crap at this, Nina. I knew I would be. You knew I would be.' His throat felt as if it was being stitched together, with needles, the thread tight. 'I'm meant to say goodbye or something, I suppose . . . Well, I can't. I'm not going to. I'll say thank you, though, for hijacking me in the library that day. I had my doubts. You know I had my doubts.' He started to chuckle, but his throat was too thick, too tight. 'It's been an odd year. I've lost an old friend I thought I couldn't lose and found a new friend I didn't think I wanted. A friend who I'm now also losing . . .' He sank his teeth into his knuckles.

'By the way, I'm going drinking after this. I should probably tell someone and it might as well be you.' He examined the red ridges in the back of his hand where he had bitten himself. One was bleeding slightly.

Nina didn't move, but there was something about her suddenly, a sense of concentration, of greater stillness. At the window the curtains swung out and back again on a light gust of air.

'Oh, so you think that's a bad idea, do you?' Dougie sneered softly. 'Well, I don't care, okay? I don't care what you think. That whole Nina School of Wisdom thing officially ends here. You've meddled enough. And as for that other business,' he snarled, working hard now to sound angry, because there was no anger left, 'that business Linda told me about, of you *loving* me . . . maybe I'm supposed to say sorry or something, fuck knows, but I'm not going to, because I am *not* sorry, okay? NOT SORRY. Are you reading me in there? I'm honoured that you love me, Nina. *Honoured.* Got that? But also grateful you never said. Because then I would have done something stupid, like have sex with you and ruined the best friendship I have ever known. So, a good secret, then, that one . . .' He was gabbling now, clinging to the sneering tone to get him through. 'So good in fact that it possibly even makes up – only a tad, mind you – for this other, not quite so good failure-to-mention-that-I'm-dying bollocks . . .'

He stumbled to his feet, kicking the chair away. 'Fuck it, Nina, that's it, I'm done here. Gotta go. Now.' His voice had grown high-pitched, not his own. He managed to plant a swift, terrified kiss on her forehead. 'Quick. Easy. That's what I wish for you, sweetheart. Okay?'

In the corridor he almost knocked over the Welsh nurse. 'Thanks.' He threw the word over his shoulder as he strode past. 'And say thanks to them,' he gasped, nodding in the direction of a glass-paned door through which he could see the blurred outline of Nina's mother and other family members.

The tyres shrieked on the tarmac as he swung the car out into the road. The thirst was like a fever, tearing at his mouth, his throat. To have it so bad, to know he was going to assuage it, was so exciting it almost eclipsed his grief. There would be no delay-the-moment mind games this time, no self-analysing taunts. Dougie drove with his neck craned, scouring the roadsides for a pub. It seemed to take an age. Red lights, foolhardy pedestrians, slow cyclists, speed limits – every possible impediment rolled across his path, almost as if some giant, invisible wand was conjuring obstacles from thin air, trying to impose the brakes he had given up on himself.

And suddenly there it was, the pub near his father's place, with the filthy food and stained carpets. The pub where he and Stevie had taken the old man earlier in the summer, only to be subjected to panegyrics on bloody

James, virtuous as usual, doing the Right Thing at every step, and now finding the Right Woman to boot. Dougie had slowed the car to a crawl for the final few yards, allowing himself one last moment of hesitation before the plunge, inspired not by negative feelings towards his younger brother but a sudden vivid memory of Stevie with her sweet, listening face tipped towards Lenny during that turgid lunch, all eyes and ears for his stories, like the lovely, loving thing she was.

Dougie blinked his eyes open. The door to the bedroom was ajar, the ill-fitting curtains had been roughly pushed to one side, allowing an injection of blinding light, of head pain. In the middle of it was the smudgy silhouette of an all-too-familiar figure.

'Wakey-wakey.'

'Dad, I –'

'You're hung-over, I know. So I'm doing a fry-up. Get your skates on.'

'Dad –' The door closed. A moment later the unmistakable smell of grilling sausages began to waft into the room. Dougie rolled his face into the pillow. Through half-closed eyes he recognized the bed linen – pale yellow, thin, dating back decades. He was in his father's spare room, then. When? How? He had no recollection of it. No recollection of anything beyond a bench in the corner of the bar and a talkative Irishman, thin and fidgety, with quick blue eyes and a grey face, keeping pace opposite him with pints of Guinness.

'Er, sorry.' Dougie shuffled into the kitchen with his head bowed, as appalled at where he had ended up as at the now volcanic pain erupting in his head, roasting his brain.

'No need,' Lenny grunted, staying busy with the frying pan. 'Eat. You'll feel better. There's juice and a coffee – only instant, none of that fancy stuff you like, but there you go.'

'Last night. How did I . . . ?' Dougie peered out of the window, afraid he might see his car.

'Night? Early morning more like. You'd had a couple of drinks down the road you said.' Lenny set two plates on the table, both heaped with sausages, eggs, fried bread and baked beans. 'You leant on the bell till I opened the door –'

'Christ, Dad, sorry.'

Lenny chuckled. 'I was glad it was you, to be honest. At two in the morning – at my age – you imagine all sorts, I can tell you.'

'I'd had a bad day . . . a friend, she . . .'

'It's okay. I don't need to know. I don't want to. You've got a problem. You fight it. Just don't give up the fight, that's all.' He offered a brief glower from under the hood of his eyebrows before returning his attention to his food, blowing air through his lips as he chewed. 'Your mother was the same, as it happens.'

Dougie, in no mood for a lecture, had been half listening, working his way with more caution through a crisp, oily corner of fried bread. He raised his head, incredulous. 'What did you say?'

Lenny's knife and fork shrieked as he scissored them across the plate. 'It's all in there.' He gestured with his fork at the window sill, where a fat manila folder was wedged between the glamorous studio picture and a chipped pot crammed with dried-up biros and blunt pencils. 'Those *memoirs* I told you about. A photocopied set are with the publishers. That's the original. I thought I'd try and get them bound and whatnot in time for James's nuptials – thought it might make a nice gift. I'll give the pair of them something else as well, no doubt, off one of those infernal lists. A Hoover – you know, something really bloody *worthwhile* . . .' He scowled.

At which point Dougie realized the old man was enjoying himself, was happy; happier, indeed, than he had seen him in years. He put down his cutlery, balancing it carefully on either side of his plate, handles down on the table, and slowly folded his arms. 'About Mum. What exactly are you saying?'

Lenny ground his jaw vigorously over his mouthful, nodding again at the folder. 'You'll get a copy, too, of course, when those vanity publishers have done their bit – costing an arm and a leg, I might add.'

'I don't want to *read* about Mum.'

Lenny sighed, reaching for a tea-towel to wipe some grease off his chin. 'No, I didn't think you should either. That's why I mentioned it. She had a problem, like yours. It didn't change how I felt about her but . . . Well, let's say it wasn't easy. Christ, you were always so like her . . .' He shook his head in wonderment at Dougie, as if the thought had never occurred to him before with such force. 'I found that hard, I must admit. Very hard. In fact, sometimes . . . but never mind that.' He steered a sliver of fried bread round his plate mopping up the last traces of egg yolk. 'When your troubles started I did used to wonder whether maybe there was something in the genes. They say that, don't they, that addictions – or at least addictive personalities – can be inherited?'

'Yes, they say that,' Dougie echoed numbly.

'Eat up,' Lenny barked, pushing his empty plate away. 'It'll get cold.'

Mechanically, Dougie picked up his knife and fork and continued with his meal. His stomach was growling to be fed and he could feel the grease on the little morsel he had swallowed already doing him good, soaking up his hangover, muffling the pain. 'It might have helped me to know that before, Dad,' he said at length. 'Did it never occur to you that it might have helped?'

'Well, I'm sorry you feel that way, Douglas, but it's not something I've ever liked to dwell on, especially not after she . . .' Lenny was gripping his mug of coffee and staring with rheumy eyes over its rim, not at Dougie but into some middle distance. 'It was bad enough losing her. The last thing I wanted was to rake up old . . . difficulties.' He blinked, sliding his gaze back into focus. 'She had got the better of it by the time you came along, anyway. In fact, having you was what sorted her.' He set the mug down firmly. 'Like I said, I'm only telling you because it's in the book and I wanted you to hear it from me first.' He paused, looking thoughtful. 'Funny how getting the facts straight – the record – suddenly starts to matter. I suppose it comes from realizing you're the only one still alive who knows them, that time is short . . .' He left the sentence hanging and blew his nose loudly into one corner of the tea-towel, studying the emission before folding it out of sight. 'Now I'm going to have a sit-down. You might like to see to the washing-up.'

Dougie left it a couple of hours and consumed another

pint of coffee before announcing his intention to retrieve his car. Lenny insisted on coming with him, saying the exercise would do him good and turning what Dougie had hoped would be a brisk head-clearing walk into a frustrating amble, his father apologizing with every step for his slowness and him having to pretend he didn't mind. It was a relief to see the Ford, with its dented bumper and rusty underskirts, quite alone in the centre of the pub car park, like flotsam washed up after a storm.

'Dad, I'll drop you back.'

'I should say no, but I won't. This damn thing . . .' Lenny delivered a begrudging slap to his left hip joint. 'On a warm day it doesn't normally give me such gyp.'

Once they were in the car, Dougie put the key into the ignition, then paused. 'Thanks, Dad, for, er, putting me up . . . or perhaps I should say putting up with me.' He shot Lenny an attempt at a rueful grin, which wasn't returned. 'Like I said, it was a bad day. I don't intend it to happen again. I've got lots of work on and Stevie's back this evening. She's great – I must bring her to visit again soon.'

'Yes, you do that.'

The engine started sweetly and Dougie drove with exaggerated care back down the grid of streets leading to the cul-de-sac that contained his father's modest semi-detached house. Leaving the engine running, he hurried round to open the passenger door, holding out a supportive arm and clamping it back to his side with irritation when it was ignored. ''Bye, then. Great breakfast. Thanks.'

Dougie patted his stomach. 'And well done on the book – I mean getting all that stuff down. That's quite an achievement. I look forward to getting my copy.'

Lenny was leaning on the bonnet to catch his breath, dabbing at his brow with a crumpled grey handkerchief. 'How's that cooking manual of yours going anyway?'

Dougie froze, not because of the off-centre remark on a sensitive subject but because his brain, weary and febrile, had chosen that moment to spin him back to his hospice visit the previous afternoon, the ghostly hollowness under Nina's cheekbones, the gauze-thinness of her skin, his hopeless attempts to say goodbye. He needed a drink, he decided, with dull inevitability – maybe he could even go back to the pub. His father need never know. 'The cook-book is going slowly,' he admitted tiredly. 'Not my natural métier, writing, I've discovered. More of a hands-on sort of guy, I guess. Not so hot on the brain-power.'

'Nonsense.' Lenny thwacked the car with his palm. 'You were the one with all the natural talent. James just worked harder.'

They managed a hug of sorts – never natural for either, but out of some mute, mutual recognition that a cog in their relationship had shifted, bringing them to an echo of an understanding, if not the real thing.

When the pub came into sight Dougie gripped the steering-wheel and drove on, pinning his thoughts instead on the extraordinary thing he had learnt about his mother, their shared weakness. And that his arrival in the world had apparently cured her. He thought about that a lot, too. What a very nice thing to have happened, and how grateful he was his father had mentioned it, albeit in a brusque fashion and a couple of decades too late. Janine would marvel, too, he mused, wondering for one wild moment if it might even serve as the pretext for calling her that he had been looking for. She knew Lenny, his family history, him, like no one else, after all. She would be as astonished as he was, intrigued, too, by the repeated pattern. It might even make her ... Dougie blocked the thought. He was hung-over and sad, he reminded himself; it wasn't a healthy or trustworthy state for clear-thinking.

Without consciously planning to, he chose the route back to London that took him past the hospice. He slowed for the big iron gates, but kept driving, doing his best to transmit some sort of telepathic message of forbearance in the direction of the upper branches of the giant tree, behind which, as he now knew, lay the window to Nina's room. A few minutes later his phone hummed with the arrival of a new text message. Wary of provoking attention in his delicate state (by no means certain he would yet pass a breathalyser test), Dougie resisted trying to decipher whatever lay behind his cracked screen until he was at a standstill in front of a red traffic light. It had to be Stevie, he decided, firing off some chirpy progress report about the timing of her return from East Anglia. Dougie's heart softened. She was why anything mattered, he reminded himself, why anything was worthwhile. He made himself savour the thought, glad that some lucidity was at last pushing through his throbbing head and drawing comfort from the notion that his mother might once have drawn similar inspiration from him.

But it wasn't Stevie: it was a number Dougie didn't recognize but which he guessed instantly to be Linda's. And there were just two words, no capitals, no punctuation: *shes gone.*

Dougie drove back to north London like an automaton. Some unmanly sobbing would have been a relief, but he felt nothing to the point of emptiness, as if he had been scraped out inside. The world – life – was draining. Nina was lucky to be out of it. He stumbled into the house wanting only to fall onto his bed. Stevie wouldn't be back until the early evening. If he closed his eyes now he could get three hours' kip, maybe four. Without sleep there was only one other thing he would end up doing, one thing yet again a scratch away from engulfing him, in spite of all his spurts of clear-thinking and resolve. He would set the alarm for five, Dougie told himself doggedly. He would wake stronger, refreshed, drink more coffee, take a shower.

But as he got to his bottom stair the silence of the house caught up with him. The pain was back between his temples. The air in the hall tasted stale and warm. The despair was rising like bile up the back of his throat. Here you are, old friend, he thought. Here you are. You never really went away. He would go out after all, then. There was no fight in him. Nothing left. Dougie turned back for the door only to find that it had swung open. A man he didn't recognize, with a comb-over hairstyle and a bright green shirt, was staring at him doubtfully. 'Sorry, it wasn't closed properly. Saw you go in.' He had an accent that was impossible to place – possibly Middle Eastern, possibly with a hint of Brummy. 'We're at number fifty-two. We got this by mistake.' He held out an envelope. 'Through our letterbox?' he prompted, when Dougie didn't move. 'Had it a while, I'm afraid – got buried, you know how it is. Someone said it was you. Dougie Easton?'

'Yes. That's me.' Dougie moved towards the man. It felt hard, as if he was swimming under water, against a tide. 'Me. Yes. Thanks.'

He took the envelope and closed the door – a good hard slam this time. The envelope was of thick white grainy paper and covered with address redirections and frankings. It had been to his and Janine's old house in Little Venice before being redirected to the wrong number up the road. As Dougie slid his finger under the flap a shower of little silver stars fell out, landing in clustered constellations across his shoes, on the doormat, over the carpet. Dougie blinked at them, his eyes bleary, feeling they contained some meaning, if only he could decipher it. Lifting the flap, he saw, written in thick, unfamiliar flourishes at the top of a gold-framed card, the words *To Douglas and Guest*. Behind it was a slip of paper, folded in two. '*Bygones, bro*,' it said, in James's loose near-illegible scrawl, '*you have tried in the past and now it's my turn. Don't you fucking dare say no.*'

'How did it go?' Amelia's voice was breathless with excitement – with consternation – for her friend. She was sitting where they had agreed to meet, on the bench halfway up the narrowest of the various tarmac paths snaking their way round the bulges of Primrose Hill. Her parents thought they were at a friend's house, enjoying a late slice of birthday cake to make up for a fictional missed party the night before. She and Stevie had hatched the lie together, talking late into the small hours, huddled under their duvets in the chilly seaside-cottage bedroom. She had been at the bench for half an hour, spreading her stuff round her to deter anyone else from sitting too close. It being a warm Sunday, the park had been packed when she arrived – joggers, dogs, families, kite-fliers – but had emptied quickly the moment the sun started to sink during the course of the late afternoon, siphoning its heat back with it. Streaks of orange and crimson cloud were slashed across the sky now, the sun a copper smudge at their heart.

Stevie threw herself onto the bench and dug around in her bag. 'It went okay, I think. I mean, weirdly okay.' She pulled two cigarettes out of a packet of ten and gave one to Amelia, who cupped her hands helpfully round the flame as she struck a match.

'What sort of weird?'

Stevie picked at a speck on the filter of her cigarette with her thumbnail. 'Calm weird. *So* calm. Kind of like . . . like she had been expecting it. She kept asking if I was okay. She tried to give me tea . . . almost like . . . like nothing had *happened*.'

'But what did you *say*?' Amelia urged, puffing inexpertly on her own cigarette, curiosity bubbling through her awe. 'I mean, *how* did you say what you had to say?'

'Dunno, really . . . not sure.' Stevie sat forwards, hugging herself. The day had grown cold with the sun gone. Her fingers were icy-stiff and her teeth were trying to chatter, but in a sort of out-of-control way that made her wonder if there was some after-shock stuff going on as

well as feeling frozen. 'I just started straight in with it —
you know, something like "I feel you should know . . . me
and Simon . . . in Spain we . . ." or something like that,
and then she just looked at me and I said, "Just the once,"
or something, and she sort of nodded and turned away
and kept nodding all through me saying, about a trillion
times, how sorry I was and how it had just happened and
no one else knew and how I couldn't feel worse about it
and I just felt I had to tell her, or something like that
anyway.'

Amelia put her arm round Stevie's shoulders, squeezing till they stopped shaking. 'It was the bravest, maddest
thing to do in the whole world,' she whispered. 'No one
but you could have done it. I couldn't have . . . ever.'

'Yeah, well, you'd never have been such an idiot in the
first place, would you?'

Amelia hesitated, her admiration and timidity almost
getting the better of her. They had had an incredible
weekend and she didn't want it to end. What had always
been a good-fun friendship had blossomed into something momentous, through mutual confessions curled
up in the attic of the Norfolk cottage, ignoring shouted
admonitions from her parents about getting fresh air.
She had told Stevie every bad thing she had ever done,
from building up a store of bloodstained underpants in
an old black sack to how she had cheated in their physics GCSE, using a biro to inscribe the formulae she could
never remember across the soft blank screens of her
inner thighs. In return, Stevie had told her about Simon
and the brief unenjoyable interlude in the pool-house.
Afterwards they had hugged and cried a little, managing

in the process to get through a quarter-bottle of vodka and a ten-pack of Marlboro Lights. They were each other's rock, they had vowed, till death.

Amelia badly wanted to prove some of that durability now, but wasn't sure how. Stevie's question about being an idiot hung in the air, one of those pretending it didn't want an answer when it did. Stevie's decision to tell the wife certainly seemed mental to Amelia – almost as mental as shagging the husband in the first place. But Stevie had also done a pretty good job of trying to make it understandable, explaining that she had been drunk and flattered and dumb, and wanted it to stop long before it had, saying how she had been sick with regret the moment afterwards and telling the wife was the only way of freeing herself from that, as well as freeing herself from her dad's friend, putting him on the back foot, showing him he had no hold over her.

'Yeah, well, maybe I *would* be such an idiot,' Amelia ventured at last, picking up a swatch of her long ebony hair and tossing it over one shoulder, 'only you haven't seen my dad's friends, have you?' She crossed her eyes and stuck out her belly, twisting herself into the grossest image she could manage.

For a moment she thought she'd got it wrong, but then Stevie burst out laughing, which set her off too. Soon they were hysterical, rolling around the bench clutching their rib-cages, their eyes streaming. An old lady walking past, with a Scottish terrier skipping at her heels, smiled fondly at the sight, thinking how heartening it was that young girls, these days, in spite of their wildness and provocative clothes, could still find the time for some old-fashioned innocent fun.

For a long time after Stevie had left, Victoria sat staring at a fixed point on the sitting-room wall, seeing nothing, feeling nothing. I'm numb because I hurt, she thought. My body is in lock-down. It is protecting me. It is clever. Clever body. She hugged herself, and her unborn child, moaning.

But when the mantelpiece clock chimed six, something inside her woke up, not to pain but to a trembling energy the like of which she had never known. Within it was rage, but also intelligence, every fibre of it she possessed. Moving with gathering speed, she uncurled herself from the chair and went into Simon's study, where she applied herself with forensic precision to the task of searching his belongings, pulling open drawers, flicking with expert fingers first through his files and then through the endless piles of paper scattered round his computer, on the shelves of his wall units and across the floor. She found copies of old articles, copies of unpublished ones, half-written incomplete ones; she found stories started and abandoned, cuttings on everything from sun-spots to hair transplants; she found work contracts and letters of rejection; she found receipts and tax returns.

Victoria did her best to sort it as she went, stacking piles, using paper clips, even making a few notes. She worked swiftly but with icy calm, aware that she was tapping into a soothing methodology with which she was familiar: collating information, evidence, trying to assemble a picture of outward actions and an inner life, trying above all to spot the gossamer threads that connected the two together. That her actions were probably futile did not bother her. It was a quest for genuine understanding, performed in the shadow of ironic acknowledgement that, while she might have become adept over the years at using research to interpret the lives and intentions of dead artists, she had clearly failed to apply the same rigour in getting to know the man she had married.

With the easy stuff done, Victoria went deeper, hunting through the back of every dusty cupboard shelf, the inside of every shoebox, every pocket. She shook out bins and books and magazines; she skimmed through every current file on Simon's computer and every recently deleted one that she could access; she checked his history of visited sites, where she found some addresses she had expected, for wine and pornography, but other much more surprising ones, too, like a place for devotees of the musician Jeff Buckley, whom she didn't know Simon liked, and another for aficionados of spaghetti westerns, in which she hadn't heard him express an interest for at least ten years.

The more Victoria laboured, the thinner grew her veneer of calm. Her fingers started to grow unruly on the keyboard, stabbing and missing the keys. For, just as she had feared, no clear picture was emerging. No clues, no explanations. There was just Simon, and his half-ordered, half-messy, hybrid life. Close to tears, the numbness of shock beginning to wear off, she returned to his inbox of emails, thinking again how little recent correspondence there was: barely anything from friends, not even Gary, or Danny . . .

Danny. Victoria looked harder, thinking about the stalled script project. There had to be a line or two about that. But there wasn't. Indeed, the only correspondence she could find with Danny was a couple of messages in mid-March relating to whether an interview with *North London Life* could be engineered for Dougie. Puzzled, she went into his documents and clicked on the file entitled 'tv script', which she had passed over. It comprised many pages, but they were loosely written, haphazardly thought through – she could have produced a better version of his gritty-lesbian-cop idea in a single afternoon. Rigid in the chair now, holding herself in, aware that she had tracked down something at last, but something so pathetic she could hardly bear to see it through, Victoria Googled Beaumont Productions, staring in grim acceptance at the screen when it became clear there was no such company, or anything approximating to it, in existence.

Victoria turned off the computer and steepled her fingers. She inhaled slowly and deeply, filling her lungs, like a diver preparing for a plunge. Then, in one fast deft motion, she tipped back Simon's expensive bendy office chair and flung both her feet at the computer screen, sending it tumbling off the desk. Love for another woman she could have understood; fixation, too, possibly even for a sixteen-year-old girl, possibly even for Dougie's outrageously pretty daughter. But there wasn't love, or anything like it, she was certain. There was just petty deceit and weakness. There was just Simon with his feeble messes, making life up as he went along.

The computer crashed onto the floor, landing awkwardly on its side. Victoria stared at it, unmoved, aware of the last small sandbag of control inside her giving way. Pain poured through it. Filling her in seconds. Choking her. Stevie. He had betrayed her with Stevie. A slip of a girl. Dougie's daughter. Victoria burst out of the study, spinning through the flat, arms and legs wild, a small, human typhoon, thrashing and smashing everything in her path, everything she could reach – pictures ornaments, books – every single outward expression of the last shared fifteen years. And when her phone started buzzing with Simon's number – excuses she guessed for running late – she threw the mobile across the room and flipped on the CD player to full volume, wanting to drown both his efforts to get in touch and the noisy violence of what she was dismantling.

The music that blasted out at her was *Don Giovanni*. Of all things. The final scene. Simon must have been listening to it at some point earlier in the week. Victoria screamed along to the aria, ripping her throat as she ripped the pictures off the walls: the expensive watercolour of Lulworth Cove, the *still life* of plums and cheese, the print of Degas' dancers, the pen-and-ink flower she loved and Simon hated, which had been relegated to a hidden slot behind the door. The opera music was galvanizing, taking her back, as only music could, to the afternoon at Glyndebourne three months before: the sun, the poppies, the droplets on their wine glasses, the arguing and making up; the normality of a marriage still zigzagging along what had still felt like a common line, heading for a common goal. It seemed a dream now. It *had* been a dream.

Victoria abandoned the pictures – they had so many – and flew into the kitchen, opening cupboards and sweeping out the crockery. Seeing Simon's new knife she picked it up and ran along the passageway and back into the sitting room, hacking at the wallpaper as she went, slicing through its silvery trellises, aware that the abyss was real, after all, and that she was falling into it alone.

Chapter Twenty-four

Simon crouched down and tried to look through the bathroom keyhole, but there was nothing, not even a pinhead of light.

'Vic? Please?' His voice was thin and high. Hours it had been now. Hours. He looked at his watch, performing the calculations again. The Sunday-night traffic back into London on the M40 had been bad – weekenders returning to their working lives – which meant he hadn't got to the Thai place until seven thirty. There had been a wait there as well – prime time for orders, the girl with the buck teeth had said, blinking shyly at him from under the long, dark panel of her fringe. So by the time he had got to the flat it was nearly eight thirty. Then there had been the broken lift, a further annoyance, given how tired he was – after the four-hour golf round, the long drive, on top of an inch too many of port with his father-in-law the night before – and the paper carrier-bag of food had been a worry too, losing more of its precious heat with every passing minute.

Opening the door, the first thing he had noticed had been his birthday statuette – the *faux*-bronze clay model of the girl on the swan, which, since its presentation, had occupied pride of place on their handsome bevelled rosewood hall table. It was still there, but with the radical difference that both rider and bird looked as if they had been under some sort of mortar attack, their once smooth black surfaces pockmarked with criss-crosses and chips. 'Vic, what the hell happened here?' he had yelled, momentarily forgetting his tiredness and hunger as he bent down to study the damage more closely.

It was only then, when there was no reply, that he peered through the archway cordoning off the hall from the rest of the flat and noticed its shocking state of disarray: pictures broken on the floor or swinging at wrong angles, scattered pieces of china, strewn clothes, magazines and books, their spines splayed, pages torn. 'Jesus Christ, Vic –' He had hurtled into the sitting room, assuming the worst sort of break-in with the worst possible consequences, understanding why Victoria hadn't answered her phone, picturing her crumpled and trembling in a corner . . .

'Simon. There you are. At last.' She was in an armchair, looking anything but crumpled, in a fresh white shirt and blue jeans. Her hands were pressed between her thighs, her feet bare. 'Well, thank goodness. I was starting to get worried. Good golf? Good fun? How was Daddy? Is that our supper? Hooray. I'm starving.'

She got up and stepped towards him through the debris covering the carpet, unhooking the paper bag of food from his fingers. 'Shall I be mother?'

'Vic, what the hell is going on? What happened here? Are you okay?'

'I'm fine. *Fine.*' She sauntered into the kitchen, casually rolling her hips, swinging the food bag round one finger.

'But I mean, shit, the state of this place. What the fuck happened? *Something*'s happened.'

'Oh, yes.' She spun on her heel, so quickly that Simon heard the squeak of her bare skin on the tiled floor. 'Something has indeed happened. You're so right there. Something truly unbelievable.' She tipped the bag upside-down and shook its contents onto the table, creating an untidy heap of silver foil cartons, pots of sauce and paper napkins. 'Let's start on this lot, shall we?' She turned and picked up his knife as she spoke, his new birthday knife, and promptly set about stabbing at the cartons of food, gashing holes into the foil and plastic lids, till the sauces, chunks of meat, rice and vegetables were slithering round the table in one messy pile. 'Very handy, this implement of yours, I've found. Look – see how good it is.'

Simon watched in fascination at first, his thoughts flying to the levels of lunacy possible for one in a pregnant state. But as her movements grew more frenzied he darted towards her. 'Hey, Vic, stop this.' He tried to take the knife, jumping back in horror as she swung it at him. 'Okay – joke over.' He held up his hands, keeping his distance. 'Now you're scaring me. You need to calm down.'

'Oh, I do, do I?' She waggled the blade, which dripped sauce, as if already responsible for some macabre deed.

Simon took another step back. 'Now, steady on there. Steady on. Okay? You need to calm –'

She came closer, waving the blade at his face, forcing him to edge backwards until, somehow, he was through the hall and half out of the still-open door, the steep stairwell just a few feet behind him. He made another lunge for her arm but she was too quick, swinging it out of reach and hopping away. And then, quite suddenly, as if a battery had died or a switch inside her had been flicked off, her shoulders fell and she dropped both her arms to her sides.

'Stevie came to see me this afternoon,' she whimpered, dangling the knife by the end of its handle, her fingers limp. There were cuts on her hands, Simon noticed for the first time, dots of blood everywhere. 'Dougie's daughter, Stevie . . . remember her, Simon? She had something to tell me.'

'Let's go inside,' he had replied huskily, never doubting, even as this worst, most unimaginable moment came at him, that he was up to dealing with it – a belief reinforced by Victoria's continued meekness, allowing him to take the knife, letting him steer her back into the bomb-site of the apartment. 'Now look . . .' He leant her up against the wall between the kitchen and the bedroom passageway, adjusting the tilt of her head and limbs as if she was a shop mannequin. 'Whatever that girl said –'

Victoria raised her head, looking at him with the blankest expression he had ever seen. 'She said you shagged her, Simon,' she said dully. 'She said the pair of you *fucked* each other that afternoon when the rest of us were running in and out of hospitals. She said she was sorry. She said she thought I had a right to know. She said she would rather die than tell Dougie. She was mortified, articulate, penitent, all in all very impressive, given that she is barely *sixteen.*'

'Vic, it wasn't like that. It –'

'Ssh. Don't speak.' She put her index finger to his lips and pressed it hard, so hard he could feel the ridges between his teeth imprinting themselves on the inside of his mouth. 'Come with me a minute, could you? Would

415

you mind? I just want to show you something. Then we'll talk some more, okay?'

Dumbfounded, glad of a moment to regroup, reorganize his thoughts, his defences, Simon had allowed himself to be led along the passageway and into the bathroom. On the threshold he had hesitated, fearful suddenly that she might be about to subject him to some further, much more ghoulish revelation – some dreadful, unthinkable red mess behind the door or in the lavatory bowl.

'That's it,' she urged, deploying an oddly sweet voice now, as if coaxing a child through some difficult chore. 'In here. Now sit there a minute, would you?' She pointed to the edge of the bath, which was draped with a mat of brightly coloured seahorses – flat and damp from recent use. Simon obeyed reluctantly, carefully choosing what looked like the least wet patch. It was during the course of this momentary distraction that she had slipped out of the room and locked the door.

That had been seven hours ago. Seven hours. 'Vic!' Simon shouted again, close to tears now, with pity for himself, for the infernal hopelessness of the situation. 'One mistake,' he croaked, for perhaps the hundredth time, sinking to his knees and pressing his mouth to the keyhole. 'One moment of madness. Isn't that allowed? Please, Vic, let me out of here now, so we can talk properly. This is just between you and me, Vic, no one else knows. No one,' he repeated, deliberately blocking the memory of the loathsome showdown with Dougie. 'For Christ's sake, it's four o'clock in the morning, Vic, have a heart. I need to sleep.'

There was nothing but silence. Simon looked about

him, trying to think straight. He had no phone. The one window in the bathroom was high and small, and over-looked roofs onto which not even the fittest, most foolhardy athlete would have attempted to launch him-self. 'I'll do anything, Vic, okay?' he tried again, in a shrivelled voice. '*Anything* to show I'm sorry. Think about that. Just think about it, okay?'

And with that, defeated, exhausted, Simon slid the sea-horse mat into the bath, gathered up the three towels – the small basin one and the two larger ones, both of which were still damp – and made what nest he could for him-self, glad for perhaps the first time in his life that his small stature meant comfort of sorts was possible, if he lay on his side in a tidy S, with his hands under his head, his feet stacked between the taps and the bath plug.

The train had soft grey seats and bright yellow tables that made Janine think of kindergarten classrooms. The car-riages were spaciously arranged and far more comfortable than any economy flight seat, with lots of leg-room, power sockets for mobiles and laptops, and seats that had head-rests, buttons for reclining and arm-rests broad enough to accommodate two sets of elbows. The one next to her was empty, although both opposite were taken, one by a white-haired man, in an immaculate dark blue suit, who had been working on a laptop from the moment he sat down, the other by a young girl with half of her head shaved and a tattoo of a snake running down her cheekbone, its tongue out towards her jaw. She had been on her phone since they moved off, her fingers working nimbly and incessantly, the nails bitten to stubs.

They had been going for three hours, which meant there were nine more ahead. That was only to Hamburg. Then there would be the hotel stop-over followed by more trains – Düsseldorf and Utrecht – to Hook, and then the ferry to Harwich. There had once been more direct ferry links from Stockholm to England, the man in the travel office had told her wistfully, using English so fluent and polished that Janine had caught herself wondering at the source of the wistfulness, whether it reached to things more personal than an apology to a would-be client.

'I need to go home,' she had told Mike, astonished at the ease with which the admission slid out of her, as if it had been waiting in the wings of her brain for acknowledgement. 'I'm not saying we're over, just that I can't be here right now.'

He had sat motionless in his chair, staring at the television. They had been eating supper on their laps – salmon, pasta, spring onions, crème fraîche, one of her staples – watching a DVD of men chasing each other over large sums of money. Janine had lost the thread of the plot early on, aware of the mood overtaking her, the need to speak.

'If you aren't here it's hard to see how we're not over,' Mike said at length, keeping his eyes fixed on the screen. He hadn't even blinked that she could see. 'What's going on? I don't understand.'

'We've not been getting on so well.'

'I've been trying.'

'I know. It's not you, it's me. I miss Stevie. I miss England.'

'Are you sure that's all you miss?'

She could see his Adam's apple working furiously, beating down his emotions. There was no question of telling him about the letter, she told herself, the extraordinary letter that had appeared like some fairytale stork delivery in their black metal post-box two weeks before, on a morning when the sea mist smoked between the pines, and the gull shrieks scraped the silence, like ghostly keening. It changed nothing in itself, but had made compelling reading.

Dear Janine,

You don't know me. I am a friend of Dougie's — I was his neighbour though I have moved away now. The point is, I think he still likes you a lot. I know it's a cheek to mention it, but I have been very unwell for a while and got a bit fed up with all the crap of people not saying what they feel until it is too late. I was pretty keen on him myself at one stage, to be honest (please don't tell!), but always knew I didn't stand a chance. He was far too busy worrying about you!

Any-hoo, all the stuff that happened between you guys — I don't think I've ever seen a man more sorry, but being an obstinate screw-up, he might never get around to telling you himself. So there — job done!

He says I meddle and he's right. Still, nothing ventured, etc. I know your daughter a bit too, btw. She is fabulous.

With best wishes,
Nina Carmichael

'I just need to go home for a while,' Janine had said aloud to Mike, dismissing the letter from her mind and focusing on the irrefutable truth of how poorly they had been connecting since his birthday dinner at the beginning of the month. In spite of their reconciliation, it was as if resentment had started in her that night, a layer on top of all the homesickness. It had made her prickly, difficult, impossible to please.

'Your home is rented to tenants,' Mike had reminded her stiffly, a trace of a sneer in his voice.

'I'll go to Cumbria,' she had replied. 'Stay with my parents till I've sorted something out.'

Janine had chosen the train–ferry option not just for economy's sake but out of a deep, intuitive sense that this journey, of all journeys in her life, was one that warranted time in its execution. To think. To readjust. To decide what exactly she thought she was going back to and why. Even so, the cheapness of the whole ticket, 195 euros, including the stop-over in Hamburg, had astonished her. Indeed, now used to Mike's habitual tightness over money, it had been the one detail of the situation she had not minded telling him.

The train sped on, so fast it seemed to cleave the flat, granite landscape as it went. Janine took out her book and tried to read – a romance Esther had lent her, with much fanfare, about an old love affair rekindled through emails – but she couldn't concentrate. For once, the narrative of her own life felt more absorbing than anything a novelist had to offer, no matter how masterful. She closed her eyes instead and tried to sleep. She should have been tired, given the virtually sleepless night she had had, the silhouette of her packed suitcase parked like an accusing shadow at the end of the bed, the ordeal of the near-wordless goodbye to Mike, the last-minute rush across the station concourse, but her brain was jumping. A plan, she needed a plan.

She put away the book and took out Nina's letter, even though she knew it by heart. It changed nothing, she reminded herself. It was merely a component part of the reconfiguration going on inside her, part of the wake-up call that nothing in her life, while she still breathed, was irrevocable; that there was no need to carry on living in a country in which she did not feel remotely at home, away from so much – people, things – that she held dear. Paths tried could be abandoned. Steps could be retraced. Being wrong, acting upon it, holding one's hand up, was allowed. Hearing from Nina that Dougie was sorry for all that had happened between them hadn't felt like a revelation either. Janine had sensed a new level of regret in him for a while, most recently in his tone during the phone call interrupting Mike's birthday dinner, the things he had hinted at but not had time to say. And that he liked her, she had known that too. Just as she was aware of liking him in return. *Liking* had never been their problem.

No, the most astonishing thing about the letter, Janine decided, spreading open the now crumpled page, admiring the solidity of the small, tidy ink writing, the dense straight lines, which she decided must have taken almost as much effort as the succinct, generous sentiments they expressed, was that Dougie should have acquired such a friend, so sweet and loyal. Platonic. Nina Carmichael. She would like to meet her. If there had been an address Janine would have written back at once to suggest it. She folded the letter away and slept, floating on a sudden certainty that the course of action she needed to take would become clear to her, step by step: all that was required was the courage to keep walking. She would get to London, see Stevie – checking in with Dougie in the process – then go north and visit her parents, give herself some space to think, just as she had told Mike.

The certainty remained intact until she had checked into the overheated, thin-walled box of one of Hamburg's cheapest hotel rooms several hours later. Closing the door and looking about her, at the cubicle shower, the Formica wardrobe, the nylon lace curtains, she found that her heart was suddenly galloping and her T-shirt – her hair – was sticking to her skin. She needed to get out, she realized, to hurry up, get on, not because the place was soulless, hideous, although it was both, but because of a violent impregnating sense of urgency about where she wanted this journey to lead, and the fear that she might already be too late.

Chapter Twenty-five

Victoria sat in the car, remembering the last time she had waited outside Dougie's house – all the usual push-pull qualms about seeing him, all the burgeoning plans for Simon's big birthday. It was like looking back at a naïve little girl, a stupid girl, with stupid ideas. Stevie, at sixteen, was already more grown-up than that, she reflected grimly, much more.

She had left it till midday, when the girl would be safely at school, when chances were he wouldn't be working. A Monday lunchtime – who on earth would book a cooking class then, even with the once-great Dougie Easton? And if he was out, there would be plenty of the afternoon left in which to wait for his return. She had cleared the day, sent work an email about being under the weather, explained that the copy for the Muñoz catalogue was going to take a bit longer than she had anticipated to get it as good as it could be. She was ahead of the game, as usual, so it was unlikely they would mind.

On the way she had stopped and bought a bag of freshly ground coffee from the expensive deli and a bunch of flowers, picking the ones she wanted out of their separate buckets: roses, chrysanthemums, lilies – yellow, pink and white, half budded. She had dressed carefully, turning up the radio so she didn't have to listen to Simon's thumps on the bathroom door, first doing a strip-wash at the basin in the second loo because she couldn't shower. She had found some dry shampoo to put bounce into her hair, rubbing at her scalp in front of her dressing-table mirror until the white dust had done its magical thing of bringing out a shine. Because it was Dougie, she slipped her feet into proper heels for once, setting them off with a swirling, calf-length burgundy skirt that hung in folds off her slim hips, and a close-fitting white top that made the best of her modest chest and still slim torso. She was sick just once, an almost mechanical evacuation she flushed away without a second glance. Afterwards, she patted her stomach, glad, for that morning at least, that the belly-swell of pregnancy was still nowhere in evidence.

Dougie was tousled, sleepy, as if getting up to see his daughter off to school might not have precluded the option of going back to bed. He was wearing a faded blue T-shirt that said 'Save Wales!' and a pair of baggy brown shorts full of zipped pockets that were too small to serve any practical purpose. There was a small crust of sleep in the corner of his left eye, which she wanted badly to remove, or tell him about. It didn't fit with what she had imagined to have it there, such a small thing, but unsightly.

'Victoria!' He looked genuinely pleased to see her.

'Hello, Dougie. Are you busy?'

'Never, when it's you.' He stepped to one side, gesturing grandly for her to enter. 'Cor! You look ... er ... smart.'

'Thanks.'

'And you've got some pong on too. Hang on, let me guess – I used to be good at this.' He closed his eyes, sniffing in the direction of her neck, but keeping a decent distance. 'Chanel No. 5. Hmm, classy. I hope that's because you're on your way to a wild lunch with someone who'll give Simon a run for his money.'

Victoria laughed, relieved that she was still able to do it. Meanwhile, she was almost equally relieved to see Dougie stab his fingers into his eyes, clearing the grit of sleep. 'It's No. 19 actually,' she retorted, feigning affront, 'much *classier* for those in the know. But, still, seven out of ten for getting the right name. Oh and these are for you. Here.' She swung the large plastic bag in which she had concealed her gifts into his stomach so he was forced to catch hold of it.

Dougie drew apart the handles and peered gingerly inside. 'These? Flowers? Coffee? Don't be ridiculous.'

'Or "Thank you" would be another possible response, I suppose.'

'Thank you – indeed. Bloody hell. This is great of you, Victoria. I've had quite a weekend, as it happens,' he confessed, twisting the bag handles shut, a brief look of torment crossing his handsome face, 'so this is really, really appreciated . . . more than you can know. Thanks.' He kissed her lightly on the cheek. 'Come on down. Have a coffee. We'll try some of this stuff, shall we? Looks rather superior to my usual tipple.'

'Coffee would be great, thanks.'

'Don't look at the mess.'

'Oh, you should see my place at the moment,' Victoria murmured, taking care on the steep kitchen steps because of her heels and having a sudden vivid image of the locked bathroom door vibrating as Simon hurled himself against it. She had stood among the debris in her passageway observing the spectacle for a few minutes before leaving the flat, thinking how small the vibrations were, how insignificant. She had double-locked the door behind her and sent a brief text to Mika, their cleaner, instructing her to take the week off and promising full pay.

Once they got to the kitchen Dougie set about clearing the sink, which was stacked with clutter as usual, then filled a jug for the flowers. 'How's Simon?' he yelled, over the noisy splash of the taps, adding, 'I haven't really seen him for a while.'

'Me neither, as it happens.'

'Pardon?' Dougie glanced over his shoulder, the filter section of his coffee percolator dripping in his hand, his face fixed in the expression of one who imagines they have misheard something important.

Victoria shrugged. It had come out more quickly than she had intended. 'Simon. Me. It looks like it might be over.'

'Jesus . . . Victoria, I'm so sorry.' Dougie slowly put down the percolator next to the other bits of his coffee-making paraphernalia and turned to face her, the colour gone from his face.

'God, don't be. I'm not.'

'You're not?'

She pointed behind him. 'If we're going to have coffee, shouldn't that lot be turned on or something?'

'Oh, yes.' Dougie hastily assembled the coffee-maker, which was quaint and old-fashioned – part-saucepan, part-filter. He poured in some water, added two scoops of her coffee, put on the lid and set it on the back ring of the hob. 'You and Simon . . . I don't know what to say . . . I mean, what . . .' He folded his arms, whistling softly. 'None of my business, of course.'

'Oh, Dougie,' Victoria cried, drawing on the manic gaiety with which she had launched herself at the day, 'you were always part of Simon's and my business. Always. We've been a merry threesome, haven't we? Ever since the early days. But as for *now*,' she sailed on, aware that Dougie was eyeing her with concern as well as curiosity, 'there's a sell-by date on most marriages, isn't there? Staleness. Dead-ends. You and Simon aren't like you used to be either. He told me.' She perched on the edge of the table, propping her feet on a chair. 'Where does trying to understand it all get one? That's what I've been asking myself. In fact, I'm done with trying to *understand* anything. Live for the moment, that's my new motto. Take what is good, what feels *right*.' She picked up the hem of her skirt as she spoke, shaking it out so that it fell in ripples over her knees.

Dougie smiled uncertainly. He was leaning against the hob, one hand doing its usual rummaging in his hair. 'Well, yes, understanding life can be a bugger, I admit . . . Er, mug or cup?' he asked, as the coffee-maker guzzled.

'Mug, please.'

'Milk? Sugar?'

'Heaps of both. Thanks. I got too thin for a while. I'm on a new gig of trying to feed myself up.' Victoria stayed where she was, watching intently as he reached for the relevant cupboards and drawers, unearthing teaspoons, a sugar bowl, two mugs, allowing herself for once to admire the big natural sturdy triangle of his torso, the slim sculpted hips, the smooth, easy grace of his long limbs, instead of trying to look past it all. He must have been a ballet dancer in a previous life, she decided, or a swimmer, or at least some kind of Olympic athlete. She let these pleasant notions swirl and settle and then, when Dougie's back was turned and he was pouring the milk, she slipped off the table and went to stand behind him, sliding her arms round his waist and pressing the side of her face against his back, in the dip between his shoulder blades. She felt him stiffen with surprise and then relax.

'Hey . . . come on, Vic.' He placed his big solid hands on her forearms. 'Do you want to tell me what happened? You've clearly had a tough time.'

'And you, too, you said. What was yours about?' She shuffled closer, fitting herself more snugly, sighing. 'Tell me about your tough time, Dougie dear.'

Dougie released a low growl. 'A friend died. Someone I liked a lot.' His grip on her arms tightened. 'Cancer, of course . . . always seems to be, these days.'

'God, sorry.' Victoria didn't care about the friend. She cared about the heat of Dougie's skin, warming her face through the thin T-shirt. Near the shoulder seam there was a small hole, possibly moth, possibly one of those snags that started to happen in washing-machines that got too old. 'This is okay, isn't it,' she murmured, 'being like this.' It was a statement not a question. She slid her hands upwards, pressing her palms against the flat of his stomach. Near her mouth the cotton of his shirt was damp from her breathing. 'You and me. I mean, it's not like we haven't . . .'

'That was a long time ago,' Dougie said gruffly. 'A very long time ago. You weren't married and I was –'

'Drunk,' she finished for him.

'Precisely.' He had hold of her fingers and was trying, very gently, to prise them off his waist. 'Come on now, tell me what happened with Simon.'

Victoria wriggled closer, gripping one of her wrists to keep him in the circle of her arms. 'If you don't mind, I'd rather not. Not right now, anyway. I was the one who ended it, if that's what you're wondering.' She paused as a shudder rippled through her, of anxiety or excitement, she couldn't tell. She had been so wired with adrenalin in the twenty-four hours since Stevie's bombshell of a visit that it was hard to be sure of anything. 'You see, the thing about you, Dougie,' she went on, enunciating her words carefully, reiterating the one clear thought that had occurred to her in the small hours of that morning, when Simon had at last stopped shouting, hatching eventually into the idea to make the visit, 'the *good* thing about you,' she began again, sensing and enjoying the intensity with which Dougie was listening, 'is that what you see is what you get. Rough or smooth. With Dougie Easton, there is never any question of not knowing where one stands. With Simon, on the other hand – at least, for me – that has never been the case. I've always found it hard to know exactly what he was thinking, where he was coming from. Early on, I think I mistook it for strength. It's only recently that I have come to realize it's more about the exact opposite, a total *absence* of strength. Simon has nothing inside, no real convictions, no ambition, no drive, no capacity for anything except pleasing himself –' Victoria broke off, aware she had started to talk too fast, to lose her rhythm.

She wasn't here to talk about Simon anyway. She was here for Dougie. Aware that he had given up trying to disentangle himself, she took the chance to press closer still, savouring the steady, manly calmness that seemed to emanate from his tall, strong frame. She wished she could suck out every last drop of it, swallow it whole, a magic draught against the turmoil in her brain.

'Kiss me, Dougie,' she whispered, tilting her hips into his, glad she had worn the heels, which meant there was only a few inches' height difference between them. 'Please. Just kiss me. Because today I need it. I really need it. And you might have been drunk all those years ago but, honestly, I've never forgotten a second of it. Not a single second.'

He said something she couldn't hear. Her head was too buried in his shirt, the blood roaring in her ears, the heat of his skin burning her lips, her face. 'Simon was never as good,' she whispered. 'Never.' She loosened her hold, just enough to give him room to turn round and take her in his arms.

By the time Janine trundled with her luggage down onto the Northern Line platform at Euston station, her sense of urgency had crystallized into a state of suspended exhaustion. One of the wheels on her suitcase was squeaking, making it harder to pull and causing heads to turn as she threaded her way through the waiting crowds. At least, Janine hoped that was why people were turning to stare, rather than because they recognized a desperate woman when they saw one, a woman in stale, mangled clothes, a woman who hadn't slept for two nights, a woman with a headache and no plan beyond a mounting realization that the heart of her emotional disarray was connected to the feelings she still had for her ex-husband.

The warmth of the weather in England had been a shock. Apart from the tell-tale drifts of leaves in the gutter, the wool and long sleeves on display in shop windows, it could have been high summer instead of mid-autumn. Down in the Underground, clad in her padded Swedish coat because her suitcase was full and she didn't have an arm free to carry it, Janine had felt her inner clothes sticking to her damp skin. Arriving on street level at Kentish Town offered little relief. Indeed, walking away from the tube station, her handbag on one shoulder, a holdall on the other, the suitcase bumping along behind her with its bad wheel, Janine could feel the perspiration starting to track freely down the inside of her arms, her ribs and into the waistband of her jeans.

It was impossible to arrive in such a lather, she decided, stopping to slide her bags from her shoulders and tearing off her coat. To face Dougie, to have the talk she had been imagining, she needed to feel cool, collected, on top of her game. Folding the coat into a cushion, not caring that she was causing yet more stares, she sat down in the doorway of a boarded-up shop to compose herself, pushing the hair off her neck and rolling up her sleeves. She checked her watch. Five o'clock. Tea time. Post school, pre-homework. It would be perfect. With a last deep breath, feeling a lot steadier, a lot cooler, she got to her knees, rammed as much of the coat as she could into the already full outer zipped section of her suitcase, and set off again. Turning into Dougie's street, she found herself grinning. Stevie. Dougie. They would both be so surprised. She must play her cards close, though, Janine warned herself, say only that she was on a whirlwind whim of a visit to the UK – soaking up a taste of home – planning to see as much of Stevie as she could, but also intending to spend a little time with her parents in Keswick. The rest of it she would leave to instinct, once she had gauged where Dougie was coming from. They knew each other so well that it wouldn't take long. In fact it would take seconds, Janine thought excitedly – *seconds* – before she knew if the absurd, obstinate hopes that had been tugging at her heart in recent weeks were shared or hers alone.

As she drew level with the house she glanced right and left, wondering which side Nina Carmichael had lived in, vowing one day to catch up with the woman and thank her for her kindness, regardless of the eventual outcome. Hearing things from other people was always good, Janine mused, especially if they clarified subjects over which one had trouble keeping perspective. She smiled to herself. What a prize it would be if she and Dougie could simply manage to be good, trusting friends again. Yes, that alone would be truly worthwhile, truly special.

On the doorstep she was joined by a black cat, which mewed as if it wanted attention, then ducked out of reach when she tried to stroke it. She rang the bell once, and a second time when there was no answer. It had just occurred to her to scour the street for any sign of Dougie's old Ford when the door opened, first a crack, and then to its full width, revealing not Dougie or Stevie but Victoria. Victoria of all people, and wearing a brown silk dressing-gown, which Janine recognized instantly because she had given it to Dougie. Victoria looked pale and unkempt, her normally smooth long hair dishevelled, her eyes wild, her lips dry and bruised. Janine took a step backwards, an involuntary cry of surprise escaping her.

'Janine?' Victoria exclaimed, clearly just as taken aback, her pallor flooding with colour, her hand rushing self-consciously to the gap between the flaps of the dressing-gown. 'Oh, my – Dougie never said. Wow – how *are* you?'

'I'm fine, thanks, Victoria, just fine,' Janine replied, in a hollow voice, blinking to absorb the shock. 'And you?' she countered feebly, as the disappointment continued to wash through her, wave after wave of it. But there was a terrible logic to it too, she told herself. Victoria had once had a thing for Dougie, after all, way back, before her time. A bitterly regretted one-off transgression between the pair of them had been one of the many confidences Dougie had bestowed on Janine during the course of early love-confessions, that happy time when any notion of future such betrayals would have had both of them guffawing. So, yes, Victoria and Dougie, it made a sort of sense; although, in her reeling state, Janine found it hard to imagine exactly what combination of conversations and revelations had induced them to renew the intimacy. Some perverse revenge for Stevie on Dougie's part? A deep soul-baring session between the two of them over Simon's callous treachery? Maybe even Real Love, carving its path after two decades?

Victoria at least had the grace to look fidgety and sheepish as she fumbled for a suitable answer. 'Oh, God, I'm not great actually. A lot has happened.' Not meeting Janine's eye, she twiddled with a strand of her messed-up hair and tugged nervously at the ties of the dressing-gown. 'Look, why don't you come in so I can explain some of it? Dougie's out getting Stevie from something – back at six, he said. I was just on my way . . . Hey, I know how it must look, my being here, but –'

Janine was already backing off the doorstep. She held up her hand. 'Please. Not my business.'

'No, honestly, Janine, please listen. Simon and I –'

'Victoria, it's none of my business.' Janine continued edging away, keeping her arm up with the authority of a policeman stopping traffic. The fingers of her other hand were locked round the pull-out handle of her suitcase, gripping it like a life-line. 'I really can't wait. It was just a spur-of-the-moment thing – passing through London. I'm on my way to see my parents – my mother isn't well,' she babbled. 'That's why I'm in the UK. So I've really got to get on . . . Can't hang around. I'll catch up with them both later. In fact, please don't mention that I called by. It might upset Stevie and I'd hate that. I mean, I will see her and tell her, obviously, but not a word about today, okay?'

Her lopsided suitcase bumped heavily over the disintegrating garden path. It was a relief to get onto the relative smoothness of the pavement. Janine set off back the way she had come, resisting the urge to run and keeping her head high so that if Victoria happened to be watching, which she hoped she wasn't, she would never guess at the tears coursing down her cheeks. At least she hadn't made a total fool of herself, though. At least there was that.

Chapter Twenty-six

Simon lay on his stomach, his head sideways, his cheek cushioned on a flannel, his arms bent, palms down, on the tiled floor, level with his collarbone. He let his gaze blur and sharpen, bringing a scuff mark on the skirting-board in and out of focus. Sleeping in the bath had given him backache and this was the most comfortable position he could find to counter it. He knew from the skylight that it was almost completely dark outside again, that soon it would be time to turn the light on. But he had begun to worry about the bulb, using it up. It was Monday night. That meant it had been over twenty-four hours now. Twenty-five, to be exact. Twenty-five hours, with not one word from Victoria and nothing but the occasional pitiful tooth-mug of water to keep him going. Even that morning, when he had heard her getting up and had called till his throat was raw, banging on the door, begging like a baby, her footsteps hadn't so much as broken stride in the passageway.

It was after that, when the front door had slammed behind her and the thick silence of the flat was ringing in his ears, that Simon had begun to be truly afraid. A marital crisis was one thing, but this was capable of becoming something much, much worse. He had tried to chase off the fear by thinking rationally. Victoria was strong-willed, highly strung, deeply hurt but, crucially, she was also pregnant – with *his* child. That alone, rampaging hormones notwithstanding, would surely bring her back to the flat, back to the bathroom door, no matter how much vitriol she spat at him in the process. And if not, if the darkness inside her was as bad as he was trying not to think it might be – if, in short, she never let him out – then that, too, could only result in his eventual release. Because, as the days ticked by, someone would realize, wouldn't they? Not Dougie, of course, not now, but Gary, Mika . . . *someone*. This was real life, after all, Simon consoled himself, not some melodrama on the telly.

But as the hours dragged by, the melodrama began to feel less melodramatic. He wasn't in regular touch with anyone, these days, that was the trouble. Weeks could pass and no one would notice his absence, or they would but Victoria would easily find ways of justifying it. She'd be good at that. It might be Christmas before anyone's suspicions were aroused. And by Christmas . . .

And where had she been all day, anyway? Simon crawled on his knees to the door pressing his ear against the wood, listening hard, even though he knew there was nothing to hear. Maybe she wasn't coming back. Maybe she would never come back. He retreated, whimpering, to his nest of towels, closing his eyes and then quickly blinking them open again as the image of the dead look in Victoria's face confronted him: Victoria as he could never have imagined her, corralling him towards the stairwell, the knife raised – *his* horrible new knife – dripping from all the craziness with the food. His wife was mad. She had lost her mind. He was going to die.

And once the panic started it was impossible to stop.

Gary and Ruth's gift, without its monetary talisman, had indeed been the unluckiest of objects, Simon reflected wretchedly. Dougie's stupid penny, immediately lost track of anyway, had arrived too late. It was from the moment of his birthday exchanges that things had started to go wrong. The damned business with Dougie's damned girl had happened the very next day, not to mention the unpleasant twists that had transpired from the couple of harmless white lies he had told Victoria after they'd got home. She was a terrier, his wife, Simon acknowledged bleakly, that was the trouble. Tenacious, unstoppable. Once she latched on to an idea she never let it go.

Simon bit into a corner of the flannel as a whimper bubbled up his throat. If he deserved to die, so did Stevie, he decided viciously: for dropping him in it, when she had been equally to blame; for wanting what had happened as much as he had. Dougie's accusation of sole culpability was bollocks; pure hypocrisy. A one-off, pleasure-seeking, no-strings – such sexual encounters happened all the time between consenting adults of all ages, as Dougie, of all people, knew only too well. So what had happened should have been okay, Simon reasoned. Stevie had done a good job of making him feel that it *was* okay. As Victoria herself had said, the girl was very mature. Even afterwards, in the sticky heat of the pool-house, when the inevitable post-coital awkwardness had kicked in, she had seemed utterly composed, sauntering off to her room to get cleaned up, picking her way back up the terrace steps, like the artful minx she was, the tassels of her bikini trailing between her fingers, the corners of her towel held so cunningly across her nakedness, granting Simon easy extra glimpses of what he had been unable to resist. He might have been forced to a point of regretting what had happened, he might die on account of it but, he vowed now, spitting out the chewed corner of his flannel, he would never, ever accept that the blame for the encounter lay with him.

The resolve lifted his spirits a little. It felt like a toehold in the dark, something on which to balance. Simon rolled over for a spell on his back, playing his blurring refocusing game with a stringy thread of old cobweb hanging from the top-left corner of the ceiling. He managed to doze like that for a bit, but woke with the room pitch black, his stomach roaring for food. He clambered onto his knees and felt his way towards the basin, not bothering to lever himself upright until he had reached it. The emptiness of his stomach was worse when he was on his feet, dizzying. How long could one live on water? Ten days? Eleven? Fourteen?

He ran cold water into the tooth-mug and slumped down on the toilet seat. Only then did he reach for the light switch. Any earlier and he would have had to face his reflection in the basin mirror, all the worse for being sketchy. His contact lenses, which were disposables, had got too sore to keep in. As bad luck would have it, his latest batch of spares was still on his bedside table. Simon sipped the water slowly, making it last, licking his lips after each swallow. A headache was threatening so he opened the small wall cabinet next to him and shook a couple of Panadol out of a packet and tossed them down his throat. Before closing the cupboard door he paused to study the remainder of its contents, panic welling again at the realization that a spare tube of toothpaste and a box of tampons were going to be of little use in the ordeal that lay ahead.

When the front door slammed an hour later, a howl of relief erupted out of him. He fell against the door with both fists. 'Vic! Vic! Please! Game over. Game totally over. Please, Vic. How sorry can I be?' Holding his breath, aware of the pumping of his heart, Simon pressed the side of his face to the door, straining to hear what was going on, praying for the tap of approaching footsteps. But there were only a few muted sounds, hard to decipher. A few minutes later the smell of food began to float into the room. Onions? Steak? Garlic? In seconds Simon's mouth had flooded with saliva. 'Vic?' he croaked. 'Fucking hell, Vic, please.' He put his back to the door and slid to the floor, dropping his forehead onto his knees, crying softly.

Janine's parents lived on the outskirts of Keswick in a detached, sandy-stoned house set half a mile back from the main road to Cockermouth. Originally a farmer's cottage, it had been added to over the years, once by previous owners and once by themselves, extensions that had required much fighting for council permission and cost almost as much to ensure conservation requirements were met as the labour and building materials. Their garden-centre business was in the middle of Keswick, among a busy parade of shops, but with plenty of space at the back for parking and a glass-roofed area for storage and display of outdoor plants and larger items. It was a non-stop physically demanding enterprise, but that had never prevented them finding time to attend, lovingly, to their own private two acres of garden and vegetables. It was here among green tepees of runner beans and raspberries, with night all but fallen, that Janine found them, after she had tumbled out of a taxi from the station.

She stood on the edge of the lawn, waiting for them to notice her, the suitcase, now without one of its wheels, parked at her side, her shoulders low from the bags they bore and the weight of the events of the last few days. Her mother spotted her first and hurried towards her, leaving her father to gather up the trugs and gardening implements lying round the borders of the vegetable beds. 'Okay, okay,' she said, peeling off her gloves, striding with difficulty because her legs were short and she had an old pair of clogs on her feet, yellow in their heyday but now blackened with age and mud. 'So long as no one's died. Has someone died?'

Janine said no and burst into tears.

A couple of hours later, after several cups of tea and a hearty supper of stew, mash and freshly picked runner beans, she had delivered an edited version of her circumstances and was a lot calmer. She had explained about Sweden and Mike – the needing to leave – but left out any reference either to Dougie or to Nina's letter, for fear of evoking ridicule rather than understanding. For, though both would have denied it, Janine knew that her parents already thought she was Hopeless with Men. It was a view that dated back to the unplanned conception of Stevie, and which the demise of her marriage had done little to discourage.

'At least you knew your own mind and acted on it,' her

mother said, in a kindly attempt to bring the evening's revelations to some sort of positive conclusion. 'That's the
main thing. And it'll be wonderful for Stevie to have you
back.' She came round the table and pulled Janine against
her ample soft stomach, stroking her hair and exchanging
a look of affection with her husband as he did his usual
thing of distancing himself from the display of emotion,
busily setting the tray for their morning tea. 'It goes without saying you can stay here as long as you need while you
get yourself sorted. Isn't that right, Alan?'

'Oh, yes. No question there.' Her dad shot a warm
smile over the top of the tea caddy.

After they had gone to bed Janine found a crusty old jar
of decaff coffee and put the kettle on. The crying had helped.
And fresh relief was creeping in, too, that, in spite of being
shocked by the turn of events on Dougie's doorstep, she
had managed not to make a total idiot of herself. The grand
sense of urgency in her box of a hotel room in Hamburg
had been self-induced, she saw wryly, the workings of an
overwrought imagination. There had been nothing to rush
for, nothing to save. She stirred her coffee, pleased to be
able to manage a dry chuckle at the recollection of Victoria's
dishevelled appearance in Dougie's dressing-gown. So he
was messing things up. And why should she be surprised?
Dougie always messed things up. How could one vaguely
emotional phone call, let alone a stupid fantastical letter
from a woman she had never met ever have allowed her to
forget that?

Janine gave the back door an angry shove and stepped
out into the garden. The moon was full, a cold marble
disc. It looked beautiful but harsh, an imperious domi-

nance to the stars dancing in attendance. She pulled the cuffs of her cardigan over her hands for warmth and swigged her coffee, which was cooling fast in the chilly night air. It was time to pick herself up. Again. Time to push on. Again. Time to be the brave, independent creature she knew she could be if she tried hard enough, dug deep enough and focused on what mattered, which wasn't anything to do with her own hopeless, malleable heart but all about the much more important business of going back to earning her own living and being as good a mother as she was able to be. She would phone the letting agents first thing in the morning, explain she had come back to the UK and check on the position *vis-à-vis* ousting her tenants. At least it was still her house and nothing to do with Mike. And Vince, her old boss at the estate agent's, she'd get on to him too, see if there was any chance of wheedling her way back into her job.

An owl hooted, startling her. And then her phone rang. Seeing Stevie's number flash on the screen, Janine hesitated for a moment, marshalling her thoughts, even wondering whether to confess yet that she was in England.

'Don't hang up.'

'Dougie, no –'

'I know you came by today. Don't hang up. Is your mum okay?'

'This is a cheap trick, using Stevie's phone.'

'Yes. Very cheap. Desperate situations call for desperate remedies or something.'

'Listen, Dougie, whatever you think you need to say, I don't need – don't want – to hear it.'

'Victoria being here today – it wasn't what you think.'

'It doesn't matter what I think. It hasn't mattered for years. You and I are divorced, remember? A quickie, rushed through due to irreconcilable differences. It absolved us of many things, including – thank God – the need to account to each other for our actions. I came to see Stevie. Obviously. I'm in the country for a bit. Thought I'd give her a surprise. A hooker could have answered the door for all I care.'

'Well, why didn't you stay to see her, then? We didn't sleep together, Janine,' he went on, when she didn't answer.

Janine laughed harshly. 'I don't *care*, Dougie. I wouldn't care if you screwed the whole fucking universe.' She cut off the call and strode deeper into the garden, not noticing the tweak of her parents' bedroom curtains behind her, or her mother's anxious face peering through the window. She arrived at the swing that lived behind the vegetable garden – kept there from her childhood for Stevie's – two still sturdy braids of rope and a slab of wood knotted round the fat limb of an oak tree by her father some thirty years before. She dropped her empty mug onto the grass before slotting herself into it. Her phone rang again.

'But we do still care.' He spoke very quickly. 'That's the thing. We've tried not to, but we do.'

'Speak for yourself.'

'I intend to. But I need you to listen, so don't hang up, okay? Please *don't* hang up, Janine. Where are you, by the way?' The owl had hooted again, somewhere from the branches overhead.

'It doesn't matter.'

'You sound . . . cold. Are you outside?'

'Yes. I'm outside and I'm cold, bloody freezing, in fact,

so you'd better hurry up,' she muttered, cursing herself even as she gave in to him. 'You can have two minutes and that's it.. Two minutes.' She twisted the swing as she talked, pushing her feet in little circles to make the ropes entwine.

'Okay. Thanks. Okay.' He sounded breathless, almost panic-stricken. 'Victoria was here because she had found out about Stevie and Simon. Stevie had *told* her, if you can believe it, just took herself round there and *told* her.' He paused, clearly wanting Janine to hear the admiration in his voice. 'Victoria, understandably, was pretty shaken, though it took me a while to realize because she didn't mention it at first. In fact . . . look, this is awkward, Janine, but she turned up out of the blue this morning, saying she and Simon had split up, and then sort of threw herself at me. It was only when I refused, fended her off, that it all came out, the full story, about what Stevie had done. She then got hysterical, totally lost it, saying she couldn't face going back to Simon, saying she felt exhausted, ill. She even threw up – Christ, Janine, you should have seen her. So I made her tea, did my best to calm her, told her she could have a lie-down if she wanted, which she did, falling properly asleep. When I had to leave to get Stevie – she does extra Spanish conversation on a Tuesday and I always pick her up – I woke Victoria, saying it would be best if she was gone before I got back, and then you must have turned up. It was only just now that she sent me a text telling me about it. She said you'd asked her not to. She said your mum was ill. Janine? Are you still there?'

Janine's phone was flashing its amber low-battery signal. She watched it for a moment, puzzling that it appeared to be in curiously perfect synchronicity with the beat of

445

her heart. 'Yes. I see. Right.' She kept her voice flat. She didn't trust it with anything else. There was a lot to take in. In fact, she didn't think Dougie had ever said so much in one burst in his life. 'Thanks for telling me. Is that it?'

'Yes, except that I want to see you. That talk on the phone we had . . . I want to finish it.'

'No can do.'

'Please, Janine, things have changed . . . so much has changed.'

'Nothing has changed. No one ever changes. Not really.'

She could hear his intake of breath. On top of the flashing yellow light, the low-battery warning was now beeping intermittently in her ear. Above her the ropes of the swing were as tightly twisted as she could make them; her legs were straining against the ground to stop the back-swing.

'Janine?' His voice had dropped to barely a whisper. 'Why did you come back to the UK?'

'A break,' she snapped. There would be no relenting from her. It was too late. It had always been too late.

There was a pause. 'From Mike?'

'A break. Touching base. To see Stevie.'

'So your mother's not ill.'

'No. I just couldn't face staying to talk to Victoria. So I lied. '

'Well, come and see Stevie then,' Dougie cried, 'whenever you like, for as long as you like –'

'My phone's about to die.'

'One meeting,' he urged. 'Just the two of us. Give me that.'

'I've already given you that. We've had loads of that.'

'I want more. One more.'

'I'm in Cumbria.'

'Come to London. Whenever you can. Whenever it suits you. I've got a bit of a week anyway – lots of work, a funeral.'

'A funeral?' Janine exclaimed, involuntary sympathetic interest leaping out of her.

'My next-door neighbour.' Dougie cleared his throat. 'I think I might have mentioned her, that day you rang and I couldn't talk – when I was in Regent's Park. Anyway, she had cancer. Lymphoma.'

'Your neighbour?' Janine repeated stupidly, sitting forwards as she digested the implications of this news. In the process she momentarily released the pressure on her feet. The swing sprang loose instantly, spinning out of the twist she had created, flinging her round. It took all her strength to stay on the seat, let alone keep the phone to her ear. By the time she came to a halt it was in her lap, its screen dead, the battery having lost the power even to issue warnings.

PART THREE

Chapter Twenty-seven

'Is this okay?'

Dougie looked up from the sofa where he was reading Nina's letter. It had arrived in the post that morning, with a little note from Linda saying, *Thought you should have this before the funeral.* Stevie had been upstairs, getting ready, for nearly an hour. Having invited her father's appraisal, she hovered in the doorway, plucking self-consciously at her outfit: a tight-fitting mid-thigh-length black skirt, a round-necked black T-shirt and a black cardigan, one of the curiously asymmetric ones that seemed to be in fashion, with a hem that zigzagged between rib-cage and thighs. Her slim legs were encased in black tights and on her feet were black ballet-pumps, with tiny bows across the toes.

'This shirt's got some writing on, but it doesn't show, does it?' She lifted one of the flaps of the cardigan to reveal the word *breathe* etched in small white letters across her chest. 'Does it show?'

Dougie shook his head, clutching the letter, smiling, not trusting himself to speak.

'And then there's this – what do you think?' She ducked behind the door and reappeared with a wide-brimmed black hat perched on the back of her head and a clowning expression on her face: a show of jaunty nonchalance that, Dougie recognized at once, arose solely from the deep, very real fear of not being taken seriously.

451

He nodded encouragingly, his smile broadening. 'Pull it forwards a bit. Yes, that's it. Wow.' He whistled softly, the admiration beaming out of him. 'I don't suppose you've heard of Audrey Hepburn, have you?'

She shook her head.

'Well, Google her one day and you'll see. You look amazing, Stevie. Better than Audrey Hepburn. Absolutely amazing.' He folded Nina's letter carefully and slid it back into its envelope. Stevie, looking happier, trotted across the room to check her reflection in the mirrored surround of a photo frame on the mantelpiece, tipping her head this way and that, trying to get a good view of the hat. Dougie watched in silence, absorbing the implications of his compliment, the irrepressible burgeoning of his daughter's film-star looks. At sixteen and a half the swan had fully emerged from the duckling, not that there had ever – in his eyes at least – been an ugly phase in the transition. A touch of gawkiness maybe, the odd patchiness in her complexion, but all of it entrancing, all of it a privilege to witness. His child. No blood tie could have made him love her more.

It would be her second ever funeral, she had reminded him gravely, as they'd sat opposite each other at the kitchen table the previous evening, spooning shepherds pie into their mouths, hers with insulting dollops of ketchup, his without. 'Ross's was the first,' she had murmured, releasing the name as a tender whisper, something that, even verbally, required the gentlest handling. 'Bad that,' she had added, not looking up, and Dougie had echoed, 'Yes, very bad,' letting the tenderness in his own voice tell her how glad he was she had mentioned it.

She was wearing more makeup than usual, he noticed now: a dusting of something faintly glittery across her cheeks, a touch of pinkish lip gloss, smudges of blue as well as a line of thick black across her upper eyelids. She was so tall that even the cheap pumps looked elegant. She had been almost-woman for some time, Dougie reminded himself. It was why the thing with Simon had happened. Why she had been able to deal with it as she had.

He shifted on the sofa, quelling an urge – by no means the first – to reveal that he not only knew of the misguided sexual engagement with Simon but was also fully *au fait* with her extraordinarily bold and brave follow-up to it. He wanted her to understand he was forgiving, and proud of how she had dealt with that, of how she was growing up. And yet he was also fearful of dismantling the new scaffolding of confidence that she had so successfully managed to build round herself since the hiatus of the summer – the light in her eye, the spring in her step: he would never forgive himself if that came crashing down again. He was already a little worried about how she would react when she heard about the aftermath of her confession to Victoria, whether she would see the separation of her and Simon as a triumph or a calamity. It had been one of the many things about which he had been hoping to consult Janine during the abruptly curtailed phone call on Monday night, once he had got past all the explaining. Janine would have a clear view on how to handle such matters. She always did.

'You outshine your old father, anyway,' he went on glibly instead, stretching out on the sofa, tucking the letter behind a cushion to read again when she had left the room.

'Actually,' Stevie replied slowly, in the tone of one making a reluctant confession, 'I was thinking you looked quite cool.' She lifted off the hat, which Amelia had lent her, or rather Amelia's mum, who had caught them rummaging in her wardrobe and offered to help rather than being cross. 'I mean, a *suit*, Dad, I didn't even know you had one. Nina would feel very honoured, I'm sure,' she added, more shyly, her eyes telling him that she knew he was cut up inside, but was going to keep on with the business – taking the cue from him – of not mentioning it.

'Nina would have laughed her head off,' Dougie corrected her swiftly. He tweaked his thigh, trying and failing to smooth out the horizontal crease left by the coat hanger over which the trousers had hung unworn for so long. It was a good suit though – the Armani, from the silly days – and he had ironed a fresh white shirt. Only a tie was beyond him. He couldn't wear a tie. 'We'll go in ten, okay? Have you eaten something? I made French toast – did you see?' It was Saturday morning so he had let her sleep in and left the toast keeping warm in the top oven.

'Yeah. Delish . . .' Stevie faltered, clearly concerned that a show of appetite might not be wholly appropriate for someone about to attend a funeral.

'Good girl.' Dougie stood up, adjusting his waistband so that it fell a little lower over his slim hips, conveniently hiding more of his shoes, which were old, of thin, weathered leather, and somewhat in danger of undermining his other sartorial efforts. 'And, er, I don't suppose you've heard any more from your mother, have you? You know, exact dates, or anything?'

'Nope. Next week, she said. But it's going to be a long visit, she promised, which will be cool.'

'Great. I wonder where she'll stay.'

'Her and Mike?'

'Yes, yes . . . her and Mike.'

'A hotel?' Stevie hazarded.

'Maybe.' Dougie sought refuge in the view out onto the street, marvelling that Janine had managed to withhold the fact of her presence in England from her daughter for an entire six days, but then wondering, on a rush of panic, whether that meant she had jetted back to Stockholm and really was back in the business of firing off texts from across the Baltic instead of northern England. He had tried calling several times during the week, but to no avail. If it rang she didn't pick up. Otherwise a computerized voice told him she was unavailable. Having at first thought a weakening battery had ended their conversation on Monday night, he now wasn't so sure.

The traffic through London was stop-start, gobbling up precious time. Dougie drove in a dazed state, with a mounting sense of unreality. If they missed the service he wouldn't care, he decided. It would make it easier to remember Nina as she had been, sprawling in the front of the rowing-boat in her daft yellow cap and dungaree-shorts, or picking like a wary kitten through one of his more exotic creations, the caution in her big eyes flaring to admiring appreciation with every bite. The silent, still creature in the hospice had already been parked in a deep, different part of him, not for visiting.

He cast a glance at Stevie, meek and quiet in the passenger seat, the hat held on her lap, like a fragile cake.

'Okay?' he asked, aware that without her at his side the world, the real world, might once again have been in danger of feeling too bleak to bother with.

'Fine. Are we going to be late?'

'Maybe. A bit. It depends on the A20. There's no point in worrying.'

'No, I know.' She tipped her head back and closed her eyes.

Dougie's thoughts drifted to Simon and Victoria, no doubt going through their own different sort of hell back in north London. The unravelling of a long relationship was a dark, drawn-out and, in the end, deeply private business, as he knew only too well. Even the way Victoria had launched herself at him at the beginning of the week had seemed an understandable, if pitiful, part of the maelstrom. She had clearly been in meltdown, seeking some sort of misguided revenge, trying to make herself feel better. Dougie's only concern had been letting her down gently and then, recognizing that he was in no position to offer advice, providing what reassurance he could during the hysteria that had followed. It had been real hysteria, too, garbled apologies on account of Stevie, mixed with suggestions first that Simon had already left, and then that he hadn't.

Afterwards Dougie had found himself reflecting on the need for a couple to have friends in such circumstances, if only as a reminder that the outside world – an oasis of humdrum ordinariness – still existed. During the prolonged misery of his breakup from Janine, Simon had provided exactly such a stalwart support service for him: perspective, laughter, sanity. Pondering this as he sat in the thick traffic on the way to Nina's funeral that Saturday morning, the weight of grief already heavy in his heart, Dougie allowed himself a moment to mourn the demise of his childhood friendship, recognizing again the magnitude of what had been lost. Simon, in these new circumstances, might well need the ballast of outside support, but it could not come from him. Some incidents laid bare the inner fibre of the participants, and Simon's decision to have sex with Stevie had proved to be one of them – not so much for the original lapse of judgement as his reactions in the aftermath, the revelation of his character under pressure. Dougie had only to think of the exchanges in the stadium pub – Simon's lewdness, his aggressive efforts at self-protection – to regain his certainty that the situation between them, for him at least, was irretrievable.

For the last few miles of the journey, winding along narrowing roads, autumn seemed to close in, a sterner and more advanced version than the one they had left in London, with leaves gusting violently at the windscreen and the sky sealing itself to a stony blank canvas. The greystone Norman church they were seeking, set in the small village where Nina's parents lived in a rural pocket off the A25, appeared suddenly as they rounded a bend. It had a squat, square tower, which, like the headstones pitched at angles in the grass around it, had the gnarled look of objects forced stoically to endure centuries of weathering and rough treatment. With only a few minutes until the service started, and the lane already thick with cars, Dougie pulled up by the little entrance gate, suggesting Stevie get out first and promising to catch her up when he had parked.

'No way.' She shrank into her seat clutching the hat.

And he was just as afraid, Dougie realized, his heart galloping as he sped along the lane, finding a space a hundred yards away, up on a bank of dead bracken. They strode back to the church together, Stevie with one palm securing the hat, now neatly slotted over her head, the wide brim flapping, Dougie trying not to slide on the tarmac in his old smooth-soled shoes. They crept through the creaking door just as the introit ended and tiptoed across to two empty seats in a back row of extra chairs.

He was sweating, Dougie noticed, sweating with dread. There was the coffin, clearly visible through the heads crowded into the pews, parked high, centre-stage, on a bed of flowers. There was the coffin and Nina was in it. It was a bigger coffin than Ross's, brown not white, but just as hard to comprehend. The heart of another dear human had stopped beating and she had been laid in a box. It happened all the time, all over the world, in a million ways. Dougie swayed, puzzling at the enormity of this, that something so commonplace should never lose the power to cause pain. Such pain. And yet this wasn't like Ross because at Ross's funeral Stevie had stood apart from him, clinging uncomprehendingly to her broken-hearted mother. Now his daughter was inches from his elbow, erect and proud as a sunflower. And though the sorrow inside him was cutting, hard to contain, it was at least pure this time, of itself, untainted by the corruption of self-disgust.

As the service progressed, though, Dougie found, much to his dismay, these noble sentiments seguing into something more like irritation. There was some good, stirring music, Mozart's 'Ave Verum' and Bach's 'Jesu, Joy of Man's Desiring', performed by the small, competent church choir and organist respectively, but also some toe-curling folksy stuff, which a motley group with bad hair and guitars played sitting cross-legged on the step in front of the altar. In between there were readings about death not being a victory and Nina not having left the world but merely taken up occupancy in another 'room'. By the time they were all on their knees Dougie's hands were clasped together in exasperation more than prayer, for the way Nina herself seemed to be getting lost among the padding and euphemism. Scrambling back into a sitting position, he felt for the letter in his pocket, as if it was the only real bit of her he had left. He kept a tight hold of it, especially as the portly vicar launched into a declamation of her manifold attributes from the pulpit, read off a card because none of the family had felt up to the harrowing job. Dougie had half hoped Linda might do it, until he spotted her hunched in the end corner of the front row, crumpled and grey-faced, her shoulders shaking under the flurries of her sandy hair.

While the vicar ploughed on, Dougie extracted the envelope and unfolded the letter behind the protective camouflage of a large flimsy prayer book, which had been tucked, like aeroplane reading matter, into the back of the pew in front of him. It was a thin, dog-eared leaflet, covered with bright colour photographs of smiling children from around the world, playing games and eating. *Reach Out*, it was headed, over the subtitle *The Power of Prayer*. Steeling himself, Dougie lowered his eyes to savour the already treasured, familiar words.

Dear Dougie,

Have you forgiven me yet? I hope so. You were such a perfect friend, arriving in my life at a perfect time, with your bloody brilliant food and messed-up life, treating me first like a bit of gum on your shoe and then like a piece of furniture of which you had, reluctantly, grown rather fond — I wouldn't have missed a single moment.

When a doctor tells you there are only months left, those months are already not as you would want them. They become too terrifyingly precious to enjoy normally, both for the 'sick' person and for those around them. You, being out of that loop, did more than you can ever know to help make it bearable.

I am tired now. Truly tired. Wanting to stay alive, it's so exhausting. In fact there's this incredible relief at the thought, soon, of being able to hold up my hands and say, okay, I give in, battle over, what will be will be and I shall no longer resist . . .

BUT first, dearest Dougie (Linda has closed her ears . . . yes, of course she is writing this — sorry, but I just couldn't manage it — who would have thought a pen could be so heavy?), there are a few things I want you to know.

(a) You are the most amazing dad. Stevie is lucky, and I think she knows it.

(b) If you ever drink again you will be fucked, so don't do it.

(c) Sort things out with that brother of yours. I've sent up a prayer or two on this, but I've never been totally sure about the receiving end of things on that score so there might still be quite a lot of uphill work for you to do. But do it, okay? Like I told you once, I always wanted a sibling, so bloody appreciate yours.

(d) I have also given some thought to your screwed-up love-life. Your trouble is you are too sexy-handsome for your own good.

If you can get over that – which I think you might even be starting to do – then I think there's hope!! Keep your heart open, that is what I would say. Never, ever give up on it. You don't know what might be around the corner.

Okay. Last words. Be nice to Linda. Be nice to Janine. Be nice to Stevie. But, above all, be very very nice to yourself.

My dearest friend, from your very dear friend,

Nina X

PS If Linda ever says I had the hots for you, she is totally making it up. x

PPS You might need to remind her to hurry up and get back to that hunky sheep-shearing husband of hers before he runs off with someone else.

Dougie held the prayer book higher, glad of its size, glad he was at least able to keep his weeping silent. He felt Stevie's hand arrive on his knee. Peering round the edge of the book, he saw that while five fingers were clamped round his leg she still had her gaze anchored on the awful trying-too-hard vicar, perhaps out of tact for her father's evident discomposure, perhaps because she was hanging on every word the reverend said. For the closing stages of the tribute Dougie did his best to offer the same respectful attention, finding that in fact there was some comfort in the platitudes, in the telescoping distance they granted to a too-short life lived well and with a generous heart.

The last hymn was 'Jerusalem', an all-time favourite of Nina's, the vicar announced, adding, as he read the final fact off his card, that she had been especially fond of Hubert Parry's music since her days of playing lead violin in her school orchestra. Dougie swung his head in aston-

461

ishment as he got to his feet, pondering the rich process of trying to get know another human being, how it was never complete, never something one could close a door on.

There was much harrumphing into handkerchiefs as the organ thundered the stirring opening chords. Strong and dry-eyed, glad his own emotions had played themselves out, Dougie sang lustily, so lustily that Stevie shot him one of her embarrassing-dad warning looks. He grinned, singing louder still, not caring that he was out of tune until, somewhere in the second verse, he caught the strain of a particularly high clear voice somewhere in the boom around him, a familiar voice that made the hairs on his neck stand on end. Lowering the volume on his own efforts, he hurriedly scanned the pews and his row of chairs, then glanced behind, where a cluster of late-comers had taken up positions next to a table of flowers and spare hymn books. But the owner of the voice was nowhere in evidence. And by the time Dougie turned back to face the altar he concluded that he must have imagined it. An open heart could imagine all sorts, if it wanted them badly enough.

A family-only group followed the coffin out of the church in preparation for the hearse-led drive to a crematorium. Dougie sought out Nina's parents to offer brief condolences before it left, then found Linda, perched on a gravestone as if it were a bar stool, drawing deeply on a cigarette.

'Aren't you invited?'

'Sure I was – Nina asked for it – but I said no frigging way. Bodies should be buried, not burnt, in my view.

I've said my farewells, thank you. Besides, I'm in charge of sausages on sticks back at the family ranch. Are you coming?'

'Sorry, not really up for that. We'll head straight back to London. This is Stevie, by the way, my daughter,' Dougie added, holding out an arm to encourage Stevie to stop hovering and make a proper approach.

'Hi, Stevie. Nice to meet you and well done, you still look human. Gorgeous, in fact.' Linda laughed wryly, patting her eyes which were visibly pink and puffy. 'Funerals. Jeez, how grim are they? And you know the worst of it? I could hear *her* snorting all the way through, telling me to stop being a dope, that we were good and done and squared, and life went on, and it *still* didn't prevent me bawling my bloody eyes out. God, and how bad were that creepy crew with tambourines? And before you ask, I've no idea,' she added, exhaling a thick upward plume of smoke and then tossing away her cigarette. 'Friends of friends or *something*. Can't be too rude because now I have to go and get drunk with them . . . Hey, I adore that hat, by the way, it totally suits you.'

Stevie grinned shyly, then shot Linda an admiring look that suggested she longed for the day when she was old enough to lounge on gravestones, smoking cigarettes, swearing and generally saying what she really thought instead of trying to be polite.

'She looks great, doesn't she?' Dougie agreed proudly. 'And we should be on our way, but . . .' he turned to Stevie '. . . would you mind giving us a moment, sweetheart? You're probably dying for one of those anyway, aren't you? Linda, can you give my daughter a fag?'

'It's okay, Dad, I've got my own,' Stevie interjected, a trace of indignation in her voice.

Dougie nodded, whistling softly. 'Of course you have. And I promise not to tell your mother. But I just need a quick word with . . .'

'I'll see you back at the car,' Stevie called, striding off down the path.

'Tell me,' Dougie asked Linda, 'is there *anything* you don't know about me? Or Nina, for that matter.' He stood squarely opposite the gravestone, folding his arms to help fight his own longing to light up.

'Heaps, I expect.' Linda smiled bleakly. 'So, you got the letter, then. Good. But you know what?' She pointed at her temple. 'I've got a terrible memory. Terrible. In fact, consider me officially brainwashed.' She ran a finger across her forehead, in the manner of one zipping up a pencil case. 'There. Hard disk erased, the few things I did know forgotten.'

Dougie chuckled. He liked her more every time he met her. 'Well, that's much appreciated, but thanks, too, by the way, for helping her write it . . . Those things Nina said, they meant – they mean – a lot. Christ, she was so . . .'

Linda stood up, dusting the back of her dress. 'None of that, okay? Or you'll set me off again and then I'll need a face lift. Let's say goodbye – get it over with. But first tell me if my bum is green.' She turned round, swiping at her backside with her palms.

'No, all clear.'

'Good.' She put her arms round him and they hugged. 'I'm taking Sam, by the way. I hope that's not going to piss you off or anything. Nina used to joke what a sun dude he

464

was, always soaking up the rays in the garden, so I'm hoping the southern hemisphere will suit him just fine. It's an admin nightmare, but I am determined.'

Dougie pulled a face. 'You're more than welcome.'

'Good luck, Dougie.' She gave him a final wave and strode off to a car waiting with an open door at the bottom of the church path.

Dougie followed slowly in the same direction, kicking at drifts of damp leaves, trying to reconnect with the belief that life still had good things to offer, that the best of his own shambolic existence was not yet done. When he got to the road, he hesitated, looking right and left, remembering the voice in the church. There had been lots of strong singers: it could have been anyone. He could just make out the Ford on the bend in the lane, pitched at an odd angle with its two inner wheels high up on the bank. Stevie was already there, standing with her back to him talking to someone. Dougie stared harder, screwing up his eyes, aware that his twenty-twenty vision was no longer quite as good as it had been. It was someone slim in a smart fitted black coat and high heels. Someone without a hat, her hair loose. Someone with the skin tone of lightest caramel and expressive hands that cut and circled the air as she talked. As he watched, the hands swooped to Stevie's head and removed the wide-brimmed hat, setting it on her own instead.

The likeness then was extraordinary. They could have been sisters. Dougie had stopped walking, overcome by so many emotions it would have been impossible to separate them, though at their heart lay a new sense of perspective, not unlike the distancing clarity afforded by the priest's presentation of Nina in church – gently setting her before the congregation like some great complete work of art, worthy only of admiration, there for the sole, sweet, pure business of cherishing. Janine, standing in the lane in the big hat, a small vibrant, silhouette against the back-drop of yellowing trees, seemed to command the same respect, the same attention.

But even as Dougie stood motionless, taking this in, a bigger, fiercer emotion rose through him, like some huge sharp splinter, surfacing after years in his system, and that was a sense of loss: a loss so acute that he could have clasped both hands to his stomach from the ache of it.

When Janine spotted him she seemed to freeze, then slowly removed the hat. With a last word to Stevie, a stroke of her arm, she set off up the lane towards him, moving purposefully, her brown eyes – when she got close enough for him to see them – stern and full of warning. She began speaking several yards before they drew level, her voice as strong as a line thrown from dry land into a cold sea. 'You wanted to talk and that's what we're going to do. But not here. I've told Stevie I heard about the funeral from you, that it coincided with my plan of a surprise visit to England, that I wanted to be here because I knew Nina had been a good friend to both of you. I came in a hire car. I'm parked back up there. I'll call you when I get back to London.'

He nodded and she walked past him, her high heels as steady as a drum beat on the narrow road.

Chapter Twenty-eight

'Ready?' Victoria unzipped her slim burgundy briefcase and pulled out several wads of papers, shaking them into orderly piles across the table, like decks of unruly cards.

'I'm all yours.' Simon hoped she would read the irony in the quip, see its deep truth now, at this point they had reached, almost exactly a week on from the implosion of their lives. But she did not look up. He took the chair opposite, resting his elbows on the table, then his wrists, then letting both arms collapse into his lap where they could twitch unseen. He couldn't read her. Somewhere in the long, dark hours of conserving the bathroom light-bulb he had lost his bearings with her, with everything.

At six o'clock on Wednesday morning she had finally unlocked the door. She had been holding a small brandy in one hand and a knife and fork in the other. 'Sorry,' she had said. 'I needed to think. I've cooked you some break-fast. Scrambled eggs, toast, bacon, mushrooms, sausages, grilled tomatoes. There's also fresh orange juice, coffee and croissants. While you eat I'm going to make a proper start at clearing up the flat. All the broken stuff – I'm sorry about that too. I was angry.'

Simon had stood in the doorway, his arms hanging limply, blinking, like an animal emerging from a burrow. 'But you're not now?' he had asked, his voice a plaintive croaky mix of hope and feeble umbrage.

'You haven't shaved,' was all she had replied, peering at the thick stubble covering the lower half of his face. 'I would have thought that was one thing you *could* have done to pass the time.' And then she had made a noise that sounded like a laugh. Except it couldn't have been, Simon had told himself, leaning against the door frame, too dizzy – from lack of food, from joy at his release – to think straight.

He brought the dining-room table and the papers back into focus. He knew he had to concentrate, say the right things. The terrors in the bathroom, the emasculation, had faded during the intervening days, like a bad dream. He had stared into a black hole and pulled back, regained an appreciation of what he had, what he had so nearly lost. Victoria had been clever in that regard, he had to admit, making sure the message, the suffering, got rammed home. He was now more ready than ever to atone, to say and do anything to get them back on track. Fidelity, parenthood, there were no doubts now: he wanted it all. He had got careless, got close to thinking Victoria was all he had – not much to be grateful for – instead of realizing that she was *all* he had, in other words, to be hung on to at all costs.

The only remaining area of disorientation was on account of her – her calmness, the inscrutability. During his incarceration she appeared to have tidied his study to the cleanliness and order of an operating theatre: everything filed, the books and clippings put away, his haphazard in-tray reduced to a few scraps, all the work surfaces polished. While a little appalled, Simon had been encouraged by the fresh-start look, the possibility it seemed to suggest of new, better beginnings. In the four days since his release they had ended up clearing much of the other mess together, carefully wrapping the shards of glass in newspaper, working out what could be salvaged. She had wanted to jettison the pockmarked statuette, but he had insisted on keeping it, 'as a memento of our best and worst', he had ventured at the time, one of many verbal offerings of peace she had studiedly ignored. Talking would happen, she kept insisting, but only when they had both had a chance to mull things over, when they were good and ready.

She had laid the table with a pot of coffee, the little cream jug that she liked to use for milk and the two large *café-au-lait* cups and saucers they had bought while holidaying in the South of France a decade or so before. They were in bright primary colours, yellow dotted with blue, their rims thick as chocolate bars. Too precious for the dishwasher, they used them on special occasions – lazy mornings, bank-holiday weekends. Simon had taken heart at the sight of them – her decision to use them – just as he had taken heart at the pancakes she had prepared for their breakfast that morning, maple syrup, fresh quarters of lemon, caster sugar, the works. Indeed, since she had released him from the bathroom she had been feeding him diligently, fussing round him in a way that was new and motherly, checking he had his favourite pillows on the spare bed, bleeding the radiator next to it when he complained how noisily it gurgled. It had been another thing to give him hope, this nurturing, allowing him to believe, in spite of her frequent absences from the flat, her hushed phone conversations behind closed doors, her refusal to talk about anything but the immediate and basic components of their shared life – food, sleep, television – that all would yet be well.

She poured the coffee, which settled in the cups as smoothly as Guinness, silky black with a thin, foamy head, and pushed one towards him.

'So what have you got there, Vic?' He nodded at the papers. 'I thought this was the full and frank discussion you've been promising me. The chance to put my case. You yours. I mean, it's been a tricky few months, you have to admit – or strange, anyway – lots of ups and downs, my cliché of a mid-life crisis, hitting forty . . . I'm not proud, I can tell you, not proud at all. No one wants to be a walking cliché – but you've been in the middle of something too, all the baby business, raging hormones and so on.'

She held her cup to her mouth with both hands, quietly sipping and swallowing, her expression, from what he could see of it over the fat bright ceramic brim, suggesting that she was waiting for him to finish more than actually listening to what he was saying. Her green eyes looked bigger than usual, fresh and purposeful; unafraid. Yes, that was it, Simon realized, with a twist of foreboding, that was the new, strange thing: she had no fear in her. Whereas his heart was suddenly thumping. 'Oh, we are going to talk,' she said, setting the cup down and dabbing the tip of her little finger into the corners of her mouth. 'Exactly like this. Exactly. You go on. Or have you finished?'

Simon felt faintly outmanoeuvred. 'Well, obviously not . . . I mean, there's so much to say, like . . . like the fact that I love you. That I'm sorry. That this whole wretched business . . . The thing with the girl was one of those moments of madness that I would undo if I possibly could. And I still question her motives,' he added viciously, 'coming round here – telling you, for fuck's sake. What sort of sick act was that – was she trying to destroy us? Jesus –'

'No, Simon. I think that was you.'

'Pardon?'

'Trying to destroy us – I think that was you, not Stevie. The child wanted me to know I was married to a shit, which is quite a different thing.' She picked up the top paper in her pile and laid it back down again, in exact alignment with the stack underneath. 'Very brave for a sixteen-year-old, if you ask me.'

'I'm not a shit,' Simon whispered. 'I love you and I made a mistake. Stepped out of line. And I think I've let you punish me, haven't I? Christ, locking me up like that – not many men . . .' He stopped, aware he was heading into unsafe ground.

'Hmm? Not many men would have put up with being imprisoned for three days in a bathroom? Is that what you were going to say? But you didn't have any choice with your "punishment", did you? Because I *locked* the door. And afterwards you were very grateful to be let out and also, understandably, very hungry, so putting up with it wasn't really the issue, was it?'

'Vic, stop this, please.'

'Stop what? Telling it like it is?'

'You're angry. Upset. I get that. I really do. I mean, of course you are. I couldn't be sorrier. I took a wrong turn. But it was months ago now and it meant nothing.'

'Ah.' She pushed aside her documents and put on her glasses, exuding the composure of some kind of legal eagle with a trick up her sleeve. 'Now there I have to disagree. It did mean something, you see. It meant a hell of a lot. It means something because it meant *nothing* to you. It means something because it demonstrates that you, as a man, as a human being, have the judgement of a mating cockroach.'

Victoria sat back, watching the effect of her words. She was in shock still, she knew. The hurt, the havoc, the humiliation. And yet driving home from Dougie's, the demeaning culmination of it all – throwing herself at him like that, being refused, *Janine* arriving, like some kind of footnote from the past, to compound the mortification, she would shudder to think of it until the day she died – an almost visionary sense of purpose had descended, a curtain opening, allowing in a chink of light, not much, but enough to see by. Simon, their new reality, needed to be faced. She had wanted to kill him. She nearly had. She had been a swipe away, so close to plunging the knife through his chest that in her mind's eye she had seen the deed done, seen how he would fall, known how the resistance of his skin and bone would feel against the blade, smelt the spilling pulses of his blood. Diminished responsibility, the court would have called it. Simon might have had his moment of madness, but that had been hers. She had got within a hair's breadth, seen the whites of its eyes and pulled back.

She had been close to throwing away the bathroom-door key too – tossing it out of a window into the street, but that had been different: much more measured, saner, a strategy to contemplate. Deciding not to do so, but not unlocking the door either, had been another reasoned act, albeit one of pure revenge, justifiable payback for suffering caused, with the add-on bonus of giving her time to think. Floating up in the newly fixed lift to their floor that Monday afternoon, it had been this prospect – the need for space inside her own head – to which Victoria had clung most keenly. Simon had left her floundering in the dark with all his slithery lying for long enough, and now it was his turn. Hearing his muffled pleadings from the bathroom as she picked her way through the broken glass in the hall, she had put some music on (Adele – she liked Adele) and shut herself in Simon's study to press on with the tail-end of her forensic search and tidy-up operation, taking her time, filling several bags of rubbish as well as filing a lot of it neatly away.

'I love you,' Simon repeated hoarsely now, pushing his hand past the cups and the cafetière to seize hers. 'I love you and I love our child.'

Victoria allowed her fingers to lie limply in his. Instinctively, she put her free arm across her lower stomach, protecting what it contained, quietly apologizing to it. She looked at Simon's hand, the familiar prehensile curve of his too-short thumb, the strong knuckles, the well-tended nails. She had really liked that about him at the beginning, all those hundreds of years ago, how he wasn't too much of a man's man to know how to wield a nail file.

'And I think you still love me,' Simon plunged on, taking encouragement from her silence and the soft look on her face.

'Love,' she replied quietly, 'real love, begins in the head.

It's a state of mind. An act of faith. And I have lost mine in you.'

'No, Vic. A bit of trust, maybe, but we can get that back —'

'I don't know you, Simon. I thought I did, but I don't. I've been trying to understand you, I really have, but I can't. Nothing about you adds up. Which is fine — I'm sure a lot of people are like that — but I'm afraid it's not something that works for me. I realize now that all I really knew about you was the version I settled on twenty years ago, the one I wanted to believe in: that you were a sort of free spirit, a little shy, but kind, laid-back . . . It's funny if you think about it —'

'But I am those things,' he cried. 'I am.'

Victoria smiled sadly. 'No, you're not. You're weak. You're deceitful. You have no fixed purpose other than your own personal gratification. You have poor judgement. You're untrustworthy. And I don't want to be married to you any more.' She stopped because her mouth had started to tremble and she did not want to allow that, not yet. She was killing their marriage, she knew, killing 'them', just as certainly as any frenzied plunge with a knife would have drained the consciousness from Simon seven days before. She had come a long way since then. She had worked through a lot of things, including the degree to which twenty years of trying to keep Simon onside, keep him happy — about his faltering career, his lack of direction, indulging his boyish ways, giving him 'manly' space — had caused her almost to lose touch with her own contrasting strengths and convictions. It had been something of a revelation to lift the blanket and find them still there. She had money. She had a good job that she loved. She was going to have a baby that she wanted. She did not need him.

She picked up her stacks of papers and began sliding them in turn across the table. They had been drawn up by lawyers. Some high-powered contact of her father's had assembled it all at lightning speed. They offered Simon financial terms that included a generous one-off payment as well as sole ownership of the flat. She, meanwhile, intended to continue with the plan of moving to Buckinghamshire. A professional property searcher had already identified four houses within a ten-mile radius of her parents', which she was viewing the following week. The last of the documents was about their child, outlining visitation rights, the number of supervised hours per week they would start with, graduating to unsupervised when the baby was weaned, but to be reviewed again in a year, and annually thereafter.

'No, Vic, no.' Simon swung his head from side to side with mulish obstinacy. 'It doesn't have to be like this.'

'Yes, Si, it does. I do not love you. You give me none of the things I need, things I deserve. I do not trust you.'

'But why?' he blazed back. 'Just because of that one –'

'Not just because of *that*, no, though let's take a moment to call *that* what it was, shall we, just this once?' She leant towards him, shaping the words with exaggerated care: 'You got drunk and had unprotected sex with your oldest friend's sixteen-year-old daughter during the birthday treat I organized for you, while I was at the bedside of a mutual friend whose life, and that of her unborn baby, was in danger. There. Not that complicated, is it?' She sat back, releasing a long breath. 'But, no, it's not *just* because of that.'

Simon was swinging his head again. 'I'm sorry,' he groaned. 'I couldn't be more sorry but . . .' He badly wanted to say how eagerly the bloody girl had sought his attentions, how he hadn't been entirely to blame, how it had taken two, but guessed that this, like any hint of self-pity, would not further his cause. 'But what else is there?' he pleaded instead, his voice strangled with the under-standing that he was back in the black hole, floundering.

'Your lying, Simon, that's what else, saying you had a script commission when you didn't, saying you'd seen Danny —'

'But we sorted the Danny thing and I can explain about the —'

'And those girlie magazines of yours, which you claimed were Dougie's —'

A snort escaped him. He folded his arms. 'Oh, right, now I get what this is really about.'

'No, Simon,' she replied, with some amazement. 'I don't think you do. It's not the pornography, it really isn't — I find some of it quite a turn-on, if you want to know — or even those sites you visit. Yes, I've been on your com-puter,' she added, in response to his sharp intake of breath, 'navigating your recent history. It's hardly rocket science. No, it's the fact of hiding it, the *way* you hid it, just carrying on lying regardless, even when I gave you every chance to come clean, and dumping the blame on Dougie, not that he gave a damn. I just don't think you know what the truth is any more. You just say what you think you need to say to get what you want, half convincing yourself in the process. But there's all the other stuff I've found too, countless receipts for things —'

'What things?'

'Oh, I can't be bothered, I really can't. You'd have answers to it all, and do you know what? I'm just not interested.'

'There have been no other "things". That's it. You know it all, Vic, I swear.'

She shook her head sadly. 'Ah, but I don't believe you. And I never will. So the truth has become irrelevant. That is what we have lost, Simon. And that is why you are going to read and sign these.' She pushed the papers at him again, beginning, in a mechanical voice, to spell out what each one contained.

'I could report you,' he burst out, pushing them back at her. 'I could report you for imprisonment and torture, not to mention threatening me with a knife.'

She leant across the table, fixing her new unafraid look on him with the force of a hammer driving home a nail. 'You fucking deserved every moment. But you go to the police if you want. Just go, and see how far it gets you.'

'*Daddy* will intervene again, no doubt,' Simon snarled, unable to restrain himself, 'as, no doubt, he intervened with this lot. Get you a hot-shot barrister. Get you off.'

'Oh, no, I don't think I'd need Daddy,' Victoria replied softly. 'I'm pretty sorted on my own.'

'And I suppose you'll meet someone else, will you, just like that?' Simon shot back bitterly, defeat injecting a tremor of panic into his voice now. 'Someone who'll be prepared to take on a pregnant woman, pregnant with *my* child?'

There was an infinitesimal pause. 'Well, that's what Dougie did, isn't it?' Victoria said quietly, a look of such vivid tenderness crossing her face that Simon found a moment, in spite of his anguish, to wonder at it. 'Or had you forgotten that?'

She wasn't inscrutable, she was hurt, Simon reminded himself frantically. She was hurt and he could still make her feel better. 'Of course I hadn't forgotten it,' he said, more calmly, 'but happily I am the father of *our* child, Vic, which is why –'

'You didn't want it,' she cut in. 'You played along to pacify me. But, yes, I can assure you, you are the father, which is why I recognize that you need to be a part of his or her life, and also why we will review how that works at every stage. As for finding someone else, I'm in no hurry – although there's someone at the RA, as it happens, someone I like who, I know, likes me a lot in return. He's called Howard. His wife died of cancer a couple of years ago. That day when I fainted in the meeting, he was first to my side.'

Victoria stood up slowly, aware that the numbness, the visionary calm that had seen her through the week, was wearing off. Her body had turned to jelly and even the simple business of standing up appeared to have applied an unbearable strain on her knees. 'I'll leave you to read that lot. The terms are generous. Lots of money, Simon. You'll be okay.'

She pushed off from the back of the chair, which got her to the doorway, then slid along the passageway, groping for balance along the wall. Once in the sanctity of the bedroom, a private sanctity since Simon's eviction to the spare room, she locked the door and fell onto the bed to cry, switching on the radio to mask the noise, although her weeping in fact made little sound, coming as it did from a place very deep inside. She wept for Simon as much as for herself, for what they had lost, for the distress she had had to inflict to ensure it was irrevocable. Never in her life had she deliberately hurt someone so much, loved or otherwise. Never had she used words to say such things, to kill something so outright. And yet, even so, there had been one blow she had withheld, one knife not thrown, and that was to do with Dougie and the memories recent months had stirred of a night shared under a boat tarpaulin twenty years before, a night when his drunken state had not prevented an encounter of intensity and pleasure the like of which Victoria had not experienced before or subsequently; a night when, for all their differences and sparring, she would have followed him to the ends of the earth had he asked.

Chapter Twenty-nine

'Your room's bigger than mine – a lot bigger,' Amelia remarked, glancing up from her encampment on the bed, where she was sprawling on her stomach, playing with Stevie's laptop, her legs bent up over her backside and locked at the ankles.

Stevie was in jeans and a bra, lost in contemplation of the deep, never-ending struggle of what to wear, a struggle compounded that evening by the last-minute, disarming twist that what had originally been planned as a girls-only trip to the cinema was now to include Paul. He was in London at last, staying with an uncle in Ladbroke Grove for a few days, prior to getting on a plane for Saõ Paulo. Amelia had kindly agreed to play gooseberry, not just because she didn't want to miss the film but because Stevie had begged her to, in a bid to keep the tryst both secret and low-key. It had been many weeks, after all, since the sunbathing on the stony fringes of Lake Kottla; weeks during which they had exchanged nothing but the occasional text message, mostly about Paul's travel plans. She wasn't sure what she felt about him any more, let alone what he felt about her. All that had really happened was a bit of hand-holding; and as the days ticked by it had felt to Stevie like an increasingly flimsy foundation for any serious hopes. Ricky, with whom Amelia had got much further, in all senses, had recently announced (in a cruelly brief phone message) that their relationship was at an end.

'You know it's an eighteen this film, don't you? We're going to need our fake IDs. But don't say anything to my mum, okay? I mean, she, like, *knows* I've got one, but sort of doesn't want to be reminded of it.'

Stevie tugged her head through the neck-hole of a tight red top, emerging pink-faced, her hair criss-crossing her face. 'Dad's the same. And he's been in an odd mood today so I don't want to stir anything up.'

'Odd in what way? He's cool, your dad.'

Stevie pushed the hair out of her eyes and posed, without conviction, in front of her wall mirror, trying and failing to imagine herself through Paul's eyes. She also checked on Amelia while she was at it. Her friend had done a lot of crying in the immediate aftermath of the Ricky business, but had actually been a lot more fun to be around as a result: less obsessive, much more open to other things. 'I dunno . . . but, like, when I went down to the kitchen just now, before you came, he was standing by the fridge just sort of talking to himself, like a total saddo.'

Amelia sat up, closing the lid of the laptop, her interest thoroughly engaged. 'What was he saying?'

'I couldn't really hear. I didn't want to, to be honest – it was kind of creepy, if you know what I mean.'

Amelia nodded solemnly. 'Totally. The black one was better by the way.' She pointed at one of the tops scattered round Stevie's feet. 'Hey, these look so great.' She scrambled off the bed and set about scrutinizing a collage of photographs that Stevie had Blu-Tacked to the wall next to the wardrobe.

'I haven't finished yet. I'm planning for it to cover literally the whole wall and go halfway round the room.'

'Oh, my God, but how gross am I in this one?' Amelia squealed, pointing at a snap that had been taken at Merryl's party earlier in the year. 'Why didn't you tell me how bad I looked in that dress?' She fell to her knees, laughing. 'No wonder you've put it right at the bottom. And who's this little dweeb here?' She craned her neck to get a proper look at a picture that was right up against the wardrobe, a waif of a baby in a blue sleep-suit.

Stevie hesitated, covering for the fact by bending down to pick up the black top. 'Remember, in Norfolk, I told you about –'

Amelia slumped down with her back against the wall, dropping her face into her hands. 'Oh, shit, of course . . . Bollocky shit – I'm a prat.'

'It's okay, Ams. I put it down there because I didn't want to make a big deal of it or anything. I mean I'm not, like, *tragic* that I lost a kid brother or anything, that would be too fake, but he was kind of sweet.'

'Oh, yes, he is . . . so sweet, and I'm really sorry, Stevie.'

'It's okay, Ams, honest.'

There was a knock on the door and Dougie put his head into the room. He looked hot and unkempt in a way that made Stevie feel slightly embarrassed for him in front of her friend. 'Dad, you've got something on your cheek –'

He swiped absently at his face. 'Are you girls ready? Amelia's mother has just tooted outside. Jolly nice of her, too. If it was up to me you'd be taking the bus.'

'Dad, you haven't got it. Go higher . . . it looks like egg. Is it egg?'

'Probably.' Dougie rubbed again, with a little more success, but not in a way that suggested he cared about getting rid of the blob. 'And Mum's running late, Stevie, so she says she probably won't catch you tonight after all.'

'Will she be here tomorrow?'

To her surprise the question seemed to make him cross. 'I have no idea what her plans are, either for tomorrow or the rest of her visit. You're the one who should know. I've barely seen her.'

'I don't know what you guys are going to talk about tonight anyway,' Stevie muttered, tweaking the black top and already starting to wish she'd stuck with the red.

'You, I expect, Dumbo,' Dougie called, already halfway down the stairs, which he was taking two at a time because a smell of something not quite right was wafting up from the lower ground floor.

'You haven't gone to any trouble, then,' Janine murmured.

They stood for a moment, both slightly in awe of what Dougie had done to transform the dingy basement of a kitchen. The old pine table was set with a crisp white tablecloth, napkins, mats and cutlery, and there were lit candles everywhere, both on the table and squeezed between the clutter on several shelves. A bunch of flowers sprouted in a haphazard fashion out of a large glass jar – yellow roses, red carnations – beside a bottle chilling in an ice bucket next to two crystal champagne flutes. 'It's non-alcoholic,' he said quickly, following her line of vision as she took it all in. 'God knows what it tastes like.'

'I'm sure it'll be fine.'

'Maybe ... Janine, I ...' Dougie faltered, aware his voice was already heavy with meaning – meaning he had meant to contain until later, when they were more into the swing of things, behaving less like strangers. 'Janine ...' But she had skipped away and was peering under saucepan lids and into the oven.

'Oh, my God, Dougie, this all looks amazing ... *ay-may-zing.*'

'To be perfectly truthful, I'm not sure it is,' he admitted ruefully. 'In fact, I don't think I've ever made such a hash of preparing a meal in my life. Even wasted, I would normally have been able to do a better job, but not today. Today I felt like a total amateur. If you don't believe me, look in the fridge – just look,' he ordered, half laughing now.

'Oh, Dougie –'

'Your favourite, right? I mean, it still *is* your favourite, isn't it? But it looks like a traffic accident, doesn't it? The filo pastry, I had to make it twice, then the vanilla cream curdled – which never, ever happens to me – and then the berries, fresh from the bloody market this morning, just sort of fell apart. They were in a brown-paper bag and I must have left them near the kettle or something, I honestly don't know, but they were mulch, as was the entire project, at every possible stage, from start to finish. It was like some kind of sick joke – which is why it now resembles something barely worthy of a chimpanzees' tea party, let alone the meal of my life.'

Janine slowly closed the fridge door. 'Meal of your life?'

Dougie hopped over to the ice bucket, his courage

draining out of him. 'Sit, okay? Just sit. Let's get on with it. I'll open this stuff. There is, of course, real wine if you prefer. White. A Chardonnay – quite good, I think. We're starting with that mussel and fish soup thing – remember the one with saffron and cream that you used to like? I nearly went for smoked haddock soufflé, but then I thought, too obvious and actually a bit easy, but I regretted it, I can tell you, at five o'clock this afternoon when –'

'Doug, stop talking for a minute, okay? Just open that bottle and shut up.'

Janine slid into a chair. It was supposed to be just a talk, the one she had finally agreed to, but already there was so much at stake it was hard to breathe. Her brain felt heavy with it, stupid. It made her vulnerable when she knew she needed to be strong. She clasped her handbag to her chest. Nina's letter was inside it. Nina's letter, which she had thought she might flourish as some sort of challenge, or proof, or simply as a huge question mark to get the ball rolling, but which she knew – quite suddenly – that she would never mention to a soul.

And now there was no prospect of meeting the poor woman either. It had taken a bit of detective work to find out about the funeral. Janine had been pleased with herself about that, but then, after the palaver of getting there, in a hire car, with a TomTom bleating instructions, had wondered what she was doing – an outsider wanting to pay her respects, hiding behind a pillar, surrounded by those who had known the woman enough to mourn her properly, including a dough-faced man with long sideboards and moist eyes, who muttered a couple of times that the best years of his life had been at her side.

By then desperate to see Stevie, but determined that, with so much to say, it should be under better circumstances, it had taken all of Janine's resolve to put her head down and scuttle out of the church on the heels of the family cortège. She had got some way down the lane when Stevie, cigarette in hand, had spotted her anyway. It had been a moment of pure joy. Stevie had thrown her cigarette into the air and run at her with a yelp of disbelief, easily buying the story of it being a planned surprise, which Janine had gabbled out as they hugged. That Dougie would co-operate deftly with the minor subterfuge had been one of the rare minor certainties in what had otherwise been a torrid few days. Holding back on Stevie had been the hardest part of it, but Janine had wanted to get her life sorted first, have some answers to the inevitable questions, and recognized that her parents' place was the best – the only – base from which to do it. By that Sunday the mist had lifted a little. She and Mike were still talking, long, agonized conversations that lasted late into the night; Donna, from the estate agent's, had kindly offered Janine a spare bed until her tenants were out; and Vince was seeing what he could do about her job. She had been planning to declare her presence in London to Stevie that night, to confess that it was not only a solo break but probably quite a long one.

'Cheers.' Dougie and Janine chinked glasses, took sips and then burst out laughing.

'Oh, wow, that is on the sweet side,' Janine cried, 'and so fizzy.'

'Look, I'll get you the decent stuff.' Dougie scrambled out of his chair.

'No, I want this.' Janine took a bigger gulp to show she was serious. 'Second time it's better, honestly. Just don't think champagne, think elderflower and a hint of sweet apple plus some sort of overripe pear.' She giggled.

'Janine, I –'

She held up a hand to silence him. 'Do you know? I'm not sure I want you to speak, because everything at this moment feels so good and if you start talking –'

'I'll balls it up.'

'Precisely.' They caught each other's eye and laughed again. 'Okay, this food, let's be having it, then. What's between the mussel soup and the traffic accident?' She gave a brisk tug to her chair to bring it closer to the table. Picking up her napkin, she suppressed an affectionate smile at the familiar clever rabbit into which it had been folded. Dougie had always been good at the rabbits; her star-turn had been doves. 'Come on, then, Master Chef Dougie Easton,' she teased, shaking out the stiff linen folds into a smooth square on her lap, 'show me what you've got. Stevie said you were writing a cookbook. How's that going? When's it likely to hit the shelves?'

'Never,' Dougie replied stoutly, now ladling out his soup. 'I've given up on it. Not my thing – words, organized thought – quite apart from the fact that the market is already overloaded with far more able, higher-profile chefs strutting their stuff in print. No, I've got another much more enjoyable plan for making money. It involves Spain and the *finca*, but not until Stevie's safely through her A levels and, no, I'm not going to say any more just now. In the meantime Xavier has at last found a rich German family to rent the place and not a moment too soon.'

'Spain? Sounds intriguing. As for the book thing, I must say when Stevie mentioned it, I did think . . .' Janine released an involuntary groan as he set the soup in front of her. It was beautiful simply to look at, since Dougie had placed the bowl on an under-plate arranged with freshly sliced red onion and snow peas. The soup itself was as smooth as cream and a nutty yellow colour from the saffron. 'Oh, God, that smells so good – *so* good – and there is dill in there, too, isn't there? I swear I can smell dill. You don't normally put that in, do you?' She held back her long hair with both hands and put her face low over the broth, her eyelids half closing as she inhaled its aromas. She was wearing a scoop-necked purple top and a purple stone in a pendant, which fell forwards, chiming faintly against the china. .

Dougie didn't think he had ever in his life seen anything more beautiful. 'Janine . . .'

She kept her eyes closed. 'You're going to "talk" any-way, aren't you? I knew you would.'

'Yes, I am. But I won't balls it up, I promise.'

She opened her eyes and picked up her spoon, slowly letting the soup flood over its edges. 'You've broken my heart, Dougie, not once but many times. So you'll under-stand if –'

'I told you, I've changed,' he whispered.

'And I told you, no one changes,' she replied, in a small voice. 'Not really.'

'Not in essence, no,' Dougie agreed eagerly, 'and thank God, because then you wouldn't like me any more, would you? But you do like me, I know you do, I can *feel* it.'

He spooned his own soup into his mouth mechanically, tasting nothing. 'But behaviour can change, that's the point – bad ways of being can be altered. Otherwise there would be no hope for anyone, would there? And with me, anyway, it's felt like I've been going *back* to something rather than doing anything different. Like, starting my own business, building it up from scratch, counting the pennies – do you remember counting the pennies, Janie?' He peered shyly at her as he used the old pet name, hoping he had injected the same good images into her head as he had in his, the little kitchen table, the sleepy book-keeping, the small, springy bed waiting for them upstairs. 'I'd forgotten the beautiful simplicity of it,' he went on, when she kept her focus on her food, 'paying what you owe, spending what you have. I've even started a small fund to pay back Simon. Very small. It'll take a while, but I'll do it. And why are you back in England anyway?' he blurted, needing to do something to release the knot of joy in his throat. 'Answer me that. It's because you've left Mike, isn't it? I know you have.'

At last she looked at him. 'I haven't, actually.' She set her spoon down. 'I've explained that it was Sweden I was leaving, not him.'

For a moment Dougie's sturdy kitchen chair seemed to melt underneath him. 'Okay.' He gripped the edge of the table, watching his nails whiten. 'Right, I see. Jesus, sorry, that was presumptuous. So much for not ballsing it up . . . but that's what I've been doing for most of my life, so what's new?' He threw down his spoon with a clatter. 'Bugger, this needs salt. Don't you think?'

'No, I don't.'

'Okay, here's another subject for you,' he tried, digging deep beneath his mounting sense of hopelessness. 'Victoria and Simon. I haven't told Stevie yet, but they really are getting a divorce. Victoria phoned me last Sunday, after the funeral, apologized for her behaviour that day she came by. She said everything was better now, more under control. She really sounded in control too, quite like her old self, in fact. She said they'd already got the paperwork under way, that she was going to make sure Simon was all right –'

'I think she was always in love with you,' Janine remarked, scraping her spoon round her bowl for the last drops. 'I think she chose Simon to be near you.'

Dougie stared at her, then laughed freely, the tension in him momentarily easing. It had been stretching across his chest, like a tight rubber band hooked between the outer edges of his ribcage. 'Don't be ridiculous.'

'I can assure you I'm not. You had that thing with her years ago. Stressed out last week, she throws herself at you. You have great *power*, Dougie,' Janine went on, in a tone of some weariness. 'It's both the best and the worst thing about you.'

Dougie was too stunned to speak. He found his thoughts swerving to Nina, to what Linda had told him about her feelings and how they fitted with her wonderful farewell letter. The power to invoke love – it should have been a matter for rejoicing, surely, and yet sitting there opposite Janine, the only one whose love he wanted, the only one who couldn't now love him back, it felt like the cruellest human blight imaginable.

'And as for Simon,' Janine continued blithely, pushing away her bowl and patting her napkin against her mouth. 'Dear, hero-worshipping Simon. God . . . sometimes I think I wanted to leave him as much as I did you. And hero-worshippers get jealous, you know that, don't you? Especially insecure small men, like him, who, as I used to tell you, feel the need to jump around to be noticed. The world fell into your lap, Dougie, while Simon spent his life chasing after it. When things started going wrong for you I even had the sneaking suspicion he was lapping it up.' She hesitated. 'I tried to tell you once, but you wouldn't listen . . . although I had no proof, obviously, then or now. And as for his behaviour in Spain this summer . . .' She sighed. 'Whatever happened – and we'll never know for sure – Stevie must have played her part. She certainly thinks she did. All that really matters is that she puts it behind her, which I think she has done.'

'Oh, yes, she has,' Dougie interjected, glad to alight upon a matter of certainty while Janine's other pronouncements continued to reverberate inside his head. Victoria holding a torch for him across so many years, it didn't seem possible. And as for Janine's take on Simon, he couldn't quite buy that either: it was too simplistic, too crude. The man had crossed a line and been unable to get back from it. He had fucked up and floundered, exposing the worst of himself. There was no bigger picture, no neat narrative of envy or anything else to explain it away.

Dougie glanced across the table, aware suddenly that he was being scrutinized, but pleased to see the scrutiny involved a smile.

'We steered her through the hoo-ha, didn't we?' Janine

491

beamed. 'Stevie. Between us, somehow, in spite of all our muddles, I think we steered her through.'

'Till the next one.'

'Oh, God, till the next one.' Her face softened. 'Stevie . . . how you love her, it's always blown me away.'

'It's always been easy,' Dougie murmured, 'the one thing I've never had to work at. Effortless, like breathing.'

For a few seconds their eyes connected, until the intensity grew too much and Dougie, his hopes ricocheting again, bounced off his chair, seizing the empty soup bowls and dropping them into the sink. 'Now, I've another surprise for you. Just listen to this.' He flicked on his iPod, which he had primed at the right point earlier in the day. 'You might just recognize this.' He spun round, clicking his fingers like a cheesy DJ, as the music, a little fuzzy from all the years since Janine's group had recorded it, spilt out of the speakers. It took him a moment to register that she wasn't sharing the fun.

'Turn it off – NOW!' she shrieked, slapping her palms over her ears. 'And for ever after.' She made a lunge towards the iPod, the legs of her chair screeching over the floor tiles, but Dougie got there first.

'I am not that girl, Dougie,' she said flatly, dropping back into the chair, the wide panels of the long white skirt she was wearing floating up and settling like rippling feathers. 'I am not,' she went on, her voice tightening, 'that silly pregnant girl who sang in a band and wore ankle bracelets and henna in her hair, that girl you fell for and who fell in love with you. I am thirty-seven. I am old and bruised. And, yes, you're right, I've realized recently that I do still . . . still have feelings for you,' she gabbled the phrase, miming quotation marks, making it sound asinine, meaningless. 'But I have no desire to do anything about them because – because all that happened, not just what *you* put me through but . . .' she paused for breath '. . . losing Ross, all of that, has made me fragile, different.'

'Ross was my fault.' Dougie had stayed by the fridge, holding himself stiffly as his hopes plummeted again. He kept his arms crossed, pinching his flesh with his fingers. 'I told you to take the night off. I told you I'd be in charge. Then I got drunk.'

She was staring up at him, her eyes clear pools glazed with sadness. 'If he'd cried I would have woken. I always woke. I always heard him, no matter how far away he was. You telling me to get some sleep that night made no difference. He made no sound, Dougie, that was the point. He just died. And though I did try to blame you at first, tried to hate you, I realized long ago that it wouldn't do, that it wasn't true, that it wasn't what I felt. Okay?'

'Okay.' He turned with hunched shoulders to start preparing the next course, working methodically, swallowing the disappointment that nothing was going to turn out as he had planned – as he had hoped – after all. The only consolation was that they did, finally, seem to be forging a proper peace, clearing out the last of the nitty-gritty, and the least he could do in honour of that achievement was to serve his dismal meal as well as was still possible. Dougie fell into a sort of trance, his fingers moving with all their customary deftness as he converted both main-course plates into two perfectly symmetrical oil paintings: a squeeze of aubergine purée in the centre, baby cod fillets round the outside, then a ring of julienne courgettes and, finally, covering the rim of each, a loosely scattered outer circle of marinated anchovies and crispy courgette flowers. He had nudged the last into place when he realized Janine had left her chair and was standing beside him.

'As for the other business . . . of still having feelings . . .' she dropped her forehead against the middle of his arm, pressing hard '. . . this isn't a game for me, Dougie,' she said, in a trembling voice. 'You need to know that. But if that's what it is for you, all this sweetness . . . courting me with this exquisite bloody meal and your exquisite bloody charm – at full bloody beam – then please, have the grace, the mercy, to tell me now so I can walk out of here, a little disappointed, but not –'

He turned round quickly and lifted her up. She clung on automatically, locking her legs round his waist, the skirt bunching out from her hips like white silky petals. 'Your turn to stop talking, I think,' he said. 'Maybe this will help.' He planted one rough kiss on her lips and then another, much gentler one, as the pleasure of recognition overcame them both, a blissful combination of familiarity and newness beyond what either had expected or could have described. 'You should know I've had the odd relapse,' he gasped, briefly pulling away, 'with drink – two this year, to be exact – but the last was The Last. I swear on – on the life of Stevie. No, shush, listen. This is important.' He nudged her face with his nose, his ice-blue eyes pierced with earnestness. 'Sometimes it takes not having something to know how badly you want it . . . need it. I need you, Janine. I've missed you so much. The number of times I've wanted to call, the number of conversations

I've had with you in my head. I love you. I've never stopped loving you. And even if you slap my face and leave now, I swear that I will never, consciously, do anything ever again to cause you pain. Do you believe me, Janine? Please say you believe me.'

She nodded because she couldn't speak, because she hadn't wanted the kissing to stop. With his arms starting to strain from the weight of her, light though she was, he shuffled to the little kitchen sofa and sat down so that she fell naturally into his lap, facing him. They nuzzled noses and kissed again, now both smiling so broadly it was hard for their mouths to get a proper grip.

'You smell good. Sugary.'

'And you . . . of fish. Nice fish.' Janine sank against him, all the fight gone, beaten out of her, as she had feared it would be, if he kissed her, when properly sober, when declaring his love, when he was being the best he could be. In her heart it was what she had been wanting for months, ever since he had started trying to be the man he had been, the one she had fallen in love with, the one in whom her faith had flared when she had received his neighbour's letter. Dear, funny, generous Nina, burdened in so many ways and making light of it, making the best of it. It seemed incredible that they both owed so much to someone she would never meet.

And yet, even as Dougie's arms closed around her, Janine's terror surged – at her submission, of what it might mean, the avenues of new suffering down which it might lead her. At the back of her head she could hear her mother's voice – and a million other sensible voices – telling her she was out of her mind, telling her to gather her skirts and run for the hills, save herself while she still could. Dougie Easton had caused her more anguish than any other creature on the planet. He was clever, funny, attractive. Women fell in love with him. His life was littered with their shadows. The ones he had responded to, the ones he hadn't. Why should she trust anything he said?

Why indeed? Janine freed herself from Dougie's mouth, but then began to kiss his hands, tenderly reacquainting herself with the long, rough fingers that worked so hard and were so good at what they did. Because they were both older and fractionally wiser, she reasoned. Because when it came to damage and neediness they seemed to have found a sort of balance. And because doubt would always be part of the package, a thread that might unravel, a thread worth fighting for. Humans might fail each other, or they might not. It was the uncertainty that gave it meaning, made it real.

'But I'm not staying the night,' she declared, pulling properly apart in one last effort to reclaim a little control. She used the chance to steer some hair back behind her ears, wanting as clear a view of him as possible, even if any capacity she might have had for emotional objectivity was lost. He was still such a handsome man, but so beaten-up, these days, too, with lines of age and suffering starting to tug round his eyes and mouth. She found them irresistible. 'One step at a time, okay?' she whispered, stroking the furrows with her fingertips.

'Yes, boss. One step at a time.'

'And we say nothing to Stevie, not yet.'

'Nothing to Stevie, not yet.' Dougie touched the end of her nose with his finger. 'And I've a request for you.'

'Go on.'

'That once you've been and gone and come back from Sweden, to pack up properly and tell Mike that you're returning to your former husband, the former love of your life –'

'*If* that's what I decide to do.'

'*If* that's what you decide to do,' Dougie echoed, managing a brief, poor attempt to look chastened. 'Then do you think you might be able to squeeze in a little pre-Christmas jaunt to Germany for a wedding?'

Janine opened her mouth in surprise. 'A wedding?'

'Brother James. He's also lost his heart to someone – this is turning into a big year for the Easton boys, though, as far as I know, it's his and her first time round as opposed to the hundredth, like you and me. At least I *think* it's their first time round.'

'A German someone?'

'A German someone. Katarina something unpronounceable. He's been stationed over there for a couple of years. There'll be lots of men in uniform waving swords and firing guns. I shall be terrified – I shall need you at my side.'

'You and James are talking again?'

'Nearly. Well, that's the plan.'

'Now you have amazed me.'

'Good. Stay amazed.'

He kissed her again and then carried her, with much hilarity and bumping of knees and elbows, upstairs, neither of them sparing a thought for the cod fillets and feathered twists of anchovy, their flavour and beauty shrivelling as they cooled. The subsiding tower of vanilla raspberry millefeuille met a more satisfactory end, serving as a much-needed snack a few hours later. They ate it with two forks straight off the plate, scattering pastry crumbs and blobs of cream among the bedclothes.

Chapter Thirty

Gary and Ruth's house wasn't really big enough for so many guests. Lois trotted between all the legs looking for attention and food before accepting that she wasn't going to get either. Whereupon she sloped under the dining-room table, her doggy brain wrestling, for by no means the first time during the course of the previous six months, to comprehend why her once perfect world seemed to have been turned upside-down.

'You said a wedding before Christmas.' Janine's eyes danced at Dougie over the rim of her champagne glass. 'There was no mention, at least in my recollection of our bargaining, of a christening within the space of the same three days. A christening, indeed, that may well make us *miss* the wedding . . .'

'Such late complaining,' Dougie countered, feigning irritation. 'How was I to know Gary and Ruth would go for a rush-job of registering Polly with the Almighty and make the extraordinary decision that I should be her god-father?'

Janine snorted. 'Extraordinary is the word. I almost felt I should warn the vicar. I mean, you barely know any hymns, let alone believe in God –'

'I *do* know hymns – I'm good at hymns.'

She giggled. 'Your singing in church certainly turned a few heads.'

'I always sing like that when I'm happy,' Dougie grumbled cheerfully. 'I've been doing the same in the shower lately, or hadn't you noticed?'

'Oh, yes.' She pulled a face. 'I'd noticed.'

'At Nina's funeral all those weeks ago,' he murmured, suddenly serious, bending over her and pressing his mouth against her ear, 'I heard your voice. I heard your voice in the crowd, Janine, and I can't tell you what that was like . . .'

She let him kiss her hair, her temple, closing her eyes with the pleasure of it, then affectionately pushed him away. 'You're impossible. We're being antisocial, standing here talking nonsense –'

'I love our nonsense.'

'So do I.' Janine paused, making herself relish the moment, one of so many when she had had to pinch herself lately, all the while vowing to treasure each and every one, nurture them like the seedlings they were, never let them wither through complacency or lack of care. 'But,' she went on, a little breathless as the love swept through her, not just for Dougie but for the certain knowledge that he shared her disbelief and gratitude, that their new connection was founded on the greatest possible mutual desire to avoid the pitfalls and make it work, 'we've only got twenty minutes or we'll be late picking up your dad, which means we'll be late for the plane, which means we'll be late for the *Schloss* pre-wedding bash –' She broke off to snatch a piece of the christening cake, which Dougie had made, off a passing plate.

'Talking of weddings . . .' Dougie absently stroked his lips where they had touched her skin.

Janine was looking at her watch. 'Yes, talking of weddings, we really *do* only have twenty minutes. This is delicious, by the way. Truly. You should become a professional cook. Oh, hang on, you already are.' She laughed at her own wit and took another bite, adding, with her mouth full, 'I'll eat this, then you and I must *circulate* if only to say our goodbyes.'

'Not James's wedding. Ours. I meant ours, Janine. Our wedding.'

She stopped chewing and looked at him, her cheeks bulging with cake. Through the french windows next to them the sun had just made its first appearance of the day, a greyish, unconvincing light, filtered by the lacy November clouds. The grass looked trampled from the most recent beating of rain, muddy in its bare patches. A squirrel scuttled and bobbed, sniffing for some secret hoard. Slowly she resumed eating and swallowing, licking the traces of icing off her fingers, her eyes filling with mischief. 'Uh-uh. No thanks. No way. In fact, I think I'm going to go and talk to someone else, escape your clutches . . .'

'But I want you in my clutches,' Dougie cried, so loudly and with such joy that a couple of guests assumed he'd had a few too many, while Stevie levered her way to his side hissing at him to behave. 'Great source of income here,' he pointed out, merrily changing tack and nodding in the direction of Polly, who had been whisked out of her christening finery into a green Baby-gro and was slumped, eyelids drooping, over her father's shoulder, a silky cobweb of spit dangling off her lower lip. She was a good, sweet baby, but he had already had more than his fill of her during the godparenting shenanigans round the font and then posing for photos outside the church afterwards, while relatives jostled for turns with phones and cameras. Now Dougie was far more interested in the view over Gary's head of Janine talking to the formidable Valerie. Dougie willed her to turn round. He had laughed at her easy dismissal of his wedding comment, but a knot of terror had formed somewhere behind his ribs. She had been teasing, hadn't she, brushing it off like that? It had to have been tease, surely. He stared hard, but Janine was laughing at something with Ruth and her mother, her head tipped back, her hair falling in ripples down her back.

'Babysitting income?' Stevie prompted, frowning, checking her phone.

'Yes. Trust me, Gary and Ruth will want their lives back soon. It happens to all the best parents eventually – heads pop up above the parapet, "Hello, world, I hope you haven't forgotten us."' Dougie started to mime putting his head over a parapet, but saw his daughter wasn't exactly gripped by his theatrics. Happiness was making him daft, he thought. It had been going on for days, weeks. He was constantly embarrassing himself. He wanted it never to stop. 'The going rate must be five or six quid an hour by now,' he went on, recognizing this might be a more obviously appealing tack for a sixteen-year-old, 'although I am a bit out of date on the subject. Still definitely worth considering, I'd say, for someone interested in saving money for trips to visit boyfriends in far-flung places.'

'But you and Mum said I couldn't go,' Stevie cried.

'Oh, yes, so we did.' Dougie scratched his head in a show of gormlessness. 'Fancy me forgetting that. But you couldn't afford to, anyway, so it was a pretty easy decision.

But maybe, if you started saving now, you could consider a gap year of your own one day . . .'

'Yeah, right . . . maybe,' Stevie conceded, either losing interest in so distant a horizon or perhaps momentarily crushed by the memory of the brief, bitter battle for permission to spend her Christmas holidays backpacking with Paul, a battle doomed from the start by her parents' united front. 'Um, Dad, is it okay if I take off now? I'll grab a bus to Amelia's. I've got a Skype planned with Paul, then we're going to Merryl's – Amelia's going to *drive* us there, can you believe it? With her mum, obviously, but she's already had, like, three, lessons.' Her fingers flew over her phone keypad as she talked. 'Could I have some too, do you think? Say, for my next birthday?'

'I expect so, if Mum agrees.' Dougie peered again through the throng for Janine. She had moved on from Ruth and Valerie and was talking to Victoria, who had also been made a godparent and who was definitely not carrying a torch for him, Dougie had decided, with some relief, when they had greeted each other outside the church with the easy amiability of old friends. A kiss on a cold cheek, a brief hug – nothing could have felt more normal. And she looked pregnant, Janine had claimed, yanking on Dougie's jacket sleeve to whisper the observation once the embrace was done with.

Dougie remained as doubtful of this as he was of Janine's other beady speculations on the subject of Simon's estranged wife. Victoria was her usual stately stick-thin self, from what he could see, perhaps a little fuller in the face, but wearing a grey silk matching coat and dress that many decidedly un-pregnant women could not have carried off. Besides, such a major longed-for event would surely have been a reason to patch things up with Simon instead of moving out, as she was reputed to have done, to a temporary place somewhere in Bayswater. No reconciliation was on the cards. Indeed, according to Ruth, phoning to issue the late godparent and christening invitation the previous week, Simon's non-attendance at the event had been a key stipulation in Victoria's co-operation.

'I guess we'll see you when we get back from Germany, then,' Dougie told Stevie, as she hugged him goodbye, the blessed phone at last having been put back in her bag. 'Have fun with Amelia . . . Oh, and well done coming to this, by the way.'

'Thanks, Dad.' They exchanged a look that was about Victoria without either of them needing to say so. There had been an embrace for Stevie outside the church from her, too, a very warm one by the look of things.

'So is it because of me that they're getting divorced?' Stevie had asked, in a thin voice, after Dougie, with Janine's blessing and spurred on by the imminent difficulties the ceremony posed, had finally revealed the full extent of his knowledge about her pregnancy scare and its aftermath.

'Divorce is never about one thing,' Dougie had replied slowly. 'It takes a while, loads of things building, but then, yes, a tipping point is reached – a final straw – and I guess in this case, Victoria and Simon, it's probably safe to assume that the tipping point was you.'

Stevie had been cradling a box of tissues at the time, ready ammunition against the tail-end of a heavy cold.

She turned away to cough long and wrenchingly, holding her chest, her eyes watering. 'And you and Mum,' she went on, even more faintly, 'what was your tipping point?'

'Ross,' Dougie said, without having to think. 'Don't get me wrong, there were plenty of other reasons, most – all of them – my fault, but losing your little brother . . .' He breathed out slowly, letting the air slide through his teeth, aware that they were at one of those rare treasured moments of transparency, of openness, and not wanting to squander it. Stevie had a right to know the truth, but maybe not every layer of it. She was their daughter and, like any child, did not deserve to be force-fed too intricate a knowledge of her parents' inner world. 'When your brother died it made us both so very sad. And when you get like that, you can't always help each other in the way you should.'

'And now?' She plucked a fresh tissue from the beaten-up box. 'What the hell is going on now?'

'We're friends, first and foremost,' Dougie answered, even more on his guard. Janine had returned to Sweden, but only briefly, to pack up the last of her things, and say a proper farewell to Mike. Since her return she had resumed her job at the estate agent's and started renting a small flat off Chalk Farm Road while her tenants used up their right to a full three months' notice. She and Dougie were now on the phone constantly, as well as in each other's beds at every available opportunity – never frequent enough for either of them – but had so far resisted any overt displays of affection in front of Stevie. 'We're friends and might want it to be more than that,' he went on, 'but neither do we want to rush in and make a mess of things. Most of all, we don't want you to get caught up in it, to have any hopes raised and dashed.'

'Well, that's just stupid,' Stevie retorted, blowing her nose hard and volubly, her voice thick with her cold. 'Of course I'm caught up in it, aren't I? Whatever happens, I'm *caught up* in it. And I'm not an idiot either, so please don't treat me like one. Mum's hair is all over the bathroom, and her perfume – I've smelt that often enough upstairs, so could you both, like, cut the crap, do you think?'

Dougie had nodded, astounded, thoroughly chastised. 'Okay. Yes. Sorry, sweetheart. All done for the best reasons . . . but, yes, consider the crap officially cut from now on. I'll, er, tell Mum.'

Remembering the conversation, Dougie held his daughter extra tightly as they said goodbye, then watched with a full heart as she set off across the room, sidling politely and issuing excuse-mes to get through the mêlée, bestowing cheek-pecks on both Gary and Ruth, before finally reaching her mother, whom she hugged, and Victoria, whose face she kissed. A moment later, Janine swung her head round and caught Dougie's eye, telling him in one glance what he had needed to know, making the knot of terror dissolve.

Simon had turned into the street with the intention of running straight past the house. He was piqued about being excluded, but nothing more. Christenings were so much mumbo-jumbo – atheist godparents, hypocrisy – that even if he had been invited (instead of told to keep away) he would have found an excuse to refuse.

But when he was parallel with Ruth and Gary's yellow front door, he couldn't resist slowing down, taking a look. Two white balloons had been tied to the letter-flap. They bounced against each other in the sharp November breeze, like the heads of two old friends, nodding together, sharing a private joke. Through the window he could see the front room was full of people, elbow to elbow, drinks in hand. Someone had the baby, or *a* baby anyway – it was hard to tell, they all looked the same to him: bald, wobbly heads, eyes that stared in a way that older kids were soon taught not to because it was rude. This one was far too young for such lessons. It was dressed in a green all-in-one and being held, tummy down, along the forearm of a stout grey-haired woman in a lilac suit. Simon felt a stab of pity for the child, being suspended face down like that, with no choice but to gawp at the floor.

He shuffled a few yards along the pavement, taking himself out of view of the window, fearful of being seen. Would Victoria want a christening for theirs? He tried to imagine it, glimpsing a village church, hats, small-talk, vicars and other horrors. Accepting the role of godparent was one thing, but she wasn't remotely religious, so maybe he would be spared. She had already made it clear she didn't want him to attend the actual birth. Simon had felt an initial stab of gratitude – all that famous gore, gaping, bleeding, stitching – it was hardly appealing, but then he had been flooded by a sense of injustice. Could she dictate that stuff? Didn't an estranged husband and father-to-be have any rights at all? When he had a moment he intended to look into it, maybe even put together enough facts for an article.

Simon stooped to tighten a lace, pondering how he might begin such a piece: the battle for equality had tipped violently the other way – yes, that would do for an intro. Women had all the power ... Victoria had certainly wielded power, shockingly, cruelly, slicing their partnership down the middle, like a ... Simon stood up, a little dizzy, disconcerted that he had wavered so quickly from his train of thought. It happened a lot, these days, when he was trying to work. He didn't need the money, of course – financial generosity had been one of his wife's many emasculating trump cards – but he still very much hoped he would get the occasional word into print, keep his hand in.

It was time to move on, Simon knew. He had sweated hard and was getting chilled. But his legs felt leaden and there was still the ache of a stitch under his rib-cage. He dropped his head forwards, holding his waist with his hands, inhaling and exhaling deeply. He was new to jogging, still learning, still hating it. It helped fill the day. He was also hoping it would get rid of the small pot-belly he had acquired in recent weeks: junk food, a little too much to drink. The reasons for its emergence were as tediously obvious as the measures it would take to see it off.

On the other side of the hedge there was a sudden burst of party hubbub. Peering through the knotty gaps in the branches, Simon saw Ruth and Gary's yellow door swing open to release a young woman onto the front path: a tall woman in a white jacket and black trousers, talking animatedly into her phone. The trousers were welded to her long legs and swallowed mid-calf by black ankle boots with towering wedge heels. She walked on them with her knees slightly bent, tottering but elegantly, like one of those thoroughbred females who earned their living on cat-walks. There was a large white flower clipped artlessly to her hair, which she plucked out as she talked, dropping it into the pocket of her jacket. Simon shrank along the hedge, turning his back on her as she came out of the gate and headed in the opposite direction.

Stevie. It had taken a moment. Adrenalin surged in his veins – flight or fight – the desire to *do* something. Her resemblance to Janine was shocking – he had never seen it so clearly before. The model figure, the beauty – cheekbones, hair, legs. Janine. Simon swallowed, marvelling again at the news that she and Dougie were apparently back together. It had seemed an odd turn of events, not just unlikely but unfair somehow, coinciding as it had with Victoria's decision to kick him out. And to secure the forgiveness of Janine was a feat indeed; Janine who was up there as one of the most seriously beautiful women Simon had met, and whom Dougie had spent the best part of two decades treating like dirt.

Simon's pulse quickened. For some people the luck never ran out and that was the galling truth. People like Dougie. Over the last couple of years Simon had actually allowed himself to forget that. He had even felt pity for his old friend – real pity – in the process rather relishing the role it allowed him, to be the stronger one for once, the more fortunate, the more blessed; the one whose help was needed as opposed to him being the supporting act for a star turn. Long before their falling out, Simon had started to understand, with some regret, that this would not last, that however strained, sober and beaten back

Dougie appeared to be, he had not lost his knack for survival and success. And he had been right. On top of the Janine thing, his new business was clearly taking off. Just that week Simon had received a cheque in the post for a thousand pounds. There would be more and soon, Dougie had scrawled on a cursory note, until he had managed full repayment of Simon's lost investment in the Black Hen.

Simon turned slowly. Stevie was twenty yards away, still walking her loose-hipped walk, bouncing on her high-heeled footwear, still chattering. It really was like going back in time, back to the early nineties, Janine reincarnated. Simon balked at the thought, fighting the dim horror that the world could go into reverse, that all the travelling forwards into the security of adulthood had been for nothing, that they were all back where they had started: Dougie with his Midas touch, Victoria with her money, himself with nothing. The one on the outside looking in. The boy whom no one wanted as a friend.

Stevie was nearly at the end of the street, about to turn out of sight. Simon's throat had constricted as if there was still something he needed to say, or shout, if only he could find the right words. But all that fell into his mind, with sudden, violent lucidity, was that he was going to have a child, which would begin as a baby – like the little green sausage-shaped creature he had seen through the window, balanced helplessly along a forearm – and would grow into something like the intimidating young adult in front of him, walking, talking, making demands. And on it would go, whether he liked it or not, for ever and fucking ever. It would go on and he would be a part of it. And thinking about that properly, for the first time, shivering in his sweat-dampened clothes, Simon felt truly afraid.

Somehow he got himself running again, aware as he did so of a gnawing tightness in his right thigh. He had got cold, that was the thing. He had got cold and now was seizing up a little. He needed to get home, get into a hot bath, use some of that lavender foam Victoria had left behind. Have a glass of something nice. Treat himself to that at least, but eat modestly – maybe rustle up some baked beans on toast or a can of soup, or one of those be-good-to-yourself ready-meals he had bought from the supermarket. He would set up camp in front of the telly, feet on the table in the way that had driven Victoria mad. He would check his phone for messages, see if allotment-Clare had got back to him yet. Clare Beazley. Yoga body, annoying voice. Hairy armpits, Dougie had told him once. Not exactly an A-lister. And Dougie's cast-off, of course, which was the worst thing of all. But, then, he was now on one of those 'new journeys' people liked to talk about, and all new journeys had to start somewhere.

Simon stopped at a lamp-post to stretch, balancing on one leg and then the other, easing the sore thigh gingerly until it felt a bit better. Even so, he set off walking instead of running, aware that he was fragile, aware that taking care of himself was something he was going to have to learn to do.

Dougie was emerging from the upstairs bathroom, en route to dig their coats out of the pile on the spare-room bed, when a woman in an electric green dress stepped into his path, a full champagne glass in each hand. He had noticed her in church. It had been hard not to. She had arrived late and noisily, thanks to screwdriver heels, which drilled the stone-tiled floor as she had made her way up the aisle to a small space in the second row. She had strikingly thick loose blonde hair and walked with a hint of a roll in her hips, her hourglass body of indents and curves easily – and deliberately – flattered by her choice of dress, a choice she had wasted no time in showing off by slipping free of her overcoat the moment she was in a pew and folding it into a tidy cushion next to her kneeler.

'You look thirsty and . . . *familiar*,' she observed smoothly now, pressing one of the glasses into Dougie's hand before he could protest and knitting the thin soft arches of her eyebrows. 'Give me a moment . . . I've definitely seen you somewhere . . . Don't tell me . . . Yes, it was on the telly, I think. Oh, yes, I've definitely got it now.' She touched his shoulder with her glass. 'It was a Sunday-night thing, barristers, court rooms – murder and mayhem – in Ipswich, I think . . . Turned out the girl was being abused by the uncle. You were the stepfather, under suspicion but a good egg in the end.'

Dougie laughed. 'I'm pleased to hear it. Except I'm afraid you're wrong. I've never acted in my life . . . except, that is . . .' he paused, letting her read the merriment in his expression '. . . when telling lies.'

'Hmm . . . telling lies, eh?' Her almond eyes flashed back at him, her neat nostrils flaring in the manner of a feline picking up an interesting scent. 'That sounds intriguing. I trust they're always in a good cause, these lies?' She cocked her head and smiled, holding out her free hand. 'I'm Isabel, by the way. Isabel Chalmers. Second cousin stray of

Ruth's – long story, for another time maybe . . . I hope . . . Cheers.' They shook hands and then she chinked her glass against his. Her fingers were slim and unadorned, Dougie noticed, apart from varnish that made her long nails glint like rubies. Seen close to, she was a little older than he had first thought, thirty-three, maybe thirty-four. There were small creases at the corners of her eyes and the fullness of her lips looked as if it might have had some recent help. She was starting to have to work at it, he guessed, the business of staying young, of enjoying herself.

Even so, he was dimly tempted. She would be fun, for a bit. And the full glass of champagne in his hand, that was even more tempting, not because he felt weak, Dougie realized, but because he felt so strong, so goofily happy, so on top of his game. He had sorted himself out at last. A brief interlude, probably, though he sincerely hoped not, but for once there were no demons to escape, no sorrows to drown. If ever there was a moment in his life when it was safe to have a drink, then that moment was now.

And yet . . . and yet . . . Dougie squeezed the spindly stem in his fingers. It wasn't safe. It was never safe. It never would be safe. He might have derived some quiet pride from having dried out without the formal aid of AA's celebrated twelve-step programme, but he had certainly, through his own stumbling and failing, become acquainted with its cardinal rules. The temptation never stopped, he reminded himself. Every moment of every day for the rest of his life it had to be resisted.

And as for the woman sparkling at him in her green dress, her eyes telling him that if he lied on her account she would have no problem with it – would welcome it, indeed – she, too, and others would need resisting now and for ever after. He had power, as the two most important women in his life had, in their different ways, pointed out. He had power and needed to be careful how he exerted it, where he let it lead him.

The temptation to stray wouldn't go away either. Men, women, sexual attraction – the world would always be a jungle in spite of its overlay of concrete and civility. No, it was the choices one made about such temptations that counted, Dougie reminded himself, amused to find an image of Laura Munro popping into his head, expounding her plans for marital fidelity across his rumpled bedclothes, prior to zipping herself back into her jeans and skipping off to her fiancé.

Isabel Chalmers was still talking, unaware their game was over, unaware that Dougie had only started playing it out of some old mindless reflex from the bad, sad days, when sex for its own sake had seemed like a plausible route to happiness instead of a blind alley.

'I'm going to have to hand this back, I'm afraid,' he interrupted her, as gallantly as he could, aware of the need to be kind, as if he had already promised something that would not now be delivered. 'It's untouched, so maybe someone else would like it. I don't drink, you see, and I have a plane to catch. With a beautiful woman who is probably, at this very minute, wondering where I've got to and who will chop me up for her dinner if we're late. She hates being late. It stresses her out. ' He smiled, nodding in the direction of the spare bedroom. 'Coats – then I'm out of here. Nice to have met you.'

'On a leash, are you?' she quipped, moving off towards the stairs, laughing, though her voice was tart.

'Oh, yes, most definitely.' Dougie grinned. 'And it's bloody marvellous. "Only in cages are we truly free." Who said that?' He glanced back at the stairs but she had gone.

Outside with Janine a few minutes later, Dougie was still puzzling over the quotation, which Janine said she had never heard. 'Well, if no one said it, someone should have done.'

'Well, you did, didn't you? So it's said, isn't it? Does that mean I'm your cage?' she asked cosily, looping her arm through his as they turned into the street.

'No, not you. Us. We're the cage. We have our rules and our love. We need nothing else.'

'Except Stevie.'

'Except Stevie.'

The street had recently been converted to Residents Only and they had had to park at some distance away. The day had closed in again, converting the sky to a dome of solid grey, the tall, leafless street trees black scratches on top of it. Janine squeezed Dougie's arm more tightly, pressing against him for warmth. He was hard to keep up with at first, but then he shortened his stride and she lengthened hers, allowing them to find a rhythm in the middle. They moved smoothly along the pavement after that, like dancers, it felt, dancers who knew each other's steps and bodies, who knew all the clever shapes they could make if they concentrated hard and stayed close.

Acknowledgements

A very special thank you goes to my agent, Lizzy Kremer, and to my editor, Clare Ledingham, for helping to make the story the best that it could be.

For matters medical, Sara Westcott was, as always, patient and generous with her knowledge; while David Ratford kindly used his bilingual expertise to put me right on my Swedish spellings.

Lastly, I would like to thank Greg Taylor, whose talk of teenage daughters and men's cooking classes set the whole idea on its way.

Reading Group Questions

1.) We discover very quickly that Dougie is a flawed man. Through Dougie himself and through his friends' eyes we see how his alcoholism ruined his marriage, his business and nearly cost him everything. Now he is trying to mend his ways to be a good father to Stevie, but temptation is always waiting in the wings. What were your first impressions of Dougie? Did your view of him change over the course of the novel?

2.) Simon betrays Dougie's friendship in one of the worst ways possible. Were you surprised by Simon's actions? Do you think that if he had handled things differently afterwards and acknowledged his wrongdoing their friendship might have survived?

3.) Stevie has her own role to play in Simon's betrayal – did you view her as a wholly innocent victim or did you feel she played a more active role?

4.) Victoria is a good and loyal friend who suffers her own heartbreak. What do you think her real feelings for Dougie are, and how might they have shaped her marriage with Simon?

5.) Janine starts the novel in a very safe and steady new relationship with Mike – at what point did you begin to wonder if her feelings for Dougie had fully been extinguished?

6.) Janine and Dougie face one of the most devastating losses life can throw at you when their baby dies. How much do you think this affected their marriage? Do you think any marriage would be strong enough to survive unscathed after that?

7.) Nina is an extraordinarily powerful character who is very instrumental in turning Dougie's life around. What did you make of her choice to keep her imminent death from him a secret? Do you think his initial anger towards her was justified?

8.) We learn that Dougie and Simon's friendship began at school, when Dougie protected Simon from classroom bullies. But how does this affect Simon in later life, and do you think we can ever outgrow the dynamics that shape our behaviour in the school playground?